PRAISE F

"I will read anything Susan Stoker puts out . . . because I know it's going to be amazing!"

—Riley Edwards, *USA Today* bestselling author

"Susan Stoker never fails to pull me out of a reading slump. With heat, action, and suspense, she weaves an incredible tale that sucks me in and doesn't let go."

—Jessica Prince, *USA Today* bestselling author

"One thing I love about Susan Stoker's books is that she knows how to deliver a perfect HEA while still making sure the villain gets what he/she deserves!"

—T.M. Frazier, *New York Times* bestselling author

"Susan Stoker's characters come alive on the page!"

—Elle James, *New York Times* bestselling author

"When you pick up a Susan Stoker book, you know exactly what you're going to get . . . a hot alpha hero and a smart, sassy heroine. I can't get enough!"

—Jessica Hawkins, *USA Today* bestselling author

"Suspenseful storytelling with characters you want as friends!"

—Meli Raine, *USA Today* bestselling author

"Susan Stoker knows what women want. A hot hero who needs to save a damsel in distress . . . even if she can save herself."

—CD Reiss, *New York Times* bestselling author

THE
Royal

The Refuge Series

Deserving Alaska

Deserving Henley

Deserving Reese

Deserving Cora (November 2023)

Deserving Lara (February 2024)

Deserving Maisy (October 2024)

Deserving Ryleigh (January 2025)

SEAL Team Hawaii Series

Finding Elodie

Finding Lexie

Finding Kenna

Finding Monica

Finding Carly

Finding Ashlyn

Finding Jodelle

Eagle Point Search & Rescue Series

Searching for Lilly

Searching for Elsie

Searching for Bristol

Searching for Caryn

Searching for Finley (October 2023)

Searching for Heather (January 2024)

Searching for Khloe (May 2024)

Delta Force Heroes Series

Rescuing Rayne

Rescuing Aimee (novella)

Rescuing Emily

Rescuing Harley

Marrying Emily (novella)

Rescuing Kassie

Rescuing Bryn

Rescuing Casey

Rescuing Sadie (novella)

Rescuing Wendy

Rescuing Mary

Rescuing Macie

Rescuing Annie

Delta Team Two Series

Shielding Gillian

Shielding Kinley

Shielding Aspen

Shielding Jayme (novella)

Shielding Riley

Shielding Devyn

Shielding Ember

Shielding Sierra

Badge of Honor: Texas Heroes Series

Justice for Mackenzie

Justice for Mickie

Justice for Corrie

Justice for Laine (novella)

Shelter for Elizabeth

Justice for Boone

Shelter for Adeline

Shelter for Sophie

Justice for Erin

Justice for Milena

Shelter for Blythe

Stand-Alone Novels

The Guardian Mist
Falling for the Delta
Nature's Rift
A Princess for Cale
A Moment in Time (a short story collection)
Another Moment in Time (a short story collection)
A Third Moment in Time (a short story collection)
Lambert's Lady

Writing as Annie George

Stepbrother Virgin (erotic novella)

THE Royal

Game of Chance, Book Two

SUSAN STOKER

Published by Montlake, Seattle

www.apub.com

Amazon, the Amazon logo, and Montlake are trademarks of Amazon.com, Inc., or its affiliates.

ISBN-13: 9781662509667 (paperback)
ISBN-13: 9781662509674 (digital)

Cover design by Hang Le
Cover photography by Michelle Lancaster
Cover image: © Edwin Remsberg / Getty

Printed in the United States of America

THE

Royal

Chapter One

Callum "Cal" Redmon pulled his Rolls-Royce Cullinan into the Greens' driveway on the outskirts of Washington, DC. Traffic had been terrible, and he'd arrived much later than he'd hoped. He was in an awful mood. His back hurt, his knees were throbbing, and he had a horrible headache. Ever since he'd been a POW and endured relentless torture, his body hadn't been the same. He felt as if he was at least twenty years older than his thirty-seven years.

The last place he wanted to be was here. He'd told his relatives that he wasn't a bodyguard. That ever since he'd gotten out of the military, he didn't want anything to do with covert operations or any kind of security. And yet . . . here he was.

Being part of the Liechtenstein royal family wasn't easy. Even though he hadn't grown up in the tiny country, and even though he barely knew the queen and king, he was still expected to be loyal. Still expected to drop everything to do their bidding when they asked. So when Carla Green had told his second cousin—who she'd met online— that she was being stalked, his cousin had reached out to Cal to see what he could do about it.

When Cal, being Cal, had told him he couldn't do *anything* about his latest online model friend's personal troubles, that she should call her local police, his cousin had ignored him. He'd talked to his mother, who'd talked to her sister, who'd spoken with the queen. She, in turn, had called Cal's parents . . . and the next thing he knew, he was being guilted into driving to DC to "investigate" the situation.

Cal wasn't qualified to do a damn thing about Carla's problem. Yes, he could shoot. Was a damn good shot, in fact. But that didn't make him qualified to be some amateur investigator and certainly not a bodyguard. He could barely handle his *own* body.

Most days, his very bones hurt. The torture he'd received as a POW had screwed him up, bad. Torn ligaments, broken bones, pulled muscles . . . those were just the tip of the iceberg. Technically, all the injuries he'd sustained had healed, but the effects were ongoing, and his scars—inside and out—were many.

Not only that, but since his release, Cal didn't particularly care for people in general. He was grumpy on the worst of days and stand-offish on the best. He'd seen the worst humanity had to offer, and he much preferred to hole up in the house he'd bought in the small Maine town where he and his friends had settled after they'd gotten out of the military.

Thanks to his royal lineage and parents who'd invested their family money carefully, Cal never had to worry about the size of his bank account. No one would know simply by looking at him that he had over a billion dollars in his extensive portfolio. Most days he wore faded jeans and long-sleeved T-shirts, and he definitely didn't flaunt the fact that he had money, and lots of it.

Yes, the Cullinan was obnoxiously expensive. No one needed a Rolls-Royce SUV. But he hadn't been able to resist. It was sleek, had all the bells and whistles, and, most importantly, was excellent on the snowy roads of Maine. Most people would assume the vehicle was just another SUV like thousands of others on the road. It was covered in dirt and looked more like a work truck at the moment than a three-hundred-thousand-dollar vehicle.

As instructed, Cal drove his SUV around the back of the fairly large house sitting on five acres and parked in the large paved area. He took a moment to reach for his phone to text JJ and let him know that he'd arrived at the Greens' safe and sound.

He'd call his friend later tonight and tell him what he'd learned after talking with Carla, but for now, after sending the brief text, he allowed himself a second to enjoy the silence that surrounded him. Closing his eyes, Cal took a deep breath. What he really wanted to do was turn around and drive right back to Maine. To hole up in his quiet house and be left alone. But he hadn't been able to say no to his mom.

He and his parents had a complicated relationship with the royal family back in Liechtenstein. His mom and dad had left the country after she'd been knocked over by a member of the media while pregnant with Cal. They hadn't been trying to take pictures of *her* but rather the queen and king, and his mom had simply been in the way. That was the last straw for his dad, and he'd moved them to England.

The queen and king hadn't been happy, but it wasn't as if his dad was ever going to be king. He was so far down the succession line, it would be nearly impossible for him to rise to the top. They'd lived a peaceful albeit public life in London, only going back to their home country now and then for short visits and official functions.

Cal had joined the British Army, eventually becoming intrigued by a team of Delta Force operatives he'd seen in action while overseas. Strings had been pulled, agreements made, and not long after, Cal had found himself in the United States training to become a Delta. It was hard work, grueling at times, but he'd loved it. He was assigned to work with Chappy, Bob, and JJ.

Cal had never clicked with anyone the way he had with his teammates. The men became inseparable, and when they'd made the decision to get out of the military after being taken hostage, there hadn't been any question in Cal's mind that he'd go wherever the others did.

They'd settled in Maine—after Cal had won a game of rock paper scissors—and had established Jack's Lumber, a tree service. And while the work could be difficult, especially with the relentless chronic pain

Cal suffered day after day, he'd been satisfied and mostly content for three long years.

Opening his eyes, Cal sighed. He was stalling. He needed to go inside and meet Carla Green and her mother. Get some facts, see what kind of evidence Carla had on her stalker, assess the seriousness of the threat. His cousin Karl had always been overdramatic, especially as a kid. If he'd stubbed his toe, he yelled and cried as if someone had chopped it off. When he'd gotten an A-minus on a test, he expected everyone to treat him as if he'd just cured cancer. He'd fallen madly in love with every girlfriend and gone into monthlong sulks when they inevitably broke up.

Cal didn't know if Karl and Carla had truly only met on the internet, but he was mostly certain his cousin was being overly dramatic once again when he'd gone up the chain of relatives to get Cal to do his bidding.

Wiping a hand over his face, Cal took another deep breath before leaning over and opening the glove box. He shook out two aspirin and swallowed them dry, praying they'd make a dent in the throbbing of his head.

He reached for the door handle and climbed out of his SUV. He arched his back, trying to stretch out the kinks from sitting for so long. Wincing at the way his movement pulled against the scars all over his torso, Cal sighed.

Every day, every movement, reminded him of the hell he'd been through. His friends had done what they could to turn their captors' attention on themselves, but once they'd realized who they had in their clutches, they'd been positively gleeful. They'd laughed as they cut him, as they'd beaten him, as they'd turned on their video cameras to show the world how low a real-life prince had fallen.

Forcing his thoughts away from the not-too-distant past, Cal started to head back around toward the front of the house . . . before movement caught his attention.

A woman exited through a side door of the home, carrying a trash bag and heading toward a bin directly opposite. Cal instinctively took a single step back, concealing himself behind the house as he studied her. She was short, perhaps a full foot under his six-foot-one frame, and full figured . . . with the kind of curves Cal loved. Probably because he'd grown up around the opposite—skinny women who did whatever was necessary in order to fit into designer dresses, to resemble society's version of what a pretty woman should look like.

Regardless, he'd always been far more attracted to women who carried some meat on their bones. He loved how they felt against him, under him, how their full tits jiggled and bounced, how their thighs and rounded stomachs were so soft in his hands. A Rubenesque woman was the epitome of sexiness.

Cal would take a curvy woman over a stick-thin one every day of the week.

Curves aside, there was nothing particularly notable about the woman he was watching at the moment. She was wearing an oversize T-shirt that she'd tied into a knot at her waist, her long brown hair pulled into a ponytail at the back of her head. A pair of well-worn, faded jeans hugged her thighs, and she had no makeup on her face, as far as he could tell. But there was something about the full effect that had Cal watching her closely.

She pushed the lid off the bin and grunted as she hefted the obviously heavy trash bag. After throwing it in, she wiped her brow on the sleeve of her shirt, then sighed deeply and turned her face upward to the sun, closing her eyes.

She stood there for a long moment, her head tilted back, a small smile on her face, as if feeling the sun on her skin was the highlight of her day.

Cal was entranced. He hadn't even said one word to the woman, and yet he could tell by the way she was enjoying the simple pleasure of the sun on her face that this was someone he wanted to know.

The first time he'd stepped outside after being rescued, he'd done the same thing she was doing now. He'd taken a deep breath, closed his eyes, and lifted his face to the hot Middle Eastern sun. It had actually hurt, the blazing sunshine burning the cuts and bruises on his skin, but even three years later, nothing had felt as good as that first breath of fresh air.

And for some reason, Cal had a sense that this woman was feeling just a little of what he had that day. As if standing out here in the weak late-winter rays, with the birds singing around her, she was free. Free of her worries and troubles.

"Juniper!"

The shrill voice screeching from inside the house made the woman jerk in surprise, and she turned her attention toward the door she'd exited. The small smile on her face disappeared, and Cal watched as she removed any expression from her face and headed back toward the house.

"Juniper! Where the hell are you?" the voice called out again.

It grated on Cal's nerves, the pitch high enough to exacerbate the throbbing in his head.

"I'm coming!" his curvy stranger called out calmly, as if she was used to being yelled at. And Cal supposed she probably was. She was most likely hired help for the household; it made sense if she was taking out the garbage. Cal's family had certainly had their share of maids, gardeners, cooks, and other staff over the years. But he couldn't remember his mom ever speaking to any of them as disrespectfully as the unseen woman inside the house, whoever she was.

Juniper. Cal smiled. It was a beautiful name.

He watched as Juniper reached for the door handle that led back into the house. She turned and looked up at the sky for another brief moment, and Cal could clearly see the expression on her face. It was no longer blank.

The longing, sorrow, and frustration he saw there spoke to him deeply. But as soon as he caught a glimpse of the emotions, they were gone, as was the woman.

Cal's heart beat fast in his chest. He wasn't sure what had just happened, but he'd never felt quite like this before. He wasn't a believer in love at first sight, like the sort found in fairy tales. Yes, he was a prince, but he wasn't going to meet his Snow White, Cinderella, or Sleeping Beauty and fall madly in love at first glance.

But . . . he couldn't deny he'd never experienced a draw toward a woman like he'd felt with the enigmatic Juniper. It wasn't just her looks, although her body was exactly what he preferred in his lovers. It was the peacefulness that exuded from her as she'd turned her face to the sun. An underlying strength as she serenely responded to the angry woman inside the house.

Shaking his head, Cal scoffed at himself. He was being ridiculous. There was no way he could've deduced all that from a woman who'd simply been taking out the rubbish.

Yet he had. His body knew, even if his mind wouldn't admit it.

Cal had no idea who Juniper was, but he knew he wanted to seek her out. Talk to her. Maybe that would bring him to his senses. She'd say something annoying or find out who he was and act like so many other women had in the past . . . simper and flirt and do everything in her power to try to make him fall in love with her.

Wasn't going to happen. He was immune to love.

But that didn't make his curiosity disappear. Or his libido. Something he'd ignored since his rescue.

For the first time in years, Cal found himself looking forward to the hours and days ahead. Yes, he had to meet Carla Green and assess her stalker situation, but now he had a second goal . . . find the enigmatic Juniper, and see if the draw he felt toward her was a momentary blip. Or something more.

The story his dad told him of the day he'd met Cal's mom popped into his head unbidden. How he'd taken one look at her and known she was the one. He'd told Cal that was how love worked for every man on his side of the family. They met the person meant to be theirs, and the stars aligned, the birds sang, and that was that.

Cal had always rolled his eyes and secretly thought his dad was making up the stories. That he was perpetuating the "royal" Disney myth about soulmates and love at first sight for his young son.

Now, for the first time in his life, he wavered in his long-held assumptions about how his parents had gotten together.

Shaking his head, Cal continued toward the front of the house as he glanced at his watch. Just after five o'clock, with evening fast approaching. And now he was actually eager to get inside . . . because on the other side of the door was a woman who'd caught his attention without even trying.

Juniper "June" Rose wiped her brow on the sleeve of her T-shirt for what seemed the thousandth time since this morning. She was exhausted. She'd been going nonstop for hours. Her stepmom and stepsister had been in a tizzy for days. Ever since they'd gotten confirmation that a real-life prince would be staying in their house.

From what June had been able to figure out from the bits and pieces of whispered gossip she'd overheard from Elaine and Carla while cleaning, Prince Redmon, from some small European country, was coming to DC to talk to Carla about her "stalker."

June snorted out loud. Stalker. Yeah, right. No one was stalking her stepsister—it was just another made-up story for attention. All Carla Green was interested in was mimicking her idols, the Kardashians. Everything she did was toward that goal. She wanted to be rich, famous, and adored.

The problem was, Carla was truly awful. June had never met a meaner, colder, more self-centered woman in her entire life. She actually enjoyed making people cry. To that end, she certainly did everything she could to make *June* miserable. She was eight years younger than June and acted more like fifteen than her actual twenty-four.

But Carla was also gorgeous. She was six feet tall and slender, had long blonde hair and big blue eyes, and when she wanted to, she could be extremely charming. June assumed that was how she'd been able to sweet-talk the man she'd met online who knew Prince Redmon.

June had accidentally interrupted her stepsister one night when she was FaceTiming with the man, Karl—and had been appalled to find Carla naked from the waist up, holding her DDD boobs aloft for the camera.

When caught, Carla had run straight to her mom and accused June of spying on her, and June had to endure an hour of being yelled at and called "ungrateful" and "jealous." Which was ridiculous, of course, but per usual, Elaine didn't give June a chance to tell her what had really happened.

June had dreamt of leaving the nasty women behind more times than she could count. She was thirty-two. She wasn't chained to the house. She could walk away at any point.

But in years past, every single time she'd worked up the nerve to leave, she'd look around and see the chair where her dad used to hold her in his lap and read to her. Or see the marks on the wall of her height throughout her childhood. He'd always made a huge deal when she grew a fraction of an inch, though she'd always been the shortest kid in her class, eventually topping off at a petite five-three.

She'd remember her dad kneeling with her in the garden out back as they pulled weeds and laughed about something or other.

Her dad had adored this house. He'd scrimped and saved in order to be able to buy it, to give his daughter a beautiful home—nothing like the cramped apartment he'd lived in during his youth. Things had been tough in her early childhood, but he'd always managed to pay the mortgage, even if they had to eat hot dogs and ramen noodles for weeks on end.

And throughout all their struggles, they'd had each other. They'd played on the five acres around the house. He'd taught her how to cook. Cleaning never seemed like a chore when he was doing it with her.

Then, when June was fourteen, he'd met Elaine and her six-year-old daughter, instantly smitten with both. A year after that, he was gone, passing away just a few months after his and Elaine's whirlwind courtship.

It wasn't fair. Every day, June still missed her dad terribly. The house, and the land itself, was all she had left of him besides her memories.

It was hard to believe he'd died so long ago. Throughout the years, her stepmom had slowly but surely sold most of the things her dad had loved so much, moving everything else to the basement or attic. The rooms looked nothing like they had when it had been just June and Dad.

As he'd lain in the hospital dying, he told June that the house was hers. That he knew she'd love and care for it as much as he did. And she'd promised to do just that. To preserve their happy memories.

When he died, she was devastated. Hadn't been able to think straight for months due to her grief. At first, her stepmom had been her rock, had kept June from falling apart. But looking back, June now knew the woman had been grooming her. Building her up only to tear her down. Somehow, she'd even convinced June that college would be a waste of time and money. Saying she'd never been academically inclined, and her dad would want her *here*, taking care of the house.

She'd had her first real moment of clarity in her early twenties and started looking into ways to kick Elaine and Carla out of the house before they removed every vestige of her father—only to learn she'd unknowingly signed away her rights to the home her dad had loved and cherished.

One day, right after she'd turned eighteen, Elaine had brought a bunch of papers home and explained they were legal documents June needed to sign for her inheritance, now that she was of age.

She'd stupidly trusted the woman, had signed page after page without reading . . . and had ended up giving ownership of her home to her stepmom without realizing what she was doing.

Reluctantly, June had stayed. Partly because she had nowhere to go and no money to rent her own place, considering Elaine and Carla had basically turned her into a servant, leaving her no time to find work elsewhere. Not that she had enough marketable skills to get a well-paying job.

But mostly she'd stayed because this was where she and her dad had been happy.

Now, with each year that passed, June's stubbornness to stay the course, to not abandon her dad's beloved house to her awful stepfamily, was waning. Carla was a bitch, her two corgis were horrible and just as nasty as their owner, and Elaine had a calculating look in her eye that June didn't trust.

She'd been squirreling money away for a few years now . . . bills she found around the house, change in the washer that Elaine and Carla had left in their pockets, leftover cash from running errands.

It still wasn't enough, not really, but June had finally reached the point where she knew she had to leave. She didn't have any friends to help her, because Elaine had skillfully isolated her long ago from the kids with whom she went to middle and high school. For years, she'd been kept busy working, doing all the cleaning, shopping, cooking, and other errands, leaving no time for a social life of her own.

When she was just out of high school and still deeply grieving the loss of her father, and when she still thought Elaine had her best interests at heart, June had been glad to help out. To do her part to help raise Carla and keep the household running as smoothly as possible.

But now she was keenly aware of just how stupid she'd been. For too many years, she'd been Elaine and Carla's slave—and she was done.

She'd miss the house, but the happy memories with her dad had been replaced by moments of humiliation and degradation. The house was no longer a cherished safe space—it had become her own version of hell.

June didn't know where she'd go or what she'd do, but *anywhere* would be better than here. She'd been researching the best places in the country to live, the cheapest places, and hadn't decided exactly where she wanted to head yet. Somewhere far from Washington, DC, that was for sure.

"Juniper!" Carla shouted as she burst into the kitchen.

June hated how Elaine and Carla insisted on calling her by the name her father always had. At first it had been comforting—it felt intimate and was a reminder of him. But now her full name on their lips was grating and made her skin crawl.

"Yes?" she asked as she turned away from the pot she was stirring on the stove.

"He's here! Finally! He's gonna stay in the room next to mine. You need to get up there and change the sheets. Make sure he has a clean towel—and make it one of the small ones." Her stepsister grinned with a mischievous glint in her eye. "Because I'm gonna *accidentally* walk in on him, and I want to see how big his dick is. Can't do that with a huge beach towel wrapped around his waist. Oh! And spray some of my perfume on his sheets. I want him to associate my smell with being in bed."

"Right now?" June asked. She wanted to roll her eyes at Carla, tell her she was disgusting and far too desperate, but she knew better. It was much easier to fade into the background, to do what she was told, than to disagree. She'd learned that from experience.

"Of course, right now! Duh! You're so stupid."

"Okay, but the dinner might burn if I do," June told her.

"Shit! That won't work. Fine—after you serve us, after the appetizers and before the dessert, while we're eating the main dish, run upstairs and get everything done. Oh, and make sure that the door between our rooms is unlocked too. How else will I be able to accidentally catch him naked?" Carla cackled. "Have you seen him?" she asked.

June shook her head. She wanted to ask her stepsister when the hell she'd possibly have had time to spy on their guest when she was busy doing last-minute chores—like sweeping dog hair from the entryway floors, taking out the trash, and cooking the four-course dinner Elaine had insisted the prince would be expecting.

"I've heard he's covered in scars. Karl actually warned me not to make a big deal about them, but I went online to see what he meant, and he's *hideous* without his clothes. I'll have to close my eyes when he's on top of me because . . . gross!" She paused to shudder dramatically. "But luckily his face is fine. I mean, his nose is crooked, and he's missing part of one of his ears, but I'll make him grow his hair long so it covers that up. As long as he has a big dick, I don't really care what the rest of him looks like. We'll still be beautiful together. I've already started looking at wedding dresses! I want to rival any other royal wedding that's ever been televised! I'm going to be a princess—and I can't wait!"

June felt a pang of pity for the prince. He had no idea the vipers' nest he'd walked into. Had no clue Carla was already planning their wedding, all while calling him "hideous" and "gross" for things he'd had no control over.

Carla stared at June for a long moment. "Well?" she finally demanded.

June knew what she wanted to hear. "You'll be a beautiful bride," she said sedately.

With a fake smile, Carla nodded. "Of course, I will. Mark my words—Prince Redmon is going to be my husband within three months. No one can resist me. I haven't had all those plastic surgeries for nothing. I'm going to be a *princess!*" she declared again.

Then she glared at June. "Don't be late with our dinner. Keep your mouth shut—and don't even look at the prince. He's *mine*, and I'll do whatever I have to in order to have him. Understand?"

June nodded immediately. "Of course."

"Good. God, you're so pathetic. As if he'd ever look twice at a fat cow like you, anyway." Then Carla turned and flounced out of the kitchen.

The second she left, June let out a breath. She'd stopped letting her stepsister's insults get to her years ago. She knew she was overweight, but as long as she was otherwise healthy, she didn't mind. Her dad had struggled slightly with his weight, and she'd seen pictures of her mom. June definitely had the Rose genes . . . she would never be tall and skinny, but she was content with that. While she didn't exercise like most people, working around the house and in the yard kept her muscles strong and her stamina up.

Turning back to the pot on the stove, June heaved a deep sigh. She really did feel bad for Prince Redmon. Carla would be relentless in her pursuit of him, and like most men who got caught in her snare, he'd be hooked before he realized exactly what kind of woman her stepsister was.

But it was none of June's business. She'd tried to warn some of the men Carla had dated in the past, and it hadn't gone well for her. Inevitably, Carla or Elaine found out what she'd said and made her life extremely miserable for weeks afterward. It was easier to just keep her mouth shut—and let Carla's suitors find out for themselves that she was a raging bitch.

June shook her head at the thought of Carla becoming a princess. She'd ruin Liechtenstein's reputation for sure. But again . . . it wasn't her business. When she left, she'd be free of Carla and Elaine Green, and she'd never look back. Her time was coming, and as Carla would say, June couldn't wait.

Chapter Two

Cal's head felt as if it was being squeezed in a vise. The headache he'd had earlier had bloomed into a full-fledged migraine. The amount of perfume Carla Green was wearing definitely wasn't helping. It smelled as if she'd bathed in the stuff.

She was beautiful—Cal couldn't deny that. She was around his height, her blonde hair elegantly done up and her face artfully painted. Her teeth were perfectly straight and unnaturally white, and he could understand why someone like his cousin would be enamored of her.

He'd spoken with Karl while on the road to DC, and his cousin told him how scared Carla was and how much he appreciated Cal doing whatever he could to keep her safe. When he'd asked Karl why *he* wasn't coming to the States to protect her himself, his cousin mumbled something about not wanting to overstep.

Which made no sense to Cal. Karl didn't want to overstep, but he was okay with *him* wading into the situation? He said as much to his cousin, and Karl replied that it was more appropriate because Cal was already stateside and could investigate discreetly. If anyone learned that Karl had flown overseas to help a gorgeous American model, the European press would make assumptions.

Cal had nearly snorted at that. Translation: The monarchy was more than a little frustrated with his cousin's exploits showing up in the tabloids. Flying to Carla's aid in the US indicated a certain amount of interest . . . maybe even enough for the family to pressure Karl into marriage, effectively ending his playboy lifestyle.

That was another reason Cal was happy not to have grown up in his home country, under the watchful eye of the royal court . . . and the paparazzi. If he ever got married—which he doubted would happen now, thanks to his captors turning his once flawless body into a repulsive mess—he'd do so for love. He'd never agree to spend the rest of his life with a woman because of pressure from the monarchy, or because it was expected of him, or because she had the right connections.

"Don't you think?" Carla asked, bringing Cal out of his internal musings. He looked up at her and nodded absently. Apparently, that was enough to satisfy her, because she continued talking about the tennis game she'd had that morning and her upcoming photo shoots.

Carla said all the right things, smiled at the right times, and frowned prettily when he'd asked about her stalker. But he could see through her as easily as if she were made out of a thin piece of plastic—which wasn't far off.

The amount of surgery she'd had was obvious, from her overly pouty lips and her tiny nose that didn't seem to match the rest of her face to an almost permanently surprised expression, probably from the overuse of Botox. Her breasts were so large, Cal was surprised she didn't fall over from the sheer weight of them, and despite being huge, they defied gravity. And she clearly liked to show them off.

After he'd greeted her earlier, she'd quickly disappeared, and he'd gotten nowhere in trying to discuss the stalker with her mother, who'd instead peppered him with questions about his service and his life in Maine. Carla had reappeared promptly at six for dinner, wearing a red dress that only reached midthigh and was cut so low in the front, Cal was afraid her tits were going to pop out of their confinement at any second. A pair of red heels completed the look, along with enough perfume to hide her scent from the most accomplished of bloodhounds.

He'd been told they would talk about the stalker after dinner . . . a pretentious four-course affair that mother and daughter were apparently extremely proud of arranging.

Cal wanted to tell them that he'd already endured too much sitting on the drive. Plus, he hated long, stuffy meals. He'd had to sit through enough of them in his lifetime and much preferred eating comfort food around a small kitchen table or in his living room while watching football—what Americans called soccer—on the telly.

But his breeding meant his manners were nothing if not impeccable, so it looked like he'd have to suffer through an extremely uncomfortable dinner before he could discuss the reason why he was here.

"So, tell us more about Liechtenstein," Elaine said.

"Not sure I can tell you much, ma'am," Cal said. "I lived there such a short while, and I was a young child at the time."

"But you've been back since then. Been to a lot of fancy balls and stuff," Elaine insisted.

"Mom!" Carla said in a fake exasperated tone. "Don't pester the man."

"What are the king and queen like?" Elaine asked, paying no attention to her daughter.

"You don't have to answer," Carla told him as she rolled her eyes.

But Cal could see both women's interest. This was nothing new. He'd been fending off gold-digging mothers and daughters for years. Less often after his capture, but he could still see right through their shenanigans. Elaine would play the "bad cop" and ask all the questions they both wanted answered, while Carla pretended to be embarrassed by her mother's eagerness.

He was just about to ask Carla a question about her friendship with Karl—anything to change the subject—when there was a loud crash to his right.

The woman Cal had seen outside was standing near the entrance to the dining room with a large tray in her hands. One of the bowls had fallen off and shattered onto the tile floor.

"What the hell?" Carla yelled. "Juniper! Clean that shit up!"

"Sorry," the woman said, not sounding very sorry to Cal's ears.

"It's impossible to find good help these days," Elaine said, punctuating the clichéd comment with a shake of her head.

Cal scooted his chair back and was half out of his chair, ready to help Juniper pick up the broken shards of the bowl, when Carla put her hand on his arm, stopping him.

"She's got it. She dropped it, she can clean it up. Just ignore her. I'm so excited about my upcoming photo shoot," she rattled on. "It's with a national retail store. When they called my agent, the rep said I was the only model they wanted, and they'd do anything to get me."

Cal tuned out Carla's conceited ramblings and, from the corner of his eye, watched Juniper deftly clean up the mess. He saw her look up and glance at his dining companions for a quick moment, before looking away with a knowing half smile.

She intrigued him. If he didn't know better, he'd think she dropped the bowl on purpose. Why? He wasn't sure, but it had been an effective distraction from Elaine's question about the king and queen.

Before he was ready to see her go, Juniper disappeared through the door, he assumed to return to the kitchen.

Carla and her mother didn't even seem to notice. They talked nonstop without giving him much of a chance to participate in the conversation, not that he wanted to. His head was still pounding, and Cal wanted nothing more than to get to a dark room, close his eyes, and soak in the silence.

Juniper returned with another tray of food and served Elaine first, then Carla, before walking toward Cal. They were seated at a rectangular table with Elaine at the head, he and Carla on either side of her. Juniper placed a steaming bowl of what looked like French onion soup in front of him, her eyes focused on the task.

Her brown hair was pulled back in the same ponytail he'd seen earlier. Wisps had escaped and were curling around her forehead and face. Her cheeks were flushed, and when he inhaled, Cal could smell onion, garlic, and other spices, obviously from the food that was being prepared in the kitchen.

It seemed as if the Greens had plenty of money . . . the big house, a servant, the immaculate grounds. He yet again wondered why the hell he—a former Special Forces soldier—had been asked to come, instead of the police or a private detective, who would be better able to track down Carla's stalker.

He felt something fall into his lap and looked down in surprise. A foil-wrapped packet of over-the-counter migraine medicine was lying on top of his napkin.

Cal looked up quickly, but Juniper was already walking away from the table.

"I hate this soup," Carla muttered. "And she knows it."

Elaine reached over and patted her daughter's hand as she pressed her lips together. "You don't have to eat it, honey."

"I know. And I'm not. If she thinks she's gonna give me onion breath all night, she's wrong."

The longer Cal spent in Carla's presence, the less he liked her. He had no idea why Karl was so obsessed with the woman. Then he mentally snorted. Of course, he knew. Karl was a boob man. Always had been. Carla probably flashed her knockers at him during one of their video chats, and he had become putty in her hands.

Also, the longer he was around the mother-daughter duo, the more Cal could no longer deny why he was *really* there. Not because of any stalker the girl might have—so far, he hadn't heard or seen any evidence there actually *was* a stalker.

No. Because of who he was. Prince Redmon.

Familiar or not, it had been a long time since he'd had to deal with this kind of shite.

Sighing, Cal picked up his spoon in one hand while grabbing the packet of pills with the other. Instinctively, he kept them hidden from Elaine and Carla. He didn't like to show any kind of weakness to anyone, not that a headache was much of a weakness, but as a POW, he'd

learned to keep his pain to himself. As he leaned in to taste the soup—
which was the best French onion soup he'd ever had—Cal glanced
down and saw something scrawled on the small packet. Presumably a
note from Juniper.

For your head.

Somewhat amusing, because what *else* would the pills be for? But
Cal was still shocked that she'd somehow known he was in pain. He'd
gotten very good at hiding his emotions from those around him, except
for his best friends back in Maine. And somehow this woman, after
being in his presence for what . . . two minutes, while serving meals,
had not only realized he was hurting but had attempted to do something about it.

The draw he felt when he'd seen her earlier increased tenfold. He
didn't know how, but he would figure out a way to talk to her. As soon
as possible.

He managed to eat his soup while half listening to Carla and keeping one eye on the door. He needed to see Juniper again. Wanted to
hear her voice. It was an uncomfortable compulsion, but one he didn't
even try to fight. No one had ever intrigued him so much.

"Are you listening?" Carla demanded.

Cal wanted to say, "No," then stand up and leave, but he'd been
trained from a young age to be polite and never make a scene. "Of
course."

"Good." Then Carla launched into another monologue about her
last photo shoot and every single thing that was wrong with it.

Cal smothered a sigh. This was hell, and he couldn't wait to be
done. He vowed to call Karl and tell him what a wanker he was. And
that he needed to start watching porn instead of chatting with desperate
American women over the internet.

He managed to open the packet of pills and swallow them down
without either woman noticing. Not sure the pills would touch the
hammering in his brain. He was still glad to have them.

The door to the dining room opened, and she was back. Juniper. She didn't look at him, just calmly picked up the soup bowls and headed back out of the room. Cal wanted to know what color her eyes were. Wanted to thank her for the pills. Wanted to see if there was any sign of the connection he felt in her gaze. But he didn't get the chance.

Juniper entered and exited the room many times over the next hour. Filling empty water glasses, removing dishes, and bringing new ones brimming with some of the best food Cal had eaten in a very long time. Meanwhile, Elaine and Carla complained about every course. The food was too cold, too spicy, had too many calories . . . the list went on and on.

But Juniper acted as if she didn't hear their complaints. She didn't say a word as she served the group, her serene expression firmly in place. Cal found himself eating more than he thought he would . . . especially since, when he had a migraine, he usually didn't feel like eating at all.

As he ate, Carla and Elaine prattled on about the modeling contracts Carla had gotten, how she was becoming one of the most well-known names in the industry.

That is, until Juniper brought in a tray of what looked like the most decadent chocolate mousse he'd ever seen, which he couldn't wait to try.

Carla stood up so fast, her chair fell to the floor behind her.

"Are you kidding me?" she screeched. "Mother! Do you see this?"

"Yes, dear," Elaine said calmly. "But I'm not sure it's a reason to lose your decorum."

"She's doing this on purpose! Trying to get me fat! Well, it won't work!" Carla glared at Juniper and said in a low, hateful tone, "*You're* the fat one around here, not me."

"Carla!" Elaine scolded in mock outrage.

Cal watched the scene with extreme interest. Juniper stood stock still, holding the tray with the three plates of dessert, staring at Carla calmly, as if she hadn't just been insulted and denigrated . . . or as if she was used to being spoken to in such a way.

21

Carla took a deep breath and seemed to realize she was making a scene. She turned away from Juniper and smiled at Cal. "I don't know about you, but I'm stuffed. I couldn't possibly eat anything else." Then, still simpering, said, "I suppose it's time to tell you about my stalker. That *is* why you're here. To keep me safe."

Elaine stood, and Cal sighed and followed suit. Despite enduring three courses and over two hours at the table with these women, he was still disappointed he wouldn't get to taste the chocolate mousse. It looked delicious. And if it was half as tasty as everything else he'd eaten tonight, it would've been a nice ending to the meal.

"You heard her. Go," Elaine said in a hard tone to Juniper.

Without a word or a glance in his direction, she turned and left the dining room.

"We'll go to the sitting room. It'll be more relaxing for us all," Elaine said smoothly.

Cal followed the two women out of the dining room, feeling uncomfortable at leaving the dirty dishes on the table. His mom had always hammered into his brain that while he might be a prince, he was still expected to do his fair share of housework. He always had chores, like clearing the table and helping the cook wash the dishes, taking out the rubbish, and keeping his bedroom tidy.

Doing his best to turn his attention to the present, Cal winced when Elaine shut the door to the sitting room a little too hard. Carla walked over to the small love seat and sat. Elaine took the large chair across from her, leaving only one place for him to sit—next to Carla. Which wasn't going to happen.

Before being taken captive, he'd been pursued by the most cunning and desperate women in all of Europe. These two were out of their league. They just had no idea.

He leaned casually against the wall and crossed his arms over his chest. "If I'm going to help, I need to know everything," he said sternly.

A look of frustration that he wasn't falling in line and doing as she wanted crossed Carla's face a second before her lip began to quiver. She reached over to grab a tissue out of the box conveniently placed next to the love seat.

She dabbed her eyes—her *dry* eyes—and sighed before speaking. "It all started about three or four weeks ago. I received some flowers here at home. They were beautiful, two dozen pink roses. The card said, 'Beautiful flowers for a beautiful woman.' I didn't think anything of it. I mean, I get gifts from admirers all the time."

"At home?" Cal asked.

"What?"

"Do you get gifts sent here to your home all the time?"

"Well . . . yeah. Where else would they send them?"

"How do people know your address?"

Carla paused, looking momentarily nonplussed, before shrugging prettily, her breasts almost jumping out of her dress. It was all Cal could do to keep his eyes on her face. It wasn't that he wanted to see her boobs; he was legitimately curious how long the tiny dress could keep them contained.

"I would think it's easy enough to find," she said, shrugging yet again . . . and Cal got a distinct feeling she was *trying* to expose herself, maybe so she could feign embarrassment while he dutifully reassured her that she was beautiful and begged her not to concern herself.

Or maybe she thought he'd be so overwhelmed at the sight of her bare flesh, he'd ask her to marry him right then and there.

That *so* wasn't happening.

"Right, so what happened next?" he asked.

"The next day, I got a letter. It was taped to the front door. It was sweet. Talking about how pretty I was and how much he admired me. Then flowers appeared on my car windshield. Every day there have been gifts. At first, I wasn't worried. Men like to give me presents. But then . . ." She shivered.

"The gifts started getting weird," Elaine said, picking up the story for her daughter. "Handcuffs, a ball gag . . . even a knife."

"A knife?" Cal asked, furrowing his brow. "That's odd."

"Right? It was one of those knives with the ridges on it too," Carla said.

"A serrated knife?"

She nodded. "Yeah, and the note that came with it said he was going to use it on me soon."

Cal's misgivings increased. He highly doubted a stalker would leave a knife for his intended victim. If anything, it would give her something to use against him, which wouldn't be smart. "Where are all the items you've received?" he asked.

"Oh, the flowers died, so I threw them away, and I couldn't bear to look at the other things, so I got rid of them as well."

"And the notes?" Cal asked.

"I was scared," Carla said with a sniff. "I thought if I got rid of them, I wouldn't have to deal with what was happening."

"Did you at least take pictures of them?"

Carla shook her head.

Cal sighed in frustration. Of *course*, there was no evidence. How convenient.

"I'm just so relieved you're here to watch over me," she said breathlessly. "When I told Karl how scared I was, and how I feel like someone's watching me every time I step out of the house, he promised you were the best person to help keep me safe. I just *know* I'll feel more secure if you're with me while I'm modeling. You'll make sure no one gets near me."

"Who do you think this is?" Cal asked. If Carla and Elaine thought he was going to hang out for weeks on end, glued to Carla's side, they were sorely mistaken. He was here as a favor to his family, to gather as much information as he could before talking to either the police or a private detective, who were much more qualified to help. If her stalker was indeed real, the police and an actual bodyguard would do her a lot more good than Cal could.

"I don't know!" Carla wailed. "I mean, I've dated my share of men who weren't happy when we broke up. I've been proposed to twice, and all of my boyfriends were practically obsessed with me, but I don't think any of them would do this."

"I'm going to need a list of names," Cal said, doing his best not to roll his eyes. "Men you've dated, modeling rivals . . . anyone who might have a reason to be upset with you."

"Of course," Elaine said. "I'll start on that tonight and get it to you in the morning."

Cal nodded. "What do you think he wants? Without seeing the notes for myself, it's hard to understand what this guy's motive is."

Carla smirked and sat up straighter, gesturing to her body with a hand. "He wants this," she said arrogantly.

Cal did his best to keep his cool. "Do they just want sex? Or do they want to kill you for some reason? Jealousy? Revenge? Money? There's always a motive, and I'm having a hard time understanding what that is. Once we figure *that* out, we can narrow down the suspects, and the cops can start interviewing any men and women who seem to have the greatest motives."

Carla opened her mouth to respond, but the door to the room opened.

Cal almost chuckled. Saved by the door, again.

Juniper entered, wearing the same jeans, T-shirt, and apron she'd had on earlier. She was carrying another tray that looked way too heavy for her, and Cal actually pushed off the wall to help her before he stopped himself. He had a feeling if he showed the slightest speck of interest in this woman, Carla and Elaine would lose their minds. So he forced himself to slump back against the wall as if he hadn't a care in the world.

He watched as she put the tray down on a low coffee table and poured two cups of what he assumed was coffee. It was so light, he knew without having to ask that it was full of cream and sugar and probably other flavoring. Then she picked up a second pot and poured steaming hot water into a third cup. She picked up the saucer it sat upon and walked toward him, holding it out.

"Peppermint tea," she said almost shyly, without meeting his gaze. "I wasn't sure if you drank coffee, since you're British and all, so I thought maybe a nice cuppa tea would hit the spot."

He grinned at her attempt to use British slang.

"It might help your head too," she said so softly, Cal barely heard her.

Before he could respond, Elaine said sharply, "That will be all, Juniper. We're in the middle of a very important and private conversation. Don't interrupt us again."

Juniper nodded and immediately turned and headed for the door.

Cal took a sip of the tea and sighed in contentment. He'd learned over the years to drink strong black coffee, since it was what his friends drank. But after getting out of the Army, he'd gotten in the habit of indulging in English tea after dinner. This hit the spot.

Once again, he marveled at how observant and considerate Juniper was. He also wondered about her story. She was older than Carla but maybe not quite as old as Cal. Maybe in her early thirties. Why would she stay here? Putting up with being talked down to and treated like shite?

He had more questions about Juniper than he did about Carla's stalker . . . which made him feel a little guilty.

"Anyway, as I was saying, I went to the police, and they said they couldn't help me, since I didn't keep any of the notes or gifts," Carla said, dabbing the tissue at her dry eyes once more as she sniffed delicately. "Basically, they told me that after I'm attacked or killed, they could start an investigation."

Cal didn't know a lot about police procedure, but that didn't sound right to him. He merely nodded and took another sip of tea.

"I wouldn't be surprised if another 'gift' was delivered tomorrow," Elaine said. "He seems to know her schedule, and since she doesn't have a shoot for another couple of days, he'll deliver whatever he wants her to have, to scare her, here at the house."

"Do you have security cameras?" Cal asked.

Elaine shook her head.

"Don't you think you should? It would catch the stalker red handed if he's delivering the gifts," Cal said rationally.

"I've talked to a few companies, but they either don't show up, or they're booked for months," Elaine said with a shrug.

"You could always go to an electronics store and pick up the battery-operated ones. Or order them online; they'd be here in a day or so," Cal pushed. He wanted to see how far they'd go in their excuses. If he or someone he loved had a stalker, he'd have security cameras hooked up as soon as possible.

"I'm n-not so good with electronics," Elaine said haltingly, with a small stutter.

"And they could be hacked into," Carla said with an enthusiastic nod. "Besides, I'm on camera all the time, and it would feel like an intrusion to have them here at home too."

Cal wanted to roll his eyes. Their excuses were ridiculous, and with every word out of their mouths, he was more and more convinced there was no stalker. He'd come all this way for nothing.

He took another sip of his tea, and his lips twitched slightly.

Well . . . maybe not *nothing*.

"Right. So what do you want me to do?" he asked bluntly.

"Keep me safe, of course," Carla simpered. "Stay by my side to make sure this freak doesn't get his hands on me."

"For how long?"

"Excuse me?" Carla asked.

"For how long?" Cal repeated. "Without cameras, it's unlikely we'll be able to catch this person very quickly. If he leaves a note, we could turn that in to the police in the hopes of getting his fingerprints, but if he wears gloves, that will be a dead end. The notes and gifts could go on for weeks. Months. How long do you expect me to stay by your side?"

"As long as it takes," Carla said, almost triumphantly.

"I'm sure you'll figure out who's harassing her sooner rather than later," Elaine said, obviously a little smarter than her daughter and understanding that Cal wanted some kind of time frame. "We know you have your little business up in Maine, and we wouldn't want to interfere with your life for too long. We're just so grateful you came down to see what you could do. So any amount of time you can stay would be appreciated."

He could almost hear the words she *didn't* say. They were hoping he'd fall madly in love with Carla while he was here and decide to never leave. And he didn't miss the bit about his *little* business back home.

"What's your schedule in the morning?"

"I usually eat breakfast around eleven," Carla said. "Then I'm going to go shopping to find some lingerie to wear for a photo shoot I've set up for later this week. My agent said he'd send the pictures to *Playboy* and that there's a good chance I could be Playmate of the Year."

Cal guessed he was supposed to be impressed by that. He wasn't. Not in the least.

"Right, so we'll regroup tomorrow after you've had breakfast. We'll see if any other gifts are left, and I'll look into getting some cameras set up, at least outside the entrances."

"Wait . . . but . . . I don't want cameras!" Carla said with a pout.

"Do you want to catch your stalker?" Cal asked.

"Of course, I do."

"Then I'll be setting up cameras," he said firmly.

Carla glowered. "Whatever."

"It'll be fine, Carla," Elaine soothed. "Prince Redmon obviously knows what he's doing. It's why he's here."

"Don't call me that," Cal said between clenched teeth.

"Oh, sorry. Of course. Cal, then," Elaine said with a smile. "First names are better, since we'll be working so closely together."

That was it. Cal glanced at his watch. It wasn't yet nine o'clock, still early, but he was over this whole evening. "I think we're done here for now. I'll see you both tomorrow." He regretted to his core agreeing to stay at the house while he was trying to figure out who Carla's stalker was. At the time, it seemed easier, and he would be better able to protect Carla from someone who was out to do her harm if he was on the premises. But now that he was pretty sure why he was *really* there—because Carla Green had aspirations to snag herself a prince—he wanted nothing more than to get back into his Rolls and head home.

"I'll show you where your room is," Carla said as she stood.

Once again, Cal wondered how the hell she wasn't falling out of the flimsy cups of the dress. She must have some sort of double-sided tape keeping them in place. Not only that, but the hem of the dress had hiked up so high while she was sitting, he could almost see her underwear.

Cal would never tell a woman what to wear—ever. And she obviously thought the dress was sexy, an opinion most heterosexual men would share. But to his eye, it was simply sleazy.

"No need," he said quickly. "Just tell me where it is. I need to get some stuff out of my car, then I want to walk the perimeter of the house and make a call or two."

Carla pouted again, but Elaine quickly intervened. "We put you in the blue room. Top of the stairs, hallway to the left, the third door on the right. It's got a full bathroom attached, and there are towels and everything you'll want inside."

"Thank you."

"And I'm right next door, if you need anything," Carla informed him.

Cal pressed his lips together. He was in literal hell. "Right. Thanks. I'm sure I'll be fine. We'll talk tomorrow. But ladies, we *will* be going back to the police station soon. They're the ones who'll be able to figure out who's stalking you, and why. Not me."

He saw the clear frustration in both women's eyes, but he was done with this farce for now. He needed some sleep and some peace and quiet. Tomorrow, hopefully when his head wasn't hurting, he'd figure out what to do next. He'd have to stay on his toes around these two—that was for sure. At least it wasn't the eighteen hundreds any longer. He had a feeling neither Elaine nor Carla would think twice about entrapping him in some sort of compromising position and insisting he marry the latter.

Cal walked over to the tray still on the table and deposited his tea-cup before taking his leave. He didn't see anyone around as he strode toward the front door. He stepped outside and walked quickly around the large house, heading straight to his SUV, where he climbed behind the wheel and rested his aching skull on the headrest. The blessed silence was heaven. The over-the-counter pills Juniper had given him had actually taken the edge off his migraine, but nothing would make it go away completely except for a good night's sleep.

He rolled his shoulders and grimaced. His muscles were still tight as hell, and he would've given anything to have a huge tree to chop up right about now. The pain from his time as a captive was always there, but the physical labor he did for Jack's Lumber sometimes helped stretch out the scar tissue and aching muscles.

He curled his hands into fists and opened his eyes. The moon was full tonight, giving him enough light to see the scars on his hands and fingers. He couldn't see the others, as he was wearing long sleeves and pants, per usual, but he could feel them.

He was a modern-day monster. His captors had beaten his face with their fists, saving their knives and other sharp implements for the rest of his body. They hadn't even spared his cock or balls. The pain had been unbelievably excruciating—it still gave him nightmares—but he hadn't given them the satisfaction of hearing a single scream or moan from his lips.

Still, the damage was done. Carla would be appalled if she saw his body. She'd shrink away from him in fear, probably cry real tears—not the fake ones she'd been attempting to squeeze out tonight. She wouldn't want anything to do with him if she knew what he looked like.

Hell, maybe he should let her accidentally catch him without a shirt on. That should be enough to have her begging Karl to make him leave. For a second, Cal seriously considered it. She was right next door. He could "accidentally" leave his door open when he heard her stirring in the morning and let her find him with his chest bare.

There was a chance she'd already cooked up a scheme to catch him naked anyway. She wouldn't be the first. He could just let her have her way, and that would be that.

Cal sighed. No, he wouldn't do that. He was a Redmon. He always followed through with his responsibilities. He said he'd do what he could to get to the bottom of Carla Green's stalker situation, even if that meant discovering no stalker existed. He couldn't leave. Not yet. Not until he had proof of either a real threat or that mother and daughter were lying in the hopes of landing a rich prince.

Taking a deep breath, Cal reached for his cell phone. He'd promised he'd keep his friends in the loop as to what was going on. He clicked on JJ's name and waited for him to answer.

Jackson "JJ" Justice was their de facto leader. He was the oldest of the four of them, and their tree service business was named after him. He was the one who'd suggested getting out of the military and starting some sort of business to begin with, and he was the glue that held them all together. Cal trusted the man with his life and was looking forward to getting his opinion on this messed-up stalker business.

"Hey, Cal. What's up? Everything good?"

"Not really."

"What's wrong? Talk to me," JJ said in a no-nonsense tone, one of a hundred reasons why Cal liked and respected him.

He told his friend and former team leader everything that had happened since he'd arrived. How he didn't think there was a stalker at all, about the Greens' reluctance to put up cameras . . . even describing Carla's overt attempts at flirting and her ridiculously revealing dress. He left out nothing. Not even the pills or tea that the mysterious Juniper had given him.

When he was done, he waited for JJ to say something, and when he didn't, Cal frowned. "JJ?"

"I'm here."

"So? What do you think?"

"I think Chappy is gonna be happy he'll be able to put his ring on Carlise's finger sooner rather than later."

"What?" Cal asked, confused. "What does that have to do with anything? I told him I'd arrange a weekend off for the wedding. That he wouldn't have to wait if this turned into an extended trip."

"I know what you told him, but I also know Chappy. He's not going to want you to drive all the way home, go to their wedding and reception, and then turn around and drive all the way back to DC, especially with the hell that'd wreak on your body. He wants to wait until you're home for good."

"That's ridiculous. I could fly. It wouldn't be a big deal," Cal muttered, but deep down, he knew JJ was right. Chappy was a protector to his core. He wouldn't do anything to stress Cal out or inconvenience him. Even if that meant waiting to marry the love of his life.

"So basically, you think they're lying and that they're hoping her magic tits will somehow win you over, and you'll ask her to marry you, and she'll get to be a princess," JJ summed up in one breath. "Is that about right?"

"Yeah."

"Then why don't you come home tomorrow?" he asked.

Cal sighed. "What if I'm wrong? What if there really *is* a stalker, and when I leave, he strikes, hurting Carla . . . or worse? I wouldn't be able to live with myself."

"Right. So you're going to stay until you know for sure."

"As much as I don't want to, yes," Cal admitted.

Another lengthy pause passed. "What's up with the Juniper chick?"

"I don't know," he said, feeling his heart rate speed up just thinking about the other woman.

"What does your gut say?"

JJ was fond of asking that. He did it all the time when they were in the military. They'd relied on their guts more often than their superiors would've been comfortable with. And since that last mission had ended on such a sour note, and JJ admitted that he'd ignored his own misgivings, he vowed never to do so again.

Even though their gut feelings were no longer life and death but more about which direction a tree might fall when cut down or who should lead which groups on the Appalachian Trail, he was constantly asking for input from the others. Cal wasn't surprised he was asking now.

"That I need to talk to her. Find out what she knows, if anything. Why she's here. Why she puts up with those two bitches. How she knew I had a migraine."

"Then stay until you find out all the answers," JJ said simply. "About the stalker, Juniper, all of it. And when you do, come home with a clear conscience."

"Right."

"I'm guessing you'll be home by Saturday."

Cal chuckled. "It's Sunday," he reminded his friend. "That's not even a week from now."

"I know," JJ said without a hint of laughter. "You're good, Cal," he said. "Damn good. You'll get to the bottom of what's going on in no time. Hell, I think you already have, but you just want more proof. And I'm guessing with how observant this Juniper woman seems to be, she'll probably have plenty of info for you. You know better than most how things work. People talk around the hired help and don't think anything of it. I bet she, and any other people who work in that house, knows all about what Carla and her mother are planning. You can be charming when you want, Cal. Turn that charm in Juniper's direction and find out what you need to know. Then come home so Chappy can get married."

"You just want me on the schedule again," Cal joked.

JJ snorted. "Whatever. You know we can handle things without you. But on that note, April's driving me crazy. She doesn't like it when all her chicks aren't in the nest."

Cal smiled. April Hoffman was their administrative assistant at Jack's Lumber. More than that, she was like a sister to them, even if she acted like their mother. She worried and hovered and generally kept them all on their toes. She ran their business as if she'd been doing it all her life, and Cal didn't know what they'd do without her.

There was also something going on with her and JJ . . . but no one knew what. They acted like they annoyed each other, but when one of them wasn't looking, they couldn't keep their eyes off each other. Cal didn't know what was holding JJ back; he wasn't normally a man who didn't go after what he wanted. But Cal had a feeling that when JJ finally made his move, April wouldn't know what hit her.

"Right. Well, we'll see," Cal told his friend.

"Keep me in the loop. I'll talk to the others, let them know what's up. If you need anything, and I mean *anything*, you call. Understand?"

His tone became hard, and Cal closed his eyes in gratitude. JJ and the others would always have his back, and it felt good. He might be in DC on his own, but they'd be here in hours if he needed them. "Yeah. Thanks."

"Go get some sleep. But watch your back. I wouldn't put it past a woman like Carla to drug you and end up pregnant."

Cal shuddered. "Not happening."

"Right. As I said, watch your back. We'll talk later."

"Later," Cal said, then clicked off the phone.

He stared at the house and sighed. He really did want to do a walk around the property's grounds, get his bearings, see if there were any places someone could sneak up to the house, and scope out the best place to put up cameras. He had a feeling the Greens didn't want security cameras because all they'd catch would be Carla or Elaine planting the "gifts" that were being received.

But again, until he could prove that, he had to operate as if the threat was real.

Taking a deep breath, Cal stepped out of his SUV and opened the back door to grab his duffel bag. He carried it to the house and placed it next to the front door. He'd grab it when he was ready to go inside. Then he turned and began walking around the house. The sooner he got some reconnaissance done, the sooner he could get some sleep.

Chapter Three

June couldn't get their guest off her mind. She was exhausted, but that was nothing new. After cleaning up dinner and making a list of what she needed to buy at the store tomorrow, she headed outside to one of her favorite places in the world.

It was cold, but that didn't bother her. Being outside in the fresh air, alone with her thoughts, away from Elaine and Carla—who might yell at her to bring them something—was heaven.

She was sitting on the old swing that her dad had put up when she was around eight, slowly pushing herself, swaying gently in the moonlit evening.

Hearing a noise to her left, June turned her head and saw a figure walking around the back of the house. For a moment she tensed, thinking maybe Carla hadn't been lying after all, and she really *did* have a stalker, but then she recognized the silhouette.

Cal.

She'd resented the man's arrival because of all the extra work it made for her . . . until he'd actually arrived. Even before Carla admitted her plans earlier that evening in the kitchen, June had overheard her stepsister's excited ramblings to her mother about how she was going to make a real-life prince fall head over heels in love with her, so she could be a princess.

She'd half hoped Carla *did* marry the man, because then she and her mom would likely move away to live in some castle or whatever, leaving June in her beloved family home.

But the second she'd laid eyes on Cal Redmon, June had a feeling the future she'd hoped for wouldn't come to fruition. For one thing, he looked anything *but* overwhelmed with love or lust for Carla. For two, she couldn't help but see the look of obvious doubt on his face when Carla's stalker was mentioned.

She was relieved the man wasn't as stupid as her stepfamily was hoping. But his disbelief meant that he'd probably leave soon, and June herself would finally have to make her move.

She thought she might actually have enough money squirreled away to leave DC. She'd never lived anywhere else and considered the city itself a big tie to her dad. And the thought of leaving the house to Elaine and Carla was still overwhelmingly repugnant.

But it was time.

She'd been nothing but unpaid labor since her father died. Talked down to. Looked down on. And she was done. It was time for her life to begin. Elaine and Carla could fend for themselves; her dad would understand. He'd probably be upset that she'd stuck around this long.

Bringing the swing to a slow stop, June watched as Cal slowly walked the entire perimeter of the house. He examined the windows, the back door, the side door, the trees . . . he left nothing unscrutinized. He disappeared around the other side of the house, toward the front, and June let out the breath she hadn't realized she'd been holding.

She wasn't sure why the man made her uneasy. It wasn't that she was scared of him. He just seemed . . . larger than life, despite what appeared to be a quiet demeanor. He'd seen and done so many things, she felt like a country bumpkin in comparison. She hadn't been anywhere. Had lived all of her thirty-two years in this house, on this property. And she'd been a doormat for her stepmother and stepsister for almost half that. She was shy, not brave in the least, and she hated herself for not having the strength to break away from the unnatural hold they had on her.

To her surprise, Cal reappeared on the other side of the house, but instead of continuing to examine the structure, he seemed to be walking straight toward *her*.

June had thought she was hidden in the shadows. Even with the branches still bare of leaves, she'd thought there was no way he'd see her in the darkness among the thick grove of trees.

But her earlier assumption had been spot on . . . he didn't miss much.

Cal strode right up to one of the large trees on the outer ring of the grove and leaned against it. He didn't say anything, which unnerved her.

She wanted to say something witty, worldly, but absolutely nothing came to mind. She wasn't good in social situations.

After a long moment, he broke the silence. "I'm Cal."

"I know," June replied.

His lips twitched. "You're Juniper?"

"June," she blurted. "Please call me June. Elaine and Carla call me Juniper, and I hate it."

He blinked in surprise. "All right. June. How'd you know?"

She frowned and remained still on the swing, looking up at him. "Know what?"

"That I had a migraine."

June relaxed. For a second, she thought he was talking about Carla's imaginary stalker. "You were squinting, and every time there was a noise, you turned your head away from it."

Cal nodded. "Thanks for the pills."

"Did they help?" she asked softly.

"Surprisingly, yes. As did the tea. Thank you."

For a moment, June was nonplussed. When was the last time some-one had actually *thanked* her? She had no idea. Which was sad and just one more reason to get the hell out of DC. "You're welcome."

"It's cold out," Cal said.

June shrugged. "It's not so bad. I like it out here."

He stared at her for so long, June began to feel uncomfortable. As if he could somehow see right through her. See all her fears, frustrations, and sorrows.

"Shouldn't you be on your way home?" he asked after a while.

It was June's turn to blink in surprise. The strange feeling that she'd met this man before, that they somehow knew each other already, had been so strong, she was actually startled to realize he had no idea who she was. "I *am* home. I live here."

"Oh," he said with a small frown. "I'm kind of surprised the Greens would hire a live-in housekeeper."

June suddenly realized he was fishing for information.

Maybe because it was dark. Maybe because she felt drawn to this man. Or maybe because she was finally ready to move on with her life. Whatever the reason, she was done tiptoeing around who she was to Carla and Elaine.

"Elaine married my father when I was fourteen," she said quietly. "Carla's my stepsister. This was my house—mine and my dad's—before it was theirs. I've lived here my entire life. And they haven't hired a live-in housekeeper. Hiring someone means paying them. I'm not only expected to clean the house, but to cook, do all the shopping, laundry, dog sitting, and simple repairs . . . and all for free."

She was practically out of breath by the time she finished speaking, and she immediately regretted being so honest. She didn't know this man. He could go inside and tell Elaine what she'd said, and then she and Carla would be even more insufferable than they were already. If she thought her life was tough now, it would be nothing after Elaine got through with her for sharing so much with the prince.

June wasn't sure what Cal's reaction to her outburst might be, but she didn't expect him to push lazily off the tree, walk toward her, nod to the swing, and ask, "May I give you a push?"

Stunned, June could only nod.

Cal pulled back on the ropes at her shoulders, then gently pushed her. Closing her eyes, she could almost pretend she was ten years old again, and her dad was the one behind her . . . the last person who'd pushed her on this swing.

It really was too cold outside, but the feel of Cal's hand on her back every time she swung his way was too unusual and comforting to give up in favor of being warm.

Several minutes went by in silence as he pushed her. The longer he went without commenting on what she'd said, the more concerned June felt. For once in her life, she'd been completely honest, but she didn't want this man to think she was a complete idiot. Who would stick around and work like a dog for free?

Finally, she couldn't take the quiet any longer. "When my dad died, I was devastated. For a while, Elaine treated me very kindly. I was fifteen, still in high school, and she came to my extracurricular activities and generally pretended to care about me. But when I graduated, she somehow convinced me to stay at the house and help out with Carla. That turned into cleaning, which turned into cooking, driving them around . . . basically doing everything.

"I wanted to go to college, but never got around to talking to anyone about my options. Elaine kept me too busy. And it felt good to be helping. My dad loved this house. I made him a promise to look after it, to never sell it. He left it to me, you see."

She fell silent, feeling ridiculous all over again. Why was she telling so much to a complete *stranger*? She pressed her lips together.

"What happened?"

Bringing her feet to the ground to stop the swing, June twisted slightly so she could see his face. "How do you know something happened?" she asked.

Cal chuckled, but it wasn't a humorous sound. "I just spent a few hours with your steps, and it's obvious they'd lie, cheat, and steal to get whatever they want."

June stared at him for a long moment, relieved beyond measure that he wasn't falling for their over-the-top charm.

"I was stupid," she finally admitted. "Elaine came to me with a bunch of papers and said they were from the lawyer. Something about my dad's estate. I had just turned eighteen, and since I was legally an adult, I needed to sign them to get my inheritance. I signed the papers without reading them. I trusted her . . . and she got it all. The house, the life insurance money, everything. I inadvertently signed away everything Dad had worked so hard for."

"That bitch," Cal muttered under his breath.

June huffed a surprised laugh, then smiled. "Yeah."

Cal studied her for a long moment. Long enough for June to get uncomfortable yet again. It didn't help that he was standing, and she was still sitting on the swing. He towered over her. She should stand up, put them on more of an equal footing, but for some reason, she stayed where she was. Her head tilted back as she stared at him.

"You stayed," he said in a tone June couldn't read.

She shrugged. "I had nowhere else to go. I didn't have any money, and I made a promise to my dad."

"How old are you?" Cal asked.

For some reason, June felt herself blushing. "Thirty-two," she admitted softly.

"Seventeen years," he said, more to himself than her.

"Yeah," she agreed. "Too damn long. But I'm leaving," she added quickly, admitting it out loud for the first time ever. "I'm done. I've let them take too much from me, and even though I promised my dad, I can't do it anymore."

"Your loyalty astounds me. It's impressive. I've only seen that kind of loyalty a few times in my life."

June couldn't read him. Wasn't sure she wanted to. "It's more like stupidity," she mumbled.

To her surprise, Cal moved until he was in front of her and squatted down. They were eye to eye now, and she couldn't take her gaze from his face. She could just make out his features in the moonlight. He didn't touch her, but she swore she could feel the heat coming off his body and seeping into her skin.

"Where will you go?"

"I haven't decided yet," she admitted, curling her hands around the ropes to prevent herself from doing something stupid . . . like reaching out to this man.

"Hmm." The sound came from deep inside his chest, and oddly, it made her blush again. "It's getting late. You probably have to wake early," he said after another moment.

June nodded. "Not as early as you think. Elaine and Carla aren't morning people. But I do need to go to the store to get some things. Is there anything you'd like? A certain kind of tea? You grew up in the UK, right? I'm sure there's something you prefer, and I can get whatever you want."

"You know about me?"

June stared at him, her mind swirling, trying to decide what to say. In the end, she went with honesty. "Some. When Carla and Elaine started talking about you coming, I wanted to learn more about you."

She caught his slight wince, and hurried on. "I only read your Wikipedia page," she told him. "I just know the basics. I didn't look at the pictures or videos from when you were captured. I know that you grew up in England, and you're bilingual, English and German, and that it's unlikely you'll ever be king because of how many people are ahead of you. You live in Maine, and you own a business with your friends, who are also POWs."

June forced herself to shut up. She'd word vomited way too much, and she was embarrassed. Biting her lip, she waited for him to stand up and storm off. She wouldn't like people prying into her life, so why would he be any different?

But he surprised her by staying right where he was. His gaze was intense, and for the life of her, she couldn't figure out what he was thinking.

"That's a pretty good summary. What the article *didn't* say was how much I love Maine. The remoteness, the physical labor of working with trees, of hiking the AT." He reached out and grabbed one of the ropes just below her left hand. "I'm not going to marry your stepsister, June. Nor am I qualified to be here. I'm not a private detective, I'm not a cop. Yes, I can shoot a gun, but that's about as far as my abilities go when it comes to being a bodyguard. I'm only here because my cousin Karl saw Carla's tits and went a little crazy, begging my parents to ask me to come here to make sure she's safe."

She barked a surprised laugh at his words. "Karl and Carla," June snorted.

Cal's lips twitched. "Yeah. It's ridiculous."

"She does have nice boobs," June mused, then shook her head. Jeez, she was being a dork. Like usual.

But Cal simply shrugged.

June stared at him for a beat. "So . . . you're leaving?"

"Is she really being stalked? Or was that a ruse to get me here, so she could try to get her hooks into me and become a princess?"

June wasn't sure what to say. There was always the possibility that Carla was being harassed; she *was* very pretty, and she was in the public eye, thanks to her modeling career and her own ambitions to become Kardashian-famous.

"They treat you like shite, and yet you're *still* loyal," Cal said with a small shake of his head. "One in a million. Wait until I tell Chappy. He'll laugh his head off."

June didn't know who Chappy was, but she didn't like the thought of this man thinking she was loyal to Carla, who was probably lying her ass off. "I've seen no evidence of a stalker, but that doesn't mean one doesn't exist. And from the little I *do* know, I'm leaning toward her wanting to be a princess.

"She's planning on 'accidentally' coming into your room after you shower," she continued. "She said she wanted to see your penis. She purposely had me put a small towel in your bathroom instead of a larger one. She also made me douse your sheets with her perfume, thinking it would make you think of her as you slept and . . . I don't know . . . become subliminally attracted to her or something?" She grimaced. "There's a linen closet in the hallway right next to your room. There are clean sheets and towels in there. Oh, and the lock to your room is broken, but the one in the bathroom still works."

When Cal didn't say anything, just continued to stare at her with that intense gaze of his, she added lamely, "The room you're in used to be mine. But Elaine decided to turn it into a guest room."

That got a reaction out of him. Cal frowned and let out a small growl.

June had always thought authors of the romance books she liked to read were ridiculous for having their heroes growl constantly. But she understood it now. Goose bumps broke out on her arms.

"Where do you sleep now?" he asked. "And if you tell me the attic, I'm not going to be happy."

June frowned. "I'm in the basement," she admitted softly.

Cal sighed and looked toward the sky as if trying to compose himself.

"It's not so bad. Sometimes I sleep in the sitting room in the winter, when it's really cold. And it's nice and cool down there in the summer, so that's a plus."

"Right," he said sarcastically.

They stared at each other for another heartbeat before Cal abruptly stood. He held out his hand. "Come on, it's cold out here, and you have to be tired."

June stared at his hand, then moved her gaze up to his face. "Be careful," she whispered. "Carla can be ruthless when she wants something, and she has her mind set on being a princess. She'll make my life hell just for talking to you."

"I have no intention of letting her get her claws into me," Cal said calmly. He wiggled his fingers. "Come on, June, let me escort you inside."

No one in recent memory had worried about her well-being or cared if she was tired or cold. She slid her fingers into Cal's large, warm hand. He helped her stand, then didn't let go before turning and heading for the door that led into the kitchen at the side of the house. He led them into the warm room and closed and locked the door behind them.

Then he turned to her and reached for her other hand. June could do nothing but stand there and get lost in his gaze.

"How do you feel about winter?"

She frowned at the surprising question. "Um . . . I'm fine with it?"

His lips twitched. "I'm assuming you don't hate the cold, since you were sitting on that swing out there."

She shook her head. "No, I don't hate the cold. There's something so peaceful and beautiful about the world when snow blankets everything."

Cal nodded.

When he was quiet for a moment, June couldn't help but take the opportunity to study him. The overhead lights in the kitchen were off, but she always left the light on over the stove just in case Elaine or Carla wanted something in the middle of the night. So she could see him a lot better, now that they were inside. His dark hair was a little long, he had stubble on his face, and his lips were way too luscious looking to belong on a man, but it wasn't a turnoff in the least.

His nose was crooked, and part of an ear was missing, just as Carla had said. June knew that was thanks to his time as a POW. His face itself was scar-free, but she could see several gnarly scars peeking over the neckline of his T-shirt. The sight of them made her heart hurt . . . as much as it made her angry. No one had the right to do that to another human being.

"I usually get up early. Will that be an issue?" he finally asked, bringing her out of her inner musings.

"Not at all. What would you like for breakfast?"

"Anything."

June frowned and asked again, a little more forcefully. "What would you like for breakfast, Cal?"

To her surprise, he grinned. Whenever she slipped and used that tone with her stepmother, she paid for it.

"A fry-up?" he asked, his grin widening.

"Fried eggs, sausage, bacon, tomatoes, mushrooms, and toast? I'm not making blood sausage, sorry. That's gross."

He laughed. "Why am I not surprised that you know what a fry-up is?"

June returned his smile. "I read a lot. Is peppermint tea all right? I think that's all we have until I go to the store. I can pick up some black tea or some other flavor if you want while I'm there."

"Peppermint is perfect. I have a feeling I'm gonna need something to keep my headache at bay while I'm here."

June nodded, very aware that he was still holding her hands in his.

"I'm thinking three days," he said.

June frowned. "For what?"

"For me to get the evidence I need that your steps are full of shite."

"Oh," June said, trying really hard to keep the disappointment out of her tone.

"Did you have a timetable for when you planned to leave?" he asked.

Blinking in surprise, June could only shake her head.

"Newton's a nice town. Small but peaceful. My mates are good chaps, and I'm sure there's a flat to let somewhere. Chappy's getting married soon, and his fiancée, Carlise, is a hoot. I don't know her all that well yet, but she'd do anything for Chappy, and that's what matters to me."

"Um . . . that's good?" June replied, thoroughly confused.

Cal gave her a small smile. "Think about it."

"About what?"

"About coming with me. To Maine."

June gaped, stunned speechless.

Then Cal shocked her further by leaning closer and kissing one cheek before brushing his lips over the other. He was still smiling when he pulled back and squeezed her hands. "It's the English way of greeting someone," he said. "Or saying 'see you later.' Sleep well, June."

Then he turned and headed out of the kitchen, presumably to go up to his room.

June stood stock still in the middle of the kitchen and stared at the doorway where he'd disappeared.

She brought a hand up to her cheek and stood there for a long moment. Then she sighed, shook her head, and headed for the basement door. It would be cold downstairs, but if Carla was going to be prowling around, trying to catch their houseguest naked, June didn't want to be caught sleeping in the sitting room.

After she'd brushed her teeth and changed into a pair of sweats, June lay on the lumpy mattress of the old pullout couch and stared into the darkness.

Go to Maine? She couldn't, right? Sure, she'd made up her mind to leave, but she wasn't ready yet.

Then again . . . why not? It had been seventeen years, and it wasn't as if Elaine or Carla were going to change. In fact, if Cal left after just three days, odds were their behavior would get a whole lot worse.

Yes, she had some money, but was it enough to get transportation to wherever she was heading, and lodging, and food until she could find a job? Maybe. But if she traveled with Cal and didn't have to pay for a plane or bus ticket, that would be money she could save. She hadn't thought about going to Maine, but why shouldn't she?

Cal had asked if she liked the winter, and she'd been honest. She did. The cold made her feel alive. Besides, being as curvy as she was made hot summers almost unbearable. Boob and thigh sweat wasn't fun, and if she was cold, she could always put on more clothes. If she was hot, there was only so much she could take off.

Was she brave enough to go with Cal?

She wasn't sure. And it would certainly piss off Elaine and Carla if she did.

As her mind went back and forth, she realized it was funny that she didn't think of him as a prince now that she'd talked to him one on one. He was so much more than a few paragraphs on the internet conveyed. She liked him. Probably more than was smart.

She'd be stupid—well, stupider than she already felt for allowing herself to be treated like crap for seventeen years—to *not* take him up on his offer.

For the first time in ages, a sense of exhilaration welled up inside June.

She was actually going to do it. Get out. Leave. The memories of her father and their good times would be with her always. She didn't need to live in their home to cherish them. It might've taken her too long to realize that she was worth more than being an unpaid servant for her stepfamily, but she was going to take the hand that she'd been offered.

Freedom was finally within her grasp—and June couldn't be more excited. But she'd have to temper that feeling. Make sure Carla and Elaine didn't have any idea that something was up. Because if they knew she was planning to leave—with their prince, at that—they'd do anything they could to prevent it. June had no doubt about that.

Elaine had proved how cunning and immoral she was by stealing June's inheritance out from under her. She was a fool for ever trusting her. She hadn't consulted a lawyer once she'd realized what happened because she had no money, and she had a feeling Elaine would twist everything to her advantage. June could only comfort herself by staying. She might not own the house, but she still lived there, just as her father had wished.

But enough was enough. June was leaving. Nothing would stop her. *Nothing.*

Chapter Four

Two days later, Cal was completely sure Carla had made up the stalker to lure him to DC so she could ensnare a prince.

Cal was used to manipulative women, but Carla and Elaine took the cake. Even *he'd* underestimated them. Until he called an acquaintance of his, a former Navy SEAL who had mad computer skills, who'd been able to hack Carla's computer and acquire a few video chats between the woman and Karl.

He would be having a serious talk with his cousin later, both for being taken in by a pair of fake boobs and a pretty face and for divulging information about Cal himself. But it was Carla's footage that really interested him. It was tough to watch the videos; the last thing Cal wanted to see was the amateur porn show Carla had put on for his cousin. But the info he gleaned was invaluable.

The things she'd told Karl directly contradicted everything she'd told Cal about her alleged stalker. She'd claimed there were cameras at the house, and they'd caught someone wearing all black, slinking around the property, and leaving her nasty notes and scary gifts. The items the stalker had allegedly left at her door were different. Even everything the police had supposedly told her was different from what she'd told Cal.

In short, everything that came out of her mouth was a lie. Cal wasn't exactly surprised, but he was still astonished by how far she and her mother would take this charade.

Cal had kept himself busy, trying to stay away from Carla as he researched the situation, but he'd still been forced to spend more time than he preferred with her and Elaine. And the more he was around them, the more disgusted he became. The way they treated June was truly appalling. That it had been going on for years was the most shocking thing of all.

He hadn't lied when he'd told June she had a loyalty he'd rarely seen. In fact, he'd only seen it in his friends. He knew to his very bones that Chappy, Bob, and JJ would die for him, just as he would for them. But June's actions . . . they went beyond that. She was loyal to a father who was no longer alive, no longer here to see how much she was suffering, all because of a deathbed promise.

Not only that, but she was hardworking, pretty in an unflashy way, and kind.

Cal had always hated any kind of movie that featured a prince . . . which were far too many. Those movies had made his life a living hell, with nearly every woman he met dreaming of riding off into the sunset with him once they learned he was royalty. It was all bullshit. He didn't live like a prince, didn't want to. Being part of a royal family had ended any chance he had of living a normal life, thanks to his captors carving him up so thoroughly.

Despite all of that . . . when he'd talked to June that first night, he couldn't help but compare her to Cinderella. He wouldn't be surprised if she had a family of mice she talked to in the basement where she'd been forced to live.

For the first time in his entire life, Cal wanted to be someone's Prince Charming.

He wanted to rescue the damsel in distress. Wanted to live happily ever after with his princess. It was utterly ridiculous, and not something he'd ever in a million years admit to anyone, even his closest friends. But the more he was around the evil stepsister and her mother and saw how patient and even keeled June remained in the face of their disdain, the more he wanted to snatch her away and make her see her own worth.

It was obvious she had no idea what an amazing person she was. She'd lived under the thumb of Elaine for so long, it was a miracle she'd remained so sweet and thoughtful.

The warning she'd given him that first night had been appreciated—especially when he'd found a damn hand towel in the bathroom, just as she'd said. The smell of perfume on his sheets had almost made him gag. Even after remaking the bed with clean sheets, he'd still had to endure the cloying odor.

Not only that, but he'd seen the doorknob to the loo rattling after he'd gotten out of his shower. The sheer nerve of Carla attempting to invade his privacy almost had Cal storming out of the house and leaving that very night.

The only thing that stopped him was June. And the promise he'd made to his parents to look into the stalking situation.

It was only Tuesday, and he was already done with this farce. Yesterday, he'd installed simple cameras outside the front and back doors, despite Carla's protests and the fact there was no proof of a stalker. It was disgusting that she'd even attempted this ruse. Thousands of men and women across the country were actually being stalked at any given moment, and anyone who lied about such a thing potentially took time away from legitimate cases.

Today, he'd spent his morning at the police station, talking to a detective about the situation and sharing the information he'd been able to learn, thanks to his retired SEAL friend. Cal had just returned to the Greens' home and was heading to the kitchen, hoping to find June and tell her that they were leaving tomorrow.

She'd decided not to tell her steps that she was leaving, had told him with a small smile that imagining the looks on their faces when they realized she was gone—and they'd have to cook and clean for themselves—was something that would sustain her for a long time.

But en route to the kitchen, Cal passed the library, where he caught the sound of Carla and Elaine's voices. The door was open a crack, allowing him to clearly hear the conversation going on inside.

Instinctively, he kept quiet, wanting to know what the bitch duo was cooking up now.

"He's suspicious!" Carla hissed.

"I know," Elaine responded, sounding equally put out.

"I've done everything I know to do, and he doesn't seem affected at all. I don't get it! I mean, I've practically shoved my boobs in his face, and he hasn't even looked twice," Carla moaned.

"Maybe he's gay?" Elaine suggested.

"He's not. Karl said that he used to hang out at the pubs in England all the time and take women home. I'm telling you, I think maybe his penis was damaged when he was captured. Maybe he can't get it up anymore. What's the word for people who have it chopped off?"

"I don't know."

"Yes, you do, in the old days . . . those men who were like religious or something?"

"A eunuch?" Elaine asked.

"Yes! That's it! Maybe he's one of them. Although I think the more current word is Bobbittized." Carla laughed at her own joke.

Personally, Cal wasn't amused. His lip curled in derision. The audacity of Carla discussing his dick, and making light of the torture he'd suffered, was almost unbelievable. But with these two, he was beginning to think anything was possible.

"Anyway, I'm thinking either his dick got cut off, or he can't get it up anymore. Those are the only reasons I can think of for why he's unaffected by my body," Carla whined.

"So we need to give him a reason to stay," Elaine said.

Cal's eyes narrowed as he listened.

"Like?"

"Leave it to me. But this time tomorrow, he'll have all the proof he needs that you have a stalker, and your life is in danger. I'll suggest that you should go into hiding and that you need a bodyguard to go with you."

"Ooooh, I like it!" Carla enthused. "We can go to a remote cabin and—wait, no. I would hate that. We can go to Vegas and check into one of the penthouse suites or something. I'll convince him we'll be safer there because there are cameras everywhere. He's so damn hung up on stupid cameras, he should love that. Then I'll seduce him. I might have to close my eyes so I don't have to see how gross he is, but I'll do whatever it fucking takes to get that crown on my head. And Karl says he's *loaded*! Do you think we'll get married in a big ceremony like Kate and Meghan had? Ooooh, I want a horse-drawn carriage and twenty-seven attendants!"

"You're getting ahead of yourself," Elaine scolded. "Right now, the man won't even look twice at you. You're going to have to act scared out of your mind and make him want to protect you."

"I can do that," Carla said firmly. "If it gets a crown on my head, I'll do whatever I have to."

Cal had heard more than enough. He was disgusted with the entire business. His cousin's infatuation with Carla, his parents insisting he come here after being pressured by the royal family, Carla and Elaine's scheming. And if anyone gave him grief for shirking his responsibility . . . well, he had those video chats between Karl and Carla in his back pocket, if necessary.

He'd fulfilled his duty, had done as promised. There was no threat to Carla, other than her overblown ego and unimaginable desperation.

Forget tomorrow. He was leaving today. Right now.

He quietly continued toward the kitchen. He knew he'd find June there, working hard without complaint to make a dinner no one would appreciate. She'd been up since before six, when he'd come downstairs to find her just finishing his breakfast. She even had a cup of tea waiting for him.

The couple of hours he'd spent with June the last two mornings hadn't changed Cal's mind about her. If anything, the time had made him more curious. Had drawn him closer. She had a comforting presence. She was just as happy to sit in silence with him as she was to chat about the many happy memories she had of her father.

Cal didn't like how quick she was to denigrate herself. To talk down about her lack of education, her lack of sophisticated clothes, her lack of job skills . . . her size.

In his eyes, she was incredibly resilient. There was more to life than a formal education. Some of the smartest people he'd ever met weren't college educated. He'd take a down-to-earth person with street smarts and common sense over someone with a PhD and a giant ego any day of the week.

And June was kind and generous. It was almost unbelievable how thoughtful she was, considering the way she was treated. She could've been bitter and angry, desperate to get back at a world that had dealt her a rotten hand. But obviously her upbringing with her father had left a lasting impression. Cal was disappointed he'd never meet the man who'd raised such an amazing daughter.

He opened the kitchen door, and just as he'd thought, he found June standing at the stove. She turned when the door opened, her cheeks flushed from the heat of the oven and her hair up in a messy bun. She had no makeup on whatsoever and was wearing an apron over a T-shirt and a pair of black leggings.

For a moment, all he could do was stare. Her legs were outlined perfectly in the clingy material, and the curves on display made his mouth water.

"Cal? What's wrong? Are you okay?" she asked with a furrow in her brow.

The fact that she was worried about him didn't escape his notice. He was more sure than ever his decision to invite her to Maine was the right one.

"We're leaving today. Now, actually."

She stared at him in surprise for a beat. "Now?" she whispered.

Cal could hear the trepidation in her tone. He wasn't letting her change her mind. No way.

He stalked toward her and took the spoon out of her hand, turned off the burner under a large pot, and put his hands on her shoulders. He turned her away from him, her gorgeous round arse on display, and pulled the tie holding the apron around her body.

It fell open immediately. It took all his willpower not to reach down and palm the healthy globes hugged by her leggings and the T-shirt that didn't quite cover them.

As Cal turned her back around to face him, he wanted to smirk when he remembered the conversation in the library. About how he might be into guys, or that he must not be able to get it up anymore. He was more aroused by a fully covered June than he'd been in . . . well, longer than he could remember.

He wanted her. All of her. But now wasn't the time or place for those kinds of thoughts.

"Yes. Now," he finally answered firmly.

"Why? What's happened? I thought you weren't leaving until the end of the week."

"Carla's not being stalked. They've made it up. I have all the proof I need. But when I was walking by the library and heard them talking, I—"

"They were in the library? They never go in there," June said in confusion.

Cal nodded. "Yes, they were in the library. Probably looking for books on witchcraft or something. I don't know. Anyway, Elaine was talking about providing proof of Carla's stalker, and I'm not going to participate in this farce anymore."

"How's she going to get proof of something that doesn't exist?"

Cal had his ideas, but what Elaine and Carla did wasn't his concern anymore. "It doesn't matter. I'm done. And we're leaving."

June bit her lip uncertainly.

Cal put his hands on her shoulders again and leaned closer. "The first time I saw you, you were looking up at the sky with the sun on your face and an expression that told me you felt free in that moment. I can help you find real freedom, June. You can feel that way every day and not only in stolen moments from working yourself into exhaustion for no payment or thanks. You can do whatever it is your heart desires. You can be who you were meant to be. All you have to do is be brave enough to say yes. To go downstairs, pack your stuff, and leave with me right now."

Cal held his breath as he waited for June's response. He would kidnap her ass if he had to—for her own good, of course—but he really wanted her to make this decision herself. She needed to. For her own peace of mind.

"I'm scared," she whispered.

"I know." And he did. He never talked about the time when he was a POW, but he found himself wanting to open up to June. "When I was rescued, I was terrified. I knew the assholes had filmed my torture. I wasn't sure who'd seen it, if anyone. And when I found out the footage had been broadcast around the world, I wanted to die. I literally didn't want to live at that moment, June. It almost felt easier to turn around and go right back into that cave. At least there I knew what to expect.

"But I had three mates who told me I'd be fine. That they'd be with me every step of the way, and not just in the scary new world of relentless media attention I found myself in for a time. But while starting a new life in Maine. Let me do the same for you, June. You're braver than you realize. I don't know many people who would've been able to survive what you've been through for so many years. Able to flourish in tiny moments of sunshine, even while locked away in a dark basement. Please let me help you find your footing."

She stared at him for so long, Cal worried that he'd overstepped. That he'd gone too far. But then she whispered, "Why?"

"Because the thought of leaving you here and just walking away makes me sick to my stomach. Hurts more than any torture those arseholes dished out. Besides . . . when Carla finds out that you're gone, and makes the connection that you left with *me*, think about how furious she's going to be." He gave her a grin.

June smiled a little. Then she sobered. "I don't know that I can live a normal life out there. Here, I know my place. My days are all the same. What if I can't find a job? What am I going to do?"

"One day at a time," Cal said firmly. "And princess, your life *here* is the one that's not normal." The endearment popped out without him thinking about it.

He couldn't read the emotions swirling in her eyes, but his entire body sagged with relief when she finally nodded.

"You'll go with me? Right now?"

"Yes."

Triumph rose within Cal. Adrenaline swam in his blood.

"But maybe after lunch? Carla and Elaine usually take a nap after they eat."

Cal wanted to leave right this second, but she had a good point. He didn't want to be in the middle of a scene if he could avoid it, and he knew without doubt that Carla would pitch one hell of a fit when she realized he was leaving.

"Okay. Can I do anything while you go pack?" he asked.

"You can cook?" she teased.

"I've been a bachelor a long time. Of course, I can cook. I can at least stir whatever it is that smells so good in that pot while you're gone."

"Are you really sure?"

He had a feeling she wasn't talking about lunch.

"More than sure. It's going to be okay, June. I promise. And as a member of the Liechtenstein royal family, you should know it's a matter of honor that I always keep my promises."

She smiled at that.

He leaned down and kissed her right cheek, then the left, loving the sweet blush that bloomed on her cheeks. "Go on. Pack your things. Bring as much as you want."

"I don't have much."

Cal wasn't surprised. "Any keepsakes from your dad you want to take?"

She nodded. "A tea set my dad always used when he would play dress-up with me."

"Where is it?"

In response, June walked across the room, knelt down on the floor, and opened a cabinet. She reached in, moving things out of her way, before sitting up with what looked like a silver teapot. "I had to hide it from Elaine. She would've sold it or had it melted down to make some stupid trinket for her to wear. It's solid silver. I asked Dad once why he let an eight-year-old use something so valuable, and he told me that it was made to be used, and he couldn't imagine a better person to use it with than the most important little girl in his life."

Tears were in her eyes as she stared at the tarnished teapot, and Cal made a vow right then and there to learn as much about her father as he could. Not only would it make her happy to talk about her beloved dad, he had a feeling he could learn a lot about how to be a better man from hearing stories of how he'd lived his life.

He walked over and crouched down next to June. "May I?" he asked, nodding to the teapot.

June handed it over without hesitation. Again, the trust she showed in him was humbling.

"Any cups to go with it?"

June shook her head. "No, they were all broken years ago."

"All right. Come on, up you go. Get your things, princess. We'll get on the road right after lunch and make as much headway as possible. It's a long drive up to Newton."

To his relief, she nodded and walked toward the basement door. "Turn the burner back on to medium and stir. Don't let the Alfredo sauce burn. I make it with full-fat cream and cheese, even though Carla and Elaine are constantly dieting," she said with a sly smirk. Then she was gone.

Two minutes later, Cal found himself still smiling at her minor defiance. His June was going to be just fine. She hadn't lost the spark for life deep down inside her.

When he realized he'd thought of June as his, Cal didn't even blink. Somehow, someway, this woman had tunneled her way under his walls . . . and he wasn't sure he hated it.

Chapter Five

June was worried that something would happen to prevent them from leaving, but surprisingly, things went remarkably smoothly. After Elaine and Carla ate lunch, they went upstairs to their rooms, as they did every day. Even though they'd literally just gotten out of bed a few hours ago, they always took a nap after they ate.

The moment their doors shut behind them, Cal was heading down the stairs to the basement to grab her suitcases. It was embarrassing that she only had enough belongings to fill two, but it wasn't as if Elaine gave her any money to shop or, God forbid, bought her any gifts. The money June had saved up over the last few years was stashed in the pockets of her oldest, rattiest pants. She figured no one would think to look there, and the cash would be safe.

Cal had already moved his duffel bag to his SUV, and he quickly and efficiently helped her into the passenger side of the luxury vehicle and shut the door before walking around the front to the driver's side.

As he drove away from the house, June couldn't help but look back at the only place she'd ever lived. It was a bittersweet moment, and she wasn't sure how to feel. There was relief, for sure, but also sorrow . . . and a good amount of uncertainty. Was she doing the right thing? Would her dad understand? Would he forgive her for giving up on their home?

It took a moment for her to realize Cal had stopped the vehicle, giving her all the time she needed to take in the house for the last time.

She glanced over and found his gaze glued to her face.

"You okay?"

She nodded.

"You want me to take a picture with my phone?"

June had a cheap old phone, but she'd left it on the counter in the kitchen. She didn't want Elaine or Carla to have any way to get ahold of her, and she didn't have any friends to call.

She hadn't even thought about taking a picture of the house, and she considered his offer for a moment before shaking her head. "No, I think I'd rather remember it as it was back when my dad was alive. When I had good memories."

"Okay." But he didn't turn his attention to the road. He remained focused on June.

Taking one last look at the house, she forced herself to face him and say, "I'm ready."

June wasn't surprised when Cal didn't ask if she was sure. Didn't offer to turn around. He'd made his thoughts on her leaving quite clear, and he wasn't going to change his mind now. Secretly, June was relieved. It was nice to let someone else make the tough decisions for her. But only for a little while, until she was back on her feet.

With every mile they drove away from the house, June felt lighter. She hadn't realized how much the responsibility of keeping up the large house had weighed on her. She felt guilty about that for a moment, then shook her head. No. Her dad wouldn't have wanted her to feel such a heavy burden. He never would've held her to her promise to keep the house if he could've foreseen the future.

"You aren't freaking out over there, are you?" Cal asked.

June turned to him and offered a small smile. "A little, but I'm okay. This is good. Great, actually. What do you think they're going to do when they wake up and realize we're gone?"

Cal chuckled. "Pitch a god-awful fit," he said.

He wasn't wrong.

"Will you get in trouble? With your family, I mean? You know she's going to go straight to your cousin and make all sorts of false claims."

"I know, and don't worry about Karl. I can handle him. I've already talked to my parents, so they know what's up. They'll deal with his folks, who, in turn, will deal with Karl."

"Will *he* get in trouble?" June couldn't help but ask.

"Would you care?" Cal countered.

June shrugged. "Yeah. I mean, he doesn't know how manipulative Carla can be. And she's really pretty. And you know . . . she's got those tits." She smiled to let him know she was kidding, even though she wasn't really. June had good-size boobs herself, but they were real and therefore showing a bit of sag. Not high and perky like Carla's.

"He's an idiot," Cal said firmly. "And it's about time his parents were clued in to the fact that he's being led around by his cock by perfect strangers he meets online."

June was a little shocked by his blunt words.

"Sorry, I probably shouldn't have said that. But it's true," Cal said quietly.

"It's okay. I mean, I've been sheltered, but I'm not *that* sheltered," June told him.

He gave her a look she couldn't interpret, but she decided it was probably in her best interest to ignore it. To let the subject drop.

"So . . . how far are we going today? And if you need me to drive, I can. I mean, I'll be scared to death I'll wreck your beautiful car, but if you get tired, I can take over."

"I don't care about the car. It's just a bunch of metal. And thank you, if I need you to drive, I'll let you know."

June ran her hand over the smooth leather of the console between them. "A bunch of metal? I heard Carla say it's a Rolls-Royce. And everyone knows that they're super expensive."

"Yeah?" Cal said almost vaguely.

"Of course. It's probably like eighty thousand dollars or something."

"Three hundred and fifty," Cal told her with a laugh.

June's eyes widened, and she gaped at him in shock. "Seriously?"

"Yup."

"Holy cow. I take it back. I'm not driving. No way. Now I'm even scared to touch anything."

Cal threw his head back and laughed so hard, June could only stare. She'd never seen him look so relaxed, so free, in the short time she'd known him. She liked it . . . a lot. And wondered what she could do or say to make him laugh like that again in the future.

"You know I'm a prince," he said, when he had control over himself.

"Yeeeah . . . ," June said, drawing out the word, wondering where he was going with that.

"I'm assuming you also know that most royal families aren't exactly hurting for money."

She nodded.

"I've got more money in the bank than I'll ever be able to spend in this lifetime," he said baldly. He didn't seem to be bragging, just stating a fact. "I wanted a car that was safe, built like a rock, and able to handle Maine winters. I also wanted to be sure I could outrun the paparazzi, if I ever had to, and get immediate attention and service when I want it, like when I check into a hotel or something. This is that car."

"Oh."

He glanced at her. "Look, I don't go around telling people how much my car costs, but it's not hard to do a search online and figure it out."

"So why did you tell me?" June asked.

"Because you're you. Because I have a feeling you have no interest in my bank account. That you'd actually prefer it if I made twenty thousand a year and used coupons when I shopped."

"It's smart to save money," she said defensively.

Cal chuckled. "You're right, princess. All I'm saying is that I trust you."

She looked over at that. "We just met."

The man next to her shrugged. "Yes. Are you going to go online and post pictures of my ride or of me?"

"What? No! I don't even have any social media accounts. And likely never will, since I don't have friends to share them with anyway."

"Right. I trust you," he said again. "And you'll have friends soon enough. I'm sure Carlise will be super excited to meet you."

June wasn't so sure about that. She had a hard time opening up in social situations.

"I think the weather's supposed to hold until we can get back to Maine, so that's good," Cal said, changing the subject, for which June was thankful.

They talked about nothing important for a few more hours. She couldn't help thinking about Carla and Elaine. They'd be awake by now. Would've seen that she and Cal were both gone. She wasn't sure what they would do, but she had a feeling her stepsister wasn't going to let go of Cal so easily. She'd had her heart set on marrying a prince, and now that he'd left without a word, she'd probably be even more determined. Especially if she discovered June had gone with him.

"What are you thinking about so hard over there?" Cal asked.

"Nothing important," June said, determined not to be a downer. She was enjoying her first road trip and didn't want to do or say anything to ruin it.

"You getting hungry?" he asked.

"If you are."

He shook his head, but June didn't know why.

"How about we go for another hour or so, then we can find a hotel and get some dinner?"

"Oh, you want to stop? Instead of driving straight to Newton?"

Cal shrugged. "It's only an eleven-hour drive. I could do it in one day, but we aren't in any hurry. And I don't need to be back until Saturday, which is when Chappy is getting married."

"Really? I mean, they're getting married *this* weekend?"

"Yup. When Chappy heard I was coming home, he immediately arranged it. He's that anxious to marry Carlise. He's flying her mom up from Cleveland, and April is planning a party after the ceremony to celebrate."

"You'll have a good time, I'm sure."

"*We'll* have a good time."

"What?"

"You'll go with me, right? Weddings aren't really my thing."

June stared at him. "I . . . they aren't mine either. I mean, I'm assuming. I've never been to one."

"Then you really need to go to this one. From what I understand, the ceremony itself will be low key. There won't be a ton of people there. It'll be fun for you."

June wasn't sure about that, but she also really, really wanted to go. She'd barely done anything for nearly two decades. She'd been left out, sitting on the sidelines, since she was fifteen. She wanted to experience *everything*. And she couldn't deny that spending time with Cal wouldn't be a hardship.

"Okay . . . if you're sure."

Cal smiled at her. "I'm sure."

Silence fell between them then, but it was comfortable. June's mind was spinning as she watched the world go by through the windows. It felt as if she was having an out-of-body experience. Like it wasn't actually her sitting in this luxury car next to a rich prince, with no job, no place to live, and no idea what was going to happen next. But surprisingly, in spite of those worries, she was content. She trusted Cal. He'd help her get on her feet.

A small smile spread over her lips as she thought about how happy her dad would be for her right about now.

～

Cal looked over at June and couldn't help but enjoy how her smile seemed to light up her entire face. Her hair was still up in a messy bun, she still had on the same T-shirt and leggings . . . and he'd never felt prouder to have a woman sitting next to him than he was right at that minute. As far as he was concerned, she was tremendously brave for taking the leap and leaving the only place she'd ever known. None of the coiffed and cultured women he'd met in the past could hold a candle to June.

She wasn't what society would call classically pretty. There was nothing exotic about her facial features, and her hairstyle was unsophisticated, the color frequently considered "mousy," but Cal didn't give a damn about such things. He was too busy noticing that her hair was the perfect length for wrapping around his fist . . .

No matter her physical features, she had a comforting and attractive internal energy that shone from her every pore. Making him want to get closer, soak up her unique vibes.

The longer he was around her, the more he *wanted* to be around her.

He really *didn't* have to stop for the night, despite how his body ached after long drives. He could drive straight through and get to Newton without having to bother with a hotel, but he could admit he wanted to prolong his time with June. He enjoyed being with her, talking with her, seeing the world through her eyes.

She hadn't been anywhere other than DC. He liked being the one to show her what else was out there. Introducing her to the possibilities of the world.

He had a feeling she was way too good for him. Yeah, he was a member of a royal family, he had plenty of money in the bank, and he was deemed handsome by women and reporters all over the world. Of course, if they only knew what the rest of his body looked like, they'd call him a monster.

His bank account and pedigree didn't matter. There were far more important things in life. June was kind and trustworthy and positive, despite years of mistreatment. And that's what made her better than most . . . including Cal.

Ultimately, he didn't know what would happen between them, but his plan at the moment was to be selfish, enjoy her company, feel normal for a while . . . then find her a place to live, a job, and watch her blossom from afar.

She deserved more than a broken man who couldn't bear to look at himself in a mirror.

The traffic around New York City was atrocious, and they ended up losing a chunk of time as they crept along at fifteen miles an hour. Cal was definitely glad they hadn't ended up there after they'd gotten out of the Army, as Bob had wanted.

A couple of hours later, deciding to stop near New Haven, Connecticut, Cal found a large chain hotel and pulled in. He turned to look at June . . . and couldn't help but smile at the sight of her. She looked extraordinarily excited to be staying the night at a hotel. It made him both sad and angry that she'd never had the opportunity. He'd bet his title and everything he owned that Elaine and Carla had stayed at plenty of hotels in their lifetimes. And they wouldn't be satisfied with a common chain.

Cal wasn't a snob, but he usually stayed at higher-end hotels as well. The ones with valets and the security he sometimes needed when someone recognized him. But he didn't want to drive into the heart of the city to find better accommodations. And while most women would be thrilled to stay in a five-star hotel and be waited on hand and foot, Cal had a feeling June would only feel uncomfortable and out of place.

"Come on, we'll go check in, then come back and grab what we need for the night," he said as he turned to climb out of the vehicle.

Without thought, he took hold of her hand when she met him in front of the SUV, and he led her into the lobby. Cal glanced at her and couldn't help but notice the slight blush in her cheeks. He couldn't remember the last time a woman blushed in front of him, especially for something as simple as holding her hand. He liked that blush. A lot.

Inside, he approached the empty counter and asked the clerk for two rooms with king-size beds for the night.

The lady behind the desk gave him a sympathetic look before turning to her computer. "I'm sorry, but there's a high school lacrosse tournament going on in town, so we're almost completely booked up."

Cal blinked, staring at her for a moment. He didn't normally use his notoriety as a tool to get what he wanted, but he was sorely tempted to try right about now.

"It's okay, I'm sure we can find somewhere else to stay," June said softly next to him. "And if you need me to, I can drive. Maybe we can make it all the way home?"

He could hear the disappointment and trepidation in her tone. It was obvious she didn't want to drive his expensive SUV, but she would if she had to. Cal opened his mouth to tell her not to worry, that they'd figure something out, but the woman behind the counter had been tapping away at her computer, and she spoke first.

"I don't have any king rooms left, but I *do* have a room with a double bed. With all the families here for the tournament, the rooms with queens are definitely all occupied, but I had a cancellation shortly before you walked in. It's a room on the ground floor, near the pool," she said, again sounding apologetic.

Cal winced. The last place he wanted to be was in a room near the pool. Especially in a hotel packed with teenagers. But maybe they'd all be resting for their tournament instead of up all night, causing mayhem in the pool area. He looked at June. "It's up to you."

"We'll take it," she told the clerk.

"Great," the woman said. "I don't suppose you have AAA or anything? It would save you ten dollars."

Cal wanted to laugh at the idea of saving ten bucks. But instead of being a pompous ass, he simply shrugged and told her that, no, he didn't have the discount auto plan.

Within minutes, the lady was handing him two keys and telling them about the free breakfast in the lobby in the morning. She leaned over and said conspiratorially, "It'll be super busy down here around seven because the tournament starts at eight-thirty. I suggest you either eat earlier than seven or wait until eight-thirty or nine if you can."

Cal nodded. "Thanks. Appreciate the tip."

The woman winked. "Your room is right down that hallway on the right. Enjoy your stay."

Cal led June back outside to the SUV and got his duffel bag out of the car. He lifted one of the two suitcases June had packed. "Will this one do? Is your overnight stuff in here, or do you need to grab something from the other one?"

"That one works. Thanks," she told him with a huge smile.

It wasn't until June had opened the door to their room and he'd followed her inside that Cal realized what a colossal mistake he'd made. He'd been so busy thinking about the possible noise level of a room next to the pool, he hadn't thought about the consequences of sharing a room with June—and a single bed.

"Feck," he swore, using the not-as-offensive British slang he used around people who may or may not be offended by the more colorful language he'd adopted while in the military.

"What? What's wrong?" June asked, her brow furrowed. She'd just set down her suitcase and was staring at him with a worried expression.

"There's only one bed," he said, pointing out the obvious.

June looked from him to the bed and back to him. She shrugged. "It's okay. I'll sleep on the floor. I'm used to it."

Cal's head almost exploded. "You are *not* sleeping on the bloody floor," he bit out.

Now she looked confused. "Why not?"

"Because!" he said, exasperated.

"Well, *your* royal butt can't sleep on the floor," she said, voicing what he could tell she thought was a perfectly reasonable argument.

"Princess, I've slept in the dirt, on a muddy riverbank, chained against a wall in a damp dark cell after having the shit beaten out of me . . . I assure you, this floor probably doesn't even rank in the top twenty nastiest places I've slept. But you? You are *not* sleeping on the floor. No fecking way."

She stared at him for a good ten seconds before shrugging again. "Fine. We'll both sleep on the bed." Then she turned around and went to the window. She threw open the curtains, only to chuckle at the view of a large pickup truck parked right outside their room.

Cal could only stare at her. Did she not realize how small the bed was? And that he was *not* a small man? That he'd probably need to sleep diagonally if he didn't want his feet hanging over the edge of the mattress?

Maybe this was part of some grand plan to somehow compromise—

He cut off that thought before it could finish forming. He hadn't known June for long, but there was no way she was anything like her steps. She just honestly didn't seem to have any reservations about sharing the bed.

Cal didn't know whether to be flattered or pissed that she was so naive.

"I thought we could order in tonight," he said.

"Okay."

She was the most agreeable woman he'd ever met in his life.

"But if you'd rather go out, that's okay too," he added, just to be contrary and see what she'd say. He had little patience for indecision or people who went along with whatever he suggested. He never knew if it was because they were trying to suck up to get in his good graces or what. He'd gotten used to his friends back home speaking their minds. If they didn't agree with something he said, they had no problem letting him know.

June studied him for a beat before shrugging.

Disappointment hit Cal. She was going to say going out was fine too. Then he'd have to try to figure out what she wanted to eat. He'd probably end up suggesting a place she hated, and she wouldn't dare say anything, but since she wasn't good at hiding her feelings, he'd still feel guilty about it all night.

To his surprise, June walked over to where he was still standing in the entryway. She put a hand on his arm and looked him in the eye. "You're tired," she said in a no-nonsense tone. "It doesn't make any sense to go back out now that we're here. We can order something to be delivered—that's fine with me. Besides, you got a good parking spot. With this place sold out for the night, I have a feeling if we leave and come back, we might not be as lucky, and someone might break into your car if it's parked in a dark corner of the lot or something, instead of under a light as it is now.

"Maybe there's a game or something on TV you can watch to relax. Would you mind if we ordered from a burger place? It's been forever since I've had a nice juicy burger. Oh! With fries smothered in cheese. And maybe chocolate cake."

Cal knew he was now grinning like an idiot, but he couldn't help it. This woman consistently surprised him. She was considerate, smart—it *would* suck to have his Rolls parked in a dark corner—and decisive. He could definitely live with that. With *her*.

"Sounds like a plan," he said as he pulled out his phone. Burgers and fries typically weren't among his favorite take-out meals. The fries tended to get soggy during the drive, but if that's what June wanted, that's what she'd get.

He scrolled through the app on his phone looking for a burger restaurant that wasn't too far away from the hotel. He found a place called Prime 16 that had great reviews and was listed as one of the top ten best places to get a burger in New Haven.

Cal asked June how she preferred her burger cooked and what she wanted on it, then added his own to the cart. He threw in extra sides of French fries, goat cheese croquette bites, buffalo cauliflower, and fried pickles for good measure. At the last minute, he remembered that she wanted chocolate cake, and while that wasn't an option on the menu, he thought she'd still enjoy the chocolate torte they offered.

Cal was obviously hungrier than he'd thought, but everything on the menu looked delicious.

"You went overboard, didn't you?" June asked with a small smile.

"Why do you think that?" he asked, genuinely curious as to how she was able to read him so well. He'd always been excellent at hiding his thoughts from others.

"You have a look in your eye that tells me I'm going to be shocked by how much food you ordered. And your lips are turned up in a half smile."

"Let's just say I got enough to put us in a food coma, so neither of us will notice any noise coming from the pool area across the hall."

"Good. Um . . . Do you mind if I take a shower while we wait for the food?" she asked with a small crinkle of her nose.

"Why would I mind?"

She looked nervous all of a sudden. "I don't know."

Cal hated to see her sudden discomfort. He walked over to where she was standing near the window, and it took every ounce of strength he had not to touch her. "You don't have to ask me if it's okay for you to do *anything*. Whatever you need, whatever you want, you go ahead and do it."

"Sorry," she said on a sigh. "I guess I'm just used to getting permission to do just about everything."

Cal held his temper in check. Damn her stepmother and stepsister. "Then I give you permission to do or say whatever you want, June."

"And if I said I wanted to go swimming?"

The thought of her in a bathing suit made his cock twitch in his jeans. It was such a surprising feeling, his mind completely blanked for a moment.

It had been over three years since he'd gotten a hard-on. After being tortured, and after those animals had taken great joy in threatening to cut his dick off, he literally hadn't been able to get an erection. Something he'd so easily taken for granted before his capture.

But at the moment, his dick was acting as if it had never been treated to the sharp side of a blade. As if it was more than happy to perform—as long as it was for the woman standing in front of him.

"You want to swim, you go swim," he said tightly.

"Will you come with me?" she asked.

And just like that, his erection disappeared in a flash. "No," he said flatly. He wasn't wearing a bathing suit. Wasn't displaying his body. Opening himself up to the disgusted stares, the pitying looks, the pictures people would be sure to take.

He was so lost in his head, he didn't realize June had stepped closer and was gripping his arm tightly. "Cal?" she asked. "Talk to me."

He had a feeling she'd said his name several times. He gave her a fake smile and a small shrug. "Sorry, I flaked out on you for a moment there. I'm good. And no, I don't swim. Ever. But if you want to, go for it. I think I'll just go and wait in the lobby for our food."

Feeling like an arse, he stepped away from her and headed for the door.

"Cal?" he heard her say, but he ignored the summons. He needed air. Needed to get away from her. Away from her concern, her soft looks, her innocence.

She wasn't for him. She was sunshine and goodness, and he was . . . Cal wasn't sure *what* he was anymore. But he refused to taint her newfound freedom with his demons.

This would've been so much easier if she was a conniving bitch. He knew how to deal with people like that. If she would've looked at him with pity. Or contempt. Or greed in her eyes.

He had no idea what to do with a woman as sweet and giving as June, no matter how much those traits appealed.

He sat down on a bench outside the lobby doors and sighed. She was driving him crazy after just hours alone, and he was suddenly regretting stopping at a hotel. How the hell was he supposed to get through the night with June in the same bed? He wouldn't. He knew that without a doubt.

Once she fell asleep, he'd move to the floor. It wasn't a big deal. As Cal had told her, he'd slept in much worse places.

He had a nagging suspicion that having Juniper Rose asleep in the same room would ruin him for all other women regardless. Would make it impossible to have a good night's sleep ever again.

"Feck," he muttered. He was screwed. She'd already gotten under his skin, and he had no idea what he was going to do about it.

Chapter Six

June bit her lip as she fretted. When Cal returned with their food, he'd seemed to have gotten over whatever had bothered him earlier. He'd laughed and joked with her as they ate as much of the delicious food as they could. He'd totally gone overboard, but June enjoyed everything he'd ordered. She'd only been able to take a few bites of the chocolate torte, but it was heaven.

Not since her father passed had anyone done something as simple as make sure she was fed. She'd been ordered around, ignored, and belittled for ages. Cal even gave her the remote and told her to find something she wanted to watch. She hadn't watched TV in years, and she had no idea what the popular shows were these days, but she ultimately settled on a cooking competition show that looked entertaining.

She'd taken a shower earlier, while Cal was outside waiting on their food, and felt much better now that she was clean.

A shower, a full belly, and a night with nothing better to do than watch a show on TV? It was enough to make a girl feel spoiled.

"What do you think they're doing right now?" she asked quietly.

She and Cal were sitting next to each other on the bed, pillows propped up behind them as they watched the program. He was scrolling through his phone, occasionally typing something, but she could practically feel the tension rolling off him and knew he wasn't relaxed.

Very unlike the man she'd sat next to in the car all day, or even the man who'd dined with her a short while ago.

"Probably pissing themselves that they had to make their own dinner," Cal said with a small smirk.

June didn't really find any amusement in his words. It wasn't that she felt guilty . . . okay, she felt a little guilty, but there was a thread of worry deep inside that she couldn't shake. She knew her stepmother. Knew the woman was mean down to her core. She wouldn't let this go. June had no doubts about that.

"Elaine's going to be mad."

That seemed to get Cal's attention. He put down his phone and turned toward her. "Probably," he said after a beat.

When he didn't elaborate, June sighed and returned her attention to the TV. "I can't believe he thinks just putting those onion straws on top is using the ingredient to its fullest," she said.

"June, look at me," Cal ordered.

She couldn't deny this man anything. She turned her head.

"Your days of worrying about your stepmother and stepsister are done. You're right, neither of them is going to be happy. They thought they'd snagged a prince, and with their toy snatched away, they're going to want someone to pay. And it sucks, but I'm guessing you'll be the one they blame. The one they try to take their frustration and anger out on. But I'm telling you here and now, that's not going to happen. You're safe with me and my friends. I'm not going to let anyone put one finger on you. You're free, princess. Of them, of feeling obligated, of being afraid. You're free to do whatever it is you want."

June couldn't stop the tears from falling. Had she ever had someone stick up for her like Cal?

Yeah . . . once. Her dad. He was her champion. Her cheerleader. She'd looked up to him, and her devastation knew no bounds when he was snatched away from her so suddenly.

Cal had appeared out of nowhere, and he'd taken her from a life she'd hated but didn't know how to escape, offering her a new beginning.

He lifted a hand and placed it on the side of her head, his thumb brushing away the tears on her cheek. "Don't cry," he pleaded. "I can't stand to see you cry."

"Then you need to stop being so awesome," she retorted.

He gave her a small smile. "Tell me you believe me. That you know you're safe and don't have to worry about them anymore."

"I believe that you'll do everything you can," she hedged.

But Cal shook his head and frowned. His fingers burrowed into her hair and tightened. "Not good enough."

June reached up and wound her fingers around his wrist and held on as she stared back. It felt as if they were the only two people on earth right now. Having his complete attention on her was a little discomfiting, but it also felt really good to be truly seen for the first time in years.

"You don't know them, Cal. They aren't going to let this go. They *hate* me. Carla is going to accuse me of stealing you away from her. They're going to want revenge."

Cal didn't look concerned in the least. "They hate you because you're the complete opposite of them. Because you're sunshine and light and everything that's good in the world, and they're bitter, moneygrubbing, fame-seeking bitches who can't stand it when good things happen to anyone else."

A small snort of laughter escaped her. He went on.

"I actually *want* them to try something. Because I have a lot of people who have my back. And not just my military friends. My parents, my cousins, the entire royal family. I don't care that they don't live here, *no one* messes with one of their own. Certainly not useless, lazy American women with overblown senses of self-worth."

Wow. That was harsh. But he wasn't wrong.

"Okay," she told him.

"Are you saying okay because you truly believe what I'm telling you, or are you saying that because you're uncomfortable and want me to shut up and don't know how to make that happen?"

"I believe you," she said honestly. And surprisingly, she found that she did. Every muscle in Cal's body seemed coiled, as if her trust in him to keep her safe was as important to him as breathing. He was intense, and she was sensing he could be a little scary, but she wasn't afraid of him.

With every minute she spent in his presence, June found herself falling deeper under his spell. She had no idea what the future held, but she suspected if he wasn't in it, she'd feel an emptiness and an ache so heartbreaking, she wasn't sure she'd survive it.

But she kept those thoughts to herself as she closed her eyes with a sigh and tilted her head into Cal's hand.

She felt the mattress shifting . . . then she felt his lips brush against hers.

Her eyes popped open, but he was already moving away.

"I'm going to shower. Do you mind if I turn the lights off?"

She shook her head and watched as he flicked off the light next to the bed on his side. Then he strode to his duffel bag, rummaging through it for a moment before disappearing into the bathroom.

June put a finger to her lips. He'd kissed her before, but it had been those light, airy cheek kisses he'd claimed were the norm in Europe. Had he simply missed her cheek?

No, she didn't think so.

Scooching under the covers, June lay down, lowered the volume on the cooking program, and was half-asleep when Cal finally emerged from the shower. From the light of the TV, she was surprised to see he was wearing flannel pants and a long-sleeved T-shirt.

She wasn't an expert, but she didn't think most men slept in so much clothing.

Then she remembered.

His scars.

This guy was the strongest, most masculine man she'd ever met in her life, and yet he was obviously still very affected by what he'd endured. She recalled the pictures she'd glossed over online. The awful ones that were still-shots from the videos his captors had posted for the world to see. The ones that showed his torso and thighs literally dripping with blood.

She remembered the remoteness of his gaze, the emptiness. She couldn't imagine what he'd been through, and it was obvious, at least to her, that he was still struggling with his scars. Probably physical, mental, *and* emotional.

Anger rose within June. She was furious that anyone had dared touch him. They had no right. And for what? For pleasure? For revenge? For fame? It made no sense.

She longed to reach over and snuggle up against his side. To reassure him that she was attracted to him no matter how many scars he had. That she trusted him, and she thought the world was a better place with him in it.

But as soon as he got under the bedding, he turned on his side and put his back to her.

June reached over and clicked off the TV. The sound of laughter coming from the pool area across the hall seemed much louder now that the television didn't drown it out. She ignored it, mostly because all she could think about was the man next to her. She could practically feel the heat coming off his body. The bed was small, but she hadn't realized how much smaller it would become with Cal lying under the covers with her.

She lay silently, listening to Cal's breathing. It was obvious he wasn't sleeping, but June had no idea what to do or say to make him relax. She supposed it was probably awkward for him to sleep next to a stranger, but she didn't feel awkward at all. Somehow in the last few days, he'd stopped being a stranger to her and had started feeling like a friend.

Which was silly, really. She didn't know him, and he didn't know her. She was probably just feeling grateful that he'd helped her. Very soon, she'd need to put on her big girl panties and figure out what to do with her life, now that she was free.

Cal had said it more than once, and she let it sink in. Free. She didn't have to put up with Carla's mean-spirited digs. She didn't have to do Elaine's bidding. She might've lost the house her dad loved, but she'd gained so much more. The ability to do what she wanted. To be who she wanted.

She was grateful to Cal, but that gratitude was mixed in with so many other feelings, she couldn't separate one from the other.

Unconsciously, she moved closer to his back. Her nose was almost touching him, and when she inhaled, she could smell the clean scent of the hotel soap he'd used in the shower. The urge to put her arm around his waist, to tell him that he didn't need to hide from her, that she accepted him exactly how he was, scars and all, was almost overwhelming, but she managed to keep her hands to herself. It would be embarrassing for him to reject her, to look at her with pity and say that she'd misunderstood his motives, that he would keep her safe, but friendship was all there would ever be between them.

The thought of losing that friendship was enough to make her roll and face the other direction, giving him as much space as she could. She needed this man in her life . . . even if it was only as a friend.

"She's a whore! A fat, ugly, deceitful bitch!" Carla raged as she paced the sitting room in agitation. "She stole him right out from under my nose! She *knew* I wanted him. That was the only reason he was here! Because I was going to marry him. I can't believe she snuck out of here without a word. After all we did for her. She's ungrateful and ugly and stupid and . . . and . . . I can't think of what else! I'm too mad!"

"Calm down, Carla," her mom said.

"How can *you* be so calm?" Carla asked in disbelief. "You raised her, gave her everything, and *this* is how she repays you?"

"She's gonna get hers," Elaine said with a glint in her eye.

Carla took a moment to study her mother, then sat beside her on the love seat. "What do you have planned?" she asked, a hint of excitement sparking.

Elaine smiled. "Well, I had something all worked out to prove that you have a stalker . . . and I talked to the guy today, after we found out what that bitch had done. Now he has a new target."

Carla gasped in delight. "Seriously? That's *awesome*! What did you tell him to do?"

"Whatever he feels like. I gave him a menu of sorts."

"What do you mean?" Carla asked with a frown.

"Scaring her with notes or leaving dead animals and other things on her doorstep will get him a hundred bucks. Beating her up will get him five hundred. Putting her in the hospital? That's good for three grand." Her mom's expression hardened. "Making sure I never have to think about her ever again—but not before she deeply regrets defying me? Ten thousand."

Carla's brow wrinkled in confusion.

Her mom rolled her eyes. "*Torture*, honey. Then killing her. The next time I see her name, I want it to be in a news story about her murder. Then you can play the poor brokenhearted sister and win the prince back."

Carla sat up straight and grinned. "Yes! I can do that. But I'm not wearing black. I look awful in black."

Elaine snorted. "Of course not, honey. But we can't talk about this to anyone."

"I won't," Carla said immediately. "Do you think he'll do all of them, though? Like, work up to torturing and killing her? I want to know she's suffering and scared out of her mind."

Her mom stared at her for a long moment.

"What?" Carla asked defensively. "She's been a pain in my ass for years. And in yours ever since you married her dad. Do you . . . ?" Carla bit her lip. "You don't think she discovered he didn't die of a heart attack, do you? That you'd put that suc . . . sucin . . ." She paused to find the right word. "Succinylcholine in his drink?"

Just like that, her mom morphed from the smirking, happy-with-herself woman she'd been a moment ago into someone Carla had never seen. Someone who actually scared her a little.

"Don't *ever* say that again. I mean it, Carla. Ever! My poor husband died of a heart attack. One careless slip, and there's always a chance someone could decide to dig him up and do an autopsy. If that happens, we're screwed. I should've had him cremated, but Juniper pitched such a fit that it would have seemed suspicious if I'd insisted. But he's dead and gone. I got the money I wanted, and you're living the life you are because of me. So don't you *dare* bring that up again. Understand?"

"Yes, Mother. Sorry," Carla said in a contrite tone. It was five years ago that her mom had admitted what she'd done, during a drunken night of celebrating with the modeling agency Carla had just signed with. She'd made her promise never to bring up the death of her step-father to anyone, and she hadn't . . . until now.

"I should've taken her out too," Elaine muttered. "But it's never too late. This will be better. This will support the story about your stalker. The prince put up those cameras, after all, so it's really *his* fault the stalker couldn't get to you and had to turn his attention on your poor sister," she said, smiling wickedly. "Hurting your loved ones in order to make you suffer. To prove what he'd do to you next."

"Where did you tell him to find her?" Carla asked, impressed by her mom's creativity. She didn't like having to think so hard herself. She was used to being the pretty face, to having people take care of her . . . not having to plan things like complicated murder plots.

"Maine. That's where your prince lives. I'm certain he's taken her to that ridiculously tiny town he lives in. It'll be easy to find her but harder to get to her there. If she was in a big city, my guy could just take her out in a robbery gone wrong. But he'll figure it out. And to answer your earlier question, he seems desperate for money. I'm sure he'll run through my menu before he gets to the dessert."

Her mom laughed, and once again, Carla felt an iota of unease. She was very glad her mother was on her side. And why wouldn't she be? She was her daughter, after all.

"So, what are we doing about breakfast in the morning?" Carla asked. She felt much calmer now that she knew Juniper was going to get what was coming to her . . . and that she'd get her chance to marry the prince. Surely, he'd realize he was gravely mistaken about the stalker and come running back to protect her.

She'd also make sure she talked to Karl soon, let him know how terrified she was and help stoke the flames.

She was going to be a damn princess if it killed her. She deserved it.

"When you get up, you can make us something," her mom said offhandedly.

Carla frowned. "Me?"

"You don't expect *me* to do it, do you?" Mother asked with a raised brow. "After everything I've done for you? You wouldn't have that modeling contract if it wasn't for me. We wouldn't be living in this big house if it wasn't for me. You know it's true, so don't try to argue."

Carla took a deep breath and nodded. She didn't know how to cook, but she could make them toast or something. She understood what her mom was saying, and the fact that she'd not only killed her second husband but knew someone willing to travel to Maine to take care of Juniper made Carla think twice about going against her wishes.

She'd just have to look into hiring someone who could cook and clean and do the shopping, everything Juniper had done before stealing her prince and taking off. She'd use her own modeling money if she had to. There was no way she was going to do all the work herself.

Satisfied with the plan for her stepsister, and the idea of hiring someone to help around the house, Carla said good night to her mom and headed upstairs. She had some pictures to take for her social media pages, a bath to enjoy . . . and then she wanted to FaceTime with Karl. Start laying the groundwork for guilting the prince about leaving her alone in her time of need.

After that, she had to pay some attention to her side hustle.

She wasn't making nearly enough money modeling. She blamed her agent, who wasn't getting her the big gigs she wanted. So she'd become a camgirl. Carla had paid good money for her boobs—well, her mom had. She wanted to get as much money out of them as she could.

Going online every night and flashing a bit of herself was like taking candy from babies. It was almost ridiculous the number of men who would literally throw money at her just to show them some tit.

Carla had no idea if her mom knew what she was doing in the wee hours of the night, but it didn't matter. All that mattered was money.

And making her stepsister pay for stealing the prince, of course, so Carla could become a princess. The end justified the means. And she was more than satisfied with the plan to end Juniper.

Chapter Seven

Cal tried to tell himself to move. To get off the bed and away from June—but he couldn't. It was as if his arms were attached to someone else.

He'd had gallant plans to move to the floor as soon as June fell asleep, but just when he was getting ready to slip out of the bed, she let out a small whimper, as if she was having a bad dream.

Cal had moved before even realizing what he was doing.

He'd hated turning his back on her last night after getting in bed, but it was for his own sanity. For the first time in years, he'd masturbated in the shower. The second he'd stepped under the hot water, he'd thought about the fact that June had been in that very space earlier. Naked, standing in the same spot he was right then.

His cock had hardened so fast, it was almost embarrassing. He'd touched himself without thought, groaning at the pleasure that coursed through his body. Ropes of come were shooting from the tip of his dick after he'd barely begun stroking, as if it had just been holding back, waiting for the right woman . . . the one lying so innocently on the bed on the other side of the wall.

He'd quickly washed up, then stood in the loo for a while, donning flannel pants and a long-sleeved T-shirt, refusing to look in the mirror. At home, he slept nude. It was the only time he felt comfortable enough to go without clothes. He had no mirrors in his room and only a small one in his loo, so he could shave without cutting himself to ribbons.

He'd wanted to give June time to fall asleep. But when he'd finally gotten up the nerve to go into the room, he instinctively knew she was still awake. He'd had to turn his back on her because he was seconds away from pulling her into his arms, and he didn't want to pressure her in any way.

Not only that, he didn't want to get used to June being around. Once she was on her feet, she'd see how broken he was. She'd eventually find someone who was much better for her than Cal. Someone who was as good and kind as she was.

He was not that man.

It took a while for her to fall asleep, and when he finally felt he could move without waking her, that whimper belayed his plans. He'd scooted closer and wrapped his arm around her waist, pulling her into the cradle of his body. She'd made a contented noise in her throat, grabbed hold of his arm, and hadn't let go . . . all night.

Now it was morning. The big truck parked outside their window had woken him up when the lights had shone into the room around the blackout curtains he'd pulled shut before dinner. His nose had been buried in June's hair, her body nestled perfectly in his arms.

Surprisingly, he'd slept well himself. He had nightmares frequently and almost always woke up at least once a night remembering the pain of knives tearing into his flesh. Some nights, when he couldn't go back to sleep, he'd pace his house for hours trying to get the images out of his head.

But last night, he'd slept like the dead while curled around June.

He'd been right; the more he was around her, the harder it would be to let her go. He knew that, but still he couldn't bring himself to leave the bed.

"What time is it?" she mumbled.

"Not time to get up yet," he told her. "Go back to sleep."

The truth was, Cal had no idea what time it was. But he didn't want to move. It would only take around four more hours, depending on traffic, to get to Newton, and he wasn't quite sure what would happen when they did. For sure, his alone time with June would come to an end. He'd already called April last night to see if she could find a place for her to live. Then he'd be alone with his tortured thoughts again.

"Okay," she said without hesitation, then shocked the shit out of Cal by turning in his embrace. Instead of pulling out of his arms, she snuggled into his chest as if she'd done it every day of her life.

Turning onto his back, Cal held her against him. Her hair was tangled in his fingers, and he could feel her warm breaths against his chest even through the shirt he wore.

Then he suddenly froze.

During the shift to his back, his shirt had risen up slightly . . . and June's hand eased its way to the bare skin of his belly.

He released a shuddering breath and closed his eyes. His torso had taken the brunt of his captors' rage. They'd taken great joy in carving into his body. In pushing their knives into his flesh hard enough to make him wonder if they were finally going to do it, just plunge a knife into his heart and kill him right then and there. But for reasons he couldn't fathom, they never did.

The scar tissue was so thick in places, he could barely feel anything. But at this moment, the heat of June's hand felt as if it was scalding him where it rested on his abs as she slept.

He felt desperate to grab hold of her hand and wrench it away from his damaged skin, but he also didn't want to wake her. The longer he lay there, the scent of the hotel's shampoo in her hair and the slight weight of her body against him, the more Cal eventually relaxed.

He remained in bed for probably another hour or so before she began to stir once more. Her fingers flexed, nails digging into the skin of his stomach.

Cal sucked in a breath and closed his eyes.

He hadn't been touched intimately since well before he was a POW. Honestly hadn't wanted to be touched this way again. But inexplicably, he felt the urge to put his hand over June's and press it into his skin, not letting her move.

June stirred again. "Um . . . maybe I should . . ." Her sentence trailed off, and she sounded unsure and embarrassed.

When her hand began to slide away, Cal's eyes shot open and he did exactly what he'd been thinking—put his hand over hers and held her still. "Stay," he ordered gently.

She stopped trying to move away, and they lay silent for a minute or two before she spoke.

"I'm sorry if I crowded you. If I *am* crowding you. I don't . . . I haven't . . . I mean, I haven't slept with anyone before."

Cal turned his head to the side, trying to see her face. He was shocked to his core. How the hell was this woman still a *virgin*? Were all the men she'd met morons?

She could clearly see his expression because she huffed out a quiet breath. "No, I mean I've . . . done *that*. You know. But I haven't *slept* slept with anyone before."

Her explanation didn't exactly make him want to revise his opinion of the men she'd known in the past. "Why not?" he asked softly.

She shrugged against him. "They weren't interested in anything but sex? I had to get back to the house before I was missed? I could probably come up with a hundred reasons, but basically . . . I didn't want to."

Cal could understand and respect that. "You weren't crowding me. I was the one who took you in my arms first," he admitted. "I'm drawn to you, June. There's something about you that I just can't resist. Honestly, it's confusing."

"I feel the same," she confessed against his chest.

A fifty-pound weight seemed to lift from his shoulders at that admission, but in the next moment, it settled back down. He shouldn't be here. Shouldn't be quite so truthful. The last thing he wanted to do was get her hopes up that anything might develop between them. Not because he didn't want her—Lord, he wanted her more than he'd wanted any woman in recent memory. Maybe *ever*.

But she could do so much better. She could have a man who wasn't screwed up in both mind and body, like he was.

Despite that ever-present mantra in his head, he couldn't make himself let go of her. For the first time in years, he felt . . . normal. As if he wasn't a scarred mess of flesh under his clothes. An unwelcome surprise waiting for anyone who dared to get close. He definitely wasn't Prince Charming; he was more like the Beast from *Beauty and the Beast*. Unfit to be seen in normal society. Grumpy. Broken. Cursed.

"We should get up, get some breakfast, get on the road," he said after a moment, making no move to escape the bed.

"Yeah," June agreed, seeming to burrow into his side further even as she said it.

Cal's lips twitched, but he didn't complain, only tightened his hold a little. After a moment, he felt her thumb start to move back and forth on his belly. He instantly tensed but forced himself to relax. It felt more like a little tickle than anything else. He couldn't feel much of the slight touch.

"They're the assholes, you know," she said quietly.

Everything in him froze again.

"Anyone who takes pleasure in hurting others has no soul. I don't care if they were born that way, or if they learned their beliefs while growing up. There's no excuse to hurt others, to look down on them, to take away their free will. I don't understand a person's need to have power over someone else. To tell them what they can and can't do. To rule a country and its people with an iron fist. It makes me sad. We're all in this together. Trying to get by, day after day—to figure out where we fit in the world." She sighed.

"And I'll *never* understand the need of some people to hurt others to get what they want. My dad taught me that the only way to reach your goals is to work hard. To help others along the way. To be nice. And I know that concept is completely foreign to a lot of people. They feel as if they have to step on others to get to the top. But why would anyone want to be up there anyway? Seems like it would just be a lot of stress and loneliness . . . people lying and taking advantage of you to get what *they* want. I'd rather stay at the bottom, happy and content, than have to deal with all that.

"Crud, where was I going with this? Oh right . . . what happened to you wasn't your fault, Cal. Your scars shame *them*, not you. They're proof of your strength. The fact that you're here is a testament to your inner fortitude, your tenacity. Feck what others think about you. Your friends know the truth—that you took the brunt of your captors' hatred to protect them."

She wasn't saying anything his friends hadn't told him throughout the last three years, or that the psychiatrists he'd gone to see hadn't said. But somehow, lying here with her in the quiet of the morning— knowing she had no agenda, that she was as good and as transparent as anyone he'd ever met—her words struck a chord deep within him.

They didn't take away the shame. Didn't change the past and didn't make it any easier to look at his body . . . but they did ease the burden he carried on his soul just a tiny bit.

"Did I use that word right?"

He blinked in surprise. "What word?"

"Feck."

He chuckled. "Yeah, princess, you did."

"I'm not, you know," she said after a moment.

"Not what?"

"A princess. I'm about as far from a princess as you can get. And honestly? I don't think I'd ever want to *be* one. Too much pressure. I'm just . . . me."

She was right. She wasn't a princess. The royal life would chew her up and spit her out. Change her into a cynical person. Make her wary and distrustful. And Cal didn't want that.

"Don't change," he whispered. "Be who you are. Who your dad raised you to be. And feck anyone who doesn't see that you're perfect exactly the way you are."

She lifted her head and smiled at him. "What other British swear words can you teach me?"

"I'm not sure I should be teaching you dirty words," he said with a small smile.

"Oh, come on. Please?"

He couldn't resist this woman. Not for a second. "Okay, let's see. There's *arse*, as in *arsehole*. *Blimey*, which is pretty mild, used as an expression of astonishment. *Bloody* is really common, made somewhat famous by Gordon Ramsay, who says 'bloody hell' all the time."

Cal was a little disappointed when June slipped her hand out from under his and sat up next to him. She crossed her legs and leaned toward him eagerly. "What else?" she asked.

Cal pushed himself to a sitting position and, without thinking about it, put his hand on her knee. When he realized what he'd done, he stared at his hand as if it belonged to someone else, thinking he should move it. But it was June's turn to put her palm over *his*, keeping him in place.

"*Bollocks* means *nonsense*, and it's another word for a man's testicles. A *wanker* is a detestable person or as a verb can mean someone who's drunk."

"Is it gender specific?" June asked.

Cal couldn't believe he was having this conversation. "Not really," he said with a shrug.

"So I could say that my stepsister is a wanker?" she asked with a grin.

Cal chuckled. "You could."

"Cool. What else?"

"*Shite* is a variation of *shit*, a *plonker* is an annoying idiot, *manky* is worthless or disgusting. It's a fairly mild descriptor. A *cock-up* is a screwup. And one of my personal favorites is *bugger*. It can be used in so many ways, kind of like how Americans use the word *fuck*. It can be a noun for jerk or a verb meaning to ruin. Or it can be an expression of annoyance."

June's eyes sparkled. "Cool!"

Cal grinned. "Your dad is probably rolling in his grave knowing I'm teaching you all these," he muttered.

"Actually, he'd be just as excited as I am," June countered. "He was wonderful. Funny and sarcastic but also loving and tenderhearted." She sighed. "I think that's how he ended up with Elaine. She probably fed him some sob story about being a single mom and he bought into it hook, line, and sinker."

"How'd he pass?" Cal asked gently, squeezing her knee lightly.

June ducked her head. "Heart attack. Which makes no sense because he was pretty healthy. He weighed a few extra pounds because he loved to eat, but he went to the doctor every year, didn't have high blood pressure or anything, and worked out regularly. I didn't understand it then, and I don't understand it now. One day he was there, and the next, he was in the hospital dying."

The hair on Cal's neck stood up, and his gut rolled. He hadn't known June long, or her stepfamily for that matter, but if what he was hearing was true—if her father had been healthy—something seemed incredibly fishy. "What did the autopsy say?"

June looked up at him with a frown. "Nothing. There wasn't one. Elaine said she didn't want to desecrate his body."

The sixth sense that had saved Cal's life more than once was screaming now. Reminding himself to make some inquiries, or at least to get a friend or two with more clout than he had to look into the situation, Cal changed the subject. "You hungry?"

She gave him a small smile. "I could eat."

"Okay. But one more thing," he said before she could move.

"Yeah?"

"You'd be an amazing princess. One any nation would be honored to have. You'd care about your people first and foremost. You'd put their well-being above all else. You'd fight for them when necessary, and cheer for them when they did great things. You'd be the kind of princess with statues erected in your honor, and you'd earn your people's deep and abiding loyalty. And you'd accomplish all of that without being anyone other than exactly who you are. The world would be a better place if there were princesses like you."

Cal wasn't normally very good with words. He was used to holding his tongue, letting his family speak for him. And while he didn't like the tears that sprang to June's eyes at his little speech, he didn't regret anything he'd said. Every word had come from his heart.

"Go ahead and use the loo first. I'm going to check my emails and let my friends know we'll be there later today, check in with April and see if she's had any luck finding you a place to live."

"Okay."

To his surprise, she leaned forward and kissed one of his cheeks, then the other.

It took every ounce of strength within Cal not to grab her neck and pull her back to him as she moved away.

"Did I do it right?" she asked shyly. "You know, the kissing thing?"

He almost blurted that, no, she'd missed his lips. Instead, he forced himself to nod. "Yeah." He wasn't about to tell her that most people didn't actually touch their lips to anyone. They gave polite air kisses when they greeted others formally.

The skin on his body might be scarred, with so many nerve endings damaged, but his face had long since healed from the abuse it was subjected to . . . and the warmth of her lips lingered.

"I won't take too long," she told him with another small smile, turning to swing her legs over the side of the bed. She disappeared into the loo after grabbing a change of clothes from her suitcase, and it was only then that Cal dared to breathe once more.

He'd known her just days, and she was already the best thing that had ever happened to him. He didn't know what her future held, but he'd cherish every minute in her presence until she decided that Newton was too small. Too remote. That she wanted to move on, do big things in her life somewhere else. He had no doubt that she'd realize her potential sooner rather than later now that she was out from under her stepfamily's thumb.

Thinking about Elaine made him scowl. He'd known she was cunning, but after hearing about the death of June's father, he feared her depravity went deeper than even he suspected.

He was out of his element with murder . . . the little he'd learned came from watching the random crime show here and there. He'd need to call someone who knew what they were doing, see if an investigation was warranted. If nothing else, having to answer questions about her husband's death might take Elaine's attention off the fact that her stepdaughter had left without a word . . . with the man she'd hoped would marry her *real* daughter.

Thinking about Elaine and Carla left a bad taste in Cal's mouth, and he refused to ruin a perfectly good day worrying about them. He reached for his phone on the nightstand. He needed to check in with JJ, make sure Jack's Lumber was holding its own, email Chappy about the details of his wedding, and ask Bob about gift ideas for the happy couple.

The ceremony was a rare chance for Cal to make a grand gesture. Lord knew his friends had refused to use his money to get their business off the ground or to buy any of the gear they'd needed. Yes, he'd chipped in a decent portion, but JJ had insisted on getting a loan and not letting Cal fund the entire operation.

But there was no way Chappy could refuse a healthy donation made in his *wife's* name. Cal knew without fail that anything that might make Carlise's life easier would be accepted without too much grumbling.

Cal owed his friends so much. Without them, he had no doubt that he wouldn't be here today. They'd kept him sane and fighting for his life while they were prisoners. He would've given up if they hadn't been there, if it hadn't meant their captors would've just turned their knives on his friends. He would have given his life for them and knew they would've done the same.

He hated what had happened, hated how he felt about himself now, but he wouldn't change anything if it meant his friends being hurt in his stead.

Cal paused while reading his emails, smiling at the sound of the water in the bathroom. June had admitted never sharing a bed with a man, and he'd never shared a hotel room with a woman. It was intimate . . . and with June, at least, he certainly didn't mind.

The best part about the day was that he had another four or more hours alone with her as they continued north. He had no idea where their conversations would lead them, but he knew he wouldn't be bored. He was eager to learn more about her, but first, they'd check out and eat some breakfast.

And he'd worry later about what would come when they reached Newton.

Chapter Eight

June was glad the clerk had told them the best time to go to breakfast, because even though there were still a good number of people in the lobby, they were able to find a seat apart from the rest of the patrons. The food wasn't anything special, but it would be enough to keep her going until they could stop for lunch on their way to Maine.

June was looking at the trip as a grand adventure, one she hadn't thought she'd ever really get a chance to take. Better still, she hadn't had to spend any of the money she'd painstakingly saved. She felt bad about Cal paying for the hotel, which was one of the reasons she hadn't balked at sharing a room. She appeased her guilt by telling herself he'd have spent money on a room even if he'd been traveling alone.

But the bigger reason she'd agreed—more time with Cal.

He was unlike any man she'd ever met. He was protective and alpha, yet she could tell that he was uncomfortable around people at the same time. He was a prince. Should be used to being around scores of people. Except he clearly wasn't. She figured that a lot of that was probably because of what he'd been through while he'd been held captive.

He was also patient and observant and didn't mind when people cut him off, both on the road and in line at the breakfast buffet. He didn't take himself too seriously, and while she was sure that if the situation called for it, he could morph into the royal he'd been raised to be, she had yet to see him be rude or inconsiderate to anyone.

If he'd been hoity-toity or impolite to others, June wouldn't like him nearly as much as she did. And she liked him a heck of a lot. More than was probably smart.

No matter what he said, she was *not* princess material. Sure, she'd probably replay his words in her head when she needed a confidence boost, but that's all they were—words. She had a feeling if he brought her home to meet his parents, they'd see right through her. Tell their son in no uncertain terms that she wasn't going to cut it in their privileged family.

And the thought of ever being introduced to the king and queen of Liechtenstein made her want to barf.

No, she and Cal came from very different worlds, and the sooner she got that through her skull, the better off she'd be. She appreciated his assistance, but she had a feeling as soon as they got to Maine, and he settled back into his routine, he'd wonder what he was thinking, rescuing her from her situation and allowing her access to his life.

In the meantime, however, she was going to enjoy the unexpected change in her circumstances as long as she could. Starting with the runny oatmeal, lukewarm eggs, and mushy hash browns in front of her. It was pretty subpar, but it was also food she didn't have to buy or prepare and therefore was extra appreciated.

"It's not great," Cal said, reading her mind with a grimace after taking a sip of the coffee he'd gotten from a large carafe in the corner of the lobby.

June couldn't help but giggle. "You should see your face." She grinned.

He smiled dryly. "I can't help it. I got used to amazing British breakfasts the two mornings I spent in DC. Although I have to say, the company here is just as good as it was there."

June felt herself blushing. This man. He had a way of saying the perfect thing. If she was more worldly, she might think he was flirting with her.

The Royal

"Ugh," he said after taking another sip. "I can't drink this. I miss your peppermint tea. I'm going to throw this in the rubbish bin and get a juice. You want anything while I'm up?"

"No, I'm good," she told him, pleased that he'd enjoyed the tea she'd made for him.

She watched as he stood and headed for the trash can in the corner of the room. She saw more than one woman's gaze follow him, and her lips turned up in a small smile when he didn't seem to notice. The man was the most oblivious attractive person she'd ever met . . . or maybe she was just used to the way Carla preened everywhere she went, how she *expected* to be stared at.

June had a feeling if Cal knew how much attention he earned—not because he was Prince Redmon, but because he was a very good-looking man—he'd be appalled. He did his best to fade into his surroundings, but it was impossible. Even if he hadn't been a prince, he'd garner respect and attention everywhere he went.

Movement to the left caught June's attention. An older man was sitting by himself attempting to eat, but his hand was shaking so much, he promptly dropped his fork on the floor. She watched as he stared at it for a moment before sighing and pushing his still-full plate away.

June was moving before she thought better of it. She picked up the extra set of cutlery on their table—Cal had brought her a set, not knowing she'd already grabbed her own—and walked over to the old man's table. She pulled out a chair and sat, saying, "Hi! I'm June."

He looked up in surprise but gave her a small smile. "Edgar."

Without making a fuss, June unwrapped the unused plastic cutlery as she spoke. "I'm from Washington, DC. I'm here with my friend—he's over there, getting some juice, because he's a tea snob." She whispered the last part, as if admitting a state secret.

The old man chuckled. "Can't blame him. I'm partial to a hot cup of tea myself."

"Are you here alone?"

"Yes," he said quietly.

"What brings you here?" she asked as she nudged the man's plate closer to him and scooped up a spoonful of eggs before placing the cutlery in his hand. She held his hand with her own, and he stared at her in disbelief mixed with what she hoped was relief, not irritation.

She held her breath, praying she was doing the right thing. She truly wasn't trying to be rude or pushy, but she couldn't sit a table away and watch someone go hungry because of a physical disability.

Finally, he moved the utensil toward his mouth. She held his hand steady as he wrapped his lips around the spoon.

"I'm on my way to visit my wife's family. She died last week," Edgar said sadly.

"Oh, I'm so sorry," June replied gently, helping him scoop up another mouthful of eggs. "Were you married a long time?" she asked.

"Sixty-one years," Edgar said proudly. "She was the love of my life. I don't know what I'm going to do without her."

"Oh, that *is* a long time." June continued to assist. It seemed as if he was lost in his memories, barely aware he was still eating. "You must miss her so much."

Edgar looked up and met her gaze. "She always helped me eat . . . just like you are."

June gave him a tender smile.

"Everything okay?" Cal asked.

June felt his hand on her shoulder and tilted her head up to look at him. "Hi, Cal. Everything's perfect. This is Edgar. He's my new friend."

"It's nice to meet you," Cal said, giving June's shoulder a squeeze. "May I join you?"

Edgar gestured to the seat across from him.

To her relief, Cal didn't question what she was doing. He simply went back to their previous table, grabbed the coffee she'd been drinking, threw away their empty plates, and joined her and Edgar.

As she helped her new friend eat, he and Cal launched into a conversation about the Army. It turned out Edgar was a veteran, and he and Cal had a lot to talk about. June didn't think Edgar even realized when he finished his breakfast. She got up to get him a hot cup of coffee, careful not to fill it so much it could spill in his shaky hands, and when she returned, he and Cal were still chatting away.

She put an elbow on the table and her chin in her hand, listening with a small smile on her face. After a while, Edgar looked over at her.

"Sorry, you must be bored out of your mind."

"Not at all," June protested. "I'm fascinated."

"How long have you two been married?" Edgar asked.

June dropped her hand and looked at Cal in embarrassment.

He didn't miss a beat. He reached over and took her hand in his, bringing it to his mouth and kissing the back before saying, "It feels like both forever ago and just yesterday that we met."

June's cheeks were burning, but she couldn't take her gaze from Cal's. Her heart was beating hard in her chest, and butterflies swam in her belly.

Edgar chuckled. "That's how I felt about my Betty," he said.

June turned her gaze back to the older man but was very aware that Cal hadn't dropped her hand. She wasn't sure what was happening at the moment, only that it felt . . . right.

The three talked for another ten minutes or so before Edgar finally looked at his watch and declared that he had to be going. They all stood, and Cal took Edgar's dishes over to the bins.

"Thank you," Edgar told her solemnly. "You didn't have to help me."

"Of course, I did," June countered. "And it was my pleasure. You've made my day, and I hope maybe when you get to where you're going, you'll keep in touch?"

"I'd like that," he said gruffly.

Cal returned, and he put his hand on the small of June's back. It felt like a brand on her skin, and she surreptitiously leaned into him the tiniest bit.

Cal held out his hand to Edgar, and the two men shook.

"You're not what I expected," the old man said seriously.

"You recognize me?" Cal asked, clearly surprised.

Edgar nodded. "From the second I saw you across the room." He gestured to June with his head. "She's one of a kind," he said. "Don't let her go."

Cal nodded. "She's definitely one in a million," he agreed.

"Are you driving to where you're going?" June asked tentatively. She couldn't imagine him behind the wheel of a vehicle, considering she had to help him eat.

"Lord, no," Edgar said. "My son-in-law is meeting me here in about ten minutes. He's driving down from Hartford this morning. My daughter dropped me off here last night."

"Okay, then," June said, feeling sad that they had to leave him.

"I'll be fine, child. But I appreciate your concern. Most people wouldn't even have taken a second glance at me."

"Well, then they're missing out," June said firmly.

"Thanks again," Edgar said. "I'll be in touch." He pocketed the business card Cal had slipped him at one point. Then he turned and limped toward the hallway that led to the lobby.

"You ready to go?" Cal asked in a tone June couldn't read.

She nodded.

They headed for their room and gathered their stuff, and June waited patiently while Cal checked out. He took her elbow in his large hand and led her to the parking lot. They stowed their stuff, then Cal walked June to the passenger side of the luxury SUV. He opened the door, and when she would've climbed in, Cal stopped her.

She looked at him, frowning when he didn't say anything. He just stared at her for a long moment.

"What? Do I have something on my face?" she asked self-consciously.

Cal shook his head and brought a hand up to palm her cheek. "The more I learn about you, June Rose, the more fascinated I become."

June shook her head, although she didn't really know why.

"You were great with him," he said.

"Edgar?" June shrugged. "He needed help."

"He was right, you know. No one in that lobby looked twice at him. Except you. And not only did you see him, you saw that he needed help, and you acted. And actually seemed to enjoy his company."

"Why wouldn't I?" she asked a little defensively. "He's old, not diseased."

"You like the elderly?"

June's brows furrowed in confusion. "Yes, why?"

"I don't know. Some people are uncomfortable around them."

"Well, that's silly. They're just people. And like you found out today, most have fascinating stories and histories to share, if we just stop long enough to listen. I think we could all learn a lot from our older generation, but most of the time, we're too busy with our faces locked on our phones and other electronics, too busy going, going, going to stop and talk to them."

"I agree," Cal said. His thumb barely brushed her lower lip.

"Why didn't you tell him we weren't . . . *together* together?" she blurted.

Cal didn't seem fazed by her question. "Didn't seem right at the time," he said easily.

His answer told her nothing, but she already knew him enough to realize that if he didn't want to explain, nothing she said would convince him to elaborate.

June took a deep breath in through her nose. She could've stood there forever, staring up at Cal, smelling his clean scent, memorizing his face, trying to figure him out. But that wasn't logical. They had places to go, things to do. "Are we leaving?" she whispered.

"Yeah," Cal said, but he didn't step away from her.

She gave him a small smile. "I'm not sure you can drive from where you're standing."

He grinned. "Probably not." Then, slowly, he leaned in. Giving her time to protest, to pull away, to ask him what the heck he was doing.

But June wasn't about to do any of those things. She knew whatever was happening at the moment couldn't last. He'd get bored with her quickly enough. She wasn't a model like Carla, and she wasn't exactly the most interesting person in the world either. She hadn't ever left DC, hadn't ever eaten a hotel's crappy breakfast. And she was almost entirely dependent on him.

He'd help her get settled; she had no doubt about that—he was too honorable not to—but then he'd figure out anything brewing between them was an aberration, and he'd get back to his life.

But he was here *now*. Standing so close she could feel his body heat. And leaning ever closer with a glint in his eye that she was sure resembled her own gaze. She lifted her chin slightly and was rewarded with the tightening of his fingers as their lips met.

At first, he merely brushed her own lightly, fleetingly. Quick and almost unsure.

June couldn't stop herself from touching him. Her hands rested on his chest as she made a small noise in her throat.

Then his lips were on her again, the polar opposite of the last kiss, moving with a confidence that took her breath away. If she were a more romantic woman, she would've called it a claiming.

His tongue licked along her seam, and she eagerly opened for him. He tasted sweet, like the juice he drank at breakfast. June felt light headed and off balance as his tongue caressed her own, and her fingers dug into the material of his shirt as she did her best to stay upright. But Cal wasn't going to let her fall. His other hand wrapped around her waist and pulled her close, holding her against him even as his head tilted, and he deepened the kiss.

June had never felt this way before. As if she wanted to devour and *be* devoured. Cal's kiss was passionate but not obscene. He didn't slobber all over her, didn't try to force his tongue down her throat. He didn't manipulate her head this way or that, just moved naturally as they explored each other.

Way before she was ready, Cal's head lifted, but he didn't go far. He rested his forehead against hers as he struggled to slow his breathing and regain his composure. June was relieved she wasn't the only one so affected by their kiss.

"I shouldn't have done that," he said after a long moment.

Every muscle in June's body tightened. He regretted kissing her?

God, how humiliating. She tried to pull away, to put some space between them, but Cal's hold tightened as he lifted his head and stared at her.

"I shouldn't have done that . . . but I've never been given a sweeter gift. You're amazing, June. You're the most giving person I've ever met. You're tying me in knots after mere days, and I'm not sure if I should be scared out of my head or if I should tie *you* up, throw you into the cargo area of my Rolls, and spirit you off to some abandoned cabin to keep you for myself until the end of my days."

June was so surprised, she burst out laughing. "You'd be bored silly in no time," she assured him, then licked her lips, loving how his flavor lingered there.

His gaze locked on her lips, and he inhaled deeply. "I seriously doubt that. Are you okay?"

She frowned. "Why wouldn't I be?"

Cal shrugged. "Just wanted to make sure you don't regret coming with me. You're safe. I won't force myself on you. I just . . . lost my head there for a moment."

June frowned. It sounded as if their kiss was a onetime thing. That he had control of himself now, and he was telling her it wouldn't happen again.

Disappointment filled her, but she patted his chest and did her best to smile. "It's okay. I trust you."

"Thank you, princess. Shall we get going?"

She nodded, shivering slightly as he dropped his hands from her, and she climbed into the passenger seat. He closed the door, and she took a deep breath, trying to get control over her emotions as he walked around the car.

She wanted him. More than she'd ever wanted anything in her life. She'd even agree to go back to DC and be an unpaid, unappreciated burden in her stepmother's life if it meant she could have one night with the man climbing into the driver's seat next to her.

And not because he was a prince.

Not because he was rich.

Not because he drove a car that cost more than most people's houses.

Because he was Cal. The kind of man who would take the time to talk with an elderly man he'd just met. Who would hold a woman all night and not try anything sexually. Who could see through Carla and Elaine's lies to the truth beneath.

And because he turned her on more with a mere kiss than others had managed with sex.

"And we're off," Cal said lightly as he started the engine. June turned her attention to the navigation system. She'd been in charge of it the day before, telling him where the rest areas were located and when they were approaching traffic. He gave her an address in Newton, and she entered it. The electronic voice of the British lady on the nav app, who managed to sound refined instead of robotic, informed them that their destination was three hours and forty-three minutes away.

A few minutes of silence went by as Cal steered them onto the highway. Then he put his hand on the console between them, palm up.

June looked at it, up at Cal, then back at his hand. She struggled internally for two seconds, then mentally sighed before placing her hand in his.

He squeezed her hand but didn't say a word.

They drove northward hand in hand, and June did her best to convince herself she wasn't falling in love with the man next to her. She couldn't be. It was too soon. She barely knew him. She was too plain. He was too . . . everything.

But no matter how she tried to argue with herself, a part of her deep down knew it was too late. She'd already fallen, hard and fast.

Closing her eyes, June rested her head on the seat back. She had no idea what her future had in store, but she was determined to enjoy her time with Cal . . . because sooner or later he'd be gone, and she'd be alone again. Until then, she'd absorb every ounce of his attention she could, and she promised herself she wouldn't make a scene when he eventually put distance between them. She was who she was . . . Cal was who *he* was. And that was as far apart as two people could get.

Tuning out the pesky part of her that was determined to fight for what she wanted, that was trying to convince her she was just as worthy of Cal as anyone else—certainly more than her stepsister would've been—June turned her thoughts elsewhere. What she'd do with herself once she got to Maine. How she could make a living. She'd do whatever it took to *not* have to go back to DC. To not fall back under Elaine's thumb.

Whether or not she succeeded depended on her ability to stand on her own two feet, and that was exactly what she was going to do.

Chapter Nine

The closer they got to Newton, the more out of sorts Cal felt.

He'd enjoyed his alone time with June. Was selfish and didn't want to share her with anyone else. His friends would want to know everything about her. April would want to make sure she had no ulterior motives; she was like a protective mother bear when it came to "her boys." And Carlise would want to be her new best friend.

All of which were good things, but Cal wanted to wrap June in a bubble and keep her to himself. It made no sense. It was bloody ridiculous. And yet, he couldn't shake the thought.

As he pulled into town, the feeling only got stronger, more urgent. It was all he could do not to drive straight to his house, haul her inside, and lock the door behind them.

But June was sitting up in her seat, looking around with wide, excited eyes. And the last thing Cal wanted to do was dim that enthusiasm.

To him, Newton wasn't terribly exciting, but it was home. It was a typical small American town, a place where he was now comfortable enough to be himself. No one here treated him as Prince Redmon. To the locals, he was an employee of Jack's Lumber who came to their aid when a tree fell across a road, or on a house, or on someone's property. He climbed into trees to rescue kittens—and kids—who'd gone a bit too high to come down safely without assistance. He wasn't born and raised there, but he was treated like one of their own.

He pointed out the various buildings and businesses that he figured she might be interested in visiting at some point. Granny's Burgers, the small grocery store, the hardware store, the one and only beauty shop in town. June nodded at each, and he figured she was making mental notes as to where everything was, so she wouldn't have to ask in the future.

He'd learned that she wasn't big on asking for help. He would have to watch out for that—

No. Cal shook his head. It wouldn't be his job in the future. She'd find someone else who would willingly keep her safe and make sure she didn't try to handle everything on her own.

"The empty room April found isn't too far from here," Cal forced himself to say. His tone was a bit gruff, but he didn't think June noticed. She was too busy taking in the sights.

It was early afternoon, and the sun was out, although it wasn't exactly warm. Spring came late to this part of Maine, and Cal was looking forward to being busy with the tree business and leading hikers on the AT once more. It would give him something to do other than obsess over the woman next to him.

"Are you sure they said there was no deposit?" June asked worriedly. "That doesn't sound right."

"If April said it, it's true," Cal told her. When they'd stopped for gas, he'd found an email from April with the address of the place and the basic details of the lease.

"Okay. I have enough for about three months' rent if the cost she mentioned is right, but not much more. I'll look for a job right away."

It took everything in Cal not to insist he'd pay for her rent, that she didn't have to worry. June had pride, which he understood, but there was no way he was going to let her go hungry or be homeless if she couldn't find a job.

"It'll work out," he said, keeping his concentration on their surroundings. He hadn't been to this area of Newton before, so he wasn't sure where he was going. The navigation system gave him turn-by-turn directions—and when it announced that they'd reached their destination, Cal frowned.

This couldn't be right. This couldn't be the room April had found for June.

They were parked in front of a house that looked as if it had seen much better days. The porch was missing a couple of boards, there was a rusted-out car in the front yard, and the place was badly in need of a paint job.

"Oh . . . it's . . . kind of cute," June said after a pregnant pause.

It wasn't. It was a disaster. June, being June, was simply trying to remain positive.

"I'm sure the room inside will be fine."

It wasn't an apartment complex, just a single room the homeowner was renting out. Cal had known as much. Rental places in such a small town were rare, and the few apartment buildings were usually full. He knew it had an attached loo and a separate entrance, as it was a room in the basement. When he'd asked about a kitchen, she'd emailed back something about a hot plate and a dorm fridge. Not ideal, though he'd agreed to look at the place.

But now? After seeing the house in person? He knew exactly where he'd take June.

Without saying a word, Cal put the Rolls in reverse and backed out of the driveway, which was full of deep ruts.

"Cal?" June asked.

He didn't respond, just pulled away from the house.

"Where are you going? Stop!"

"You aren't living there," he said firmly.

"I know the outside needs some work, but I'm sure the room is perfectly adequate. If nothing else, it'll be *mine*. I won't have to be at someone's beck and call. I can do what I want, when I want—"

"You can do that where I'm taking you too," he said as calmly as possible.

He was making a mistake. He knew that. The more time he spent around this woman, the harder it would be to walk away. But he wasn't going to let her live somewhere that didn't look safe. Where *she* wasn't safe.

Maybe he wasn't being fair; he hadn't seen the room, after all, and he hadn't met her prospective landlord. But he couldn't leave her in that shithole of a house. He just couldn't.

"You know of another room? Did April send you more than one place for us to check out?"

"Yes," Cal lied, not feeling the least bit remorseful about it. He had a few choice words for April, but they could wait. Sure, he'd given her only a day's notice to find something, but he couldn't understand why she'd ever think *that* place was appropriate. He could only guess she hadn't seen it firsthand . . . but that wasn't like their admin. She was nothing if not thorough.

"Okay," June said quietly.

It didn't take Cal long to get to his destination. He pulled into the long driveway and glanced over at June.

She was staring at the house with wide eyes. "Holy crap, Cal. This is gorgeous! This can't be right. There's no way I can afford whatever the rent is to live here."

Satisfaction swam through his veins along with relief that she liked the look of the house. It was his pride and joy. He'd bought it when he'd first moved to Newton and had done a lot of work to make it into what it was today. He'd spent every waking moment that first year fixing it up when he wasn't working his day job. The result of hours of online instructional videos, and a lot of blood, sweat, and tears, it was a house he was proud to call home.

"You can," he assured her as he stopped the Rolls.

June stepped out of the SUV and continued to stare in wide-eyed wonder at his house. The wraparound porch had a swing on it usually, but it was currently in the garage for the winter. He had a couple of chairs on the wooden deck, though, and even a wreath on his front door—one that April had bought for him.

The two-story house looked as if it came straight out of an architectural magazine. It was part of the reason Cal had bought it. He'd loved the old-fashioned woodwork, even if it made upkeep a bitch in the harsh Maine climate.

It had an open floor plan, cathedral ceilings, a chef's kitchen, crown molding, and yellow birch hardwood floors. He had two fireplaces, one in the master bedroom and another in the great room.

"Come on, I'll show you around."

"Wait—what?" June asked, finally clueing in.

But Cal didn't give her a chance to balk. He took her hand in his, ignoring how right it felt, and towed her toward the front door.

"I usually use the back door, as it's closer to the detached garage, but I figure you'd get the most out of the tour if we went in through the front."

"Wait, Cal, *you* live here?" she asked.

"Yes."

"And you rent out rooms?" she persisted.

"No. Not usually. But apparently now I do."

"I can't—" June started.

Cal turned to her once they'd cleared the three steps to the porch. He yanked her toward him, ignoring the small *oof* when she hit his chest. "Yes, you can. And you will. There's no way I'm leaving you at that poor excuse for a house. I don't care if the rooms inside are immaculate. The roof probably leaks, and the neighborhood looks dodgy as hell.

"You'll be safe here. I give you my word as a member of the Liechtenstein royal family. You can get on your feet, find a job, save some money, then find your own place. Please, June . . . don't make me take you back there. I wouldn't be able to sleep. I'd stop eating from worry. Waste away to nothing." He was laying it on thick, with a small grin for her benefit . . . but he was being completely honest too.

June rolled her eyes. "I really shouldn't," she said.

"You should," he countered. "At least take a look. I have a guest suite on the second floor—it has a little sitting area and your own en suite loo. We'll have to share the kitchen, but if that makes you uncomfortable, we can get you a small fridge and whatever other appliances you need or want for your room."

"I don't mind sharing a kitchen with you, Cal," she said with a huff. "Jeez. We slept together last night. Why would I care about sharing your kitchen?"

As soon as the words were out of her mouth, she blushed a fiery red.

"I mean . . . I . . . um . . . *shoot.*"

Cal let her off the hook, even though her words brought memories of holding her to the forefront of his mind. "I know what you meant, and I'm glad. I'm not a slob, I clean up after myself, and there will be times when I'm not here for several days and nights in a row, if I'm on a job out on the AT. You won't even know I'm here much of the time."

But he'd know *she* was there for sure.

Reluctantly letting go of her, he turned to the door and put his key into the lock. "At least give it a look," he cajoled.

"All right. But if at any time you change your mind, you have to promise to tell me," she fretted.

"I will," Cal said, knowing he'd never reach that point. He might encourage her to go, to spread her wings and fly, but he'd never kick her out from a lack of wanting her there.

He held his breath as she entered his home. He wanted her to like the inside as well, which was a new feeling. He didn't care what others thought about his house, but he desperately wanted June to feel comfortable.

She strolled around the great room with wide eyes, touching things here and there as she explored. When she went into the kitchen, he heard her quick indrawn breath.

"Wow, Cal. This is . . . I don't even *know* what this is."

"It's a kitchen," he deadpanned.

He'd spared no expense when he'd redone the space. He wasn't the best cook, but he wanted a kitchen that was well organized, beautiful, and functional.

He had a deep farmhouse sink, long counters, custom woodworked cabinets, deluxe appliances, a small food prep sink, marble countertops, a Bertazzoni freestanding gas range, a double refrigerator, a wine cooler, custom-designed storage for pots, pans, and lids, and every other gadget and kitchen utensil known to man.

Now that he thought about it, Cal realized he'd gone way over the top. But he liked what he liked. The kitchen was easy to get around and looked damn good as well.

She turned to him, shaking her head. "You know, up until this moment, I didn't really think about the fact that you were rich. I mean, you mentioned having plenty of money. And I would've figured it out if you hadn't, what with your car and all, but . . . I guess I blocked it out. Now? Seeing this?" She waved her hand, indicating the large kitchen. "It's really hitting home. I don't think I can live up to all this." She looked around again, frowning as she swallowed nervously.

Cal walked toward her. She backed up until she was against the counter and couldn't go any farther. He got close enough to touch, without actually doing so. But he was definitely crowding her.

"Not live up to it? You already do," he insisted, hoping she could hear the sincerity in his tone. "You're one of the most inspiring people I've ever met . . . and that's after being around you for less than a week. Your loyalty, even to people who haven't done one iota to deserve it, is mind blowing. Your ability to feel empathy for others, to treat them with kindness, to smile when your world is bleak, to find joy in the moment, to be humble—all of those things make me feel as if I'm completely failing at this whole living thing.

"This kitchen? This house? My car, my bank account, and everything else . . . I'd give it all up in a second if it meant being able to change my past. To be anonymous. To not have been a target simply because of my heritage. But I can't. So I've hidden out here alone. Built this beautiful house, because I thought it would make me content and happy.

"It's only after meeting you that I've remembered *things* can't do that . . . only people can. I've been more relaxed, more settled, in the few days I've spent with you than I have in years in this house. *You've* done that. Not the material things I've collected or the lofty title hanging over my head. And again . . . I'd give it all up today if I could be the kind of person you are. To live a life free of bitterness and wariness toward my fellow man."

Cal realized he was babbling. Talking about stuff that had little to do with the elegant, expensive kitchen that had started this conversation. But he couldn't seem to hold back around June.

He flinched slightly when she lifted a hand, but relaxed when she placed it on his cheek.

"Cal," she whispered.

She didn't say anything else for the longest moment. Finally, when she spoke, her brown eyes held so much emotion and intensity, he couldn't look away.

"I *am* bitter," she told him. "I'm angry that my dad died and left me alone with Elaine. I don't trust people pretty much *ever*, but you were an exception. And your family, your experiences . . . they've all made you into the man you are today."

Cal couldn't help but wince at that.

June shook her head. "No, it's not a bad thing. You're protective and watchful. Wary of other people and always on alert. And you might think those are negative traits, but in my eyes, they're a gift. For so long, I've had no one to rely on but myself. I've had to watch my own back, fend for myself. But around you, I've been able to relax. Let down my guard just a little, simply because I know you're there. Paying attention to the people around us, the cars, the very *space*.

"Don't you get it? If you weren't who you are now, if you hadn't experienced what you have experienced . . . I wouldn't be here. I wouldn't have trusted you when you said you wanted to help me. So don't be ashamed of your past. It's there. It can't be changed any more than mine can. All we can do is be grateful for the lessons we've learned and move forward."

Cal wanted to nod. To tell her she was wise and that he fully agreed. But he was still too swamped with bitterness. With shame. Her words felt good, really good . . . but he wasn't ready to completely believe them. Not yet, and maybe not ever.

"And as far as this kitchen goes . . . I'm thinking I could probably get used to it," she teased with a small smile.

Cal covered her hand where it lay on his cheek. He kissed her palm after lifting it, keeping her hand tightly in his. "You aren't a house cleaner," he warned her. "Not my cook, not my maid. This is your *home*. You want to leave your shoes in the middle of the floor, feel free. You want to invite people over to visit? Go for it. I'll get you a key so you can come and go as you please, and we'll see what we can do about getting you a reliable vehicle as well. In the meantime, you can use mine when you want, and if I need to go anywhere, I'll get a ride from one of my friends. I want you to be comfortable here, princess. Don't feel as if you can't touch or use anything in this house. It's all just stuff. Understand?"

"Why are you being so generous?" she whispered.

"You don't know?" he asked.

She gave a small shake of her head.

There was so much Cal wanted to say. So much he wanted to admit.

But she'd run scared if he told her that he could easily imagine June as his future. That he could practically see his unborn children in her eyes. That after mere days, he already knew he'd become a shell of a man without her in his life.

And he wouldn't admit any of that, even if she was willing to hear it. He wasn't good enough for her. Money and a title weren't enough to hold this woman's interest. To satisfy her huge personality. Her sunny disposition. He didn't want to taint her. Hold her back. Drag her into his darkness.

"Because you deserve so much more than you've gotten in life thus far," Cal settled on saying.

"So do you," she said softly.

Cal almost laughed at that. Ninety-nine percent of the people in the world would disagree with her. They'd take one look at his bank account, at his family, and assume he was the spoiled rich prince the media loved to exploit with fabricated stories about his life.

"You'll stay?" he couldn't help but ask. "Even though my car scares you, and my kitchen makes you afraid to touch anything?"

She smiled, and Cal realized he'd do anything, *anything*, to keep that happy look on her face.

"Well, I haven't seen the rest of the house, but I'm thinking I could move into this kitchen and sleep on the floor and be completely content."

"So that's a yes?" he pressed.

"Yes, Cal. I'd be honored to stay here for a while."

For a while. God, he hated hearing those three words, but she was right. Eventually, she'd want a place of her own. A good man in her life. She might even find Newton not to her liking and decide to move to a bigger city. It would kill him to let her go, but he would. He liked her more than enough to want the best for her, and he knew deep in his heart that it wasn't him.

"Good. If you want to go upstairs and explore the rest of the house, I'll get our bags and move the car into the garage. I thought I'd grill up some steaks tonight, if you're interested . . ."

Cal did his best to sound nonchalant, but the simple act of discussing what to have for dinner with this woman felt so right.

"I can help with the bags and dinner," she offered immediately.

"I know you can, but you don't have to. I've got it. Let me treat you. First night in your new place and all," he said somewhat lamely.

"All this and being waited on . . . ," she teased. "I'm not sure I'm ever going to want to leave."

A pang hit Cal hard and fast. He didn't want her to leave either. But he recognized that she was making a joke, so he grinned. "The guest suite is upstairs to the left. Take your time. I'll bring your suitcases upstairs in a few minutes."

Then he forced himself to let go of her hand and turn his back on her as he headed to the front door.

"Cal?"

Her voice stopped him in his tracks, and he turned around. "Yeah?"

"Thank you."

The two words were whispered and so full of gratitude—and some other emotion he couldn't read—that they made Cal's insides ache. He hated that so few people had been kind to this woman. She'd lived in a pit of vipers, and it made him angry that she'd been so underappreciated. He swore to make sure she never felt that way ever again. "You're welcome, princess. I'll be back in a jiffy."

He continued to the entrance and reached for the doorknob. It took every ounce of willpower he possessed not to turn around and take June in his arms. Having her here—in his home, in his space—was something he thought he'd never experience. Sharing his life and home with a woman. She wasn't his, and the circumstances weren't romantic, but he was having a hard time telling his heart that.

Now that he was home, he had several calls to make. To his parents, to Karl, to his friends. He wanted to put out feelers to help June find some sort of job where she could feel needed and stay busy. He already knew she was just like him in that regard—didn't like to be idle.

He also wanted to have a chat with the police chief, Alfred Rutkey, about what little he knew of June's situation. There may not be anything that could be done about the questionable death of her father, but he couldn't rest until he'd looked into it. If Elaine Green had done something to the man, he wanted to make sure she didn't get away with it.

Not only that, but the fact the two women had fabricated an entire ruse and lied so easily to his face about a stalker still didn't sit well with him.

He wanted to talk to Carlise and Chappy, find out the details about their wedding ceremony, and see if Carlise, or maybe April, would be willing to help June find something pretty to wear. He didn't care *what* she wore, himself, but he had a feeling she'd want to look nice for the occasion.

Yes, there were plenty of things Cal needed to accomplish, but all of that would have to wait—until he managed to stop thinking about the woman inside his home.

He'd gone to Washington, DC, thinking he was simply doing his family a favor, and it had ended up changing his life.

Did he regret it? No. He'd gotten June away from her situation, and he'd make sure she was able to stand on her own two feet. But he wasn't going to be in her life forever. She needed to fly, and she couldn't do that if she was tethered to him.

Cal suspected she might be the best thing that had ever happened to him . . . and if he thought being tortured and cut to ribbons was painful, he had a feeling it would be nothing compared to letting her go.

Tim Dotson had driven straight through the night to get to Newton so he could check out the area and make a plan. He'd stocked up on enough pot to last several days, though he didn't think it would take nearly that long to do what he had to do. The money the old broad offered him was too good to drag this out.

He'd met Elaine Green when she was buying coke from one of his acquaintances. Tim was what most people would probably call a hit man of sorts. He hired himself out to take care of problematic clients for many of the drug dealers he knew, including Elaine's supplier. But mostly he just beat people up and scared the piss out of them for a small fee and a steady supply of weed.

He'd just finished a job for a particular dealer and was collecting payment when Elaine pranced into the trap house. She looked ridiculously out of place in one of the most run-down neighborhoods in the nation's capital, but he supposed her money spent just as well as anyone else's.

Despite appearances, she seemed totally comfortable around the nasty dregs of society hanging at his dealer's house. Tim couldn't help being intrigued by both her arrogance and confidence. They'd gotten to talking, and she'd told him she was buying for her daughter Carla, a model who apparently used coke to stay thin.

When she'd asked for his number to keep in touch, in case she had an emergency need for cocaine and their mutual friend wasn't available, he'd given it to her. Tim wasn't offended she thought he was a dealer. He liked keeping people on their toes and off balance.

She'd called him a few times over the last year or so, desperate for a hit for her daughter. It wasn't difficult to get what she needed, to perpetuate the ruse that he was a dealer. And he added a sweet "service fee" for his trouble.

The truth was, Tim was far more skilled as a con man than anything else. Happy to be whatever someone wanted or needed . . . as long as the price was right.

To that end, Elaine had called a few days ago with an opportunity he couldn't pass up. Turned out her daughter—who sounded like a first-class bitch—was planning to marry a real-life prince, but there were complications in the courtship. Reading between the lines of her rambling story, Tim realized the old broad had tried to trick the man. She'd managed to get him to DC on the pretense that the daughter was being stalked, but the guy quickly decided that it was all bullshit. So Elaine needed to provide proof.

For his part, Tim was tasked with heading to her fancy-pants neighborhood to fake-scare the shit out of the daughter. He was preparing to do just that when Elaine called a second time.

The prince had apparently skipped town—stolen away by some dowdy stepdaughter. The flood of swear words the old bag had used was actually impressive. That's when she told him there was a change of plans.

Elaine wanted payback.

She seemed to think that hurting the stepsister would make the prince fall madly in love with Carla or some shit. He wasn't clear on the particulars, and personally, Tim thought the bitch was wacked. He'd been on the verge of telling her to fuck off—it was all getting too complicated for his taste—until she told him how much money she was willing to pay to be rid of the stepdaughter.

It was an offer Tim literally couldn't refuse. The plan the old woman concocted was ridiculous, but money was money, so he was all in.

He'd immediately set out for Newton, Maine, preparing to earn an easy paycheck.

Except now that he was here, he realized it wasn't going to be so easy after all.

Newton was the smallest town he'd ever been in. No stoplights, older houses everywhere. There was a ski resort not too far from the town, but it looked like any money it brought in hadn't really trickled down to this backwater burg. It was quaint, quiet . . . the sort of place where everyone knew everyone else and their business.

There was no way Tim could blend in like he'd planned. Hell, he'd stopped into a burger joint to get a bite, since he'd been up for over thirty hours and was starving, and he'd been greeted with hellos from every single patron *and* the owner of the joint. A broad who actually went by the name of "Granny," who had asked him a million questions about who he was, where he was from, and what had brought him to town.

He'd had to make up shit on the fly—not so easy when he was dead tired. He ended up blurting that he was down on his luck and looking for work.

To his amazement, Granny had given him three contact numbers for people who were looking to hire.

Tim didn't like working. Hated getting up early. Didn't care for people telling him what to do and how to do it. He liked easy money, getting laid, smoking the occasional joint, and . . . that was about it. But he needed a reason to stay in town. Taking some menial job would be great cover for the real reason he was there.

He'd thanked the woman and headed back to the house with the ROOM FOR RENT sign he'd seen while driving around and getting a feel for the place. It was a shitty-looking house, but it would be better than living in his truck.

He briefly thought about the "menu" of stuff Elaine suggested he do to the stepdaughter. She was itching to make the girl suffer. The longer he stayed to check off the items, the greater his chances of being caught and thrown in some tiny Mayberry jail.

But Elaine Green wasn't here, and because she was kind of stupid, her idea of "proof" wasn't exactly conclusive. She'd never know if he *actually* did everything he claimed.

Tim had done some shit in his life he *almost* regretted, but conning an old rich broad who spoiled her daughter and thought she could get away with anything would never be one of them.

He could write a note, take a picture of it hanging on his own door, and send it to Elaine. *Cha-ching.* A hundred bucks.

He'd punch a wall, take a picture of his raw knuckles, claim he'd robbed the bitch and punched her in the face . . . and Elaine would slide him five hundred.

He probably couldn't get away with lying about putting the step-daughter in the hospital, but he'd happily forgo that money to get the mother lode. Ten K for killing her? Tim was totally down. He'd never made so much money at one time, and he'd do just about anything to get it.

Maybe he could fake-stalk the stepdaughter for a short while, at least. See how many times he could bleed the mom for a hundred bucks. Getting a C-note for every fake claim of harassment would be worth staying in this hick town a few days.

It would also give him time to follow the bitch and figure out her routine. He'd strike when she least expected it, head home, and collect his money.

Smiling, Tim nodded to himself. He didn't care about Elaine, the model, or the unsuspecting stepdaughter. All he cared about was a life of leisure. In order to avoid a real job and go where he wanted when he wanted, he needed money. If he had to freeze his ass off in Maine, he'd do it. Because the reward would be worth the effort.

The fact that someone had to die in order for him to get ten grand wasn't even a blip on his conscience.

Chapter Ten

June pinched herself to make sure she wasn't dreaming.

It wasn't that long ago that she was stressing about when she'd be able to leave DC and where she was going to go. Now, here she was in Maine, with the most amazing man she'd ever known, with a roof over her head—a very fancy and comfortable roof, at that—and sitting around a huge table with six of the nicest people she'd ever met.

She'd slept like a rock the night before in the comfortable guest bed, waking up this morning to the smell of bacon and coffee. The hotel aside, she couldn't recall the last time someone had made *her* breakfast. She was feeling well and truly spoiled. In fact, the only downside to staying with Cal was that she was lonely. Going to bed in the huge guest room, sleeping in the king-size bed by herself, felt . . . wrong.

All it had taken was one night in Cal's arms, and she'd been ruined.

But she wouldn't complain. Not one word of protest would ever leave her lips. She'd never pressure Cal for anything he didn't want to give freely, even if her heart ached for it.

They'd spent the morning talking about Newton, his life growing up in England, the king and queen of Liechtenstein, his job at Jack's Lumber, his friends, and some of the trips he'd guided on the Appalachian Trail.

June soaked in every scrap of information. Cal was fascinating, and she loved hearing about his experiences. The only thing he wouldn't talk about was his time in the Army, but June understood. His military career had ended so abruptly, and horrifically, she didn't blame him for not wanting to talk about it.

She'd had a harder time talking about herself. Compared to him, she was utterly humdrum. She'd lived her entire life in DC and didn't feel like she'd done anything. But with his gentle urging, she'd told him more about her dad. She didn't remember her mom but shared the things her father had told her about the woman. She'd talked about her love of kids and the elderly. About her favorite meals to cook, how she adored winter and disliked the heat and humidity of summer.

After lunch, Cal had gone into his office to make a few phone calls. June entertained herself with one of the hundreds of books he had in his library. He'd come out of his office a few hours later and informed her that they were going to have company for dinner. JJ, Bob, Chappy, Carlise, and April were coming over.

She'd immediately panicked, her brain going a million miles an hour with all the things she'd need to do to get ready to entertain. Of course, Cal had noticed. He'd put his hands on her shoulders and reminded her that she wasn't in DC, she wasn't working for her stepmother anymore, and she didn't need to make sure everything was spotless or cook a four-course meal.

His reassurances went right in one ear and out the other. These were his *friends*. She had a feeling they were coming over to make sure she wasn't taking advantage of Cal . . . and she didn't blame them. He was rich. And a prince. And she was nobody.

Despite being a skilled cook, June was in for a new experience preparing the meal. It had been a long time since she'd had help, and Cal made her laugh nonstop. Not to mention his constant bumping into her and brushing against her. Even though the kitchen was large, and they had plenty of room to maneuver, she still found him in her personal space every time she turned around. Not that she minded.

His friends had arrived just as they finished prepping the meal, and now they were all sitting around a large table in the open space between the kitchen and the sitting area.

"So, tell us about yourself, June," April said with a friendly smile.

"No," Cal said before June could say anything. "We aren't doing this."

"Doing what?" April asked innocently. "I'm trying to get to know her."

"No, you aren't, you're preparing to interrogate her."

April laughed. "If I was doing that, I'd ask for her age, her mom's maiden name, her social security number, and how much money she has in the bank," she said, without sounding the least bit annoyed. "Come on, Cal, loosen up."

"It's okay," June said, giving him a small smile.

Chappy laughed abruptly, winking at Cal. He was sitting on the other side of the table, next to Carlise. He'd barely taken his eyes off his fiancée all night, and June thought it was sweet. "The shoe's on the other foot now, isn't it?" he said.

"Can it, mate," Cal growled.

Carlise smiled. "They all came up to Riggs's, I call Chappy Riggs, cabin to check me out," she told June. "There was a huge blizzard, and when JJ realized that I was alone up there with Riggs, he freaked out. They all came up to make sure I wasn't a serial killer or torturing their friend. I thought it was sweet, but Riggs was highly annoyed."

June understood. They didn't know her. The last thing they knew, Cal was going to DC for some kind of bodyguard job, and now he was back with a stowaway. They understandably wanted to know what was going on. She was glad Cal had such good friends.

"I'm not a serial killer," she said. "My name is Juniper Rose, but please call me June. My mom's maiden name was Smith. She died when I was little; I don't really remember her. My stepsister was the one Cal went to DC to protect, but she and my stepmother were lying about a stalker, and Cal figured that out pretty fast. I had already been planning to leave the only home I've ever known, and Cal offered to help me. So . . . here I am. I'm not planning to take advantage of his generosity. As soon as I can find a job and get on my feet, I'll get out of his hair."

She thought she heard Cal growl again under his breath, but then he was speaking. "April, we need to have words about that hovel you thought would be appropriate for June," he said.

"Easy, man," JJ muttered.

June was surprised to hear a thread of warning in the other man's tone. He'd been nothing but gracious and friendly from the moment she'd met him tonight. But now he sounded as if he was two seconds from challenging Cal.

"You didn't see it, JJ," Cal said, apparently not fazed by his friend's tone. "The house was practically falling apart."

"It was within the budget you gave me," April argued. "And also, the only place available last minute without a background check."

"You could've told me it was a piece of shite," he countered, his volume rising.

June reached over and put her hand on his thigh without thinking, only wanting to comfort him. "It wasn't that bad," she said calmly.

"Not that bad? If there was heat, I'd be surprised," Cal grumbled.

"Well, it looks like things turned out all right in the end," April said, shrugging.

Cal narrowed his eyes at her, and his expression said perhaps something had just occurred to him . . . but he didn't say anything more.

"I truly appreciate you trying to help. I mean, you don't know me at all," June added, wanting to smooth over the awkwardness. She didn't like that these longtime friends were disagreeing.

"What did you do down in DC?" Carlise asked, filling the ensuing silence. "Maybe we can help find something for you here."

"Not much *to* do here," Bob muttered under his breath.

That's what June was afraid of. She already loved the small town, what little she'd seen of it, but if she couldn't find a job, she'd probably have to move to a bigger city. Looking around the table, she felt her embarrassment spike and her cheeks warm. These men and women were probably much more educated than she was. She hadn't done *anything* with her life. Not really.

"Um," she hedged, trying to figure out a way to change the subject.

"She was an unpaid servant under her stepmother's thumb," Cal said, his voice rife with irritation. "She did all the cooking, shopping, cleaning, errands—everything."

June felt her cheeks grow hotter. She was so embarrassed. It wasn't as if she'd been a prisoner. She could've left at any time. But she'd chosen to stay. She felt incredibly stupid at the moment.

April spoke, unwittingly preventing June from literally running away from the table. "Hmm, do you guys know Meg King?"

"Doesn't she run Hill's House?" JJ asked.

"Oh yeah, I knew the name sounded familiar," Bob agreed.

"That's her. I ran into her at the store last weekend, and she was telling me she's having the hardest time finding someone to help keep the residents entertained during the day," April said.

"Hill's House is a private retirement home of sorts," JJ explained to June. "There are only six people who live there at any one time. There's a permanent employee who lives with them, Meg, making sure they're taking their meds and seeing to anything else they might need. It's not a nursing home. Everyone who lives there is ambulatory, they just need a little help to make sure they're safe."

"Oh, that sounds nice," Carlise said.

"I've been there," Bob agreed. "It *is* nice. It doesn't smell like a lot of old folks' places do."

"That's rude," April said with a frown.

"What?" Bob argued. "I'm just saying that it's a nice place for people who shouldn't live on their own anymore, but don't want to go into a nursing home or assisted living."

June bit back a grin. She liked how honest everyone was with each other. Aside from JJ's protectiveness where April was concerned, they didn't take offense when people disagreed with them, and they bantered back and forth like she imagined brothers and sisters might. Once upon a time, she'd hoped to have the same kind of relationship with Carla, but of course that hadn't happened.

"Anyway," April said, turning back to June. "Meg said she couldn't find anyone willing to come in during the day and help out."

"Why not?" Carlise asked.

April shrugged. "I'm guessing it probably doesn't pay a ton, and most of the younger people around here are looking to leave—go to Bangor or other larger cities, or work at the ski resort. And people get weird about working with the elderly."

"Why?" JJ blurted.

"No idea."

"What would the job entail?" Cal asked.

June glanced at him, surprised at how interested he seemed. Was he that eager to see her leave? She swallowed hard, trying to keep her disappointment from showing on her face.

"Nothing medical," April said. "Playing games, talking with the residents, maybe taking them on outings . . . stuff that will help keep them busy so they're not sleeping all day."

"You'd be great at that," Cal said, turning to June. "You had no problem starting up a conversation with Edgar at the hotel. You helped him eat without hesitation and made him feel as if he was the most important person in the room."

She stared at him, trying to read his expression.

"If nothing else, you could work there while you looked for something you might enjoy more and build your savings at the same time. And living here will save on rent money."

June let out the breath she'd been holding, so relieved she felt almost light headed. He didn't want her to move out immediately. Thank goodness.

"If you think you might be interested, I can introduce you to Meg," April said. "She's super sweet."

June pried her gaze from Cal's and turned to look at April. "I think I might like that. Thank you so much."

"You're more than welcome," April said with a smile.

June jerked in surprise when she felt Cal's large hand cover hers on his leg. She hadn't even realized she was still touching him. His thumb caressed the sensitive skin on the back of her hand, and goose bumps broke out on her arm.

"Have you started translating a new book lately?" April asked Carlise.

"She translates books from French into English," Cal said quietly in June's ear as Carlise began to talk about the last book she'd finished.

June was impressed. But she also felt a little more intimidated. April and Carlise definitely had their lives together. They had great jobs, and she . . . well, she didn't really know how to do anything.

She nodded and smiled in all the right places as Carlise wound up her discussion about the book she'd just turned in.

"You guys ready to get hitched?" Bob asked when she was done.

"Yes!" Both Carlise and Chappy said at the same time.

Everyone laughed.

"My mom couldn't get a flight until Saturday morning though," Carlise said. "JJ's picking her up in Bangor and bringing her straight to the cabin. We'll have the ceremony there, and she'll stay with April— thank you so much for that! Oh, and just a reminder, this is not a dress-up kind of wedding," Carlise said sternly. "Jeans are perfectly fine."

"Thank God," Bob said.

JJ leaned over and smacked his friend on the back of the head, and everyone laughed again.

"Having it at the cabin where you guys met and fell in love is perfect," April said. "And I for one am grateful I don't have to put on a dress. I can't remember the last time I wore one, and I don't intend to change that anytime soon."

"You'd look good no matter what you wore," JJ said.

June blinked at the undercurrent of . . . well, she wasn't sure *what* she heard in JJ's voice.

She didn't get a chance to think about it long before April asked, "You're coming, right, June?"

"Oh, um . . ." Cal had asked her to go, but now she wasn't sure. It was going to be a very small and intimate affair, and she didn't want to intrude.

"She is," Cal answered for her.

"Yay!" Carlise said. "I can't wait for you to meet Baxter and to see Riggs's cabin. It's so cute and awesome. And it's gorgeous up there. You're going to love it!"

April asked Carlise how her mom was doing, which gave June the opportunity to turn to Cal and ask, "Baxter?"

"Their dog. Long story, but he was a stray who saved her life . . . twice."

June blinked at that. "Really?"

"Really."

"Wow. Okay."

"And if you don't want that job at Hill's House, we'll find you something else. You don't have to take it just to be polite," he said earnestly.

"I think I *do* want it," June reassured him. "But I don't have any experience with anything like that."

"You're perfect for it. You're kind, and everyone who meets you loves you."

She wasn't sure about that, but warmth bloomed inside her at the compliment.

"I'll find an apartment or something as soon as I can," she felt obligated to say. "You didn't go to DC expecting to come home with a roommate."

"No rush. You can stay here for as long as you want. That is . . . *if* you want."

June nodded before she'd even thought about it. "I want to stay."

He smiled at her. "Good. I want you to stay too."

She felt as if she was drowning in his eyes. His hand was still on hers, and she wondered if he could feel her blood pumping faster through her veins. If she twisted her wrist, they'd be holding hands. For a moment, it felt as if they were the only two people in the world.

"What do you think, Cal?" JJ asked.

His gaze left hers, and he turned to his friend.

It took June a second to regain her senses. The short moment between them was intense, but she'd seen the sincerity in his eyes when he'd told her she didn't have to leave his home. It should've felt awkward to be living with a man she barely knew, but she felt as if she'd known Cal for years. Around him, she felt safe . . . the same feeling her dad always gave her. Except Cal definitely didn't feel like a father figure.

Talk around the table turned to the weather and the upcoming hiking season. It seemed people were requesting reservations for guides on the AT earlier than they had in the last couple of years. Which meant the guys would be busy making sure the section of trail they were responsible for maintaining was cleared of debris and the white swatches of paint on the trees were clear and easy to see. It also meant they'd be gone more often, taking turns leading the hikers.

It sounded like Chappy, Cal, Bob, and JJ's business was extremely successful. They'd survived an unbelievably horrific ordeal and come out on the other side stronger than before. June was proud of them, even if she didn't really know them all that well.

"That was delicious," Carlise exclaimed when they were all finished with dinner. She patted her belly. "If I'm not careful, I'm gonna put on a hundred pounds living here. It's not like I'm out hiking and chopping up trees like some people," she teased.

June flushed uncomfortably. Any time the topic of weight had come up when she'd lived with her stepmother and stepsister, she ended up on the receiving end of some very nasty comments. Carla constantly complained that June's dishes were too calorific, accusing her of trying to make her fat like June was. Elaine frequently mentioned how June could be cute—not pretty, mind you, but simply cute—if she lost weight. A lot of it.

Her mom was a big woman. June took after her, and even though she tried to watch what she ate and was constantly busy, she never

The Royal

seemed to be able to lose the extra pounds. It was frustrating, and being around Carla hammered the point home even more that she would never be the kind of woman society deemed acceptable.

"You'd be beautiful no matter what you weighed," Chappy reassured Carlise. "And when you're pregnant with our child, you'll be even more irresistible."

"Wait, are you pregnant?" April practically shouted.

"No, no, no. Not yet. It's been like a second and a half since Riggs and I even got together," she said with a laugh. "But yeah, we want kids," she said a little dreamily, looking up at her fiancé.

"This is so exciting," April said with a huge smile.

June couldn't help but smile as well. Seeing Chappy and Carlise together, and blissfully happy, made her a little envious.

She felt Cal's gaze and turned to see him staring at her with an unreadable expression.

"What?" she whispered.

He shook his head. "Nothing. Just thinking."

June didn't have a chance to question him further, as the guys all stood up and started clearing the table.

"Oh, I can get that," she insisted, standing and reaching for the plates Bob held.

"We've got it. You go and relax with Carlise and April," Cal ordered.

"But—"

"Come on," Carlise said, coming over to June's side and linking their arms. "The guys'll take care of it. I want to talk to you more. Get to know you."

The thought of not cleaning up after a meal was so foreign, June felt almost weird just standing there, watching the guys all shuffling toward the kitchen with dirty plates. Their willingness to help was so . . . *nice*.

Escorted by Carlise, June sat on the end of the couch.

April sat on the other end, smiling gently at her. "You haven't had it easy, have you?" she asked.

June was momentarily surprised. She figured they'd start out with polite small talk. But April sounded serious. She shrugged. "Not as bad as others, I'd guess."

"When did your dad pass?"

"A long time ago. I was fifteen, he'd been married to Elaine about a year."

"Oh, I'm so sorry. That had to have been incredibly hard," Carlise said with a frown.

"Yeah. He was my world. I was lost for a while and threw myself into helping around the house. The next thing I knew, I blinked, and I was turning thirty. That sounds really crazy, but it's true. I was so entrenched, helping to raise Carla and doing everything to make my stepmother's life easier, that I didn't realize how much of myself I'd lost."

"It's never too late to make changes in your life," April said. "I'm forty-six and was married to a guy who took everything I did for granted, then he barely blinked when I said I wanted a divorce. I started over, and I can't tell you how much happier I am now."

"How old is your stepsister?" Carlise asked.

"Twenty-four."

"Oh, so she's quite a bit younger than you."

"Yeah."

"Well, you're here now, and it's awesome," April said firmly. "No looking back."

June smiled at them.

"Your family was really lying about having a stalker?" Carlise asked.

"Unfortunately, yes. Carla kind of had Cal's cousin wrapped around her finger. Then I overheard them talking about 'catching' a prince and all the things Carla would do when she was a princess," June admitted.

April's easygoing countenance turned hard. "Did they even know that Cal has practically nothing to do with the royal family? That he pretty much only participates in that kind of stuff when there's a coronation or an important wedding or something?"

"They don't care. Carla loves attention. Craves it. She decided she wants to be a princess, so she and my stepmother will do pretty much anything to make that happen," June told them.

"I don't think it works like that," Carlise said. "I mean, what, did she think Cal would arrive, feel sorry for her that she had a stalker, and propose?"

June shrugged. "Kind of? She's very pretty—on the outside, I mean. She's slender, has beautiful blonde hair and big blue eyes. She's tall. Oh, and of course she has big boobs too . . . fake, but big. I'm pretty sure she planned on using sex to help her case."

June hated to think of Carla and Cal together in that way, but she had little doubt it was a big part of her stepsister's strategy. To mesmerize him with her body and give him blow jobs until he couldn't see straight, as if that would make marrying her a foregone conclusion.

Although she supposed there were plenty of men in the world who could be swayed with good sex. She just didn't see Cal as being one of them.

"Well, she was doomed to fail in that regard," April said with a huff. "Cal's too sensitive about how he looks to get naked with anyone. Forget about a woman he just met."

"I've never seen him in anything but long pants and shirts since I met him," Carlise said softly.

"I saw his back. Just once. He was changing his shirt after he and the others were caught in a rainstorm last summer while on a job. It was awful," April said with a small shudder. "It looked as if he'd been whipped over and over and over."

June wasn't comfortable talking about Cal like this. And knowing he was sensitive about how he looked wasn't a revelation. She'd definitely figured that out for herself, even in the short time she'd spent with him.

"Anyway," she said, trying to move the topic away from his scars, "Carla and Elaine probably aren't happy in the least that Cal left."

"And even less happy that you went with him, I'd guess," Carlise said.

"So you think they'll do anything to retaliate?" April asked, her brows furrowing.

"I'm thinking Carla will contact Cal's cousin, the one she met online, and try to get him to intervene on her behalf. She and Elaine might even go so far as to mail threatening letters to themselves to make it look like there really is a stalker. Cal overheard them plotting to provide some kind of proof. But I doubt they'd come all the way up here to do anything to either of us. Carla will probably cry a lot and put on quite a show to urge Cal to go back."

"It won't work," April said with a firm shake of her head.

"You don't think so?" June asked.

"Nope. Once Cal's done, he's done. Nothing they say will entice him to return to DC. Especially now that he knows how they treated you."

"I don't know if that matters . . . ," she hedged.

"Seriously?" April asked, looking incredulous. "You don't see the way he looks at you?"

June swallowed hard. "He just feels sorry for me. He's helping me out until I can get back on my feet."

"Nope," April said with a shake of her head. Then she turned to Carlise. "How much time was it, exactly, between when you met Chappy and when he proposed?"

"Counting the three days he was unconscious or not?" she asked with a laugh.

"Not."

"About eleven days."

June's eyes widened.

"See?" April asked.

June didn't. She hadn't realized how fast Carlise and Chappy's relationship had progressed, but regardless, that had nothing to do with Cal.

"The guys . . . when they fall, they fall hard. And fast. And Cal's halfway there already. I can tell just by looking at him. You guys didn't drive straight here from DC, did you?"

"No. We stayed at a hotel."

"One room or two?" April asked.

Now June was definitely uncomfortable. "One. There was some sort of athletic competition going on, and there weren't any more rooms."

"Right. Look, I'll be blunt here. I've known Cal and the others for a while now. They're good men. The best. After what they went through, they're each a little broken in their own way. But Cal . . ." She paused and shook her head. "It would be tough for anyone to break through the walls he's got up. Between women wanting him for his money or title, and because of the hell he went through—which I don't even know much about, because those guys are loyal to a fault and don't talk about it—I think Cal planned to be alone forever. But you can't give up, not with the way he looks at you. Even if he tries to push you away for your own good. Push back. Make him see that his scars don't matter. That you don't care."

June wrung her hands in agitation, clearly distressed now. She hated talking about Cal behind his back, and she didn't like gossip. Nothing good ever came from it. She'd learned that from Carla.

"And now I've freaked you out. I'm sorry," April said contritely. "I just . . . I love Cal like a brother, and I've never seen him as captivated with someone as he is with you. All I'm saying is not to give up on him. Don't listen to him if he tries to tell you he doesn't want anything serious. He does. I can tell. And if you want him back the same way, you need to hold on tight. Understand?"

June wasn't convinced April was seeing the reality between her and Cal. But the thought of him liking her, even a little, felt good. Really good. And if she actually thought Cal wanted her but was denying himself because of some belief that he wasn't good enough, or because she might push him away after what had happened to him, she'd hold on for all she was worth.

For now, she simply nodded, wanting this conversation to be over.

"I know this is short notice, but would you guys like to come over to Riggs's apartment and hang out with me tomorrow night? As a kind of bachelorette party? I don't know anyone else here, and if I tell Riggs that I'm having a girls' night in, he can go and hang out with his friends without feeling guilty. Things *did* move really fast with us, and I want his friends to know that just because we're getting married, their relationship is still solid. He's not going to spend all his time with me and not hang out with them anymore."

"I'd love that," April said, then added wryly, "Although are you sure you want someone old like me at your bachelorette party?"

"You aren't old!" Carlise scolded.

"Girl, you could be my daughter," April returned.

"Hardly," Carlise said with a snort.

"You're sixteen years younger than me. My comment stands."

"Fine, but seriously, April, it's not as if you have one foot in the grave, and you aren't ready to move into Hill's House or anything yet."

"Sometimes around the guys, I feel ancient," April said quietly, looking over to the kitchen where the four friends were laughing and talking, obviously giving the girls time to have their own chat.

June saw that her eyes were locked on one man in particular. "JJ doesn't look much younger than you," she ventured.

April turned her head and laughed, although it sounded forced to June.

"Right. Men like younger women, period. Stories about older women getting the young hot guys are only for romance novels." She turned to Carlise. "What time do you want us there tomorrow? And what do we need to bring?"

"I was thinking around dinnertime? Six or so? We could eat, then break out the drinks. So just bring whatever drink you enjoy. We can hang out, watch movies, talk, whatever."

"Sounds great," April said. "I'm happy for you, Carlise. You and Chappy are perfect together."

"Thanks."

"I think I'm going to head out," April said. "I'll see you both tomorrow night. It was so nice to meet you, June, and I'll talk to Meg about that job at Hill's House and get you two in touch. Do you have a phone?"

June frowned. "No. I had one, but I left it in DC because I didn't want Elaine or Carla to be able to get in touch with me. All they'd do is yell, insult me, and insist I come back to make their breakfast and do their laundry."

"Smart. Okay, I'll have her get in touch with Cal so you can discuss a time and a place for you two to meet up and talk about the position," April said.

June wasn't surprised that she was so good at her job. She seemed incredibly organized and decisive.

After they all stood, April gave Carlise a quick hug and, to June's surprise, leaned in and hugged her as well.

"You going?" JJ asked April as he approached.

"Yeah, it's getting late, and I want to get an early start at the office tomorrow."

"I'll follow you home," JJ told her.

"Not necessary," April said.

"Even so, I'm still going to. See you guys tomorrow?" JJ asked the men.

"I need to head up to the cabin to make sure things are all set out there," Chappy told him.

"I was thinking about taking June over to Rumford to shop for necessities she didn't get to bring with her," Cal said.

June blinked in surprise at that. He hadn't talked to her about going anywhere. Not that she'd mind—there *were* some things she could use that she didn't bring. But she hadn't expected him to want to spend the day with her after he'd been gone for a few days.

"I'll be in the office as usual," Bob said with a grin.

"April and June said they'd come over for a bachelorette night," Carlise told her fiancé. "So you guys can hang out tomorrow night and do . . . guy things."

"Whoooo! Strippers!" Bob teased. When no one laughed, he shrugged his shoulders. "It was a joke, jeez! It's not like there are any strippers around here anyway. And with me being the only unattached guy, it wouldn't be any fun."

June frowned at that. Bob wasn't the only single guy. There was JJ—though on second thought, he seemed very interested in April. And there was Cal. She looked at the man in question and found him glaring at Bob.

"Right, so . . . where should we meet?" Chappy said with a grin.

"We can hang out here," Cal offered.

"Cool," Chappy told him, then slapped him on the back. "It's a plan. I'll bring the beer. If you want something else, you're on your own."

"Beer sounds good to me," Bob said.

"I'll be DD," Chappy told his friends.

"Always the protector," Carlise said with a smile, snuggling into his side.

"It's your bachelor party," Bob protested. "You should be able to drink."

But Chappy merely shrugged. "Not really interested in getting hammered the night before I get married."

"Oh, all right. On that note, I'm going to jet too," Bob said. Then he smiled and turned to June. "It was nice to meet you." To her surprise, he leaned in and kissed her cheek, then kissed the other one.

"Bob," Cal practically growled.

"What? It's the English way, right?"

Grinning, JJ approached and did the same thing.

Chappy quickly followed suit.

June knew she was blushing, but it wasn't every day she was kissed six times by three extremely handsome men.

"You guys are arseholes," Cal muttered.

His friends didn't seem fazed by the insult. They simply waved goodbye and all headed out the door.

When everyone left, she glanced at Cal after he shut the door behind them. "Are you mad?"

"No."

"You *look* mad," she observed. And he did. His brows were furrowed, and his lips turned down.

"They were messing with me," he told her.

"How so?"

"Kissing you like that."

"Oh. But they were just following your customs, weren't they?"

"Yes and no. They mostly kissed you because they knew it would irritate me."

June shook her head. "Why would that irritate you?" she asked.

"Because I don't want anyone kissing you but me," he said bluntly.

June stared at him in disbelief . . . and a little bit of excitement. "It didn't mean anything," she said softly.

"I know. But I still didn't like it." Cal moved closer and lifted a hand to swipe his thumb over one of her cheeks, as if he could wipe away anyone else's touch.

Feeling brave, and not sure where it was coming from, she placed her hands on his chest. When it came to this man, she found herself wanting to be different. Wanting to be the kind of woman he'd consider being with. "Maybe you should do something to erase the feel of their lips on my cheeks."

"Like?" he asked with a grin and a raised brow.

June shrugged. "Maybe cover their kisses with your own?"

She held her breath as she waited for his response. To her dismay, he didn't move for a long moment.

Just when humiliation was creeping in, he stepped further into her personal space. He didn't speak, just lowered his head ever so slowly.

June held her breath as his lips brushed her right cheek. Then he nuzzled her hair out of his way, and she felt him kiss the sensitive skin under her ear. She tilted her head, one hand clutching the material of his T-shirt. A small, desperate noise escaped her throat.

Cal moved to her other cheek, kissing her there as well. He lifted a hand to the back of her neck, holding her tightly, and kissed her forehead. Then her nose, then back to the first cheek.

She was breathing fast, and tingles shot through her body. Everywhere his lips touched, she felt branded. She'd been kissed before, but it had never felt like *this*. As if the anticipation might just kill her.

"Cal," she whispered—then his lips were on hers. He sipped and nipped at her lips, but he didn't enter her mouth. Even though the kiss was chaste, she felt it all the way to her toes. It was the most romantic kiss she'd ever received, and June wanted more.

He lifted his head before she could beg him to continue. His breath sighed over her as he asked, "Like that?"

She opened her eyes and stared up at Cal. "Huh?"

"Do you still feel their kisses on your skin?"

She couldn't feel anything but Cal. She shook her head.

"Good. You have a nice chat with April and Carlise?"

June wanted to insist she didn't want to talk about the other women . . . about *anything*. That she only wanted to continue what they were currently doing. That she wanted his tongue in her mouth, his hands on her body. She wanted everything. But she swallowed hard and said huskily, "Yeah."

"Things looked intense at one point. You were frowning so hard, I almost came over to see if you were okay."

The notion that he was watching out for her felt good. "It was fine. We were talking about Elaine and Carla." She had a feeling that wasn't what had made her frown so much. It was April's revelations about Cal. The ones that made her feel both guilty and protective.

"You don't have to worry about them anymore. I'll take care of them."

June nodded.

He hadn't moved away from her, still had his hand on the back of her neck. It felt amazingly possessive, and June had never felt safer than she did at that moment.

He stared down at her for a long moment. Then slowly pulled her into a hug.

June went willingly, burrowing her nose in the side of his neck as he leaned over her. She was enveloped by him, and she wasn't sure what had brought on this small intimacy, but she would treasure this moment for as long as it lasted.

"What are you doing to me?" he mumbled into her hair.

She didn't get a chance to answer, not that he probably expected her to, because Cal pulled back and gave her a tender smile. "I'm going to head up to shower. Kitchen's all cleaned up, doors are locked. I'll see you in the morning. Okay?"

Surprised, because it was still pretty early, all June could do was nod yet again.

He let go of her and turned toward the stairs that led up to the second floor and the bedrooms. It seemed to June that he was running, even if his pace was unhurried. But from what? Her? That seemed impossible. She was completely harmless.

It was confusing being around Cal. One second, he was kissing and hugging her, and the next, he acted as if he couldn't stand to be in the same room.

Sighing, June wandered into the kitchen. He'd said everything was put away, but she had to check for herself. She wiped down the already clean counters and looked around for something else to do. Not finding anything, she went into the sitting area and picked up the book she'd been reading earlier.

She heard the water turn on upstairs, and instantly the words on the page lost all interest. All she could think about was Cal, naked in his shower.

April's words about the scars on his back sprang to her mind, and June found her eyes filling with tears. She hated to think about Cal being hurt. She hated even more that he might think less of himself because of what others had done. Didn't he know he was the most incredible man she'd ever met? That she didn't care one second about what he looked like under his clothes?

Probably not. His entire life had been about outward appearances, something June understood more than most people. Being a member of the royal family meant being in the limelight, being held to different standards than others. Any imperfection could be seen as a flaw, something to criticize. She hated that for him and vowed to do what she could to make him understand that she wouldn't judge him for *anything*.

After the water turned off, June waited to see if maybe Cal would join her back downstairs. When he didn't, she eventually headed up to her own room. She'd enjoyed meeting his friends and looked forward to spending more time with April and Carlise and the guys, but the one person she wanted to get to know better was the man she was living with . . . who seemed a million miles away right now.

Chapter Eleven

Cal kicked himself for volunteering to take June shopping. It wasn't that he didn't want to spend time with her—hell, he wanted to spend *all* his spare time with her. It was because the more he was around her, the more he wanted to be.

The night before, he'd fled upstairs before he did something that would scare the crap out of her. Like pick her up, throw her on the couch, and make love to her right then and there. Putting his lips on her was both heaven and hell. She had the softest skin, and the little noises she'd made in her throat while he'd been kissing her made his cock stand up and take notice. It had taken all the strength he had to control himself and not go any further.

She'd been isolated, mistreated, and she was finally getting to spread her wings. The last thing Cal wanted to do was stifle her. She could have any man she wanted now. He couldn't be selfish and not give her a chance to date, fall in love . . . be happy.

But just thinking about her with any other man made him want to snatch her up and lock her away. She was *his*, damn it.

Except she wasn't.

His friends had purposely gotten under his skin with their stunt last night. Kissing her right in front of him. Customs be damned—they hadn't kissed anyone else like that before, ever. And the thing was, their shenanigans worked. He'd hated seeing their lips on her. Chappy was taken, and JJ might as well be, with how he couldn't look away from April, but it didn't matter.

Cal had been thrilled when June suggested he cover their kisses with his own. She was shy but not paralyzingly so. And she'd felt so damn perfect in his arms. Just as she had the night in the hotel, when he'd held her as they slept.

But no matter how much he might want her, he couldn't be with her like a normal man should be with a woman. He couldn't bear to look at himself in the mirror; how could he expose his ruined flesh to June? He'd rather die than see a look of disgust or pity in her eyes.

So now he was torturing himself by spending the day with her in Rumford. Shopping, of all things. He wasn't a man who shopped. If he needed something, he went online and ordered it. Other than for groceries, he couldn't remember the last time he'd walked into an actual store.

"This is fun," she said from next to him, jolting him out of his thoughts.

Looking over at her, Cal saw June was smiling. Her cheeks were flushed from walking in the chilly air, and her eyes sparkled. It took so little to make her happy. "Yeah?" he asked.

She nodded. There wasn't a mall in Rumford. No designer shops. Nothing that compared to the stores she could shop at back in DC. But it didn't seem to matter. June was taking pleasure in just being out in the world, a concept that was mostly foreign to Cal. Outside of the occasional tranquil hike, it had been a very long time since he'd enjoyed simply living.

When June glanced over at him, she suddenly came to a halt and put her hand on his arm to stop him as well. "Cal?" she asked.

He tilted his head in response, even as he clenched his fists to keep from wrapping an arm around her waist and pulling her into him.

"Are you all right?"

"Of course."

"I mean, you probably have more important things you need to be doing other than hanging out with me. We can go back to Newton."

Cal mentally kicked himself. He didn't want his unsettled mood to rub off on her, but it apparently had. "No, I have nothing better to do right now," he reassured her.

Her brows furrowed as she watched him. Finally, she said, "I've had a lifetime of studying people. Of figuring out what they want without them needing to say it. I know when someone doesn't like what I've served them for dinner, when they're in a bad mood . . . or when they're simply being polite, and deep down they want to be anywhere but where they are. You don't have to lie to me, Cal. I can tell you're uncomfortable shopping."

She inhaled deeply, as if summoning the courage to say her next words. "And I can also tell you're uncomfortable around *me*. Take me back, and I'll stay out of your hair for the rest of the day. I'll talk to April tonight when I go to Chappy's and see if she can help me find other living arrangements."

Cal moved before she'd finished her last sentence. He backed June up two steps, until she was pressed to a brick wall behind her. They were on a fairly busy street—people were walking and driving by—but to Cal, it felt like they were the only two people in the world at that moment.

He'd messed up badly. He hated that she'd lost her excitement of just a moment ago.

"It's not you," he said fervently. "I just . . . being with you, watching you get more excited over a damn throw pillow than I've been about anything in years . . . it's making me realize how much of my life I've been missing out on. You find joy in everything around you, and I can't remember the last time I've felt even one iota of that emotion."

"I'm sorry," she whispered, looking at him with concern swimming in her eyes.

"No," he said, immediately shaking his head. "Don't be."

"Something changed when we got to Newton," she said softly. "We were fine in DC, then when we were on the road. But since we've been in Maine, you seem to have trouble being around me. I don't know what I did, but if you tell me, I'll stop."

Cal's heart dropped. It killed him that she felt that way. But she wasn't wrong either. What changed was the fact that she was in his home—and she felt so damn right there. He'd been home two days and had already started dreaming about the future. About having her there permanently. About sharing her life. But he just couldn't see it actually happening.

He reached out and cradled her head in his palms. She immediately put her own hands on his waist, gripping his jacket in her fists as she waited for him to say something.

Cal had planned to tell her that maybe it *would* be best if she talked to April about an apartment. It would be less painful if she left now than if they got any closer.

But what came out of his mouth was something completely different. Thoughts and feelings he'd buried for years.

"It's not that I don't want to be around you. I do. More than you could ever know. But from the second you stepped across my threshold, I wanted to bolt the door and never let you leave. You bring light and good energy into my house that haven't been there since the day I moved in. But I can't do that to you. Not when you've just gotten away from a home that was more of a prison.

"Don't you see, June? I'm trying to give you the space and freedom you haven't had before. I'm terrified my screwed-up psyche will damage you. Will hold you back from everything you can be."

Cal closed his eyes and took a deep breath. Feck, this wasn't going how he wanted. He'd wanted to reassure her that he *liked* being with her, that it was *his* life that was too messed up to deal with. Instead, he'd word vomited things he never meant to say.

She covered one of the hands still resting on her face. He opened his eyes and stared into her beautiful brown gaze.

"Can I be honest?"

"I'd be upset if you weren't," he told her.

"I'm scared."

Cal frowned and immediately tensed. "Of what?"

"Everything," June admitted. "I have maybe a couple months' rent to my name. I don't have a car. I only have two suitcases worth of belongings. I have no friends. I'm completely reliant on you. My stepmother and stepsister hate my guts, and I wouldn't be surprised if right this moment, they were trying to find me to make me pay for leaving them.

"And I've never felt about *anyone* the way I do about you. Like if I don't see you, can't touch you, I'll break into a million pieces and float away. I know I'm too plain, that people don't look twice at me. I'm short, overweight, and have no fashion sense whatsoever. But my heart doesn't care that I'll never fit into your world. It just . . . wants what it wants."

Cal's mouth was so dry, he couldn't even swallow. "What does it want?" he whispered, holding his breath as he waited for her response.

And June being June, she didn't try to be coy. Didn't prevaricate. She had the strength and the bravery to say what was in her heart.

"You. It wants *you*, Cal."

A torrent of emotions almost overwhelmed him. Joy. Satisfaction. Possessiveness. The need to take this woman home and drag her to his bed and show her exactly how much he admired, respected, and longed for her.

"But if you don't enjoy spending time with me—and don't lie, I can tell you aren't having fun right now—I'll be okay. I'm not going to be the type of woman who begs and sobs and goes crazy. Or invents a stalker to try to get you to like me," she finished dryly.

Cal's fingers tightened slightly as he leaned in. "I'm going to kiss you now," he informed her.

Her brows furrowed in confusion, but she didn't pull away. Didn't tell him he was being ridiculous or giving her whiplash with his mood swings. No, the hand at his waist clenched as she tried to pull him closer, and her chin lifted a fraction of an inch.

This kiss was nothing like the gentle ones from last night. He didn't ease into it. There was no tender brushing of lips. He took her with all the desperation he felt in his conflicted soul. He should let her go, but he needed her in his arms, his bed, his life.

He took her mouth as if he was a man starving, and she was the sustenance he needed to survive. And his June gave as good as she got. She wasn't content to passively accept what he gave her. She tilted her head to deepen the kiss and seemed to be just as desperate as Cal.

Their tongues dueled, their teeth nipped, and little moans of pleasure erupted from them both as they kissed. One of Cal's hands eased to the back of June's head, protecting her as he pressed her harder into the bricks with his body. The other slipped under her jacket and shirt to rest on her lower back.

As soon as his cold fingers touched her warm bare skin, she arched sharply and went a little crazy in his arms. Her fingers speared into his hair and pulled on the strands, adding a small element of pain to his passion, ramping up his need even more. Her other hand copied his own, moving to his back and finding its way under his clothes to his flesh.

He didn't feel her touch exactly, but the sensation of her cold fingers on his shredded skin was like a bucket of freezing water to his libido. His cock, which had been hard as a pike a moment earlier, wilted, and he pulled his mouth from hers with a gasp.

They were both breathing hard, and Cal couldn't help but notice how his hand had mussed her hair. She looked like what he imagined she might after tossing her head back and forth on his pillow as they made love.

"Cal?" she said tentatively after a moment.

He was very aware that she hadn't moved her hand from his back, but then again, he hadn't moved his either. They were wrapped around each other like two vines growing in the wild.

"I . . . Can you please move your hand from my back?" he whispered.

She nodded, and when she was no longer touching his skin, he felt as if he could breathe again. Feeling ashamed and weak, Cal took a deep breath and tilted his head back, looking up at the sky as he tried to control his emotions.

After what seemed like forever, but was probably only a minute or so, he looked back down at June. She hadn't wrenched herself out of his arms. Hadn't questioned what was happening or asked why he didn't want her to touch him. Her knowing gaze was glued on his, and he had a feeling she'd stand there with him for as long as he needed.

"I—" he started, but she shook her head.

"I'm sorry. I should've known better than to touch you. Cal, what happened to you was awful. Absolutely horrific. And something I'll never be able to understand. But as I already told you—and will keep telling you until you believe it—your scars shame *them*, not you. I'm not going to be so ignorant as to say you should wear them with pride. But they're a part of you now. Your history. What makes you Cal Redmon.

"And they make absolutely no difference in how I feel about you. Wait—no, that's not true. Knowing what happened, what they did, and seeing the man standing in front of me today? Those scars make me admire you even more. You were already someone deeply impressive. But knowing what I know about your history, about what you survived? I'm in awe of you."

Cal shook his head. "You have no idea how bad it is," he told her.

"You're right, I don't. But I still don't care."

Cal didn't believe that. Couldn't. She *would* care. If she saw how ravaged his skin was. How utterly disgusting the scars looked. She'd care. How could she not?

"If the roles were reversed, if it was my body covered in scars, would it make a difference?"

Everything within Cal revolted at the thought of the woman in his arms going through even a fraction of the torture he'd endured. Nausea welled up inside him, and all he could do was shake his head violently.

149

"Then why would you think it makes a difference to me?" she asked quietly.

Cal closed his eyes again and swallowed hard. He wanted to believe their attraction and lust would be the same after she saw him without his long-sleeved shirts and pants, but he was afraid to take that chance. Having her recoil would destroy him.

He felt June go up on her tiptoes, and he braced, making sure she was steady against him. Her lips brushed his cheek before she moved to whisper in his ear.

"I want you, Cal. Even though I know I'll never live up to your expectations. Even though you're light-years better than me. I want you on me, over me, inside me. If you need the darkness in order to make that happen, or if you need to be fully clothed, I'm okay with that. I'll take you however I can get you."

And just like that, Cal's cock sprang to life once more. His eyes popped open, and he drew his head back so he could see her face. She was blushing again, which was so fecking precious. But he could see the certainty and lust in her gaze.

"Nothing about you could ever turn me off," she continued, looking him straight in the eye as she said it. This woman was definitely braver than he'd ever be. "You are the sexiest man I've ever met. *Period.* You're generous, loyal, hardworking, protective . . . in short, everything I've ever dreamt about in a man but never thought existed in one person."

"You forgot wealthy and a prince," he said, teasing her.

June was somber as she said, "No, I didn't. Because I couldn't give a damn about those things. I've seen what money can do to people—my stepmother, for instance—and I'd want you if you were nothing more than a lumberjack. And . . . truth be told, being royalty is the one thing about you that makes me want to turn tail and run. I can't live up to that. Could never live up to your family's expectations. And I don't want to be a princess. I would make a terrible one. I want *you*, Cal. The man who makes me feel safe and free for the first time in my life."

How could he resist that?

He couldn't. He was going to have her.

Then he'd let her go. It would be shitty of him and possibly the most difficult thing he'd ever done. Even the torture he'd endured wouldn't be as painful as letting her go. But he would have to, for June's sake.

Cal leaned down and kissed her again. A sweet, tender kiss this time. "There's a cute little gift shop down the road a bit that I think you'll like," he told her. "Then we can go to the big-box store and get the other necessities you need. I'd like to make a stop at the home-improvement store too. After that, we can head home, and you can get ready for Carlise's bachelorette party thing. That sound okay?"

She stared at him for a long moment before nodding. "If you're sure I'm not being a pain."

"You aren't being a pain. Not even in the smallest, remotest sense of the word. I'm not used to this, to shopping with no real goal in mind as to what I need to buy, but spending time with you is . . . everything. I'm enjoying it."

"Okay."

"Okay," he agreed.

Then he slowly slid his hand out of her hair and stepped away. But he reached for her hand and tucked it in the crook of his elbow, pressing it against his side as they started walking once more.

She leaned against him, and it was the sweetest feeling in the world to have her so close. How he'd gone from being steadfastly single and resigned to that status quo to wanting a woman so badly it made every bone in his body ache with need, Cal had no clue. But even knowing the pain would crush his soul when it was time to part wouldn't keep him from accepting everything she offered.

Soon.

He'd prefer to give them time, to let the anticipation build, to enjoy wooing her. But Cal had a feeling neither of them would be able to wait for long. And the fact that she was willing to give him what he needed—namely, the dark—just to have him, made it even more clear that this woman was perfect for him.

Tonight, she was hanging out with her new friends, and he'd be chillin' with his mates. Tomorrow, they'd be occupied with the wedding. June would soon meet with Meg and likely start working, and he needed to do his fair share of work at Jack's Lumber. But somehow, someway, they'd figure out a time to connect. Cal had no doubt about that.

Just as he had no doubt that once he touched June, once she let him inside her body, he'd never be the same.

Chapter Twelve

June looked over at Carlise and smiled a little tipsily. She hadn't planned on drinking tonight, just on getting to know April and Carlise. But April had made an amazing drink with pineapple juice, flavored rum, Sprite, and who knew what else. She couldn't taste the alcohol in the drink at all, and before she knew it, she'd sucked down two cups of the stuff and was now on her third.

"Oh! Before I forget, I called Meg, and she's super anxious to meet you," April said excitedly. "And if it's okay, she wants you to come by Hill's House on Monday and meet with her."

"So soon?" June asked.

"Yup. She just hired a new janitor, but she's been looking for months for the right person to fill the entertainment coordinator position and is almost giddy that you're here."

"She doesn't even know me. I mean, doesn't she want a résumé or references or anything?" June asked.

April waved her hand in the air and shook her head. "Not necessarily. I told her all about you. Where you were before, what you did. You'll be perfect."

"But what if she doesn't like it there and doesn't want to take the job?" Carlise asked. Her words were also slightly slurred. They were all feeling mellow, but weren't knockout drunk. No one wanted to be hungover for the wedding the next day.

"Why wouldn't she like it?" April asked.

"I don't know. But interviews are supposed to be for both sides. And we all know Cal will let her stay for as long as she wants, so she doesn't have to worry about money."

"I'm not a mooch," June said a little more forcefully than she'd meant to.

"Oh, I didn't mean to imply that," Carlise said with a frown.

"She just means that with the way Cal looks at you, you could tell him you wanted a jet plane, and he'd go out and not only buy it for you but build a hangar and an airstrip in his backyard," April said with a huge smile on her face.

"That's not true," June protested.

"Girl, please," Carlise said after taking a sip of her drink. "He looks at you as if you hung the moon and control the stars."

Pleasure swept through June at the other woman's words. Still . . .

"We've only known each other a few days," she protested.

Carlise burst out laughing. "Do we need to go over this again?" She lifted her arm and looked at her bare wrist, pantomiming checking a watch for the time. "Riggs and I have known each other for a hot minute, and we're getting *married* tomorrow. Time doesn't matter, it's how he makes you feel deep inside. When your belly does somersaults when you see him. When his voice makes you wet between the legs, and the way he constantly watches you, as if he's afraid little green men will come down out of the sky and steal you away at any moment."

"Is that how it is with you and Chappy?" April asked.

A dreamy look crossed Carlise's face. "Oh yeah. And when he kisses me and . . . *you know* . . . it's as if there's no one in the world but the two of us. Has Cal kissed you yet, June?"

She couldn't help but lick her lips and remember the amazing and passionate kiss they'd shared earlier that very day. She nodded.

"And did the earth move?"

"Definitely."

"And the sex?"

June blushed and shook her head.

"Right, well . . . it'll happen. Soon, I'm sure. Because Cal is just like my Riggs. He doesn't mess around when it comes to what he wants. And that man wants *you*. He practically drools when you're around."

"Oh, that was a nice picture . . . not," April said with a roll of her eyes.

"I meant it in a good way. He wants her," Carlise said. Then she smirked. "And should we talk about you and JJ?"

April choked on the drink she was sipping. She turned to Carlise and shook her head. "We aren't going there."

"Why not? I mean, it's obvious by the way Cal looks at June that he wants her, just as it's obvious by the way JJ looks at you."

"He doesn't look at me in *any* way," April said stubbornly.

It was Carlise's turn to roll her eyes. "You're kidding, right? The man can't take his eyes off you. And Riggs told me all about how that stranger came into the office the other week and harassed you, and JJ nearly lost his mind. His voice got all growly and scary, and he chased the guy off."

"It wasn't that big of a deal. He overreacted," April insisted, but she wouldn't look either June or Carlise in the eye.

"All I'm saying is that the man likes you, April," Carlise said in a softer tone. "If you gave him even the smallest sign that you were interested, he'd jump on that . . . and on you." She giggled at her own joke.

"I'm too old for him," April insisted.

"What?" June asked, not sure she heard right.

"I'm almost fifty," she said mournfully.

"I thought you were like forty-five or forty-six," Carlise said, confused.

"Forty-six. Which is almost fifty." April sighed.

"Oh my God, no it isn't," Carlise said with a shake of her head. "Besides, JJ is going to be forty soon. I think his birthday is in a month or something like that."

April's head came up at that. "He is?"

"How do you *not* know this?" Carlise asked with a laugh. "I mean, you know everything about everything. I can't tell you how many times Riggs has said that without you, Jack's Lumber would've crashed and burned. You keep them all straight, organize the work schedules, and you've even started arranging their AT hikes. How do you not know how old JJ is?"

"I thought he was in his early thirties," April said. "I mean, have you seen him? He's in amazing shape. And he doesn't have any gray hair at all."

"That doesn't mean anything. The gray hair, I mean," Carlise said. Then she put her drink down and leaned toward April. She was sitting cross legged on the floor in front of the sofa, where June and April had sat before opting for the comfort of the couch. "You are not too old for anyone. I don't care if JJ *was* thirty-two or something. Look at you— you're beautiful. And smart. And you don't put up with his crap, which I think he really needs."

"He sees me as a mother figure," April protested.

June couldn't stop the burst of laughter that escaped her lips.

"What? He *does!*" April insisted. "He even calls me 'mom' sometimes."

"He's teasing about that!" Carlise told her.

"If JJ thinks of you as a mother figure, I'll call Elaine and tell her where I am and agree to work for her for free for the rest of my life," June said solemnly. "And since she's the last person I ever want to see again, I'm *that* sure of what I'm saying."

April stared at her with so much hope in her gaze, it made June's heart hurt.

"Look at me," she reasoned. "I'm short, fat, have never gone to college, and have lived in the same house my entire life. And somehow, a billionaire prince is interested in me. *Me.*" June shook her head. "Not only that, but for some reason, he's worried that I'm going to think his scars are a turnoff, which I don't get.

"But I want him, so I'm going to have him. It probably won't last, and there's no way he'd ever want to marry me, but I'm not willing to let this opportunity pass me by because I'm scared. And I am. I'm terrified. But I know deep down that if I chicken out, if I don't go after what I want, I'll regret it for the rest of my life. And you will too, April, if you don't give JJ a chance."

She was practically out of breath by the time she was done, but she really wanted April to hear her.

"You aren't fat. Or short. And . . . I'll think about it," April said.

"Says the woman who's five-nine and has probably never had to wear any clothing with an X in front of the size," June muttered.

To her surprise, April put her glass down on the small table next to the sofa and practically threw herself at June.

She barely managed to not spill her drink as April hugged her tightly.

"Hey, I want in on this hug fest!" Carlise protested as she squeezed in on June's other side.

"I feel like a squished bug," June said with a laugh, as she was embraced by the two women.

Carlise pulled back and smiled at her. "I like you, June."

"Me too," April agreed.

"And I like you guys. I've never really had friends before, actually. Never had time, and the girls I knew in high school all went on with their lives after we graduated."

"Your stepmother sounds like a total bitch," April said firmly.

"That's because she is," June said with a shrug.

They all laughed. Carlise went back to her spot on the floor and took another sip of her drink, and April scooted back to her side of the couch.

"I can't believe you're getting married up at the cabin where you almost died," April said almost nonchalantly. "If it was me, I'm not sure I'd ever want to go up there again."

"Wait, *what*?" June practically shouted. "You almost *died*?"

Carlise shrugged. "Yup. But Baxter saved me." She reached over and petted the black pit bull who'd followed her around the apartment all night, only settling down when Carlise had.

"Start at the beginning!" June insisted. She couldn't explain why she was so upset about learning her new friend had almost died. Maybe it was because she seemed so . . . full of life. The thought of not knowing her was painful.

June sat and listened with wide eyes as Carlise explained what had transpired just a month earlier. How she'd first been caught in a storm, and Baxter led Chappy right to her. Then how her best friend had been stalking her and ended up coming to Maine and the cabin and tried to kidnap and kill her. The rest of the story involved a bunker, an avalanche, and Baxter once again helping to save her life.

"It's not as if we're getting married in the bunker," Carlise told April when she'd finished telling the story of her ordeal. "We're doing it outside at the cabin. And trust me, I have a lot of *very* good memories in that cabin and can't wait to make more after Riggs marries me." She had a satisfied smile on her face.

"God, can we please not talk about sex when I'm not getting any?" April begged.

"You could be if you took your head out of your ass and gave JJ the green light," Carlise fired back.

"Nope, not going there again. We've already talked about that tonight," April said with a shake of her head.

"You were the one who brought up sex," Carlise reminded her.

"Whatever."

June couldn't keep the smile off her face.

"I don't know what *you're* smiling about," April muttered. "You aren't getting any either."

"Not yet," she said coyly.

Carlise giggled. "One bed," she said.

"What?" June asked with a frown.

"It worked for me. And you said that you and Cal shared a bed on your way up here to Maine. I have a feeling he'll be stubborn, and if you finagled some way to get into his bed to sleep again, I'm thinking he wouldn't be able to keep his distance from you for long."

"You have a good point," June said.

"I know. It's that forced-proximity thing," Carlise said firmly.

"The what?" April asked.

"It's a trope. I've translated a few romance books that used it. When the hero and heroine are forced to spend time together, especially in a bed, things tend to happen. Hey! How can we get JJ and April into a bed together? I guess putting a cot in his office and then somehow breaking the lock when April's in there with him would be a bit too obvious?" Carlise seemed entirely too excited about the idea of trapping her friends together.

"As if JJ wouldn't be able to figure out some way to get free. He was Special Forces, you know," April said with a shrug. "He'd have us out within five minutes."

"Hmm, you're probably right. I'll have to think of something else," Carlise mused.

June thought it was telling that April didn't immediately protest Carlise's idea in general. She made a mental note to talk to Carlise later—when she wasn't about to get married and when they both weren't tipsy. There had to be something they could do to help April and JJ get together, especially when it seemed as if they both liked each other.

She may have only met these women yesterday, but they were so friendly and welcoming, she felt as if she'd known them a lot longer. It didn't even seem weird to be talking about their love lives or setting up their friends.

"That leaves Bob," June said.

"What about him?" Carlise asked.

"We need to find someone to set him up with," June said.

"Oh! You're right. But I don't think he's interested in anyone around here," Carlise said, frowning.

"Maybe one of the people who need a guide on the AT?" April mused. "Most of the requests are from women. I could vet them a little more closely, schedule him with women who might catch his eye."

"Great idea!" June said a little too enthusiastically. "But that name . . . Bob . . . I'm not sure that's the sexiest name."

Carlise and April both laughed uproariously.

"His real name is Kendric," April informed her.

"Oh my gosh, that's so much better! Why in the world does he go by Bob?" June asked.

"Kendric is totally a romance hero name," Carlise agreed. "And I don't know why everyone calls him Bob."

"His last name is Evans," April supplied.

Both June and Carlise looked at her blankly.

"Jeez, you guys. Bob Evans? The restaurant?"

"Oh!" Carlise said.

June simply shook her head. "Boys. I swear, they have the most juvenile minds."

Everyone giggled.

"I could totally tell the client I schedule him with that his name is Kendric. That way she wouldn't know about the Bob thing unless he tells her. But by that time, she'd already be calling him Kendric in her head."

"Yeah, like with me and Riggs. He told me his name was Riggs and then passed out on me for three days. So when JJ called and demanded to know what I'd done to Chappy, I was so confused. To this day, I can't call him anything but Riggs."

"Sounds like a plan," June agreed. "April will schedule Bob . . . er . . . Kendric with a single woman who loves the outdoors—because why else would she want a hiking guide?—and they'll fall in love, and she'll move to Newton, and they'll live happily ever after."

June knew she was being ridiculous, but the alcohol in her veins and the happiness she was feeling hanging out with her new friends had her convinced everything would work out perfectly. "I wonder what the guys are doing?" she mused.

"Should we call them?" Carlise asked a little too eagerly.

"No! It's too soon. We want them to wonder what *we're* doing," April said with a smile.

"But we're just hanging out," Carlise said with a shrug.

"They don't have to know that. Maybe they'll think we're having a wild party or something."

June wasn't so sure about that, but she didn't comment. She simply took another sip of her delicious drink and smiled. She was happy, almost scarily so, and refused to think about the other times in her life when she was content and how things usually turned to crap. That wouldn't happen here. She hoped.

Chapter Thirteen

"What do you think the girls are doing?" JJ asked.

Cal had lit the firepit in his backyard, and they were all sitting around enjoying the chilly air. They'd each had a beer or two earlier but had switched to water so they'd be sober enough to drive later.

Now, it wasn't lost on him that JJ was probably asking because he was interested in one woman in particular.

"They probably fell asleep," Chappy said with a chuckle. "Carlise has been exhausted recently, stressing about the ceremony, even though I've purposely tried to make it as low key as possible, so she wouldn't worry. But . . ." His words trailed off.

Cal couldn't help but compare tomorrow's ceremony with some of his own family weddings in the past. Because of who they were, his family planned weddings that were expected to be traditional, huge, expensive shindigs. He'd always shied away from that kind of attention, even before he was a POW. And when he tried to picture June wearing an elaborate dress with a twenty-foot train and long veil in front of a thousand guests in an extremely old church in Liechtenstein . . . he just couldn't do it. She'd hate it. Would be paralyzed with nerves. And he couldn't blame her. His parents weren't exactly the simple mom and dad next door.

But if he broke with tradition and didn't have the paparazzi-filled ceremony that his countrymen and women seemed to love, maybe he could still find a compromise. Give June something that would make her feel like the princess she'd become but that wouldn't completely freak her out.

He couldn't deny that he'd love to show June off. Let the people of his country see how amazing she was. He also couldn't help but think about his own situation. The need to show his countrymen and women that he'd risen above everything he'd endured. Prove that he'd come a long way from the tortured man seen in those awful video clips the terrorists had shared with the world.

It took a moment for the content of his daydreams to actually sink in. When it did, when he realized he was actually planning his and June's fictitious wedding, he sighed deeply, suddenly overcome with sorrow.

"Cal? What do you think?"

He jerked and realized he'd completely zoned out of the conversation going on around him. "Sorry, I wasn't listening. What do I think about what?"

His three friends laughed.

"Never mind. More importantly, what were you thinking about? Or should I say *who*?" Chappy asked with a smile.

Cal normally wasn't one to discuss his feelings, but he didn't mind talking to his mates a bit. He was actually relieved to unload some of his confusing thoughts about June. "She's driving me crazy," he admitted.

"You need us to come up with a reason why she can't stay anymore?" JJ asked. "Because we will. Just say the word, and she'll be out of here."

"No!" Cal practically shouted. Then he took a deep breath. "No. I don't want her gone. That's the problem."

"Ah," JJ said with a nod.

"It's just that . . . we only recently met. And those steps of hers, her mother and sister, they treated her like shite. She hasn't had a chance to live. And now I've dragged her *here*. To Newton. Where nothing happens, and there isn't even a proper shop for her to visit when she wants a new outfit."

"How did shopping go today? Was she upset that there weren't enough lady boutiques or whatever in Rumford?" Bob asked.

"Not at all. It went fine. I swear, she was excited by the tiniest things. Being around her is like being with someone who just got out of prison after decades inside, and everything is shiny and new," Cal said.

"That probably *is* what it's like for her," Chappy said. "Given what you've told us about her circumstances."

"Don't get me wrong, she knows about the world, had to do all the shopping and stuff for her family. But she still seems so . . . innocent compared to me." Cal knew he wasn't explaining himself well.

"Does she seem happy here?" JJ asked.

"I think so."

"Then stop worrying."

"It's not that easy," Cal protested.

"Sure, it is. You like her, she seems to like you. Just go with it," Bob said with a shrug.

"You guys have seen me," Cal blurted. "You *know* what those arse-holes did to me. How the hell can I expose her to that? Show her physical proof of the evil that exists in the world? Every inch of my body is a wreck." He didn't talk about *this*. Ever. But his need to spare June any kind of pain made him willing to broach the one subject that was off limits. His scars.

Chappy leaned forward and stared intently at Cal from across the fire. "You think she cares about your scars?"

"How could she not? They're fecking hideous," Cal said.

"They are *not*," Chappy said heatedly. "You got those scars from protecting us. And if she so much as wrinkles her nose at them, I'll personally escort her out of this house, away from Newton, and tell her never to return."

Cal wanted to be grateful. Chappy had always been the protector of the group. It had gratified Cal to be able to take on that role for a short time when they'd been captives, to protect his friends for once, but the instincts ran deep within his mate, and Cal loved him all the more for it.

"June isn't going to give the smallest shit about your scars," Bob said before Cal could answer Chappy. "The woman's head over heels in love with you."

Cal stared at his friend in disbelief.

"It's obvious," he drawled, shifting in his chair. "Her eyes are always on you, all soft and pining and whatnot. I think she'd face down the devil himself if it meant keeping you from getting hurt."

The longing that hit Cal surprised him. He *wanted* June to love him. Because as daft as it seemed, he was pretty sure he already loved *her*.

"It's easy for us to sit here and say that your scars don't matter," JJ said matter of factly. "But the truth is, the only one who has to come to terms with the physical evidence of what happened is *you*, Cal. My instinct is to recommend saying 'fuck you' to anyone who can't deal with the repercussions of you literally saving our lives. Because that's what you did. You saved our damn lives, and there's not a day that goes by that I'm not grateful to you because of it.

"But I hate that it took such a toll on your psyche. We're here for you. Whatever you need, whenever you need it, we're here. If that means protecting you from being hurt by a woman, that's what we'll do. We'll take our cues from you. Understand?"

Cal sucked in a deep breath. He wasn't sure he'd actually saved his friends' lives, but when he was being tortured, he refused to let a sound pass his lips, because if he broke, he knew his captors would turn on Chappy, JJ, and Bob.

They'd all suffered in their own ways, including physically, and as much as Cal wanted to put the entire experience behind him, he couldn't. Because every time he looked in a mirror, he was transported right back there. To that hellhole. He'd heard the taunts of their captors. Telling him he'd never be "Prettymon," as the press had dubbed him, ever again. That he was a weak, pathetic piece of shite.

"Cal? Do you understand?" JJ asked.

"Ten-four," he told his friend.

"Good. If things progress, and you bare yourself to the woman . . . and June looks at you with *anything* other than the love and respect we see in her eyes when you're fully clothed, she's not the one for you. Period. Full stop. All it'll take is one look, and you'll know. It'll suck if it happens, but at least you'll have your answer. You can call one of us, and we'll come get her, set her up in an apartment or a room somewhere else, and you can get on with your life.

"But if she isn't fazed, if the love in her eyes doesn't dim when you're alone and butt-ass naked, give yourself permission to love her back— and hold on to her like your life depends on it."

Cal nodded. He wanted that. So much. But he was terrified to find out one way or another.

"Right, can we stop talking about Cal being naked now?" Bob joked. "I mean, scars or not, it's not something I think we should be discussing at a damn bachelor party. Naked *women*, sure, but Cal's hairy ass? No, thank you."

Everyone chuckled, and Cal suddenly felt exhausted. He was relieved they were done talking about him and his mental issues.

"You all set for tomorrow?" JJ asked Chappy.

"Yup. I'm more than ready to get my ring on Carlise's finger."

"Any plans for a honeymoon?" Bob asked.

"Not immediately. Carlise has a deadline she needs to meet, and we want her mom to spend a few days here. I was thinking about taking her somewhere warm. I mean, as much as I love snuggling with her in the cabin, I wouldn't mind seeing her frolicking in the ocean in a swimsuit."

Everyone grinned. Talk turned to the best tropical places that Chappy might take Carlise. But after a while, the conversation inevitably circled back to Cal and June.

"So . . . you heard anything from the stepmonster and her daughter?" JJ asked.

"No. But what I've heard from Tex, who's still monitoring her online activity, is that Carla is apparently flashing her boobs at Karl, crying, and telling him how scared she is. She even showed him some note she supposedly received after I left, from her alleged stalker."

"She was crying and showing her tits at the same time? How does that work? I mean, when most women are upset, the last thing they're thinking about is not so accidentally letting their tits fall out of their bra," Bob said with a roll of his eyes.

"Exactly. I haven't talked to Karl yet, but it's on my agenda. I spoke with my parents and explained the entire situation, and they mentioned doing what they could to rein him in and get him to cut ties," Cal said.

"You think that's smart?" JJ asked. "Maybe it's best if your cousin keeps an eye on her. This Carla chick obviously craves attention, and if she has her heart set on you, and if you aren't attainable anymore, would she do something drastic?"

"Like?" Chappy asked.

"I don't know. Like make this fake stalker a reality?"

"As in, stalk *herself*?" Cal asked.

"I was thinking more along the lines of hiring someone to make it look like she's being harassed. You said you overheard her and the mom talking about something like that, right?"

"To what end? I'm not going back," Cal said. "She and her awful mother could hire someone to leave them notes all day long, and it's not going to make a difference."

"Hmm."

"What does 'hmm' mean?" Cal demanded.

"You mentioned looking into the death of June's father," JJ answered after a moment. "So . . . just hear me out. If a woman is crazy enough to kill her husband, to steal the house and insurance money out from under his unsuspecting daughter, and she gets away with it, why wouldn't she do something just as drastic to obtain an incredibly wealthy husband—one who has royal blood, no less—for her own daughter?"

"She can't force me to marry that silly cow," Cal said angrily.

"Maybe not—but she could do everything possible to get rid of any competition."

Cal stared at his friend, his gut twisting. He respected and trusted JJ. He'd been their team leader in the Army, and his track record was damn good. "She doesn't know where June is."

"But she could find *you*," Chappy argued. "You aren't exactly the media darling you once were, but it's not a secret that we started a business here in Newton."

"And if she finds you, it won't take long to figure out you have a new roommate," Bob added.

"Shite," Cal swore. "That bitch isn't going to touch one hair on June's head ever again. I'll fecking kill her with my bare hands if she even tries!"

"Easy, bro," Bob said.

"I'm thinking we need to cut her off before she gets any grand ideas," JJ suggested.

"How?"

"If she actually killed her husband, and we can prove it, she'd have bigger problems to deal with than trying to marry off her daughter or find her stepdaughter," Cal said.

"I'll call Tex for you," Bob said. "No need to scare June if she overhears your call. Tex knows people. Lots of people. He can plant a seed with a detective down in DC. You think June would agree to an exhumation?"

Cal pressed his lips together. He didn't even want to think about having to discuss such a thing with June. About digging up her beloved father for an autopsy, even if he'd already given thought to having the man's death investigated. "If it means proving Elaine killed him, yes—but I hope it doesn't come to that."

"Let's not rush things. I think the first step is getting the cops to listen to our theories. And making Elaine nervous enough that she forgets about you and June," JJ said.

Cal was more than all right with that.

"I'll call Tex tomorrow, before the wedding," Bob said.

"I appreciate it," Cal said.

Bob shook his head. "It's what we do. You'd do it for me."

He wasn't wrong.

Talk turned to work after that. About the upcoming hiking season, weather, and if there were any more storms predicted.

Cal kept surreptitiously looking at his watch, checking the time. It wasn't that he didn't enjoy spending the evening with his mates, but he was anxious to see June. To check on her, make sure things weren't awkward between her and Carlise and April. Not that he thought they would be, but he knew she'd been a little nervous about tonight.

When it got to be ten-thirty, and no one had heard from the women, he was more than relieved when Chappy picked up his phone and muttered, "Screw it." He looked up with a smile a minute or so later and announced, "The girls are ready to go."

JJ stood so fast, Cal could only blink in surprise. "You want me to drive June back here when I pick up April?" he asked.

"No, it's out of your way. I'll head in and get her. Thanks, though." Cal knew he was being ridiculous; it wasn't as if Newton was all that large. It would only take JJ an extra four minutes, max, to drive June to his house. But that was four additional minutes before Cal got to see her, to make sure all was well.

"You guys are pathetic," Bob said with a shake of his head, as he helped pour water and sand on the firepit before they headed out.

"Just wait," Chappy told him. "When you find your woman, you'll be the same way."

"Whatever," he retorted. "I'll leave the love to you guys."

"Who said anything about love?" JJ protested.

Cal snorted as Chappy and Bob chuckled.

Within five minutes, the fire was out, the doors were locked, and all four men were headed down Cal's driveway. Bob peeled away when they got to his street, and the other three continued to Chappy's apartment complex.

Susan Stoker

~

Ten minutes later, Cal was helping a tipsy and fecking adorable June into his SUV.

"I had *such* a good time," she gushed happily.

"I'm glad, princess."

"Carlise and April are *so* nice. And Baxter . . . he's a hero! Did you hear what he did? How he saved Carlise *twice*?"

"I did," he told her, leaning inside to fasten her seat belt.

He couldn't make himself step back when he was done. He stayed close, one hand resting on the seat next to her hip. Her head was resting on the seat back, her cheeks were flushed, and she was smiling at him lazily.

"What?" she asked. "I'm all belted in," she informed him, as if he hadn't been the one to strap her in himself. "Besides, I'm safe with you. Don't even need this," she declared, pulling on the belt across her chest. "If something happened, you'd reach your superstrong arm across the car and catch me before I could face plant into the windshield . . . screen . . . whatever you call it."

He'd certainly try. But it wasn't going to be an issue, because there was no way she was going anywhere without her seat belt. "How do you feel?" he asked.

One brow lifted. "Fine. Why?"

"Is the world spinning? Are you nauseous at all? Do you think you'll throw up?"

"Scared I'm gonna get your grossly expensive car all nasty?" she giggled.

"Don't care about that. I'm more worried about *you*, June."

She stared at him for a long moment before she sighed. "I can't remember a time when someone was more worried about me than their car."

Her words made him sad, but Cal simply lifted his hand and touched her cheek with the backs of his fingers. "You didn't answer the question," he reminded her.

170

"I'm okay. I'm tipsy, but not drunk."

"Good. I'll have us home in a jiffy." Then Cal stepped back and shut her door. By the time he was in the driver's seat, June's eyes were closed. He thought she was asleep already, until he started the car and began to back out of the parking spot.

"Cal?"

"Yeah?"

"Thank you."

"For what?"

"Everything. For taking me with you when you left DC. For not assuming I'm like Carla. For letting me stay with you. For kissing me senseless. For being so wonderful. For letting me share your friends . . . all of it."

Cal grinned. "You're welcome."

"I feel as if I've done nothing but take from you since we met."

"That's not true," he told her honestly. "You've given me more than you'll ever know."

"Like what?"

"My faith back in humanity."

She blinked her eyes open, startled.

He shook his head. "Close your eyes, princess. We'll be home soon, and you can get some sleep."

She sighed again and did as he suggested, closing her eyes but keeping her face turned toward him.

Cal divided his attention between June and the road until he pulled into his driveway. Thankfully, Newton wasn't very busy as far as traffic went.

Her eyes opened, and she said, "Oh! That was fast."

"Keep telling you that Newton's not that big."

"I know, but that took like two seconds to get here."

"A little longer than that," Cal said with a chuckle. He pulled into the detached garage and turned off the engine. "Stay put. I'll come around," he ordered.

171

June nodded, and he jumped out and jogged around to her side. She was still sitting with her seat belt on when he opened the door. He unsnapped it and held her elbow as she hopped out of the seat. She immediately stumbled and would've fallen if he hadn't had a good grip on her.

"Easy."

"Sorry. The ground is moving."

Cal laughed. "Right. Just tipsy, huh?"

June held up a hand, her thumb and index finger almost touching. He chuckled again. Hell, he'd laughed more in the last five minutes than he had all night.

He walked her into the house and immediately headed for the stairs. He paused at the door to her room . . . then, making a split-second decision, continued walking her toward the master instead.

"Cal?" she asked.

"You've had quite a bit to drink. I don't feel comfortable leaving you on your own. You could get sick in the middle of the night and choke. If it wouldn't make you too uneasy, I'd prefer if you slept in my room."

"Okay."

"Okay?" he asked, wanting to make sure she was really all right with the suggestion.

June nodded. They were already at the side of his bed, and she happily tumbled onto the mattress and turned onto her side, burrowing her nose in one of his pillows. She turned her face after a moment and smiled up at him. "It smells like you."

Cal smiled back. She was so damn cute. "I'll get you a shirt to sleep in," he told her before forcing himself to turn away.

He brought her a T-shirt and a pair of his sweats. They'd be huge on her, but the alternative was leaving her legs bare, and he wasn't sure he had enough self-control for that. He left her for a few minutes as he went downstairs to check the locks and grab a cup of water and some headache pills.

When he returned, the clothes June had been wearing were in a heap on the floor by his bed, and she was under his covers. He noticed the sweatpants still lying on the mattress. "June?" he asked.

She didn't answer. She was already sound asleep.

He should really wake her up and make her put on the sweats. At least make sure she drank the water and took the pills. But seeing her bra on the pile of clothes—and her underwear—had him momentarily gobsmacked.

She was practically naked . . . in his bed . . . wearing nothing but his T-shirt.

Cal stood there for a long moment, his dick throbbing, his control slipping. But, of course, he wasn't going to take advantage of the situation. No matter how much he wanted her.

He took his time in the loo, brushing his teeth and avoiding the small mirror as he put on the sweatpants he'd given to June and a T-shirt. The scars on his forearms were visible, and it took everything within Cal not to change into a long-sleeved shirt. But he didn't want to hide his arms nearly as much as he wanted to feel June against him, skin on skin, even in the smallest way.

He went back into his bedroom and clicked off the bedside light before climbing under the covers.

June immediately mumbled something in her sleep and turned toward him. One of her legs hiked up over his thigh and her arm went across his belly. She shoved her nose into his neck and sighed as if she was finally content.

"June?" he whispered.

She didn't answer verbally but tightened her hold on him, as if she thought he was going to shove her away.

As if.

That wasn't going to happen.

"Good night," he said, turning his head and kissing her forehead.

"'Night," she whispered sleepily.

It took Cal over an hour to fall asleep, simply because he was enjoying holding the woman in his arms too much to do something so mundane. He didn't want to miss a minute of the experience. But eventually, his body shut down.

The last thing he remembered was inhaling the flowery scent of whatever shampoo June had used and knowing he'd never be able to smell a flower again and *not* think about this moment.

Chapter Fourteen

June was having the best dream. She and Cal were married and had a little girl. Now they were trying for a second child, and he'd been extremely eager in his attempts to knock her up again. They were currently lying in bed, sweaty and sated after an especially vigorous baby-making session, and she felt amazing.

June shifted and smiled as she felt Cal against her. She turned and kissed his chest . . . then frowned. She felt material under her lips instead of the warm skin she'd just been caressing.

It took her a moment to wake up enough to be cognizant of where she was.

The first emotion that hit her was disappointment. She and Cal weren't married, they didn't have a child, and they weren't trying for a second.

The next thing that sank in . . . while she and Cal might not be a couple, she was actually lying in his bed, practically on top of him.

Memories from last night returned in a flash. Her night with Carlise and April, the delicious pineapple rum drink she'd had way too many of. Cal showing up to drive her back to his house.

She didn't really remember how she'd ended up in his bed. Licking her lips, June lifted her head—only to come face to face with a grinning Cal.

"Good morning. How do you feel?"

"Um . . . fine."

"No headache? You aren't hungover?"

June shrugged. "No, I'm good. I should get up," she said, feeling her cheeks warm and certain her face was bright red.

"No rush," Cal replied, his arm tightening around her.

June cautiously lowered her head, so it was lying on his shirt-covered chest once more. One of her legs was thrown over his, and she could feel his sweats against her skin. God, she wasn't wearing any pants! Could this get any more embarrassing?

His fingers lazily caressed her back where they held her against him, and his other hand covered the arm lying over his belly. Goose bumps immediately rose on her skin where he touched her.

"Are you cold?" he asked.

Yeah, this *could* get more embarrassing. Wanting to hide the fact that her body's reaction wasn't due to the cold, but because he was touching her, June said, "A little."

He shifted under her, and she could feel his every muscle flexing and contracting as he reached for the blanket that she'd probably kicked down at some point in the night. He covered them both.

Great, now they were in an intimate little cocoon . . . in his bed.

"You have a good time last night?" he asked.

June nodded. "Carlise and April are awesome. So nice. I feel as if I've known them forever."

"I'm not surprised. You're very likable, June."

The compliment spread through her. She wasn't used to hearing them. Elaine and Carla preferred to point out her worst traits.

"I'm supposed to meet Meg, from Hill's House, on Monday," she told him.

"That's good. I'm sure she'll want you to start right away, but you don't have to take the job," Cal warned. "You'll always have a place to stay here, so if it doesn't seem right, or you don't take to Meg or the residents, don't feel obligated to say yes, even if she wants to hire you."

"That's what Carlise said."

"It's good advice," Cal told her.

June couldn't help but think of the other advice her new friends had given her. About Cal. About going for what she wanted. She still felt inadequate, but she *was* in his bed. For some reason, last night, he'd either brought her here or, at the very least, hadn't kicked her out when she'd climbed into his bed. She might not be completely sure they'd work out in the long run, but she wasn't an idiot either. Men didn't do this. Didn't engage in small talk, extending their time in bed, if they weren't at least a little interested in the woman they were cuddling with.

And that's definitely what she and Cal were doing. She never would've guessed this man—this amazing, gorgeous, rich prince—would be a cuddler. And especially not with *her*. But there was no mistaking his determination to keep her right where she was.

Same as when they'd woken up together in the hotel.

She thought about what she'd said to Carlise and April last night. How she'd decided not to let the opportunity to be with Cal pass. That she didn't want to have any regrets. Now seemed as good a time as any to take the first step toward getting what she wanted . . . namely, to be Cal's lover for as long as he'd have her.

Coming up on an elbow, June stared down at him. His hair was mussed, and he had a five-o'clock shadow on his handsome face. His brown eyes were fixed on her, and it made her feel like the only woman in the world at that moment.

"June?" he asked, his brows coming down in concern. "Are you all right?"

"I want you," she blurted—promptly regretting her bluntness.

To her relief, Cal didn't reject her.

"I want you too," he said quietly.

She stared at him, wondering how to do this. She'd never made the first move before. And even though she was half naked and lying in his bed, in his arms, she still felt awkward and unsure.

He rolled suddenly, and June squeaked in surprise when she found herself on her back with Cal hovering over her. She licked her lips, then frowned. Crap. She hadn't brushed her teeth yet. Her hair was probably all over the place, and suddenly she had to pee.

Cal chuckled. "Why do you look like you're regretting what you just told me?"

"I don't regret it, per se. But my mouth tastes like something crawled in there and died. I'd kill for a drink of water, I have to use the restroom and probably shower, and I just . . . I don't want to give you any reason to regret . . . um . . . anything."

"Not possible. And while I want you more than I've ever wanted another woman, I'm thinking now isn't exactly the best timing."

June was relieved but kind of sad too.

"Don't look like that," Cal said with a small smile. "Now that I know you're on board with this . . . with us . . . it's going to happen. But maybe not after you've been drinking with your friends. And I need some time to . . . come to terms with things."

"Come to terms? Cal, if you aren't sure, or if you're just agreeing because you feel sorry for me or something, I don't want—"

Cal interrupted her by swooping down and kissing her neck. Her words stopped as if he'd unplugged her or something. June inhaled deeply as his lips caressed the sensitive skin of her jaw. She tilted her head to give him more room.

She felt one of his hands on her leg, and it slid up the outside of her thigh to her hip, then pushed under her shirt. She sucked in her belly, aware of how *not* flat or toned she was.

Cal lifted his head and said, "I'm sure. And there's no reason for me to feel sorry for you," he said firmly. "Your skin is so soft, so warm. And feeling your reaction to my touch, your goose bumps, is the best compliment I've ever received."

June wrinkled her nose. "I was cold?" It came out more a question than the rebuttal she wanted it to be.

He smirked, then leaned down and kissed her nose. "You react more strongly to my touch than anyone ever has. It's a complete turn-on, princess. But I'm not like that," he said more seriously. "I've got so much scar tissue, it's hard for me to feel much of *anything* in places. I want you, but I'm nervous about how it's going to go. I haven't been with anyone since before I was taken captive."

June's heart bled for this man. "It's going to go just fine," she said firmly. "We'll go at whatever speed you need, and I told you before that if you need to, we don't have to turn the lights on. But you should know, Cal, scars or not, you're the most beautiful man I've ever met. And it's not just your physical looks, which are stunning enough. It's who you are as a man. It's your personality. Kindness goes a lot further in my book than a hot body or pretty face—but lucky for me, you've got all three."

He stared at her for a long moment. "You're too good for me," he told her.

June laughed. She rolled her eyes. "Whatever. I know what I am and what I'm not. But we're two people who have an attraction toward each other and chemistry to boot."

"This is very true. And truth be told, the other reason why right now isn't a good time for us to explore this connection is because I don't have any condoms."

June blinked up at him. "Oh, I didn't think about that."

"I'm clean," he went on. "I wasn't kidding about not being with anyone in years, but I don't want to risk getting you pregnant."

She'd never had a conversation like this with a man. She knew it was the smart and adult thing to do, but it was also awkward. Fortunately, it never came up because the few men she'd slept with used condoms.

"I . . . I'm protected," June told him shyly. "Not because I've been out there having wild monkey sex with strangers or anything, but I wanted to regulate my period. It's nice knowing exactly when it'll be here, and the pill helps with my cramps."

"Wild monkey sex?" Cal echoed with a grin.

June smiled up at him and shrugged.

He got serious again. "You're okay with not using condoms?" he asked.

"Do you trust me when I tell you that I'm on the pill?" she countered. "I imagine there are plenty of women who would lie about that in the hopes they *would* get pregnant, if it meant getting some of your money and maybe becoming a princess."

"You aren't one of them," Cal said without any doubt.

His trust in her made June want to cry. "No, I'm not. I can show you my pill pack if you want."

Cal shook his head. "No need. And just the thought of being inside you bare, feeling every inch of you, is fecking exciting. But June, I should warn you. My captors . . . they didn't spare me . . . down there. I might not be able to stay hard for long."

Instead of feeling sorry for Cal, she was furious at the men who felt as if they had the right to hurt another human being the way they had. "It doesn't matter," she told him. "We'll figure things out as we go."

He stared at her with an expression she couldn't read. Then he murmured, "So kind."

June opened her mouth to tell him she wasn't always so nice. That she could be mean when the situation warranted it, but the words were lost when his hand moved again.

His gaze stayed glued on her face as he palmed one of her breasts under her shirt. Well . . . his shirt.

June inhaled sharply and dug her fingernails into his biceps. For the first time, she realized he was wearing short sleeves. She'd never seen him in anything but long-sleeved tees. She didn't have time to speculate on that because he was tweaking her nipple, making her gasp again.

"You're sensitive," he observed.

June nodded.

"Have you ever come by nipple stimulation alone?" he asked.

With any other person, in any other situation, June would've been blushing furiously and trying to scramble off the bed. But this was Cal. She loved him.

The revelation hit her—hard. She was lying under him, he was touching her intimately for the first time . . . and she already knew she loved him more than life itself. Belatedly, she shook her head in answer to his question.

"Now's not the time, but rest assured, I'm going to make that my mission in life," he teased. His gaze dropped to her chest, watching as his hand moved under the thin shirt, his breathing speeding up as he played with her nipple.

"Cal!" she whimpered.

He sighed. "I know, I'm not being fair. But having you pressed up against me all night, smelling your flowery scent, dreaming about having you under me, just like this . . . it's got me worked up."

June could *feel* how worked up he was. His cock was pressing against her thigh. It felt long and hot and . . . "You're so hard," she whispered.

He grinned. "Yeah. But I'm not sure how long it'll last. My erection seems to come and go . . . no pun intended. But it definitely has a mind of its own when it comes to you. I just . . . I'm not sure what will happen once I'm . . . naked. I just—"

"Shhhh," June murmured. "We'll deal with it when the time comes."

"Yeah," he agreed. "Soon. I want to see these beauties," he said, giving her breast a tight squeeze. "Taste them. Suck on them."

June was a little surprised by his blunt talk, but she probably shouldn't have been. He was a man who knew what he wanted. The fact that *she* was what he wanted right now was a gift. One she wasn't going to squander. She'd take anything he'd willingly give her and treasure it for the rest of her life.

The dream she'd been having when she woke up flashed through her brain, but she quickly blocked it. She and Cal weren't going to have children. Weren't going to live happily ever after like in the movies. She could never be enough for him long term. So she'd be satisfied with a happy for now.

With a sigh, Cal slipped his hand out from under her shirt, and June frowned unhappily.

"I know," he told her. "It's been too long for me. I want to rip this shirt off and keep you prisoner in this bed for hours, making up for lost time. But we need to get up and get going. The ceremony is in a few hours, and I told Chappy we'd head to the cabin early in case he or Carlise needed any help."

Once again, his loyalty and consideration struck June hard. She hadn't had much of that in her life until now, and seeing it in the man she loved was everything.

She grabbed his wrist. "Cal?"

"Yeah?"

June wasn't sure what she wanted to say. Thank you? Don't stop? When can we finish what we started? In the end, all she murmured was, "I'm looking forward to spending the day with you and your friends."

"Our friends," he said with a small smile.

"Our friends," she agreed.

Then Cal leaned down and kissed her forehead. "I'll greet you properly once we've both gotten dressed and have brushed our teeth."

"Deal," she said immediately.

He smiled again, then rolled to the side and stood. June drank him in. He really was a beautiful man.

When he held out his hand to her, she realized that she was going to have to stand up in front of him half-dressed. The fact that her thighs brushed together when she walked, that she wasn't svelte and slender, made her panic for a moment.

Until she realized Cal was purposely letting himself be vulnerable with her.

His forearm was on full display, without the usual clothing that covered it. At first glance, it was difficult to take in. Scars wound from his hand up his arm, snaking under the sleeve of his T-shirt.

Moving without thought, June got to her knees on the mattress and took his hand in hers. Slowly, she leaned in and kissed his wrist. Then his forearm. She ran her fingers over the scarred flesh, lightly caressing, kissing every inch as she moved upward.

Cal had stepped closer to the bed, letting her do as she wished, and she knew that was another gift. When she got to his biceps and saw the ugly circular scar there, she couldn't stop the small distressed sound that left her throat.

"Cigar," Cal said with zero emotion in his voice.

June placed her lips right over the obscene mark on his flesh, stroking lightly with her tongue. Without looking up, she said in a tone she hardly recognized as her own, "I hope whoever did this to you died a horrific, painful death, with his eyes plucked out and his innards spilling from his body to be feasted on by a hundred hungry carrion birds."

She was jolted back to the present by Cal's loud bark of laughter. She looked up at him, worried she'd gone too far. That maybe she should've ignored his scars altogether.

"I hope I never piss you off," he said with a somewhat mystified expression.

Relieved that he didn't seem to be upset, June shrugged. She sat on her butt on the bed and shifted to stand. Cal's hand was there to keep her steady. When she was on her feet, she worked up the nerve to look at him. She was keenly aware that she had no bra on, that her boobs weren't exactly small enough to ever be called perky, that her legs were on full display . . .

"Damn, woman. You were made to wear miniskirts. Those legs—they're lethal." He swallowed hard. "I'm gonna shower. You want anything special for breakfast before we head out?"

The way he couldn't stop staring at her legs went a long way toward boosting June's confidence. "Anything's good."

He nodded and took a deep breath. "Take your time, we've got an hour or so before we need to get on the road." Then he turned and headed for the en suite bathroom.

Smiling, not put off by his abrupt departure, June turned to head to her own room. This morning was surprising, and only partly because she'd woken up in his bed. She had a little more confidence that she and Cal would actually end up together at some point. She would still be cautious, because she knew better than most that life had a way of throwing curveballs, but maybe, just maybe, she'd get what she wanted . . . at least for a little while.

Chapter Fifteen

"Do you, Riggs Chapman, take this woman for your lawfully wedded wife? To have and hold, for better, for worse, for richer, for poorer, in sickness and in health, to love and to cherish, until death do you part?"

"I do," Chappy said fervently.

The officiant turned to Carlise, who was wearing a pair of jeans and a puffy white coat, a white stocking cap, and a pair of white mittens. "Do you, Carlise Edwards, take this man for your lawfully wedded husband? To have and hold, for better, for worse, for richer, for poorer, in sickness and in health, to love and to cherish, until death do you part?"

"Absolutely, yes," she said with a huge smile.

"I now pronounce you husband and wife. You may kiss the bride," the beaming woman told them.

Cal watched as his friend bent his new wife over his arm and kissed her long, hard, and thoroughly. Everyone cheered and clapped as he brought her upright and turned to face them.

There weren't many people in attendance—their circle of friends, Carlise's mom, and Alfred Rutkey. And, of course, Baxter, who was sitting next to Carlise, looking uneasily at all the people around them but unwilling to leave his favorite human's side.

The weather was perfect for a wedding. Chilly, but the sun was shining. There was still some snow on the ground, but almost all of the two feet that had fallen in the most recent blizzard had melted.

Cal had arrived earlier with June, who'd disappeared inside the cabin to help Carlise. He and Chappy, along with their friends, had hung out in the detached garage with a roaring fire to keep them warm. They'd spent the few hours there, waiting for the ceremony to start, and reminisced about how they'd gotten to where they were and speculated about what would've happened if they'd ended up anywhere but in Maine.

Carlise was beautiful, glowing with happiness, but Cal couldn't help thinking that June outshone everyone there. She wore figure-hugging jeans and a purple long-sleeved V-neck shirt she'd picked up while shopping. Her cheeks were rosy from the chilly air and excitement of the occasion, and she had an almost permanent smile on her face.

Cal had given her space all day, so she could hang out with the women and strengthen their friendship, but he couldn't stay away from her any longer. As everyone headed for the cabin and the food Carlise had insisted on serving before they headed back to Newton, he wrapped an arm around June's waist.

"That went well," he observed.

"It was perfect," she exclaimed, looking up at him with a huge smile. "Carlise was beautiful, and Chappy couldn't take his eyes off her for even a second. Even the little bow tie Baxter had on was adorable!"

Cal had been to many weddings in his day. Not so many recently, but before he'd been captured, he'd been required to go to just about all of the royal weddings in his family. They were ostentatious and over the top, but none could compare to the intimate, simple ceremony he'd had the pleasure of observing today.

Chappy and Carlise were obviously madly in love, and they'd survived a terrible ordeal to get where they were. It was an honor to celebrate them. Some would scoff and say they'd never last. That they hadn't known each other long enough for a meaningful connection or long-term relationship. But Cal thought differently.

He'd seen his cousins marry people they'd been dating for years, only to have things fall apart almost as soon as they'd put rings on their spouses' fingers. The way Chappy looked at Carlise, and vice versa, made him certain they'd be together forever.

"I'm going to go congratulate them. I'll be right back," June told him before rushing over to Carlise.

Cal watched as she hugged the other woman. June was innately good, and every time he thought about her stepmother and stepsister treating her like they had, he wanted to drive right back to Washington, DC, and give them a piece of his mind.

"Why the scowl?" JJ asked. "You aren't happy for them?"

Wiping the irritated look off his face, Cal shook his head. "No, I'm thrilled. I've never seen Chappy so happy or content. I was just thinking about June's situation."

JJ nodded. "Yeah. I'm thinking her family probably isn't taking her leaving and stealing their prince out from under their noses lightly."

Cal scowled at his friend. "She didn't have to steal someone who wanted to be hers. And I was never Carla's to begin with, no matter what they'd cooked up in their daft heads."

"I didn't mean anything by it," JJ said easily. "Although I'm happy to hear that things are working out for you and June."

Cal snorted. He'd walked right into that trap, even if admitting that he belonged to June didn't exactly *feel* like a trap. "You know, I've spent my entire life dreading falling in love. It always seemed like a lot of trouble. Getting the approval from the king and queen, the courtship, dealing with the media, planning a huge, extravagant wedding that costs too much, and having to entertain people I don't even know and definitely don't care about. I'm never going to be king, not even close, and it just seemed like too much work to deal with it all."

"But love finds you whether you want it or not," JJ finished for him.

"Yeah." Cal didn't feel the least bit weird admitting he was in love with June. How could he? It felt too right to hide, to deny.

"So . . . you gonna introduce her to the king and queen?" JJ asked nonchalantly.

Cal winced. It wasn't that he didn't want to, or that he wasn't proud of her. There was just too much unresolved between them. And he knew without a doubt that meeting the leaders of his country would completely stress June out. Besides . . . it was way too early for any of that.

Cal realized suddenly that he'd gone from thinking it would be best for June's sake to let her go, that she could do better than him, to wanting to be with her forever. He loved the woman. Maybe being at his friend's wedding and seeing how happy he was with his bride had subconsciously sunk into his own psyche. "Eventually," he settled on telling JJ.

His friend beamed and slapped him on the back. "Happy for you, bro."

Cal was happy too, although definitely apprehensive. He wanted June. All of her. But he was still reluctant to expose his body. Although the way she'd kissed his scars, and her reaction to the burn on his biceps, made him feel as if maybe, just maybe, she wouldn't react to the rest of him the way he'd assumed she would. She'd been upset on his behalf. And remembering how she'd wanted to eviscerate the arsehole who'd burned him somehow soothed a bit of the hurt and pain he carried in his heart.

There were times he'd dreamt of finding every single one of his captors and torturing them the way they'd tortured him, but that would've made him just as bad. He had too much pride to stoop so low.

And besides . . . the rescue unit made sure those bastards would never harm anyone again.

But knowing June felt a fraction of the same thing he did, the need for revenge, made him suspect she was meant to be his.

"Cal! JJ! Get over here! They're going to cut the cake!" April called out from across the room.

JJ rolled his eyes. "She's so bossy," he mock complained.

"And you love it," Cal said.

JJ didn't respond but did as April demanded and headed in her direction.

Everyone was standing around the table where a simple two-tier cake stood. It had white frosting and was a little crooked on the stand. Chappy took Carlise's hand, and they picked up a knife. They cut into the cake but obviously used a little too much pressure, because the entire thing tilted, and the top tier fell off the pedestal and plopped onto the floor.

Everyone stood frozen, staring at it for a long moment, before Baxter finally moved. He nonchalantly grabbed the entire tier and retreated to his pillow next to the fireplace to enjoy his unexpected treat.

Cal was afraid Carlise would be upset, but she suddenly started laughing so hard, Chappy had to hold her up.

Jerking when an arm wrapped around his waist, Cal looked down to find June snuggling against him, smiling at the scene. He immediately pulled her closer as they watched their friends cut another piece of cake and successfully feed it to each other. Carlise in her jeans and white sweater. Chappy in jeans as well and a black shirt. They were like yin and yang together and looked like the perfect pair.

The difference between this wedding and all the others he'd attended hit home for Cal once more. A cake this size would be unfathomable to the royal family. They always had at least two cakes, each several tiers high, impeccably decorated, and enough to feed hundreds of guests. Nothing ever seemed to go wrong at any of the ceremonies. Royal protocol was practiced at all times, everything ran with strict precision, and no one would dare show up in anything other than the most current couture fashion.

"This has to be very different from what you're used to, huh?" June asked.

Her question was proof that they were very much on the same wavelength. "Yeah. But you know what? This is so much better," he said, meaning every word.

"Yeah," she agreed.

"We're going to do the toasts," Carlise announced to the room with a huge smile. She waited until everyone had a glass in their hand. "To the best friends anyone could have," she said as she held up a glass of champagne.

"Hear, hear!" everyone said and took a sip of their drinks.

"To blizzards!" Chappy added.

Everyone took another sip.

"To a stray dog some jerk dumped and who ended up being my guardian angel," Carlise said.

Cal chuckled into his glass. At this rate, they'd be there all afternoon.

He wasn't exactly wrong. Everyone took a turn toasting the couple and wishing them well. The mood was happy and festive and full of love. There were a ton of pictures taken and everyone was beaming as they shared in their friends' special day.

Eventually, April turned on a stereo in the corner and a cheesy eighties dance song began to play.

"Yay! Dance time!" Carlise announced.

The sofa was pushed back, and before long, April, Carlise, June, and Carlise's mom were dancing in the middle of the room.

Chappy was watching them with a goofy look on his face, and once more Cal thought that this was the best wedding and reception he'd ever attended. Spending time with his friends was something he'd always enjoyed, but the addition of the women made it even more fun. They encouraged the guys to relax and let go more than they ever would if left to their own devices.

They all danced, laughed, and, at one point, even did the limbo. Cal couldn't remember having a better day.

The officiant and the police chief went home shortly after the dancing started, and the women were once again tipsy by the time the party wound down.

"It was great having you all here, but it's time for you to go," Chappy announced around seven. It was just getting dark outside, and it was more than obvious he wanted to get his wedding night started. Since the cabin only had one room, he couldn't exactly do that with his friends and new mother-in-law partying in the living area.

JJ drove April, Carlise's mom, and Bob back to town, which left Cal alone with June once again. He didn't mind, not in the least.

As soon as she was settled into her seat in his SUV, she reached for his hand and held on tightly as he drove toward Newton.

"That was awesome," she said with a sigh. "Although my feet hurt, my ears are ringing from the loud music, and I'll probably be hoarse from singing."

"You know that you can't carry a tune, right?" Cal asked with a laugh.

June giggled. "Yeah, but who cares? That was fun. I'm so happy for Carlise and Chappy."

"Me too."

She turned to him with a smile on her face. "For the record? I'm not drunk," she informed him.

"But you're tipsy. I never thought the toasts were going to be done."

She laughed once more, and Cal loved hearing the lighthearted sound. He already knew she hadn't had enough laughter in her life for years. "Right? I mean, when they started toasting to generators and peanut butter and jelly, I figured it had gone too far."

Cal smiled at the memory.

"What I'm trying to say is, I might be tipsy, but not so far gone that I don't know what's going on," June informed him.

He glanced over at her and found she was staring at him intently. "Okay?"

"You seem like the kind of man who'd be too honorable to take advantage of a woman when she's had too much to drink. So I'm just making sure you're aware that while I can feel the effects of the champagne, the dancing did a good job of sobering me up a bit. I know what I'm saying . . . and what I want."

Cal finally clued in to what she was getting at—and his cock immediately twitched to life between his legs, even as trepidation swamped him. It was the most bizarre thing ever, feeling both horny and anxious at the same time.

He wanted this, *her*, but for some reason, he thought he'd have more time to prepare. Get himself mentally ready for her to see his ravaged body.

"But if you don't want to, it's okay," she said quietly when he didn't reply.

"No!" he blurted. "I do, I just . . . June, I can't help but worry about you seeing me."

"Cal, don't you think I have the same worries? I'm not skinny. In fact, I'm what most people would call fat. I try to keep in shape, but I got my parents' genes. I'm always going to be heavy. But don't you think I *want* to be slender for you? Be the kind of woman you'd be proud to have at your side? Who you can't wait to be alone with and tear her clothes off? That's just not me."

"If you think I didn't want to peel those skintight jeans down your legs and bury my face between your thighs all night, you're crazy," Cal nearly growled.

"Oh," she said after a lengthy pause.

It was adorable as hell.

"We'll keep the lights off for our first time," Cal said. "That way, the pressure is off both of us."

"Okay," June said breathlessly.

"I *do* want you," Cal told her with all the emotion he felt in his soul. "I've never wanted someone even half as much. We'll make it work, June. I know it."

"Me too," June agreed.

A minute or two went by before she asked, "Can you drive any faster?"

It was Cal's turn to chuckle, as he pressed a little harder on the gas. "Eager?" he teased.

"You have no idea. Using my fingers or a toy is fine and all, but I have a feeling you're going to ruin me for any kind of self-stimulation."

Her words made his cock fully engorge. It was painful as hell, as he was confined in his jeans. He shifted in his seat, trying to give his dick some room, but it was hopeless. "Bloody hell, woman, you're lethal."

She grinned and squeezed his hand. "I'd offer to help you out with that," she said, nodding at his lap. "But this console is too big between us."

"I'm selling this car tomorrow and getting an old beater with a bench seat," he deadpanned.

June's giggle made his cock even harder. "No, you aren't," she scolded. "Besides, I'm probably not even any good at that."

"You've never sucked cock?" Cal blurted.

She shrugged. "Hasn't really been something I've wanted to do . . . until now."

"Feck, you're killing me."

"I'm looking forward to this, Cal," she said seriously.

"Me too," he reassured her. "Now, be a good girl and sit there quietly before I come in my pants," he begged.

"That would be a shame," she teased.

Cal smiled and realized he was having even more fun than he'd had at the wedding. In a million years, he didn't think he'd be laughing and teasing before getting naked with a woman for the first time since his capture.

In years past, sex had been almost . . . guarded. Yes, it was enjoyable, but he'd always worried about the woman's motives. If she was angling for a marriage proposal or had designs to mooch off him for money. He had none of those concerns with June. In fact, he had a feeling his worries would be more along the lines of her not asking *enough* of him. Of not wanting to be with him long term.

Though hadn't he already decided they wouldn't work out long term? That he was going to give her room to fly? Damn. Perhaps the wedding had messed with his head in ways he hadn't prepared for.

In his heart, she already belonged to him. But he couldn't be selfish. He had to let her go, right? Let her experience all the world had to offer?

His cock deflated a bit.

Tonight, however, she was all his—and he was going to do everything in his power to make sure she knew how sexy and desirable she was to him. How amazing. How utterly perfect. He'd deal with the future later. For tonight, all he wanted was to love the woman sitting next to him.

Chapter Sixteen

June was excited. This was really happening. She'd gone out on a limb and made sure Cal knew she wanted tonight to be the night, and he'd agreed!

She wasn't thinking about how they came from such disparate worlds, or the pressure of his royal title, or how they were so physically mismatched. Or how pissed her stepsister would be that she was in Cal's bed and Carla wasn't. All she could concentrate on was how much she loved him . . . and the fact she'd soon get a chance to show him.

He pulled into the garage and was out of the car and at her side before she even blinked. Giggling, she let him help her out, and when he wrapped an arm around her waist and pulled her close, she snuggled against him happily.

Before she knew it, they were behind his locked door, and he'd pushed her up against the wall, where he held her for a long moment, studying her, as if he could read her mind.

"Kiss me, Cal," she whispered, desperate to have him touch her.

Without a word, he lowered his head, and as soon as his lips landed on hers, she was a goner. Whimpering, June plastered herself against him and raised one of her legs.

"Easy," Cal said, pulling back. "We've got all night."

"I need you," she whined.

To her surprise, he smiled . . . and June was a little confused, because she wasn't being humorous in the least.

"You'll have me, just as I'll have you . . . but I don't want to rush this."

June sighed. She wanted Cal just as desperate as she was, but it seemed as if he was equally determined to take his time. Darn it.

He turned and escorted her toward the stairs. She was more than willing to go wherever he led, especially if it was to his bed. She stumbled in her hurry while heading up the stairs, but Cal was there to catch her before she fell flat on her face.

He had one hand on the small of her back, and June felt almost branded by him. She couldn't imagine how she'd feel once she'd taken him inside her body.

He walked straight to his room and shut the door behind them. "I'll give you first dibs on the loo," he told her.

June didn't want to be separated from him for even a minute. She didn't want to risk anything that might stop what was about to happen. But she reluctantly nodded and headed for the bathroom.

Once inside, she frowned. All her stuff was in the bathroom attached to the guest room. She didn't have any of her makeup remover or even her own toothbrush. And there was no way she was going to use his. Gross.

Looking around, she was surprised that there wasn't the usual big bathroom mirror, just a small one that he probably used to shave. And just like that, sorrow swamped her, making some of the desire that had been coursing through her body ebb.

She'd known that Cal was self-conscious about his looks, but that he had gone so far as to remove the bathroom mirror . . . that really hammered it home.

A knock on the door startled June so much, she almost fell over when she jerked at the sound.

"June? I went over and got some of your things from your loo . . . if you want them."

Her heart melted. Cal Redmon was a good man. Considerate. And tonight, he was all hers. Making a mental vow to be the best he'd ever had, even if she had no idea how to do that, she reached for the doorknob.

Cal was standing there, looking especially delicious, holding her small bag of toiletries.

"Thanks," she said with a smile.

"You're welcome." Then he slipped past her, grabbed his toothbrush and toothpaste, and grinned. "I figured I'd go ahead and take my stuff to the other loo so we could get on with our night sooner rather than later."

In the past, if she'd indicated she wanted to have sex with a guy, he would've taken her straight to bed. There wouldn't have been any of this pre-bed preparation stuff. But just like the mirror, she understood this as well. He was stalling. Doing what he could to delay getting naked.

"I could've just gone to my own bathroom and left you this one. It would've been faster."

"I like you in here. In my space." Cal shrugged. "Meet you in bed?"

Wow, how four words could make her want to melt into a puddle of goo, June had no idea.

"Last one there's a rotten egg," she teased.

Cal chuckled. Then he backed toward the bathroom door, not taking his eyes off her. Of course, he ran into the doorjamb, because he wasn't watching where he was going, and June giggled.

He smiled at her, then turned and left her standing there, staring at his luscious ass as he walked down the hall toward her room.

As soon as he was out of sight, June sprang into action. She rushed through removing her makeup and brushing her teeth. She used some of the mouthwash sitting on the counter, then the toilet. When she finished running a brush through her boring brown hair, she took a deep breath.

After a moment of hesitation, she pushed her jeans over her hips and left them in a heap on the bathroom floor. Some women would be braver, would probably remove all their clothes, but June couldn't quite get up the nerve to go that far.

Which was silly, considering what she and Cal were about to do, but a lifetime of feeling fat and inadequate couldn't be conquered with a little bit of champagne and the anticipation of a night with the man she loved.

Taking another deep breath, she headed into the bedroom—and stopped in her tracks as she looked toward the bed. Cal was already there. She hadn't heard him return.

From the light of the bathroom, she could see him lying in bed, still wearing his long-sleeved T-shirt. The covers were pulled up over his legs, and one arm was behind his head, propping it slightly as he smiled at her lazily.

"Guess you're the rotten egg," he quipped.

June didn't even hesitate. She flicked off the light, ran toward the bed, and leaped, landing pretty much on top of Cal. He let out an *oof*, but recovered immediately and rolled until she was under him, the covers tangled around his legs.

"Hi," she said like a big goof.

Cal didn't seem to find her too ridiculous. "Hey," he returned with a grin. Despite the darkness of the room, muted light from the windows allowed her to see the gleam of his eyes, the white of his teeth as he smiled.

"You're so beautiful," he said in a low, earnest tone.

June's gaze skittered to the side, over his shoulder. She never knew how to respond to compliments, especially ones she knew weren't true.

"Look at me," Cal demanded.

June brought her gaze back to his.

"You're. Beautiful," he enunciated slowly.

"You don't have to butter me up," she joked. "I'm a sure thing."

But he went on as if she hadn't spoken. "It was all I could do tonight not to drag you out of Chappy's cabin. You were completely at ease. Laughing, smiling, dancing. Uninhibited."

June wrinkled her nose. She wasn't sure if that was a compliment or not.

"You have no idea how beautiful that is to me. If you'd been to even one of the formal weddings or parties I've had to attend over the years, you'd understand," he said quietly. "Women standing around, sipping tea, gossiping about everyone's clothes, never raising their voices, never singing, never looking like they're having a good time. Their idea of dancing is to sway back and forth while trying to cop a feel on the dance floor.

"Then there's you . . . having fun, living life to the fullest, enjoying yourself . . . it was everything I never knew I was missing, and now that I do know, I can't ever go back."

June wasn't sure what he meant by that last part, but she was relieved she hadn't made a fool out of herself.

"I'm going to make love to you, Juniper Rose. I'm going to do my best to ruin you for anyone else. I want to imprint myself on your body and in your psyche. Because I already know that's what'll happen to me. I want to be so deep inside you that you don't know where I stop and you start. I pray my body won't let me down, but if it does, I'll still make sure you're satisfied."

"I'm already satisfied," she told him honestly. "Even if this is all we do, lie in each other's arms and hold each other all night. Do I want to feel you inside me? Yes. But if that doesn't happen, it'll be okay."

He pressed his lips together and shook his head.

"Shhhh, stop thinking so hard," she scolded. "This isn't one of your stuffy balls. This is you and me. There are no rules with us. We're being rebels and making things up as we go. And you should know . . . you've already ruined me for anyone else, Cal," she said, with no intention of shielding her heart from this man.

There was more she wanted to say, but all the words flew from her mind when he lowered his head and took her lips roughly. And she gave as good as she got. She loved this aggressive side of Cal.

He rolled them again, kicking free of the covers as he did, and for the first time, June felt the bare skin of his legs against her own.

He pushed her upright so she was straddling his belly, and she could feel his hard erection against her ass. He didn't ask, just reached for the hem of her shirt and pushed it upward.

Excited by his eagerness, June pulled the material over her head. When she was straddling him bare, except for her underwear and bra, she blushed. She was grateful for the weak light in the room.

Without a word, he snaked an arm around her and pressed on her lower back, bringing her closer. He pulled one of the cups of her bra down with his free hand before closing his lips over her nipple.

"Oh!" June exclaimed, catching herself with a hand on the mattress. She couldn't help but arch into his touch. It had been so long since anyone had touched her sexually. And no one had put as much effort into pleasing her as Cal was right now. He'd been right before when he'd said her breasts were sensitive. They were . . . extremely.

"Cal," she moaned as her nipples tingled, and she felt herself grow slick between her legs.

"So damn beautiful," Cal murmured before pulling her remaining bra cup down and paying attention to her other nipple.

She writhed on top of him, wanting more, while at the same time not wanting him to ever stop what he was doing.

She jerked when she felt the hand at her back push under the elastic of her undies to palm one of her ass cheeks. For a split second, she couldn't help but think about how big her butt was, but all thoughts of her size flew out the window when his fingers brushed against her soaking-wet folds from behind.

His hand was gone before she had time to fully enjoy his touch. He rolled so she was once again lying flat on her back, looking up at him. He didn't say anything, simply hovered over her, staring.

"Cal?" she questioned.

"You're so wet."

June blushed. "I thought that was the goal," she quipped.

"No, I mean you're *soaked*. You could take me right this second, couldn't you?"

Unable to read his tone, June asked, "Are you . . . mad?"

"No."

"You sound mad," she said, confused.

Cal huffed what sounded like a laugh and rested his forehead against hers. He was breathing hard, and even though arousal still swam in June's veins, she patiently waited for him to continue.

"I've never been with a woman who's gotten so wet so fast."

June opened her mouth to apologize, still unsure what he was getting at, but he raised his head and stilled her words with a look.

"Women sleep with me because they want a prince. A billionaire. No one's ever been *this* excited to be with me," he said, cupping her pussy and squeezing possessively. "And now, they certainly wouldn't want a scarred, fucked-up former soldier who'd rather spend his time chopping down trees than immersing himself in the politics and lifestyle he'd been born into."

All embarrassment over how much she wanted this man disappeared. "I just want you, Cal. *You.* I'd still want you if you were just a lumberjack. But . . . you'll never be 'just' anything. You're too kind and giving. Too sexy, regardless of how you see yourself. God, you turned me on more than I thought possible with just your lips on my breast. I'm not even sure I can handle much more."

"Oh, you can," he said with a small smile.

June brought a hand to his cheek, caressing lightly before thrusting her fingers into his hair and fisting the soft strands. "Stop thinking so hard," she ordered. "Sex is supposed to be fun. At least that's what I've heard."

"I'm going to make this so damn good for you," he said.

June wasn't sure if that was a threat or a promise, but it didn't really matter. She knew whatever this man did, she'd love it and beg for more.

"I'm going to do the same for you," she told him, then tightened her hold on his hair. "Kiss me, Cal. There's no one in this bed but the two of us . . . understand?"

"Yes," he said solemnly, staring into her eyes for another beat before lowering his head.

He kissed her again, long and hard.

June held her breath as he tore his lips from hers, then rose to his knees and reached for the hem of his shirt, whipping it off. He maneuvered to one hip and shoved his boxers down, tossing his clothes to the floor before straddling her once again.

Even in the darkness of the room, June could see glimpses of his ravaged skin. She didn't get a chance to say anything, or even touch him, because he'd rolled them yet again.

"Off. Take your underwear off," he ordered in a gruff tone.

This wasn't exactly how she'd imagined things going. She'd assumed, because of his reticence when it came to getting naked, that they'd progress a little more slowly. But June gladly echoed his movements and kicked off her undies. She reached behind her to undo the clasp of her bra, inhaling sharply when Cal palmed her breasts.

She paused, staring at his huge hands on her flesh.

"A perfect handful," he said reverently as he played with her.

June managed to get her bra off and threw it over the side of the bed, not caring where it landed. All she could think about was the feel of Cal's calloused palms on her smooth, sensitive skin.

"Lean down," he whispered, and June was helpless to do anything but obey. She hovered over him, practically on her hands and knees, her heavy breasts hanging as he squeezed and caressed them.

"They're so lush, so damn gorgeous," he breathed.

June wanted to complain that they were too big, too droopy, but she couldn't get any words out as he tweaked her nipples.

She could feel her pussy practically dripping, and she squirmed over him.

"Come here," he said, letting go of her boobs and grasping her hips, dragging her up his chest. She moved forward and grabbed the headboard as he urged her to sit up on her knees.

By the time she realized his intent, it was too late to protest.

He groaned deep in his throat as he licked her pussy lips. "So goddamn wet. And it's all for me, isn't it, princess?"

June couldn't speak. She was embarrassed, knowing Cal could see every inch of extra flesh around her middle. And God forbid, she didn't want to risk suffocating him. But in the end, she couldn't complain, couldn't find her words. Couldn't do *anything* but hold on for dear life as Cal ate her out like a starving man.

He held her hips tightly, keeping her from moving away, but June wasn't going anywhere. Everything he did felt too good. She'd never experienced anything like the pleasure he was giving her, and her embarrassment disappeared as he licked, sucked, and probed as deeply inside her as his tongue could manage.

His nose brushed against her clit, and June jolted in his arms.

"You like that," he mumbled from between her legs.

"Yes," she whispered and couldn't help but shift over him, looking for more stimulation on her clit.

"That's it, princess . . . ride my face," he ordered.

It sounded so dirty. So *carnal*. But when his tongue swiped over her clit once more, June's body moved without any input from her brain, searching out the orgasm that was just out of reach.

When she realized she was writhing on his face shamelessly, trying to get more pressure on her clit, she froze in place, mortified—and so desperate to come she wasn't sure what to do.

But Cal knew exactly what she needed. He gripped her hips so tightly she was sure she'd have bruises in the morning and yanked her even harder down on his face.

Her inner thighs burning from the awkward position, June held her breath as he took her clit between his lips and sucked . . . hard.

An embarrassingly loud wail left her lips as June came. She humped his face desperately as her thighs shook with both her release and the effort it took to keep her entire weight from landing on top of him.

Her heart beating a million miles an hour, her body sweating more than she liked, June was barely aware when Cal shifted her back down his body and hugged her close to lie on top of him. It took a full minute or two for her to come back to her senses and raise her head to look at him.

He didn't give her time to say anything, just kissed her voraciously. June could taste herself on his lips and tongue, and it only ramped up her desire. In the past, after she'd come, she was done. Ready to sleep. But sleep was the furthest thing from her mind at the moment. She wanted to give this man everything he'd given her.

She moved without thought, pulling her lips from his and immediately moving down his body. She licked and kissed her way toward his groin, feeling more than seeing the ridges and bumps of his ruined flesh. That he was even allowing her to touch his scars was a surprise, and she wanted to linger . . . but nothing would distract her from her goal.

When she was between his legs, she finally looked up. She could just see the frown on Cal's face, the fists clenched at his side. For a moment, she doubted herself. It didn't look like he was enjoying her touch. But she was determined to do this for him. To show him how much she loved him.

"Tell me if I do it wrong," she begged right before she took his cock in her hand.

"What do you mean?" he asked.

June's cheeks blazed, and she was once again glad for the darkness of the room. "I've never done this, so you're going to have to tell me if I do something you don't like." June opened her mouth and licked the top of his dick, moaning as a salty, musky taste bloomed in her mouth.

"I can't believe I forgot. You told me in the car . . . You've really never taken a man's cock in your mouth?"

"No," she told him, gently tonguing the tip.

"Bloody hell!" he swore.

She hesitated, not sure what the curse meant. She felt one of his hands push into her hair. He didn't pull away, but he didn't shove her down on him either.

"I'm honored to be your first," he breathed. "I'm probably less sensitive than most men because of the scar tissue, but even still . . . no teeth. Okay?"

Now that he'd said something, she could feel thin ridges against her palm that shouldn't be there as she ran it up and down his hard shaft.

Hatred welled in her heart toward the men who'd hurt him, but she pushed it down. There was no place for that kind of emotion right now. All she wanted to do was please Cal.

"The underside is the most sensitive," he went on. Deep down, June loved being instructed. It took the pressure off. If he told her what to do, she couldn't mess it up . . . hopefully.

"Take the head in your mouth—feck, *yes*, like that. Now suck, gently at first, then harder. Bloody hell, woman, you're a natural."

She smiled as she did as he instructed. She began to bob up and down, mimicking women she'd seen in porn videos. She used her hand to stroke him where her mouth couldn't reach, and she actually felt him grow in her mouth. It was an undeniably powerful feeling.

She rose on her knees so she could get more leverage. Her nipples brushed against his thighs as she moved, and the friction felt amazingly good.

"Suck as you come up and off my cock. Yes! Exactly like that. Squeeze harder with your hand as you stroke me, move it with your mouth . . . Oh Lord, that feels so good."

A spurt of precome filled her mouth, and June wasn't sure whether or not she should swallow. In her moment of indecision, some of it leaked back onto his dick, lubricating her hand as she stroked him.

Her heart was beating fast in her chest, and she felt as if she was on top of the world. Tilting her head, she looked at Cal, and found his gaze glued to what she was doing.

"I can't believe I'm going to say this, but I'm regretting not having the lights on," he panted. "I bet you look so damn sexy with your lips stretched around my dick."

Instinctively, June took her mouth off him and licked up the underside of his cock, feeling wetness smear against her cheek.

"Suck my balls," he pleaded.

Pushing his cock up against his stomach, June leaned down to take one of his balls into her mouth. It was soft and warm, and his back arched as she sucked.

"Feck. *Feck!*" he swore as his ass came off the bed. "Your mouth is like heaven! Come here."

Confused, June let go of him as he pulled her up and away from his groin. He flipped them again, so she was beneath him.

"Wasn't that . . . You didn't like it?" she couldn't help but ask.

"Not like it? Woman, I was two seconds away from coming all over my stomach," he told her.

June couldn't stop the small smile from forming on her face.

"Proud of yourself?" he asked.

She shrugged. "Yeah. For my first time . . . I wasn't too bad, was I?"

"You're perfect," he breathed. "And I'm going to come in your mouth sooner or later. On your tits. All over your pussy. I want to cover you with my come, mark you so thoroughly you won't ever be able to get me off your skin. But not tonight. Tonight, I need to be inside you. Fill you up. Mark you from the inside out."

His words turned her on so much, June shifted under him and grabbed his biceps, digging her fingernails in. "Do it, Cal. Please. I need you."

He rose above her, and June took him in greedily. Even in the dark, he was so damn perfect she could barely breathe, his very silhouette imposing. She couldn't believe a man like him was interested in her. "Make me yours," she whispered as she lay under him.

He paused for a moment, before letting out a groan and moving.

∼

"Make me yours."

Her words speared into his soul, and Cal could only stare down at her for a split second. She was everything he'd ever wanted in a woman. Curvy, soft, so incredibly passionate. When he'd eaten her out, she'd soaked his skin. And when she'd come on his face, it was the most satisfying and carnal thing he'd ever experienced . . . until she'd shyly reminded him that she'd never sucked a man's cock before.

He was her first, and it was something he'd always treasure. It hadn't lasted long enough. If she'd have put her mouth on him again after sucking his balls, he would've exploded immediately.

He didn't think she was ready for that. And he hadn't lied when he'd told her he wanted to be inside her when he came for the first time.

Cal could hardly believe how close he was to exploding. He'd thought experiencing this kind of pleasure was a thing of the past. After his captors had taken their knives to his dick, he wasn't sure he'd ever be able to get it up or have a normal sex life again. And until he met June, he'd figured he'd been right.

But he was so hard right now, so ready to come, that it was all he could do to hold himself back.

He groaned deep in his throat and grasped the base of his cock as he used his knees to spread her legs farther apart. He stared down at her and wished for about the tenth time that he could see her pussy in the light. Of course, seeing her clearly meant she'd be able to see *him* too, which he wasn't ready for.

He moved forward, and the second his cock head brushed against her pubic hair, another burst of precome shot from the tip.

"Feck," he swore. He was two seconds from coming, and he hadn't even made sure she was ready for him. Yes, she'd been so wet earlier, but that didn't necessarily mean she could take him.

Keeping one hand on his dick, Cal reached between her folds and gently probed. Relief almost overwhelmed him. She was still incredibly wet. Dripping, in fact. He ran his thumb over her clit, and she jerked.

"Cal," she protested. "Please!"

One of her hands gripped his thigh, and he grabbed the other with his free hand and brought it down to his cock. "You do it. Put me inside you, June. Put me where you want me."

It took every ounce of his control not to blow when her soft hand wrapped around his dick, and she widened her legs even more. She notched him between her legs and whispered, "Come inside me, Cal."

With a groan, he pierced her with one long, hard thrust.

Then he froze. *Feck.* He hadn't meant to do that. He'd meant to go slow, give her time to adjust. But he just couldn't wait a single moment.

To his relief, she made an adorable squeaking noise in her throat, threw her head back, and wrapped her legs around him. He could feel her heels digging into his ass.

"You good?" he couldn't help but ask as he propped himself over her forearms on the mattress.

"Good. Perfect. Fantastic!" she told him. Her tits quivered as she panted under him. "You're so big."

He smiled. Those were words every man longed to hear from his woman.

And she was tight. *Really* tight. She clenched him with her inner muscles, and he saw stars. It was all he could do not to move.

Looking down, Cal could faintly see their pubic hair meshed together. It was erotic as hell, and he never wanted to leave this spot. He wanted to stay there, deep inside her, for the rest of his life. But his instincts took over, and his hips flexed, pulling back an inch before surging forward.

"Oh, yeah . . . Cal! That feels amazing. More!"

He set a slow and steady pace, determined to make this last as long as possible. His head spun, he felt dizzy, and the pleasure was nearly overwhelming. This woman was perfect. Made for him.

She smiled dreamily as he made love to her.

Their slow and easy pace lasted only a few minutes before her hips began thrusting to meet his every time he sank inside her.

"You want more?" he asked.

"Yes. Please!"

His June was so polite.

His next thrust was a little harder—testing the waters, so to speak—and when she moaned and dug her nails into his biceps, he smiled.

He pushed inside her again. And again. Harder, faster. Until the crack of their flesh smacking together echoed in the room. He could hear how wet she was by the sounds coming from between their legs. He could feel her juices on his balls. Every time he bottomed out inside her, they got more and more soaked from the wetness seeping out of her body.

His heart was beating so hard, he could feel it in his fingertips. Not wanting this to be over, Cal clutched June's ass with one hand and rolled, putting her on top. She sat up, and they both groaned as the movement pushed him even deeper.

"Cal?" she panted.

"Your turn," he said in a gruff voice. "Take me, June."

"I . . . this is another one of those things I've never done," she admitted.

Possessiveness swept through him. "You ever ridden a horse?" he asked with a grin.

"No."

He couldn't stop smiling now. "Right. Just move, princess. Rock, bounce . . . do whatever feels good. You're in charge."

"Yeah, right. I don't think I've been in charge from the moment I met you," she breathed.

Cal's smile died as pleasure swamped his veins when June started to move. At first, she was a bit uncoordinated, and it took her a beat to get the hang of being on top, to find her pleasure. But when she did, she blew his mind.

She smiled at him as she braced her hands on his chest. He didn't even register that she was touching his scars. All he could do was focus his gaze between their bodies and watch as his cock slid in and out, glistening with her juices in the dim light.

"Faster," he begged.

She complied. Soon, her ass was slapping against his thighs as she rode him hard. Her tits bounced and jiggled as she moved, and Cal's

209

Susan Stoker

mouth watered with the need to feast on the healthy globes. He'd never been with a woman with such a large rack . . . not a natural one, that is. And there was a huge difference between fake tits and the bountiful, natural beauties his June had.

Cal was ready to come. Was right on the verge, but he wanted her to come first. On his cock. Wanted her to drench him with her essence. He reached for her hips and halted her movements.

"What's wrong?"

"Stay right there," he ordered. "Don't move. I want to feel you come on my cock."

"I'm not sure—oh!" she exclaimed as Cal moved a hand between her legs. With every brush of his fingers on her clit, he could feel where they were joined. She jolted against him and grabbed hold of his wrist with a death grip. "I don't know . . . I can't . . ."

"Am I hurting you?" he asked gruffly.

She shook her head.

Cal moved his fingers once more, but she didn't release his wrist. It felt as if she was helping, as if she was stroking herself with his hand. "That's it, princess, let it happen. Close your eyes, let it overtake you."

She immediately did as he ordered, and another wave of possessiveness swamped Cal. He could feel her orgasm rising. Felt it in the way her muscles tensed around him, the way she gripped his cock deep within her body. If he thought her coming on his face was intimate, this was a thousand times more so.

"Cal! I'm . . . *oh!*"

Her muscles tightened around his dick so hard, Cal wasn't sure he'd ever be able to pull out. Even as she was still coming, he rolled her onto her back and began to thrust like a man possessed.

Her mouth open in an O, June stared at him with glazed eyes as he fucked her hard.

All it took was a few more thrusts, and he was there. Cal buried himself deep inside her body and let loose. Pulse after pulse of come

210

released inside her. It was almost painful, but he didn't pull out. He wanted this. *Needed* this.

Finally forcing himself to move, he supported himself with an elbow beside her head, then moved his other hand between them. He was insatiable, needed to feel her coming again. It was a feeling he'd never get tired of. He roughly tweaked June's clit, and she jerked as he forced another orgasm from her body.

She wailed and thrust her hips, biting down on his arm as she flew over the edge once more. Her muscles twitched around him, a little weaker this time, but he still reveled in her loss of control, in her extreme pleasure . . . with him.

Cal had never been with a woman without a condom, and he was so glad that he didn't need to get up and deal with one. Instead, he stayed deep inside her body as his dick softened.

Propping himself up, making sure not to crush June, Cal felt caveman-like pride in the sweaty mess he'd made of her. Her face glistened, and strands of her hair were stuck to her forehead and cheeks. She was breathing hard and still had a death grip on him. Glancing at his arm, he realized he could still feel the teeth marks in his flesh, could faintly see them in the feeble light.

For the first time in his life, seeing a mark on his body that someone else had inflicted made him smile.

"You killed me," she said wearily.

Cal chuckled, and the movement made his cock twitch deep inside her.

"That was amazing," he said, leaning down and kissing her forehead. "Thank you."

Her eyes opened. "It was good for you?"

"Good? Princess, if it was any better, *I'd* be dead."

She smiled. "Yeah. Um . . . what was that one part about?"

"Which part?" he asked, still smiling. He had a feeling he knew what she was asking, but he wanted to make her say it.

"That . . . I was really sensitive, and I didn't think I could . . . you know."

"Did I hurt you? Did you hate it?"

"No. And no. I was just surprised. I'm usually a one-orgasm kind of girl."

"Not anymore. I couldn't help myself," Cal admitted. "I loved feeling you come around me, and I wanted to feel it one more time."

She eyed him shyly. "You could feel it?"

Cal started to nod—then he stilled. He *had*. He'd felt it. Even with his cock being as messed up as it was, he'd felt every squeeze, every contraction, the hot flood of her come. "Yeah," he whispered. "I felt it all."

"Good," she said, the satisfaction easy to hear in her tone. "Then any time you want to feel that again, I'm giving you carte blanche to do what you need to do."

Cal huffed out a laugh. He was gobsmacked. This woman slayed him. He wasn't sure if she truly enjoyed the last orgasm, but she gave him permission to do it again regardless.

He lowered himself on top of her, resting his head next to her own on the pillow. "Am I crushing you?" he asked.

He stiffened for a moment when her hands began caressing his back, but he took a deep breath and forced himself to relax. "No. I love feeling you on top of me. Inside me."

He wanted to tell her that was a good thing, because this was his new favorite place in the entire world, but he didn't want to freak her out. "I'll move in a bit. I just want to stay here for a while."

"It's fine," she soothed.

He hadn't realized how much he missed human touch until right at that moment. Having her skin on skin with him, from head to toe, felt like coming home. It made him feel fully human for the first time in years. He'd needed this. Needed *her*.

He fell asleep with the scent of sweet shampoo and sex in his nostrils. And he'd never slept better.

Chapter Seventeen

June woke up and winced when the rising sun hit her eyes. She turned her head and slowly realized where she was . . . and what had happened the night before. She was sore between her legs, but it was the most delicious feeling. She was lying against Cal, her cheek on his chest, her arm around his belly. But something was different.

Lifting her head, she saw the difference immediately. She and Cal were completely naked this morning.

Looking at his face, she saw he was still asleep. No surprise. He woke her last night after what seemed like just minutes and reached for her in the dark. They'd stayed up late making love again, talking, and learning what the other liked when it came to erotic touches. June had orgasmed more than she ever had before, and yet she still wanted this man. It was almost a compulsion.

The covers had been kicked off them both, and when June ran her eyes down his body, she could see every inch. His cock was flaccid, but even soft, it was impressive.

But that wasn't what caught her attention most, of course. It was the layers and layers of scars across nearly every inch of his body. She'd felt them the night before. How could she not when she'd run her hands all over him? But seeing them in the light of day made her fully understand for the first time the hell her man had lived through. Understand why he was reluctant to bare himself to her. Why he'd wanted the lights out.

But what *he* didn't understand was that seeing his ruined flesh made her love him *more*, not less.

She felt no pity for Cal. No disgust. All she felt was an overwhelming sense of pride. He'd endured what would've broken most men. And he wasn't broken, not even close. Bent, maybe, but definitely not broken.

She moved down his body, managing to get out of his hold without waking him and kneeling between his legs, much as she'd done the night before. She'd enjoyed taking him in her mouth. She wasn't so sure about finishing him off that way, but she knew without having to think about it that he'd never force her to do so or anything else she didn't want to do.

She began to play with his cock, lightly running a finger down the side, frowning when she saw the scars on his sensitive flesh. Pushing away the hatred for his captors that welled inside her, she concentrated on making him feel good.

Eventually, she took him into her mouth and sucked gingerly. It wasn't long before he started to harden.

"June?" he croaked in a hoarse tone as he stirred. "What are you doing?"

"What does it feel like?" she countered.

He let her play for another minute or so before lunging, turning her away from him on her hands and knees. He ate her out from behind until she was dripping, then took her hard and fast.

It wasn't until they were once more on their backs on the bed, and she was snuggled against his chest, that he seemed to realize how light it was in the room.

Cal tried to slip out of bed, but June moved before he could. She straddled his belly and frowned down at him. "No," she said firmly.

"Let me up," Cal said, not meeting her gaze.

"You see this?" she asked, swallowing down her uneasiness in a bid to make her man feel better.

His eyes went to where she was squeezing the extra flesh of her stomach.

"I'm fat. This is *fat*, and it's ugly, but no matter how many sit-ups I do—which admittedly isn't a lot—it won't go away. And these?" she continued, holding her breasts in her hands. "They're saggy. If I don't wear a bra, it'll look like they're around my belly button, which, trust me, isn't a good look. And this"—she pointed to her nose—"is too big."

"Stop it," Cal ordered.

"*No.* We're all flawed," she said.

He snorted. "The difference is that you're lush. I'm horrific," he told her, sounding utterly defeated.

"Bollocks," she said angrily.

He stared up at her in surprise. Then his lips twitched. "Bollocks?" he echoed.

She shrugged. "I figured if I used one of your words, maybe it would sink in. Cal, you're beautiful. No—don't look away from me. I mean it. You know what I see when I look at your scars?"

"Hideousness?" he deadpanned.

June ignored him. "Courage. Bravery. Loyalty. Strength and a will that I can't even imagine. You went through hell, and you're still here. You're a living, breathing example of how good can triumph over evil. I know you think your scars are a turnoff, but they're not. Not for me."

"I hate pity," he told her.

"Good, because you aren't getting any from me. You want to know what emotions I'm feeling right now, seeing you for the first time?"

He didn't move under her. He was as still as stone.

"I'm furious. So damn *angry* that anyone felt they had the right to do this to you, I want to get on a plane and hunt them down."

His lips twitched again, and June had never been as relieved as when she felt his hands grip her hips.

"I wouldn't advise that. You wouldn't like it over there. It's hot. Really hot."

EADERER

"Whatever. I'd do it for you if I could. But anger aside, when I look at you, see you in the light, I remember all the things you did to me last night. How your hands felt, your tongue, your cock buried deep inside my body. You turn me on more than anyone I've ever met, Cal. Your scars aren't the sum of you; they've simply helped make you into the man you are today. A man who I want more than I want to breathe. A man who makes me smile. Who makes me feel safe. Who I trust. Who makes me want to put all my worries and fears aside and jump with him into the great unknown."

June was speaking too fast, but she needed Cal to understand. To truly get that she didn't give one little hoot about his scars.

He stared up at her for so long, she began to feel uncomfortable. She was sitting on his lap naked, after all, which wasn't something she fully enjoyed.

"You sore?" he asked.

June frowned. That wasn't what she'd expected him to say after her little speech. Not even close. "What?"

"Are you sore?" he repeated. "Because I need you again. Right now."

"But we just . . ." June's words dropped off when Cal pushed her backward a bit on his thighs, reached between his legs and stroked his now hard and ready-to-go cock. "Um . . . no?"

"I know I'm being an arsehole, but I have to be inside you, June. Right this second. In the light. Where I can watch my cock thrusting into your pussy."

He was talking dirty again, but since it turned June on even more, she didn't complain. She lifted up, and Cal ran the mushroom head of his cock between her folds. She did her best not to wince as he entered, because truthfully, she *was* sore. But Cal needed her, and she'd always give herself to him.

She sighed deeply when he was all the way inside her body.

"This is gonna be fast," he muttered, not taking his eyes from between her legs.

"Okay," she said.

And it was. But Cal didn't forget to make sure she felt just as much pleasure as he did. He thrust into her from below, watching his cock disappear again and again, all while using his thumb on her clit. By the time they'd both come again, she felt boneless.

"It's a good thing it's Sunday," she said, her words slurring a bit.

"Sleep, princess," Cal ordered, kissing her temple.

"Will you stay with me for a while?" she asked, clutching Cal's arms. She felt sweaty and wanted a shower, but she was too tired and replete to move.

"Yeah."

That was all she needed to hear to let go. To fall asleep again, happier than she'd been in her entire life.

～

Cal watched June sleep. He couldn't believe he was lying there, completely naked in the light of day, with a woman cuddled up against him.

He'd been terrified when he'd finally come to his senses and realized June could see every inch of his body. He'd been too distracted at first, waking up with her mouth on his cock, to understand that it was morning, and his body was on display. It wasn't until they were once again nestled in each other's arms that he came to his senses.

He'd never actually intended for June to see him. Had planned to keep the lights off in bed for as long as they were together. But he'd screwed that up from the get-go, obviously.

Once again, he was surprised by her anger on his behalf. He genuinely believed that if she knew how to get to the men who'd hurt him, she'd go after them. They were long since dead, killed in the raid to free him and his friends, but her need for vengeance on his behalf felt . . . good.

June was so different from any woman he'd ever known. He couldn't get the image out of his head of her astride him, pointing out what she saw as her own flaws . . . as if that would make him feel better about his ravaged flesh. As far as Cal was concerned, June was a goddess. He'd take her tits and stomach and all the other things she didn't like about herself over his scars any day.

She shifted in his arms, and Cal grinned. She was a right mess . . . but he only smiled wider at the thought. *He'd* made her that way. And he couldn't help but be pleased.

He hadn't missed her slight flinch as he'd penetrated her, though, and he made a mental note to take it easy on her for a while. He hated that he'd hurt her, and the fact that she'd understood he needed to be inside her that last time made him love her all the more.

Love.

Bloody hell.

He'd fallen for her so fast. Almost from the first moment he saw her in DC. Had already admitted his feelings to JJ, and knew the rest of his mates could see it as well. But . . . he couldn't keep this woman. She was destined for bigger and better things than living with a damaged man.

Despite that fact, he couldn't bring himself to pull away from her. Now that he'd seen the passion within her, had experienced it for himself . . . he couldn't let go. Not yet.

He'd wait until she was on her feet. Until she'd saved up enough money to make it on her own. And he'd figure out a way to pad her bank account further, if at all possible. Lord knew, he had more money than he could ever spend in his lifetime. She had a lot of pride, though, and he didn't want to belittle her or make her feel as if he didn't think she could take care of herself.

How long Cal lay in bed, holding a sleeping June, he had no idea. But eventually his bladder made itself known. He needed to get up, make breakfast, and start the ball rolling on investigating her stepmother and stepsister. The last thing he wanted was the pair of them rearing their ugly heads in their lives again. But he had a sinking feeling JJ was right. Carla wasn't going to give up on being a princess so easily.

He just prayed they would simply be a nuisance and nothing more dangerous.

Slipping out from under June's body, he smiled when she protested in her sleep. Cal remained next to his bed, staring down at her for a full minute. She was gorgeous, and all his . . . for the moment.

He straightened the sheet that had been kicked to the end of the bed and pulled it over her before leaning down and kissing her temple once more.

He strode to the loo, grabbing some clothes along the way. Hesitating over the T-shirt drawer, Cal surprised himself by selecting a short-sleeved Jack's Lumber shirt instead of one of the many long-sleeved shirts he normally wore. He wasn't about to start wearing shorts and parading himself around town anytime soon, but seeing the small teeth marks from her bite on his skin made him smile. Yes, his scars would be visible, but he'd ignore those as best he could and concentrate on the memories from last night instead.

∾

Tim Dotson picked up the burner phone he'd bought before driving north to Maine and dialed the only stored number.

"You better have good news for me," the woman on the other end said in lieu of a greeting.

"Happy Sunday to you too, Elaine," he drawled.

"Whatever. I'm fucking hungry. I had to make my own breakfast, which burned. It's not a good morning," she growled. "Now tell me you have news."

"I have news," Tim echoed, grinning.

"Talk," Elaine ordered.

"She's here, like you thought. And she and the prince seemed mighty chummy last night."

"Damn it!" Elaine swore. "What happened?"

"Well, word from the locals is that they went to a friend's wedding yesterday. Up in the woods somewhere. They were smiling at each other and seemed to be getting along just fine when they came back into town." He wasn't stalking the chick, as Elaine assumed. It was sheer dumb luck that he happened to be leaving Granny's when the prince's sweet ride paused at a light. He could see the couple making cow eyes at each other, oblivious to anyone around them.

"No! That can't happen! Please tell me you did something," Elaine begged.

"Of course, I did," Tim lied. This was the first call of many that would make his pockets a little fuller. "While they were partying it up, I went to the prince's house and left a little present for your darling daughter."

"Stepdaughter," Elaine corrected immediately. "What was it? Did she see it? Was she scared?"

"Just a little note. I don't want to start out too strong right out of the gate. It just said she needed to watch herself. Implied that since Carla's *admirer* couldn't get to her, he might wanna play with her sister a little while first."

Elaine cackled, and Tim couldn't help but shake his head in a mixture of amusement and disgust. He wasn't the most upstanding man in the world, but he honestly didn't understand this bitch's need to terrorize the stepdaughter she'd lived with for nearly two decades.

"Oh, I wish I could've seen her face—and the prince's—when they realized Carla wasn't lying about having a stalker."

Tim rolled his eyes but didn't interrupt.

"Okay, this is good. You need to leave another note. Maybe something that says he's thinking he chose the wrong sister. That he has to sample the pussy the prince apparently can't resist."

Tim nearly scoffed. This woman was crazy. That wouldn't make the bitch run back to DC. From what he understood about the dynamics of Elaine's family and the relationship between Carla and her stepsister, it would probably just push the chick further into the protective arms of the new boyfriend.

He didn't let his skepticism bleed into his voice as he said, "Sounds good. But first . . . we need to talk about payment. You said for everything I left, I'd get a C-note."

"Right. And you will. But I need proof. How do I know you aren't conning me?"

The old broad was just as stupid as he'd thought. "I'm not," he lied. "But to prove it, I took a picture of the note on the prince's door so you can see it." He'd taped a folded piece of blank paper to his own door for the picture, but Elaine wouldn't know that.

She laughed again. "This is going to work out perfectly. I just know it. When I get your proof, I'll send the money via that app we talked about."

"I'll shoot it over as soon as we're done talking," Tim assured her.

"So more notes, then what? A dead animal next?" Elaine asked.

"Sure," Tim agreed, his mind already going to where he might find something dead to photograph. He supposed he could find some critter along the road that was struck by a car.

Elaine cackled again. "Good. I hope that ungrateful bitch is terrified out of her mind. But more importantly, we need to make sure the prince feels guilty for doubting my Carla. I'll hire a makeup artist to make it look like she has a black eye or something. A parting gift before her stalker went to Maine. That second-rate royal, the prince's cousin, will run straight to Prince Redmon the second he sees it, and he'll be back down here to protect her before we can blink."

"Right," Tim said, trying to keep the disbelief out of his tone. From what he'd heard about Cal Redmon, the man was smart. He may be a recluse and living in a rinky-dink town like Newton, but he wasn't stupid. He was a Special Forces soldier, for shit's sake. He'd seen through Elaine's ruse in less than two days. The old broad was delusional, and none of her ideas made any sense. But as long as he kept getting paid, she could think whatever she wanted.

Nope. In his opinion, the guy wouldn't be returning to DC anytime soon, especially if he suspected Juniper Rose was in danger. Not that he had a clue. No. Tim wouldn't be alerting anyone to his presence before he took out the stepdaughter. In the meantime, the prince could keep right on fucking her, blissfully unaware.

Fat chicks weren't Tim's thing, but he supposed pussy was pussy, especially living in such a small town. The prince was probably just getting his dick wet while he could. Tim would wait a little bit, until it looked like maybe he was done with the broad, before offing her to get his big payday from Elaine.

He felt downright magnanimous, giving the prince time to get laid and dump the bitch before Tim killed her.

"Oh! And Carla had an idea . . ."

Tim listened with a smirk as Elaine told him a story about a prank Carla had played on her stepsister when she was younger. It wasn't a bad idea, but he'd have to give it some thought. He might even be able to use it to kill the broad, but there would have to be a way to get much closer to the bitch to make Elaine's suggestion work.

"I'll see what I can do," he told her.

"Good. We'll talk soon. I can't wait to see the picture—and to see what else you come up with."

"As long as I get the money you promised, she'll be terrified out of her mind," Tim told her.

"Knowing she's dead and can't ever steal Carla's man again can't happen too soon for me," Elaine seethed.

Tim actually shivered. Up until now, he'd seen this job as a walk in the park. But hearing the crazy in Elaine's voice made him second-guess his opinion of her intelligence for the first time.

It was too late to back out now. He was too involved. He had no money to get back to DC, to his normal life. He had to keep going.

Mentally shrugging, he decided it didn't matter if the bitch died. She was fat and ugly. No one would miss her when she kicked the bucket.

Ready to get off the phone with the crazy old broad, Tim abruptly said goodbye and clicked off the connection. He emailed the picture he'd taken of the "note" he'd supposedly left on the prince's door and took a deep breath.

After smoking a joint, he sat in his rented room and sighed. He needed to figure out a way to get closer to his target. It was always better to befriend people before killing them, because that way, they weren't as suspicious. He could surprise them. Having to break into a house was a pain in the ass. He much preferred to be let in voluntarily or to have his target let their guard down because he was the last person they thought would hurt them.

This job wasn't turning out to be as easy as he'd hoped. The money was good—that was the only reason he'd taken it. All he had to do was continue to agree with whatever Elaine said, keep fake-stalking her stepdaughter, and keep the money train rolling. There would come a time when he'd need to do more than take pictures of notes and dead animals, but until then, he'd ride this out as long as he could.

When the time came, he'd take care of the stepdaughter, get his big payout, and head south to a warmer climate.

Chapter Eighteen

June felt as if she was floating on air. She'd woken up later Sunday morning feeling relaxed and excited about the direction her life was going. She showered, got dressed, and wandered down the stairs to find Cal waiting for her with a huge homemade breakfast. It didn't matter that it was almost lunchtime. Then they spent the rest of the day and evening hanging out, watching TV, talking. Doing things any other couple would.

For a moment last night, June was worried about where she should sleep, but Cal took the decision out of her hands when he'd led her to his room. They didn't have sex; he'd refused, saying he knew she was sore, and he was determined to let her rest, but sleeping in his arms was just as good . . . almost.

June had no idea sex could be so overwhelming or amazing. It was cliché to describe what they'd done together that way, but her mind frequently blanked when she thought about everything they'd done.

Today, Cal was taking her to meet with Meg at Hill's House for her interview. She was nervous because she'd never had an interview before. Cal gave her some pointers, but every last one seemed to fly from her head as he pulled up in front of the cute house. There was a handmade sign in the yard that said HILL'S HOUSE, but that was the only indication that it was a business instead of a personal home.

"You'll be fine," Cal told her.

June took a deep breath. "Yeah."

"I mean it. If Meg doesn't hire you, she's an idiot. But either way, you have a place to stay . . . with me. At least until you get bored and want to strike out on your own."

June frowned. "You don't bore me, Cal. Far from it."

He shrugged. "You've been here for less than a week. And Newton isn't exactly a hub of things to do. Anyway, just be yourself, you'll do fine."

June wanted to continue the conversation, ask him if he thought he'd get bored with *her*, but Cal said he had some phone calls to make while she was at her interview, and she didn't want to hold him up. "Thanks," she said. "Here goes nothing."

Before she could open the door, Cal reached out and wrapped his hand around the back of her neck. He pulled her toward him and kissed her long and hard. Her lips were tingling and her cheeks were flushed by the time he pulled back.

"A kiss for good luck," he whispered.

She smiled. "With a kiss like that, there's no way I *can't* get the job," she teased.

Cal stared at her for a beat before sliding his hand off her skin.

She took that as her cue to get out and reached for the door handle. She waved at Cal, then took a deep breath as she turned toward the front porch.

The house was two stories and fairly large. The porch ran all the way around the front and on one side of the house. The door was painted red, which June thought was a nice touch. She knocked and almost immediately was greeted by a woman who couldn't possibly be Meg. She was around the same height as June, kind of stooped over, with bright-purple hair. She was also about thirty years older than what June understood Meg to be.

"Hi! I'm Jara! Welcome to Hill's House. Hill was the name of the man who first opened his home to local residents who were getting up there in age and didn't have any place to go, nobody to help look after them. And now, eighty years later, Hill's House is still here. Come in, come in. You look like a sturdy gal, which is good. Sometimes we fall and need help getting up."

"Jara! I told you to let me open the door," a woman scolded as she rushed toward them once they were inside.

"I'm old, not helpless," Jara grumbled as she shut the door. "Besides, you were busy chatting with Austin."

The other woman shook her head at Jara, then turned to June. "Hi, I'm Meg. You've met Jara, she's one of our residents."

"The matriarch," Jara corrected. "I'm the oldest, at ninety-four, so that gives me the right to the title."

"It's very nice to meet you both," June said, not able to keep the smile from her face. "And there's no way you're ninety-four, you don't look a day over seventy."

Jara beamed. "It's the hair," she said knowingly. "I just had it redone. I used to have pink, but I like the purple so much better."

"It's amazing," June praised, and she wasn't lying. Jara had long thick hair that practically screamed for a bright color.

"I like you," Jara announced. She turned to Meg. "I like her," she repeated.

"I heard you. I saw Banks and Sofia setting up a Cards Against Humanity game in the dining room. Why don't you go and join them while I have a chat with Ms. Rose?"

"Ooooh," Jara breathed. "Cards Against Humanity, how come no one told me?" Then she turned and ever so slowly made her way toward the other room.

"I'm so sorry," Meg said with a small shake of her head. "I meant to watch for you, but Austin and I got talking about Scott's leg—he's another resident. Austin is our nurse. He's here every day, and honestly, we wouldn't be able to run this place without him. Come in. I told everyone to be on their best behavior while we're talking, but with them playing that game, I'm not sure how long we have."

Meg leaned in conspiratorially. "They get a little rowdy, and Banks is super competitive, so any game he plays generally ends when he accuses someone of cheating, but it should keep them occupied for at least a little bit."

June liked Meg immediately. She was bubbly and friendly and seemed to like her job. June followed her to a small office and sat in a chair in front of a desk that was overflowing with papers.

"Sorry about the mess. I meant to clean things up, but something always gets in the way. If you take the job, I expect I'll have more time to do things like organize and pick up around here. Which is a good segue into telling you all about what the job entails. You won't be a maid. Or a cook. Or a nurse. Your job would be to keep the six residents entertained, which, trust me, will keep you more than busy.

"There are three men and three women living here at the moment. You met Jara, and as she said, she's ninety-four but as spry and lively as someone in her sixties. Her husband died about eight years ago, and even though she really doesn't need to live in a place like this, she was lonely and didn't want to leave Newton for Florida, as her kids urged her to do.

"Brenda is seventy-seven and is pretty soft spoken, never married, and never had any kids. She fell a few years ago and wasn't found for two days, and that scared her enough to want to move here. And Sofia is eighty-four and loves reading and gardening, although the latter isn't something she can do much anymore. But we try to have lots of plants in the house she can look after.

"As far as the men go, Banks is eighty-two and the joker of the bunch. He loves telling stories and is always the life of the party. Jeremy is seventy-five and cantankerous . . . but in a nice way. Which I know doesn't really make sense, but I think he just likes disagreeing with people to see what they'll do. And last, there's Scott. He's ninety and one of the nicest people I've ever met.

"Oh, and we just hired a new janitor. That's not a full-time job. Tim works late in the afternoons and into the early evening. His responsibilities include mopping, sweeping, taking out the trash, wiping down all the surfaces in the home, and generally keeping things tidy. As a bonus, he said he's done some handyman kinds of stuff, so we'll have him do other small tasks as well. And trust me, a house as old as this one *constantly* has things in need of fixing."

June listened with a small smile on her face. She loved the affection she heard in Meg's voice when she talked about the men and women who lived there. It was easy to tell that this wasn't just a job for her, that she truly enjoyed interacting with the residents.

"Anyway, your job would be to find things for the residents to do. Cards, outings that won't be too taxing, planning birthday parties, working with the relatives of the residents when they want to visit, and basically just finding things to do to make the days go by. Your hours would generally be from ten to three, Monday through Saturday, which I know isn't full time, but it's what our budget will allow. I'm very flexible though, so if there's something you need to do during work hours, we can always figure it out.

"Oh, and there might also be some times when you'll need to be here later. Like on Halloween, for instance. The highlight of our residents' year is sitting on the porch watching all the kiddos in their costumes. We also go all out and decorate this place from top to bottom, and many times the residents want to get dressed up too. Shoot, I'm babbling. Do you have any questions?"

June asked about the pay, and her eyes widened at the figure. Maybe it was because she hadn't ever had a paying job before, but the salary Meg quoted was way more than she thought it would be. Especially for what she'd be doing. She'd worked her butt off for twelve or more hours a day back in DC and hadn't gotten a penny.

They talked about the activities the residents enjoyed, and June's mind immediately began spinning, thinking about all the fun new things she could plan. Meg asked about her work history, and June found herself opening up to the friendly woman about her past. About how she'd never had a "real" job but had been responsible for every part of running a household when she'd lived with her stepmother and stepsister.

After forty-five minutes of talking, Meg officially offered June the job, and she happily accepted.

"When can you start?" Meg asked.

"Oh, well . . . right now, if you need me to."

"Really? That would be great! There are forms and stuff that I need you to fill out, but once you do that, you can join us for lunch. We have another lady who comes in to cook for us, but you probably won't see her a lot, as she pops in and out the back door and keeps to herself. Margaret's a gem, but she's not very sociable."

"You're cheating!" a deep voice shouted from the other side of the closed door.

Meg sighed. "I swear, some days they're like a bunch of toddlers. I'll go check on them, and when you're done with the paperwork, come on out and join us."

"May I make a quick phone call?"

"Of course. While I don't expect staff to have their noses stuck in their phones all day, you can certainly have time to yourself when needed."

"I don't have a cell phone," June admitted. "I'm planning on getting one, I just haven't gotten around to it yet."

"No worries. Go ahead and use the phone on the desk. I'll see you in fifteen minutes or so."

When there was more yelling in the other room, Meg gave her a quick hug and said, "Welcome to the family," then disappeared through the door.

June smiled. Yes, that's what this place felt like. A big family. The kind where everyone didn't get along all the time, but there was still love . . . which was something she'd always wanted to be a part of and something she hadn't known how much she'd missed until coming to Newton.

She set aside the papers Meg gave her and reached for the phone. She'd memorized Cal's number and now dialed it quickly.

"Cal," he said when he answered.

"Hi, it's me," she said, realizing this was the first time she'd spoken with him on a phone. She'd practically been with him every minute of every day since they'd left Washington, DC.

"Hi," he said, his voice full of warmth. "Are you done? How'd it go?"

"I'm done with the interview, she offered me the job, and I thought I'd stay for a while. Is that okay?"

"Of course, it is. You think you'll like it? You aren't just taking the job because you think you have to?"

"I haven't met all the residents yet, but I really like Meg. And the pay is amazing." She told Cal how much Meg was offering, then wrinkled her nose, suddenly unsure. "Isn't it?"

Cal chuckled. "It sounds above average for what you'll be doing, for sure."

June sighed in relief. "My hours are generally ten to three, so do you think you could pick me up this afternoon?"

"Definitely. I'm looking forward to meeting your new charges. I'm sure you'll have them wrapped around your little finger by the time I get there later."

June chuckled. "I'm not so sure about that. They seem to be a handful."

"You'll be fine. And June?"

"Yeah?"

"I'm proud of you. You haven't even been in town a week, and you've already found a job that I know you're going to be incredible at."

"Well, it's thanks to April that I even knew about it."

"That's generally how things work. Finding jobs is about who you know, and a bit of being in the right place at the right time, not necessarily about your résumé."

"Which is a good thing, since I don't even *have* a résumé," June said dryly.

Cal laughed. "Meg's obviously a smart woman who knows she found a gem in you. Have a good time, and if you need anything or want me to pick you up earlier than three, just let me know. I'd suggest using today as a trial day. If you hate it, or it's not what you thought, you can always tell Meg that you don't think it'll work out."

June sighed. She didn't want to do that. It would be rude. But she was done being taken advantage of. Done spending time doing something she hated. She'd managed to escape out from under her stepmother's thumb, and she wouldn't live like that again. While this was only a part-time job, she'd be spending quite a bit of time here. "Okay."

"I'll see you later."

"Later," June echoed. She hung up, staring into space for a moment as she considered her good luck, then grabbed the papers she needed to fill out and picked up a pen.

Cal rested his chin on his hand and listened with a small smile as June told him about her day.

"Banks is hysterical. He's got all sorts of stories. I'm not quite sure what's the truth and what he's making up. Today he told me that he once held the middleweight boxing title. I don't know what that is, but he went on and on about the bouts, matches, or whatever it is he used to do. Claimed he was a ladies' man and never went back to his hotel with the same girl twice . . . which I believe, because he's constantly flirting with everyone. Even Margaret, the cook.

"Sofia told me later that Banks was full of crap, and no one believed any of his stories, but since it was harmless to let him go on and on, they usually didn't call him on it. Brenda said she used to work with her hands, but didn't say exactly what she did. Scott's ninety, and he has the most amazing stories about his father, who was in World War II. I think he served in Vietnam, but he doesn't talk about it. Oh! Do you think you might come one day and talk to everyone about your service in the Army? Not the specifics, because I know you can't really talk about that, but in general?"

Cal's smile grew. "Sure."

"Awesome! I don't think it's going to be hard to find things to do. I mean, all six of the residents seem like they're up for anything, even if some are pretty quiet compared to others. I was thinking about having a themed movie afternoon, when we could watch some oldies from the sixties and seventies. And maybe have a sock hop kind of thing. And I want to talk to the principal at the elementary school and see if I can arrange to bring the residents and have kids read to them. I've always heard that it's super healthy for older people to be around younger kids, and vice versa."

Cal pushed back from the table and pulled June from her seat.

"Cal?" she asked. But he didn't stop as he hurried her toward the stairs.

"The dishes!" she exclaimed with a small laugh, as she did her best to keep up with him.

The more he was around this woman, the more he needed her.

He'd spent the day talking with a detective in DC about Elaine Green—and getting nowhere. There was simply no proof that Elaine had done anything wrong. Nothing that would make the detective give up precious time on other cases to look into a seventeen-year-old death that had been ruled a heart attack. Though he did point out that June could take on all the red tape and the steep cost of an exhumation on her own.

Cal had been frustrated and irritated, but as soon as he'd picked up June from Hill's House, his bad mood dissipated. Simply being around her made him feel better.

It was a dangerous precedent though, sleeping with her. Sooner or later, she'd leave. She'd realize how much of the world she wanted to experience, and she'd get restless, feel stifled by living in Newton. Cal knew he should let her go before he got too attached, but tonight, he couldn't. He needed her.

He closed his bedroom door, and she turned to face him. He took a step forward, and she took one back. Then again. It was like its own form of foreplay.

"Cal?" she asked, looking up at him with a sly smile.

"Yeah?"

"Are you tired? You want to go to sleep?"

"Nope."

"Your feet hurt, and you need to get off them?" she teased.

She'd backed up as far as she could and was now standing at the edge of his bed.

"No." Then he shocked himself—and her, if the look on her face was anything to go by—when he whipped his shirt over his head.

Her eyes went straight to his chest, and he had a perverse moment of satisfaction when a look of anger flashed across her face. He much preferred she be angry on his behalf than disgusted by his scars . . . or worse, pity him.

"You saw me before and didn't freak out. You didn't run, and you definitely had a chance. I want you in the light again. As much as possible. I want to see all of you, and in return, I'll give you all of me. That is . . . if you still want me like this."

She moved immediately, stepping close and kissing an especially gnarly scar on his chest. It went from his breastbone down to his groin. Cal vividly remembered the arsehole who'd done it, how he'd threatened to disembowel him from neck to dick.

"I want you," she reassured him. She struggled with the button of his jeans for a moment before he brushed her hands away and undid the button and zipper himself.

She smiled at him and went to her knees. She shyly pulled down his pants and boxers, and Cal kicked them away. He'd never been as naked with someone, figuratively, as he'd been with June. He'd gotten naked with women, yes. Before his capture. But he'd never in his life been so vulnerable.

Licking her lips, she leaned in and took hold of his flaccid cock. It immediately twitched. All her concentration was on his dick. She didn't seem to even notice how torn up his thighs were. Or the imperfections on the cock itself.

She leaned in and took all of him in her mouth. Cal groaned, and his hands immediately tangled in her hair, more to hold on to something than to control her. He loved her enthusiastic, uncoordinated movements. The fact that she'd so obviously never done this to anyone else made him feel a little crazy.

He grew in her mouth, and before long, she was bobbing up and down on half his length as if she was born to it. At one point, she looked up at him with his cock in her mouth and grinned.

It was more than he could take. Cal wanted to explode, wanted her to swallow everything he gave her, but he needed to be inside her more.

He lifted her easily and stripped her in record time. He practically threw her onto the mattress, and she giggled.

The next twenty minutes were full of sighs and moans and cries . . . and more pleasure than Cal could ever remember.

But when they were both replete, with June snuggled into his side, panic quickly set in.

Every time he had her, she got further under his skin. He needed her *more*, not less. He knew that the longer she lived here, slept in his bed, the more time he spent buried in her hot, wet depths, the harder it would be to lose her. Eventually, he'd get to a point where he wouldn't be able to fathom such a thing. He'd likely become one of those men who stalked an ex and declared that if he couldn't have her, no one could.

He closed his eyes as June breathed deeply, already asleep.

He loved her. Might never love another woman like this again— but he had to let her go. For her own good. She'd be upset at first, but eventually she'd be grateful. He wouldn't be selfish. He'd let her go so she could find her place in the world, somewhere as wondrous and vibrant as June herself.

Newton, Maine, just wasn't it.

One of her hands rested on his chest, right over his heart, and even as she slept, her fingers moved, caressing him. He needed her more than he needed air to breathe, but he'd be damned if he did anything to hold her back from her full potential.

Chapter Nineteen

Almost a week later, June couldn't shake the feeling that something was terribly wrong with Cal. It wasn't anything he'd said, but it was obvious something had occurred . . . or that he'd had an abrupt change of heart.

Ever since the morning after she'd taken the job at Hill's House, and she'd again woken up in his arms, he'd been different. Quieter. Spending less time with her.

He was distancing himself, and she had no idea why.

Maybe he was reconsidering how fast their relationship had progressed. Maybe he was regretting his asking her to move in with him. Maybe, since there had been no word from her stepmother or stepsister, he'd decided she didn't need his protection.

Maybe the sex wasn't good for him, and he decided he didn't want to be with her anymore.

Whatever it was, June had never felt so depressed.

It really started in earnest when he drove her home from Hill's House on her third day—barely saying two words—then letting her know he had to go out and cut down a huge tree that had fallen across a road. He hadn't gotten home until after she was asleep.

The next night, he'd said he wasn't tired, and she should go on up to bed. June ended up going to the guest room she'd used her first night in Newton, feeling too uncertain to be in the master without him for a second night in a row. When Cal hadn't appeared or woken her up to take her to his bed, she felt extremely awkward about sleeping there again . . . unless she was specifically invited.

And so it went. Every night, he had some excuse or another for staying up late, and, not being stupid, June took the hint and continued to go upstairs hours before he did, sleeping in the guest bed.

Finally, last night he'd told her that he had to walk a section of the Appalachian Trail today and do some maintenance and that he'd be gone overnight. He arranged for Bob to take her to work and pick her up afterward.

June decided she was done. She was an expert at knowing when she was wanted and when she wasn't. She'd learned from the best, her stepmother. As much as it hurt, she wasn't going to continue to stay in Cal's house when it was obvious he no longer wanted her there.

Her heart physically ached. Things had seemed so promising. Of course, she should've known better. They'd moved faster than lightning. Cal had probably found himself caught up in the excitement of his first physical relationship in years, the thrill of saving her from her awful situation.

Now that the dust had settled, he clearly realized she was a burden—just like her stepmother had always claimed.

It sucked—hard. June already loved Cal deeply. She just wished she was . . . more attractive? Better? Smarter? Something. Wished she could've kept his interest for more than a week.

She thought they'd truly connected, instantly and profoundly. And for her, at least, the sex had been out-of-this-world amazing. She couldn't imagine it being any better. Then again, she didn't have much experience to draw on. She must not have been that good herself, if he could so easily drop her.

After all they'd done, after he'd bared himself to her, after she thought she'd finally gotten through the extremely thick shields he'd built around himself, it was obvious he was done. And it hurt. A lot.

She needed to call April, or maybe talk to Meg, and see what her living options were. She couldn't continue to stay in Cal's house knowing he didn't really want her there. It was torture to see him every day and have him remain so distant.

It would still be painful to live in Newton and see him around, but she loved this little town and the people in it. Loved her job. She'd only known the residents a short time, but they were as important to her as she supposed grandparents were to their loved ones. They were funny, caring, and incredibly interesting. She couldn't imagine quitting and going to some huge city, where no one cared about anyone, and everyone was always in a big rush. She'd always felt like a tiny little insignificant bug in Washington, DC, but here . . . everywhere she went, people said hello to her and genuinely seemed interested in how she was doing.

There had to be an apartment or room she could afford to rent.

Cal had left for his overnight hike on the AT before she woke, and the house felt empty and lonely without him. She ate her breakfast alone, and it was almost scary how fast similar memories of DC emerged, of June dining by herself as she waited for Elaine and Carla to wake up and start ordering her around.

Eight forty-five didn't come fast enough, and when Bob finally pulled up outside Cal's house, June was more than ready to leave. She carefully locked the door behind her and climbed into Bob's truck with a forced smile.

"Good morning," she told him.

"Morning," he returned as he waited for her to fasten her seat belt. Then he started down Cal's driveway.

"Can I ask you something?" she asked.

"Of course."

"Is . . . is Cal okay?" She hadn't really meant to bring this up, because she'd be mortified if it got back to Cal that she was talking about him behind his back. But Bob was one of his best friends, and if something was wrong, he'd know.

Bob's head jerked quickly to look at her. "Why? Has he said something?"

"I just . . . I mean, I haven't known him that long, but he seems . . . I don't know . . . off?"

Bob continued to divide his attention between her and the road as he drove. "He seems okay to me."

And there it was. Cal was just fine. It was only around *her* that he was being weird. That hurt even more. "Okay. I'm sure I'm just seeing something that isn't there," she said as nonchalantly as she could.

But Bob shook his head. "No, if you think something's up, then something's up. You've been around him more than the rest of us recently. I'll talk to him, see if I can get him to tell me what's wrong."

"No!" June blurted, earning herself another penetrating look from Bob. "I just . . . I think it's me. That he's ready for me to go and doesn't know how to tell me. That he's regretting asking me to stay at all. So I'd appreciate it if you didn't mention anything. But do you know of any-one who's leasing a room? Or maybe an empty apartment somewhere?"

June had never been so glad the ride to Hill's House was a short one. Bob pulled to the curb near the walkway that led up to the porch before turning to look at her.

"He doesn't want you to go," Bob said firmly.

June shook her head and opened her mouth to disagree, but he didn't give her a chance to speak.

"I mean it, June. He doesn't. I've never seen Cal so . . . settled. He's always been a little twitchy, and I can't blame him after everything. But the other day, he actually wore a *short-sleeved T-shirt* to work! I can't remember the last time he bared his arms or any other part of himself to the team. No, that's not true. I can. It was before we were POWs. *You* did that, June. Somehow, you chiseled under that brick wall he hides behind. He definitely doesn't want you to leave," he finished.

"You don't understand," June whispered.

"Then *help* me understand," Bob said calmly.

June didn't exactly want to admit that she was, apparently, not very good in bed, but she needed to talk to someone. "Things were good. Great, actually. Then after we . . . had sex . . . things changed. After the second time, he started to distance himself. *Quickly.* Found things to do at night, sending me to bed without him. Or stayed out late working. And he's barely spoken a dozen words to me in the last week, including while driving me to and from work.

"It was obviously really bad for him, or maybe I seemed too promiscuous and pushy or something. And now he left to go on that overnight trip. I just . . . I love him," June admitted softly. "And I hate making him uncomfortable . . . *hate* chasing him from his own home."

"I suck at this," Bob said with a sigh. "Look, Cal hasn't dated since we got out of the Army. Since he was tortured. Even before that, I've never seen him as . . . animated . . . as he is with you. Whatever happened, it's not on you, June. I know that for certain.

"Cal's life hasn't been easy. He's had a lot of pressure put on him to be the perfect son his entire life. From the royal family, the media. It doesn't matter that everyone knows he'll never be king, he's still endured the pressure. And after he was tortured and publicly humiliated with those videos, he changed completely. Retreated inside his head. He spent a lot of time hiking and being alone.

"Since you've arrived, he's more social. Happier. Whatever is going on in his head, it's nothing you've done. I can promise you that. But . . . don't give up on him," Bob begged. "He needs you, June. I can't see into the future. I don't know if you guys will get married, have a family, and live happily ever after. But a lot has been thrown at him in a short period of time, and I'm sure he's simply processing everything. Talk to him. Don't let him push you away, because from what you've described, it's obvious that's what he's doing. He's probably trying to be noble or something. Don't let him."

June stared at Bob. What he said actually made sense. Things had progressed so fast, and if Cal was used to holding people at arm's length, then the speed at which things between them had moved would probably be quite a jolt.

She loved the man, and she wanted things between them to work out. She wasn't sure they would. But she was stubborn—look at how long she'd hung on to the house she'd lived in with her dad—and she wanted to at least give her and Cal a chance to be happy.

"Okay," she said after a long moment.

"Okay?" Bob asked. "You'll make him sit down and talk?"

"Yeah."

"Thank God! You're good for him, June. And trust me, I wouldn't say that if I didn't believe it down to my bones. The man has been through enough, and if I thought you were nothing but a passing fancy, a way to scratch an itch, I wouldn't be encouraging you to pursue him. I'd be finding you a place to live so fast, your head would spin. But him wearing that T-shirt at the office . . . that speaks volumes. He needs you."

June shook her head. "He doesn't need me. If anything, I need *him*."

"Fine, then you guys need each other. Whatever. Just talk to him. Don't let him put you off. Strip naked and parade yourself in front of him. Do whatever it takes."

June laughed for the first time in days. "That's not happening," she said.

"I'm sure it would distract him." He grinned.

"I need to get inside," she replied, shaking her head ruefully.

"Okay. I'll be back at three to pick you up. Just let me know if you need me to come earlier or later."

"I will."

"Have a good day."

"You too. And thank you, Bob," June told him solemnly, then climbed out of his truck. As she walked toward the front door, she once again realized how lucky Cal was to have such a good friend in Bob. And JJ and Chappy, for that matter. The four men really were like brothers, and she wasn't jealous in the least. She was glad Cal had that.

"Good morning!" Banks said loudly when he opened the door as she approached. "We've been waiting for you. We're all ready for our cornhole tournament today! We've been doing our stretches, and I can't *wait* to kick everyone's butts. I mean, I had years and years of training when I was a boxer."

June resisted the urge to roll her eyes. She couldn't believe Banks did half the things he claimed he did, but like everyone else, since he was amusing, she went with it. "I don't know," she teased. "I'm thinking Sofia is probably a dark horse."

Banks scoffed as he shut the door behind her. "No way, I'll bury her!"

One of the things she'd been surprised about was how cutthroat everyone in the house was when it came to games. They might be older, but they had no shortage of competitive spirit. Whether it was playing Uno, or finishing a word search first, or winning at cornhole, everyone wanted to be on top. It was actually pretty cute.

"Banks, give June some room to breathe," Meg scolded as she came into the foyer to greet her. "Jeez, the poor woman just arrived. She might want a cup of coffee or something. And she certainly wants to greet everyone else before you drag her out into the yard. Besides, we all agreed we'd wait a couple hours for it to warm up a bit. We don't want Scott's fingers falling off from the cold."

"Won't be his fingers that fall off. It'll be his tallyho," Banks muttered.

June could see Meg trying not to laugh as she said, "That's not nice, Banks."

But Banks didn't seem chastened in the least. "Come on, June, let's get the meet and greet done so we can get on with the day."

June let herself be dragged farther into the house. Meg met her eyes and mouthed "Sorry," but all June could do was smile. She actually loved this. Loved that every day was different. Loved how eager the residents were. They seemed genuinely excited to see her each morning, and that made all the difference. She didn't mind working hard, didn't mind not taking a break during the day, because there was always someone who was eager to talk to her, to tell a story about something they'd done or seen in the past, and she felt needed.

If things between her and Cal didn't work out, she wasn't going anywhere. She couldn't imagine finding a job better than this one. Or one that made her even happier.

Of course, as much as June loved her job, she was always tired by the time three o'clock rolled around. Today was no different. The cornhole tournament had been a huge hit, and she was already planning more outdoor activities as the weather warmed up. It was good to see the residents out getting fresh air, using their muscles, and having a great time. Banks did end up winning, but to June's surprise, Jara wasn't that far behind.

She was in the kitchen cleaning dishes from the snacks everyone had just enjoyed when Tim walked in. He was the janitor Meg had hired, and he came in every day shortly before June's quitting time. She didn't know a lot about him, but he was always pleasant to her and the residents, which made him okay in her eyes.

"Hey," he said as he entered the room. "How was the tournament?"

June chuckled. "Good, although I had to break up two almost-fights, and everyone accused everyone else of cheating at least once."

Tim laughed. "Sounds about right. I brought you something," he said, holding out a foil-covered plate. "I mean, since we're both new in town and all, I figured it would be a nice gesture from one newbie to another. I can't cook worth a darn, but none of my ex-girlfriends ever complained about my superspecial double-chocolate brownies."

June stared at the plate for a moment. "Um . . . I'm kind of dating someone," she told him, not wanting him to get any ideas about the two of them.

"Oh, these aren't a come-on," he said quickly. "I broke up with a woman right before I moved to town, so I don't want to get into another relationship. I'm planning on going home to New York by summer anyway. I just figured, you work so hard . . . I thought you might appreciate a treat. All women like chocolate, right?"

"Right," June said, feeling better about his motives.

She didn't have the heart to tell him that she wasn't going to eat the brownies. She suppressed a small shiver when she thought of the reason why.

"If you don't want them, I can leave them for the residents, I suppose."

"No! I do. Want them. Thank you, Tim. That was really nice of you," June said as she stepped forward.

He smiled at her, and their fingers brushed as he handed over the paper plate. For the first time since she'd met him, June suddenly felt uneasy. She didn't really have a reason to feel that way, but she'd always had pretty good intuition. She accepted the plate and backed away. "Thanks again."

"Aren't you going to try one?" he asked with a lopsided grin.

"Not right now," she hedged. "We just had snacks. I'll save them for tonight after dinner."

"Okay," Tim said with a shrug. "I'll see you tomorrow."

"It's Sunday. I'm off," June reminded him.

"Oh, that's right. Then I'll see you Tuesday, since Monday's my day off," Tim said easily. "Have a good rest of the weekend."

"You too," June told him before heading out of the kitchen. She waved goodbye to Jeremy and Brenda, who were watching reruns of *Jeopardy!* and actually keeping track of who had the most money as the game progressed. They waved back and returned their attention to the television. The other residents weren't anywhere to be seen, and June figured they were probably taking a nap after the eventful day.

Meg appeared, and she held the plate of brownies for her as June put on her coat.

"These look good," she said, lifting the edge of the foil.

"Tim brought them for me. Said it was from one newbie to another," June told her.

"That was nice of him. Enjoy your Sunday. But I don't need to tell *you* that, I'm sure. Not when you're living with Cal Redmon." She

243

grinned. "That guy is delicious. And so polite and considerate. You couldn't have found a better man."

"Thanks," June said. She wished she was looking forward to going home to a happy and welcoming Cal, but he was sleeping out in the wilderness somewhere, most likely to avoid her. The thought sucked.

When she walked outside, Bob was waiting at the curb. She got into his truck and smiled over at him. "Thanks again for hauling me around. I really need a car, but I can't afford one right now. Maybe I'll get a bike," she mused.

"It's not a big deal. It's not like I'm driving thirty minutes out of my way or anything. It takes five minutes, tops, to take you home or to work."

He wasn't wrong, but June hated feeling like a burden. They were quiet as they drove toward Cal's house.

When Bob pulled into the drive, stopping as close to the front porch as he could, he nodded to the plate on her lap. "What's that?"

"Brownies."

"You make them at work today?" he asked.

June shook her head. "No. Tim, the janitor, brought them for me."

Bob looked surprised.

June shook her head, not wanting him to get the wrong idea. "He's not interested in me. Because of my size, people tend to think food is the best gift. Not that I've gotten that many presents in my life. It's just that he's new here, and I am too, and he wanted to do something to welcome me to town, I guess? I'm not even going to eat them," she added, not liking the expression on Bob's face. She didn't want him to think for a moment that she was in any way cheating on Cal. "I don't eat food that others have made. I mean . . . not things like this. I eat in restaurants because they're safe."

"Safe?" Bob asked with a raised brow.

"Yeah. I don't know what the environment was like where these brownies were made," she hedged. "Like, does Tim have a hundred cats, and they walk all over the countertops? Does he have a roach infestation? Can't tell the difference between salt and sugar? It's just not always safe to eat food that comes from someone else's kitchen. But I took them because I wanted to be nice and didn't want to hurt his feelings. Do you want them?"

Bob recoiled. "After what you just said? No, thank you. Now . . . how about you tell me the *real* reason why?"

"Why what?" she asked.

"What happened to make you so distrustful of baked goods from other people?"

June stared at him for a moment. She didn't want to talk about this, but after she'd spilled her guts this morning, she supposed she trusted Bob.

She sighed. "It's stupid."

"If it's made you wary, it's not stupid," Bob said. "Now spill."

"It was a few years ago. Carla made cookies when I was out running errands, and when I got back, she told me she wanted a truce. That she didn't like how we'd been fighting so much lately. I was actually happy, because at one time, when my dad was alive, we were kind of close. She urged me to eat a couple, and I did because she seemed so proud of herself for having made them."

"And?" Bob asked when June paused.

"She laced them with a synthetic marijuana. I ended up having horrible hallucinations, and Carla and her friends laughed at how petrified I was. They filmed me cowering in a corner and crying hysterically. They thought it was hilarious, passing the video around to all of their friends, and she even posted it on her social media accounts.

"I literally thought I was dying. It was awful. And I vowed never to eat anything anyone made for me—that I hadn't seen them cook—ever again."

June was staring down at the plate in her lap as she told her story, but when she finished, and Bob didn't comment after a long moment, she glanced over at him. He was clenching the steering wheel so tightly, she could see the whites of his knuckles. A muscle in his jaw was flexing repeatedly, and his lips were pressed together.

He took a deep breath, then turned to her. "Have you told Cal that story?"

"No," she said with a small shake of her head.

"Don't," he bit out. "He'd literally lose his mind and would probably drive back to DC and do something that would make us have to collect bail."

The thought of Cal being thrown in jail wasn't something June wanted to think about. "Okay," she said.

Bob shook his head a little. "Cal's an idiot for being out in the cold tonight instead of in a warm bed with you," he said. "Talk to him when he gets back tomorrow. Promise me."

"I will. But I wouldn't be surprised if he decides to spend another night on the trail," she said, voicing her worry for the first time.

"He won't. If I have to hike out there and get him myself, he'll be home," Bob promised.

June studied the man at her side for a long moment. She wasn't interested in him romantically, because she was head over heels in love with Cal, but she knew for certain he'd be an amazing man for some woman to have at her side. On the outside, he projected a happy-go-lucky countenance. He went out of his way to be the life of the party and make everyone laugh. But in just the small amount of time she'd spent with him today, after their short conversations, June had a feeling there was a lot more to the man than he showed the rest of the world.

"Thanks," she said.

"Sleep well. And if you need anything, don't hesitate to call me. You want me to take those brownies with me, so you don't have to deal with them?" he asked.

"No. I'll throw them away."

"Okay. June?"

"Yeah?"

"I've said it before, and I'm saying it again. Cal needs you. Whatever's going on in his head . . . it has nothing to do with you. Okay?"

"Okay."

"Now scoot. I've got things to do. Clubs to go to, five-star restaurants to eat at, art galleries to visit . . . you know. Stuff."

June laughed. As if Newton had any of those things. "Right. Have fun."

"I meant what I said. If you need anything, call. I'll be pissed if you don't."

"I'll be fine. But thank you."

"Later, June."

"Bye."

June reached the door and unlocked it, turning and waving at Bob, who hadn't pulled away from the house, as he was waiting to make sure she got inside all right. She closed the door behind her and sighed. The house felt too big without Cal.

She kicked off her shoes and went into the kitchen. She put the plate of brownies on the counter, then went upstairs to change into a pair of leggings and one of Cal's sweatshirts. She wasn't sure Cal's change of attitude was really about him, not her, as Bob insisted. But she definitely couldn't continue this way. She needed to find out what was going on with him. Even if what she learned broke her heart, at least she'd know.

And if Bob was right, and Cal was trying to be noble or holding himself back because of his own insecurities, she'd set him straight . . . and maybe they could be happy once again.

Her mind made up and feeling lighter than she thought possible, considering she'd be spending the night alone for the first time in years, June headed back downstairs.

∼

Tim couldn't keep the grin off his face. He wished he could be there when June tripped out after eating the brownies. Her stepmother had sent him a video of her in a fetal position, crying uncontrollably, while she'd been tripping after eating cookies her stepsister had made for her.

Elaine loved the idea of it happening again and had pressured him to make a batch of brownies for June.

So he had . . . for a mere three hundred bucks. Tim would do anything the bitch asked him to do, as long as she was willing to back it up with some green.

Apparently, the conversation about secretly feeding June marijuana had loosened Elaine's tongue, because she'd gone on and on about the best way to kill her stepdaughter. In a way that would cause her the most pain. She really wanted him to poison her. Had told him about all the painful side effects of certain drugs.

He'd started to ask how she knew so much about it but didn't have to. The crazy bitch actually told him how she'd used too much succinylcholine when she'd poisoned her husband! Who the fuck shared that kind of juicy info? The miscalculation caused him to die way faster than she'd intended. She'd muttered something about being lucky the symptoms mimicked a heart attack.

As stupid as he thought Elaine was, Tim was still shocked she'd so nonchalantly admit to killing her husband. He insisted that killing June with the same poison wouldn't work because he couldn't dose her in any reliable and methodical way. She grunted, but eventually agreed.

Truthfully, that wasn't really why Tim didn't want to poison June. He wouldn't be able to get his hands on a drug like succinylcholine. He'd have to use something like antifreeze, which was easy to get but would take too damn long. He wanted his money, and making June sick week after week would mean he wouldn't get paid for who knew how long. He much preferred something quick and easy . . . that wouldn't potentially send her running to the hospital for a bunch of tests.

He still wasn't sure how he was going to do it, but it was going to happen soon. He was sick of this town. Hated his job—though he couldn't believe his dumb luck when June was hired just days after him. He especially hated old people. They were slow, smelly, and argumentative. And being in Hill's House surrounded by them was not his idea of a good time. Besides, working in general wasn't exactly his jam. He preferred to do as little as possible for his money.

He continued to lie to Elaine about what he was doing here in Newton and how the stalking was going. He'd sent her another picture of a threatening note on a door, then a dead squirrel with a knife through its head on a doormat. He'd been reluctant to damage his own hand but eventually decided the money was worth it, so he punched a wall to scrape up his knuckles and sent "proof" to Elaine that he'd sucker punched June from behind while she was walking home one day.

Elaine was gullible as hell, and more importantly, she was prompt with her payments. This was one of the easiest jobs Tim had ever done. He was actually a little disappointed that his gravy train would be ending soon. But he was over living in the sticks, so it was almost time to do what he'd been sent to do—take out Juniper Rose and get his ten thousand dollars.

"It's not personal," he muttered as he rested his head against the back of the couch. He'd left work early tonight, not feeling it. He'd overheard June telling one of the old broads who lived at Hill's House that the prince was spending the night on the AT. It would be a perfect opportunity to head to the house and scare the shit out of her . . . but honestly, he was feeling too lazy. And he didn't want to give her any reason to start being more careful.

In his opinion, Elaine's whole plan was flawed from the get-go. If he really was a stalker, he had a feeling the prince and his military friends would rally after just one note. Close ranks around June so he'd never have a chance to get anywhere near her. It would actually make the guy spend *more* time with June instead of running back to the other daughter.

Elaine's bullshit would eventually backfire in a big way, and she'd probably try to frame Tim.

Which wasn't happening.

Nope. Tim wouldn't do a damn thing to give June or the prince any reason to be wary. He'd strike hard and fast and out of the blue.

She'd have no idea what was coming for her, which was better all the way around. What happened after she was dead wasn't his concern. As long as he got his money, Tim would be happy.

Maybe the prince *would* run back to DC, as Elaine hoped . . . but he doubted it. Her suggestion that he leave one last note after killing June, implying Carla was next, wouldn't wash. The man would see through Elaine's plan easily. But again, either way, Tim would be gone and a hundred C-notes richer.

Chapter Twenty

June was nervous. She'd slept like crap the night before. Partly because she was keenly aware she was alone in the house, and partly because she was nervous about talking to Cal when he got home today.

She felt restless, not knowing what to do with a full day off. She'd already vacuumed, swept, dusted, and started a load of dirty clothes. Not sure when Cal would be home, all she could do was try to keep busy until he arrived.

June supposed she should be relaxing—reading a book or watching a movie—but she couldn't. So she went through the house and gathered all the trash. She bundled it up and headed outside to the trash cans, which were inside the detached garage. Cal had told her he kept the bins in there to protect them from the wildlife in the area.

June was halfway across the yard to the garage when she heard something to her right. Turning, she froze in her tracks.

There was a large black bear moseying along, headed in the same direction she was going.

It wasn't paying any attention to her, but June still couldn't move. If she went back to the house, it would see her and charge. If she tried to make it to the garage, it would also see her and would definitely be able to get to her before she made it to safety.

And, to make matters worse, she was holding a bag full of smelly leftovers and other food scraps that would certainly interest the animal.

As soon as she had the thought, the bear picked up his head and sniffed, clearly catching a scent of either her fear or the food, she couldn't be sure. But the animal turned toward her regardless. He went up on his hind legs—she just assumed it was male, because it was so huge—and sniffed the air again.

Forgetting everything she'd ever learned about what to do when confronted with a bear—run? Play dead? Back away slowly? Yell and wave her arms?—June dropped the garbage bag and fled back the way she'd come.

At any second, she expected to be tackled and find herself facedown in the dirt and grass with a million-pound bear mauling her back. But that didn't happen. She ran at the door full tilt, smacking her nose against the hard wood, before scrambling for the handle.

"Please, please, please!" she pleaded as she tried to get inside. Her hands were shaking, and she felt as uncoordinated as a baby.

The relief she felt when the door slammed shut behind her was so intense, she immediately fell to her knees. "Holy crap," she whispered.

After a few minutes, she pulled herself to her feet and peered out the window next to the door. The bear was still there. It had found the garbage bag and torn it open. He was sitting happily in the yard, munching on the old food inside.

June shivered. He could be feasting on her body right about now. Moose, she could handle. Elk? No problem. Mountain lions, bobcats, feral hogs . . . easy peasy. Hell, she could even handle Bigfoot, would probably want to have a conversation with the elusive creature. But bears?

No. Just no.

As she stood at the window and watched the bear consume the garbage, a flash of doubt flew through her brain. What was she doing? Maine was *full* of bears. Did she really want to live here? Permanently?

Just when she was considering packing up her suitcases and calling Bob to come get her and drop her off at the nearest bus station—which she had a feeling wasn't anywhere near Newton—she heard another sound from outside.

A vehicle.

"No!" she whispered, then spun and ran toward the front door.

Cal was home, and he was going to be eaten by a bear if she didn't warn him!

She barreled toward the front door and almost hit her nose once more but stopped herself just in time. She opened the door a crack, and when she didn't see the bear, she bolted outside. Cal usually parked in front of the porch while he unloaded his SUV, then drove to the garage. But the bear was between the garage and the house, and it would surely attack if Cal drove down there, right?

"Cal!" she whisper-yelled as she ran down the stairs of the porch. Her heart was beating a million miles a minute. She expected the bear to charge them any second now.

"What's wrong?" Cal asked as he turned toward her.

"Come on, come on, come on!" she ordered, grabbing his arm and frantically pulling him toward the house.

Thankfully, he followed her without protest, allowing her to drag him behind her. It wasn't until they were behind the closed door that June allowed herself to breathe out a sigh of relief.

"Talk to me," Cal ordered. "What's wrong?" He grabbed her shoulders and turned her to face him. "You have two seconds to tell me what's wrong before I call Chief Rutkey."

"Bear!" she managed to squeak out.

"What?"

"There's a bear out there. Huge! With claws the size of my head. It's by the garage. It would've eaten you!"

To her utter disbelief, Cal smiled.

"This isn't funny!" she shouted.

"Yes, it is."

"Cal! It would've *eaten* you! It got the trash I was taking out, and I thought I was going to die!"

Without a word, he turned, taking her hand in his and walking to the back door. He looked out the window at the bear, who was still sitting exactly where June had last seen him. He seemed perfectly content to hang out and chow down on the unexpected treat he'd been given.

"It's an adolescent. Probably just came out of hibernation," Cal said calmly.

"What? No way. It's huge!" June protested.

Cal turned to her, the smile still on his face. "This is a side of you I haven't seen," he said.

"How can you be so calm about this?" June cried.

But he went on as if she hadn't spoken. "If asked, I would've said that you weren't afraid of anything. You've met all the recent changes in your life head on. But apparently, bears are your weakness."

"They're *deadly*. They'll freakin' kill you! They have huge claws and fangs, what's not to be scared of?"

"They're generally more afraid of you than you are of them," he told her.

June snorted. "That's what they want you to think. It's their plan—get humans to let down their guard, and that's when they'll strike."

Cal laughed.

For the first time, June took in his appearance. His clothes were dirty, he had a five-o'clock shadow on his jaw, there was a streak of dirt on his cheek, and his hair was in disarray. He looked about as far from a prince at this moment as she'd ever seen him. But he also looked more relaxed than he'd been for the past several days. Being out in the wilderness suited him.

His smile slowly dimmed as he studied her as well. He raised his hand and brushed his fingers against her cheek. "You're really scared, aren't you?"

"Um . . . duh!" she said.

"It's kind of cute," he told her.

June shook her head in exasperation, but she couldn't help loving how close he was standing to her, how he was touching her again. It had been a long week since he'd touched her like this.

"I need to shower," he said, but he didn't move away.

"Did you get done what you needed to get done?" she asked.

He nodded.

June took a deep breath. "Can we talk? I mean, when you're done? I'm sure you're hungry. I can make you waffles while you're in the shower," she suggested, knowing they were one of his favorites.

The distance she'd gotten used to seeing in his eyes returned, and she once again mourned the loss of the Cal she'd grown to love.

"Yeah, we should talk," he agreed. He turned and headed toward the stairs, but he stopped at the bottom and turned back toward her. "If you're so scared of that bear, why'd you come outside?"

June frowned. "Because I didn't want it to hurt you. Haven't you figured it out yet, Cal? I'd do *anything* to keep you safe. To make sure no one and nothing puts one more scar on your body, ever again."

He stared at her for so long, June wanted to look away. But she forced herself to hold his gaze. Then, rather anticlimactically, he turned and went upstairs without another word.

June let out her breath in a long *whoosh*. She couldn't stop herself from looking out the window once more, swallowing hard when there was no sign of the bear, only the garbage bag ripped to shreds with trash strewn about the yard. It was almost worse not knowing where the bear was. He could be hiding behind the corner of the garage, waiting to rush out and eat Cal when he went back out to move his SUV.

If she had her way, he wouldn't be going out anytime soon. She had a breakfast to make that he needed to eat; then they'd talk. She was dreading it, but Bob was right. It had to happen.

If Cal didn't want her there anymore, if she was stifling him, she'd go. Without making a fuss. She never wanted to be one of those women who couldn't take a hint. If she'd outstayed her welcome, she'd leave

immediately. She'd lived enough of her life as an unwanted poor rela-
tion; she wasn't going to do it again.

~

Cal took his time in the shower. The hot water felt good on his sore
muscles. He admitted to himself that he was spoiled, that he much preferred his soft bed to the hard ground along the Appalachian Trail. He
put his hands against the tile and let the water beat down on his shoulders, forcing himself to stand there. To not rush through his shower and
back downstairs so he could see June.

This last week had been torture. All he wanted was to hold her. Talk
to her. Listen to her stories about the residents at Hill's House who she
was getting to know. But he'd forced himself to keep his distance. To
try to reduce his obsession with her.

But it was no use. He loved her more now than he did a week ago.
Even though she was sleeping in the guest room again, he could still
smell her on his sheets. It was literal torture to walk past her room at
night and not barge in, pick her up, and carry her to his bed.

The knives his captors had used were excruciating . . . but not like
this. It felt as if he was ripping his own heart out of his chest, second
by second. Seeing how worried she was for him, even if he'd thought it
was cute, had brought the point home that no matter how much of an
arsehole he was, she would always be the beautiful soul he'd fallen for.
She'd still care about him, still worry about him . . . just from a distance.

A distance that he was creating.

He'd gone out on the AT to get some real separation. It hadn't
worked. He was miserable being away from her, even if they'd barely
spoken for the past week. And the second he returned, she'd gone and
shown him once more why there'd never be anyone else like her.

He had a decision to make, and he instinctively knew when he
went downstairs, it would be time. He either needed to stop trying to
push June away, accept the fact she'd eventually want more than he or

Newton could give her, and deal with the heartbreak when that happened. Or he could pretend she meant nothing to him and end things here and now.

The thought of doing the latter hurt so badly, Cal put a hand to his chest, over his fast-beating heart.

He was still just as conflicted when he stepped out of the shower five minutes later. He changed into sweats and a long-sleeved T-shirt, needing the protection the cotton would provide. It was as if he was putting on armor.

His cell phone, which was on the bed, alerted him to an incoming text. Grateful for anything that would put off the inevitable talk he needed to have with June, Cal picked it up and looked down at the message. It was from Bob.

Bob: Did June tell you about the brownies?

Cal frowned and quickly typed a response.

Cal: No. What brownies?

Bob: Right, to make a long story short, Tim, the janitor at HH, made her brownies as a welcome to town thing. She won't eat them because her bitch of a stepsister once gave her cookies laced with pot and laughed when she had a bad trip.

Cal's hand tightened around the phone so hard, he was actually surprised when it didn't break into a hundred pieces.

Bob: I'm just giving you a heads-up so you don't freak if she does tell you. What's the word on Elaine and Carla? Have you heard from them? We need to step things up because I'm not feeling warm and fuzzy about her having anything to do with them ever again.

Bob wasn't the only one. Cal pressed his lips together and did his best to gain control over his rioting emotions, then he pressed Bob's name. He wasn't going to text about this shit. It would take too long, and he needed to get downstairs.

"Yo," Bob said as he answered.

"I talked to Karl, my cousin, just this morning. Carla's been trying to get hold of him every day. He finally answered the last video chat when she called, and she was wearing a bikini top, her tits overflowing the damn thing. Karl said he could see her damn nipples. Anyway, she was crying and saying that she was scared to death and that she'd been getting more threatening notes. I'd already talked to Karl shortly after returning from DC. Told him what the real situation was. He's decided to play along with her for a while longer, see what he can learn . . . but more likely because he's a sucker for blondes. Regardless, he's also promised to keep in touch."

"So she hasn't given up," Bob said.

"Doesn't look like it," Cal agreed.

"You know what would make her shut the hell up fast?" Bob asked.

"What?"

"You getting married."

In the past, Cal would've told his friend to bugger off, that there was no way he was marrying someone in order to get some too-eager bitch off his back. But now? The thought of making June his princess for real shot a pang of longing through him.

"Think about it," Bob said, not giving Cal a chance to respond. "Just knowing she's still sticking to the stalker story is worrisome. We need to nip this in the bud. Get her to understand once and for all that you won't be manipulated and that if she really wants help with some mythical stalker, she needs to go to the police and let them sort it out."

"Yeah, well, any ideas short of marriage? Because I've already told both Carla and her mother pretty much all of that," Cal told his friend.

"Well, I know JJ thought keeping the cousin involved was a good idea. But I'm having doubts. If your cousin cut her off, if she doesn't have an audience and a way to get to you, she might give up this crackpot story."

"And if she doesn't?" Cal asked. "The last thing I want is for her or her mother to show up in Newton."

"I think we talk to Chief Rutkey. See if he has any connections down in DC."

Cal sighed. "Right. I got nowhere with the detective I spoke to, but I'll still do that tomorrow."

"Sounds good."

"Thanks for telling me about the brownies," Cal told his friend.

"I wasn't sure June would tell you, because I warned her you wouldn't be happy. Not because another man gave her a present, but because of what her stepsister did to her."

Honestly, Cal wasn't happy about either. The only person who should be giving her gifts was *him*. Though he'd done a shite job of that so far. "I gotta go," he told his friend.

"Right. If you need me to give June a ride again, just let me know. She's an amazing woman, and Newton is damn lucky to have her. Oh, and heads up, April's chomping at the bit to get us all together so she can talk about the schedule. People want to book guides for their AT hikes, and thanks to that last snowstorm, locals are eager to get their trees pruned before they fall on their houses. I'm thinking later this week we can sit down and hash it all out."

"Right, thanks."

"Talk to you tomorrow."

Cal hung up and stood in the middle of his room for a long moment. His gaze went to the bed, where he'd spent a very restless week sleeping by himself.

And suddenly, like a flash, he realized what a colossal idiot he'd been.

Spinning on his heel, he strode toward the door. He practically ran down the stairs, for some reason terrified that in the twenty minutes or so he'd been away from her, June would've decided she was done. That she didn't want to talk, and she was leaving.

To his relief, she was sitting on the couch with a book in her lap when he practically burst into the room. Cal went to the sofa and took a seat on the other end. The four feet between them suddenly felt like twenty. Even more so when she straightened and leaned against the arm of the couch, as if to increase the distance.

And *he'd* done that. He'd made her feel uncomfortable around him. He felt like a complete arsehole.

"Feel better?" she asked tentatively.

"No," Cal told her honestly.

She blinked in surprise.

"I've been a dick to you," he blurted. He wasn't surprised when she shook her head to deny his words.

"You've been busy. And stressed," she said, letting him off the hook. But Cal wouldn't let her.

"You got brownies yesterday from the janitor?" he asked.

She frowned in confusion at the change of topic and shrugged. "Yeah."

"But you didn't eat them."

June shook her head.

"I'd ask why, but I just talked to Bob," Cal said. "Were you going to tell me about them? About what happened to you?"

"No," she said. "Bob said you wouldn't be happy."

"I'm *not* happy," Cal agreed. "But it's not because some arsehole gave you brownies when I've done nothing but give you grief for the last week. It's because you had that horrible experience with Carla, and I had to learn about it from someone else."

"You haven't exactly been around much lately," she hedged.

"No. I haven't. Do you know why?"

"Because you aren't used to sharing your house. Because you're having second thoughts about me being here. Because after we had sex, it wasn't what you were expecting, and you didn't know how to tell me that you weren't interested anymore." June's hands were clenched in her lap as she spoke, and her face had practically no color.

Cal felt a thousand times worse for hurting her. For letting her think for one second that his confusing behavior was because of anything *she'd* done. He shook his head. "No, that's not why."

"I get it," she said in a rush before he could explain. "I haven't been with many guys—okay, it's only been three, including you—and things between us happened really fast. I practically threw myself at you like some whore, and I'm sure the sex wasn't that great. And after Carla, you're probably thinking I'm only here because I want your money or have some fantasy about being a royal, but that's not why I slept with you. Not at all."

Cal couldn't stand it anymore. He scooted closer, lifted his hand, and covered her mouth, stopping her from saying another awful thing about herself.

"No, listen to me, June. Are you listening?"

She nodded.

Cal moved his hand, spearing his fingers into her hair, his thumb resting on her cheek. "I haven't been avoiding you because the sex wasn't good. It was actually because it was *too* good.

"Being with you is nothing like I imagined it would be. It was so much better. I swear I saw stars and fireworks and little birds and all the other cheesy things people claim they see when they make love—and it freaked me out. I started second-guessing myself. You can do so much better than me, June. You're good down to your core, and I'm . . . not.

"You haven't dated much. You've lived in the same house your entire life. I don't want to be the one to hold you back. Don't want to be the reason you don't find what you were always meant to do. You should share your kindness and grace and huge heart with others. Have the chance to meet other men. And being here with me, in Newton, won't allow you to do that."

"Who says?" she asked, sounding completely serious.

"You've seen this place. There's not even a stoplight. We don't have a mall, the most exciting thing that happens is when someone has too much to drink at the Honky Tonk, and the police chief has to take them to the station to sober up for the night."

"So . . . let me get this straight. You *want* me to leave? You *want* me to date other people?"

"No!" Cal practically roared. Then he took a deep, calming breath. "I just . . . I'm broken inside, June. And scarred outside. And I don't want to hold you back from living your life."

She sat up straighter, and Cal let his hand drop from her face.

"First of all, I don't want to meet other men elsewhere. I want *you*. Second, it's almost laughable that you don't think you're a good man. Cal, you drove down to Washington, DC, to protect a complete stranger simply because your family asked you to. You let another stranger—*me*—come with you to Newton because you felt bad about my situation. Then you let me *live* with you. Your actions speak so much louder than your words, Cal. And I also see how your friends are with you, how the people in Newton interact with you. All of them can see the goodness in you, even if you can't.

"And . . . I don't want to change the world," she admitted softly. "I may have lived in the same place my entire life, but I've seen more than my share of evil . . . starting with the people who call themselves my family. I love it here. I love everything about this small town. The fresh air, how people say good morning even when they don't know you, how they actually stop to let you cross the street instead of giving you the finger when you're in a crosswalk and have the right of way. I love working at Hill's House. Jara, Banks, Scott . . . all the residents . . . they're amazing. I could talk with them every day for thirty years and still never hear all their stories."

She stopped and looked at him with tears in her eyes. Tears that tore Cal's heart out when he saw them.

"Then there's *you*, Cal. You make me feel as if I'm truly living for the first time ever . . . and I love you."

His heart nearly stopped at her confession.

"But this last week has been the hardest of my life. Harder than anything I endured with Carla and Elaine. Seeing you every day but not being able to touch you, knowing that you're actively avoiding me . . . it's the most painful thing I've ever experienced.

"So if you don't want me here, I just need you to tell me. And I'd understand. I know I'm not worldly. I'm not beautiful. I'm awkward and sheltered. Then there's your family. I *understand* your reluctance to get involved with someone who's probably unacceptable to royals. Can you imagine introducing me to the king and queen of Liechtenstein?" She let out a self-deprecating huff of laughter.

"Yes," Cal said without hesitation. "They'd love you, because every big emotion you feel is on your face for all to see. You're real—and trust me, they're used to dealing with conniving and deceitful people twenty-four hours a day.

"I'm so sorry, June. I'm sorry I freaked out. You were already everything I've ever wanted in a partner, and when the sex was so good, and I found myself craving it, craving *you*, every minute of every damn day, I panicked. I'm *terrified* of losing you. So I pushed you away to protect myself. It was a bloody awful thing to do . . . and it didn't work anyway. The harder I pushed you away, the more desperately I wanted you."

June sighed and licked her lips. "So where do we go from here? I can't handle you pushing me away one minute and apologizing and wanting to be with me the next."

"I'm done keeping my distance. I love you, Juniper Rose. I want you with me. By my side. In my bed, in my life. I won't be a bloody fool again. If you forgive me, I'll be the best boyfriend you've ever had. I'll make sure you don't want anyone else, ever."

The tears he'd seen in her eyes finally overflowed and streamed down her cheeks. He had a split second to worry she'd reject *him* this time, before she threw herself into his arms.

"I love you, Cal. So much! I'll make a horrible princess, but I'll love you more than anyone ever has or ever could."

Cal held her tightly against his chest and buried his face in her hair, inhaling deeply, bringing her essence into his soul.

He'd had a close call, and he knew it. He'd been such an arse, and his June had found it in her heart to forgive him. He'd never give her another reason to doubt him. Not ever again.

He stood, taking her with him. Then he leaned over and picked her up. She shrieked a little and clutched his shoulders as he strode toward the stairs.

"Cal! Put me down! The food—"

"I'm hungry for something other than waffles," he told her.

"I'm too heavy!" she protested.

"Like hell you are," he told her. "The day I can't carry my woman is the day I get a walker and call myself over the hill," he said with a growl.

"No one's ever carried me before," she said, sounding awestruck as they went up the stairs.

Truthfully, she wasn't light for most men, but Cal had lifted too many trees and worn too many heavy rucksacks throughout his military career for her to feel like anything more than the perfect handful.

He brought her straight to his bedroom and to his bed, where he let her bounce to the surface before joining her. He caged her in with his body and said, "I need you, June. I need to be inside you *right now*, to feel your pussy clinging to my cock. I was a massive idiot, and I've missed you so much. I don't think I've slept more than two hours a night since I made up those stupid excuses to keep my distance."

He stared down at her, his mouth watering to taste her once again. But he wasn't going to make one move until she let him know she wanted him just as much. He'd screwed up, bad. He was lucky she'd forgiven him, but he wasn't going to mistake her forgiveness for consent. If he had to work harder to find his way back into her bed, he'd do whatever it took.

But Cal should've known his June . . . his tenderhearted, kind June . . . wouldn't make him grovel.

She squirmed under him, pushing her leggings down and kicking them off.

"I'm yours, Cal. I've always been yours. Make love to me. Please."

Relief swam through his veins . . . along with lust. "This is going to be fast," he warned as he began to strip off his own clothes. He seemed to say that to her a lot. Too often. He had no control around this woman.

"Good. We can get it over with and then go slow the second time."

More proof that she was made to be his. He grinned as they raced to see who could get naked first.

June lay against Cal's sweaty chest and absently traced a finger over one of the multitude of scars. She felt boneless. Their first time had indeed been fast. Cal had taken her hard, almost brutally, and she'd loved every second. After they'd both come within minutes of him getting inside her, he'd taken his time and caressed every inch of her body. He'd made her come with his mouth, then his fingers, and she played with his cock and balls but not enough to make him climax. He was too eager to get inside her again at that point.

He'd taken her from behind. Switched and put her on top, facing his feet. Then they'd ended up in missionary style as he ever so slowly made sweet love to her, until she'd begged him to move faster.

She'd come then, and he'd joined her soon after. They were both sweaty, the covers were strewn all over the bed and half on the floor, and the overhead light was shining bright. But June didn't even think about moving, about covering up. She was with the man she loved more than life.

"The light's on," Cal said quietly, as if he could read her mind.

"Yeah," she agreed, coming up on an elbow. "Want me to grab the sheet?"

He shook his head. "I used to think the most horrifying thing in the world would be to expose myself to a woman, to a potential bedmate. It was bad enough when I had to take my shirt or pants off to be examined by a doctor. But letting a woman I wanted to make love to see my scars wasn't something I ever thought I'd be able to do. You made it doable. You made it all right, June."

"There's nothing wrong with your body, Cal," June told him fiercely. "You're in better shape than probably eighty-five percent of the men in the world. You chop down trees, you work out, you hike." She ran a hand down his chest, feeling the bumps and ridges as she went. "But I wouldn't care if you had a beer belly and saggy boobs. You'd still be the man I love."

She felt him tense up, and she prayed he wouldn't shut down on her.

"I love you," he whispered. "I have no idea how I got through each day of the last few years without you to look forward to coming home to. I promise I'll never give you a reason to doubt my love for you ever again. In the morning, we'll move your stuff into this room, and you'll sleep here, in my arms, our bed, every night going forward. Anything you want changed in the room, the house, the yard, we'll do. We'll get you a car, go shopping for clothes, upgrade the furniture if you want."

"Easy there, tiger," June said with a laugh. "I don't want or need anything."

"You have to want *something*," Cal said with a frown.

"I do. You," she said.

He stared at her for a beat before shaking his head. "Of all the women in the world, I managed to fall in love with the one who doesn't care one whit about my money."

"You could be broke, and I'd still be head over heels for you," she told him.

Amazingly, she felt her lust returning. She smiled down at him and moved so she was straddling his thighs. "You haven't let me taste you yet," she said, feeling her face warm with a blush.

"I'm always too desperate to get inside you," he replied. "And if I come in your mouth, I won't be able to get it up for a while to do just that."

"I'm sure you can get creative," she told him, moving backward.

"Feck." He gasped as she began to stroke his cock. "I'm putty in your hands," he told her. "You aren't disgusted with . . . I mean . . . I'm disfigured," he finished softly.

"Here?" she asked, licking him from base to tip. "Not as far as I'm concerned."

Cal shook his head in disbelief. "Perfect for me," he murmured.

"Yup. I am," June agreed happily, then lowered her head, determined to show her man what he'd been missing for the last week. She wanted to experience something she instinctively knew she'd never share with another man ever again.

Thirty minutes later, after they were once again sweaty and satisfied, June lay in Cal's arms, almost comatose. The week of worry had finally caught up with her, and she was half-asleep. This time, he'd gotten up after he'd given her another orgasm and covered them both with the comforter.

"June?" he said.

"Hmm?" she murmured.

"No more presents from other men."

She smiled against him. "I threw the brownies away."

"Good. Because you're mine. And I plan to give you so many gifts, you'll be buried in them."

She sighed. "You're going to go overboard, aren't you?"

"Definitely," he answered.

"All I want is you, Cal. You're the best present I've ever gotten."

She felt more than heard a low, satisfied rumble come from his chest. "Sleep, princess. Tomorrow's a new day. The start of the rest of our lives."

She liked that. A lot. Turning, she kissed his chest, right above his nipple, then lay her head back down. With his arm tight around her, his scent in her nostrils and all over her skin, she slept better than she had in a week, secure in the knowledge that everything was right in her world for once.

Chapter Twenty-One

June couldn't stop smiling. She literally couldn't. If she'd thought she was happy in the day or two after she and Cal had first made love, that was nothing compared to how she felt now. She had a job she absolutely adored and friends in April, Carlise, and even Meg. And a man who was attentive and considerate, who she loved with a passion that surprised her with its intensity. And, icing on the cake, he loved her back the same way.

There were times when June second-guessed what the hell she was doing. Cal was an honest-to-God *prince*. She'd heard him talking with his parents one night, and it hit home that if things truly did work out with them—which she'd fight to the death to make happen—at some point, she'd have to meet them. She'd have to go to Liechtenstein and attend the occasional formal function. The thought of doing either scared the crap out of her, but losing Cal frightened her more.

She could suck it up and go to one of his fancy balls, as long as he was by her side. And she had no reason to think Cal would be anywhere but. They'd been practically attached at the hip from the second she got off work in the afternoons until he dropped her off at Hill's House each morning.

It was probably good that she had a job to go to, because otherwise she and Cal would probably spend all their time in bed . . . which wasn't a bad thing, but he had a business to help run. One of the many things she loved about her man was that even though he had more money than he could spend, he still wanted to do his part for Jack's Lumber. And he hadn't once hinted that maybe she shouldn't work either.

Which was a relief because June loved Hill's House. The more time she spent there, the more she fell in love with all the residents. They were ornery, sometimes petulant, but they treated her as a friend, not as an employee or a second-class citizen like she'd been treated back in DC.

She had a soft spot for Banks. She never knew what the older man was going to say next. What stories he would make up about the things he'd done in his life. She took them all with a grain of salt, but he was so earnest about having met certain celebrities and whatnot, it was hard not to get swept up in his enthusiasm.

She hadn't seen much of Tim in the last week, but that wasn't too surprising, since he usually came into work around the time she was leaving. He *did* ask if she'd liked the brownies he'd made for her, and she'd politely told him she had. He'd given her a look she couldn't interpret but had no time to analyze, because Cal had arrived to pick her up, actually coming inside to say hello to the residents.

He'd put his arm around her shoulders, pulled her into his side, and made it very clear to Tim that if he had any ideas about hitting on her, they wouldn't be welcome.

It had been a blissful week since she and Cal had cleared the air, and now he was dropping June off at Hill's House once more.

"Three o'clock, right?" he asked, just like he did every morning.

"Yup," she said. "If our paper airplane tournament goes late, I'll call."

He chuckled. "Right."

"You have no idea how competitive everyone is. I swear Jara's become the worst of the bunch. Even worse than Banks. She threatened to cut the toes out of all of Scott's socks if he didn't stop trying to distract her while she was cutting out snowflakes the other day."

They'd had a competition to see who could make the "best" snowflake—and June quickly realized that being so vague with the parameters wasn't the smartest thing she'd ever done. In the end, she'd brought in Margaret and Austin to be judges—and had to cheat and quietly tell them whose snowflake was whose, so everyone won at least one of the categories she'd made up on the fly.

"I'm looking forward to sled day," Cal said with a smile.

"Another thing I'm sure I'll regret, but *everyone* is so looking forward to that." She'd gotten the idea after seeing a video online. The guys at Jack's Lumber had agreed to come to Hill's House with one of their four-wheelers to pull the residents behind it on a modified sled. It didn't matter that there wasn't any snow on the ground now. It was kind of insane and ridiculous, but when she'd suggested it, everyone had been so excited, there was no way she could deny them.

"We'll be careful. Won't go over like three miles an hour," he promised. "You being here is the highlight of their day, June," he said. "You know how I told you I was holding back because I wanted you to go out and change the world?"

June hated to think about that day, but she nodded anyway.

"You're doing it already. Changing the world right here in Newton. At Hill's House."

His words made her feel good. "Cal," she whispered, feeling overwhelmed.

He leaned over the console and put his hand on the back of her neck, pulling her toward him. She loved it when he did that. It was a possessive gesture, an alpha move, and it reminded her of how he was in bed . . . dominant and sure of himself.

He kissed her hard and only pulled back far enough to say, "Tonight, after dinner, I want to try out a new position. One I read about online."

"Okay," she said breathlessly.

"You don't want to know what it is?" he asked with a smile.

"Doesn't matter. I have no doubt you'll make it pleasurable for both of us."

"Damn straight I will." Cal took a deep breath as his hand slowly slid out from under her hair, and it took everything June had not to grab it and put it back on her nape.

"I thought I'd stop by with lunch . . . if you have time."

"I always have time for you," June said honestly. "Besides, Sofia will be thrilled to be able to ogle your body again."

He rolled his eyes. "She makes me nervous."

"She's harmless," June said with a giggle.

"Granny's Burgers?" he asked.

"Sounds awesome. Although I should probably get a salad," she said with a little frown.

"No. I love your curves—and apparently you'll need a reminder tonight of how much I love every inch of your body and never want you to change."

June smiled. It was hard to believe Cal didn't think she needed to lose weight. She did, and she was working on that, if only to be healthy and live a long, happy life at Cal's side. "Right. A burger, but no fries. I'll eat a side salad that Margaret will make."

"All right. Around twelve-thirty sound okay?"

"Perfect. I'll be able to take a half-hour break. You're finally having that meeting with April this morning about who's doing which upcoming hikes, right?" she asked.

Cal wrinkled his nose. "Yup."

"It won't be that bad," June said, patting his arm. "You said yourself that April is a natural at pairing up guides with guests."

"She is. I just don't like the thought of spending the night away from home. From you."

June just about melted into a puddle at the way he pouted the words.

"Me either. But I'll be fine. And think about how nice it'll be when you get home."

"Oh yeah . . . *nice*," Cal said with a smirk.

June rolled her eyes. "On that note, I'm getting out."

She opened the door of his Rolls and slipped out of the seat.

"June?"

She turned and saw Cal looking at her intensely. "Yeah?"

"I love you."

She smiled. "I love you too." He was being extra mushy today, and June couldn't get enough. Her dad had told her that he loved her all the time, and it had been years since she'd heard the words. Cal was usually all business when he dropped her off, telling her to have a good day and he'd see her later, his mind already on Jack's Lumber tasks. Perhaps he was feeling more emotional today because they'd actually made love this morning before showering. Whatever the reason, June wouldn't question it.

"See you later. Be safe."

She resisted the urge to roll her eyes again. As if there was anything to worry about around a bunch of seniors. "You too. Later."

She shut the door, gave Cal a little wave, then turned and started up the sidewalk toward the house. When Meg opened the door for her, June turned and waved at Cal once more. He was still sitting in his SUV at the curb, as he always did, waiting for her to get inside before he left.

He was protective, but not in an overbearing way. June blossomed under his care and love.

An hour later, her phone vibrated in her pocket, and when she had a break to check her messages between rounds of paper airplane throwing and refereeing the competitors, June smiled as she read a text from Cal.

He'd gotten her a phone a few days ago and made a big deal out of programming all their friends' names and numbers into it. He'd texted her on and off since, just letting her know he was thinking about her. It felt good not only to read his messages but just to have a phone again. It made her feel a little more independent.

Cal: Just wanted to let you know how beautiful you looked this morning. That white blouse brings out the gold in your eyes and those jeans highlight your arse in a way that makes me regret we both have to work.

June giggled out loud at the two dozen emojis he'd included at the end of the message, including several eggplants, smiley faces, and hearts.

"Another message from your man?" Banks asked.

"Yeah," June said, trying really hard to keep from blushing.

"In my day, we didn't have those fancy phones and messages. We had to write letters. I've lost the ones I got from all my women, but they definitely got my motor running, if you know what I mean."

June shook her head at him and grinned. Banks had told her more than once how popular he'd been with the ladies. He'd never married—claimed he couldn't settle down with just one.

"Whatever, Banks. Are you done with your second plane?"

"Yup. I'm ready to kick some booty."

Making a mental note to respond to Cal's text later with a suggestive one of her own, she turned her attention to the task at hand, making sure no one cheated as they tried to improve their paper airplane designs.

∾

Tim's hands shook slightly as he paced his room, wishing he had some weed to take the edge off his current shitty mood. He'd been sending Elaine all sorts of "evidence" of stalking the mousy bitch he was officially sick of hearing about, but she'd stopped sending him money through the app four days ago. He wasn't sure if she didn't believe him anymore, or if she was out of money, or if she was simply trying to get him to hurry up and get rid of her stepdaughter once and for all, deciding not to pay him for any more little shit.

Whatever the reason, Tim was done. He was sick of being in this fucking town, sick of mopping floors at Hill's House, and *very* sick of cleaning up after old people. It was time to make his move.

Juniper would be dead before the end of the day—and he'd be gone. He'd go back to DC and collect his money personally. And if Elaine didn't want to pay up, he'd threaten her spoiled bitch of a daughter for real. The old hag doted on Carla—and he'd turn into their worst fucking nightmare if she didn't live up to her end of the bargain.

He had an ace in his pocket. The fact that she'd offed her second husband. If she didn't pony up his ten grand, he'd play that damn card—by making sure the recordings of their conversations made it into the right hands.

The woman was so dumb. No *way* would he have taken this job without covering his own ass. Yes, those recordings would incriminate him as well, but if he had to go down, he'd take that bitch with him.

But it wouldn't come to that. Elaine would never give up her cushy lifestyle. One listen to that particular conversation about murdering her husband and he'd have the dumb cunt right where he wanted her. Maybe he'd hold it over her head for years to come. She'd pay him to keep quiet, otherwise she'd join him behind bars.

Looking around the shitty room, Tim made sure he'd packed everything. He'd sneak into Hill's House when he wasn't expected, shoot the bitch, and leave while everyone was freaking out and panicking.

Easy peasy.

Soon, he'd be ten thousand dollars richer, Elaine would be done with the stepdaughter she hated so much, her daughter could cry in the arms of the prince—super unlikely, but Tim would let Elaine enjoy her delusions—and he'd be back in DC, making plans to head south to a warmer climate.

June laughed as quiet, soft-spoken Brenda threw her arms in the air and yelped in satisfaction when her plane outflew everyone else's by several feet.

"Woooo!" she exclaimed happily.

"How the heck did you do that?" Jeremy asked, sounding baffled.

"I was an engineer," Brenda said with a shrug. "I'm good at building stuff."

"Yes, you are," June told her with a huge smile. "And because you won, you get the first ride on the sled next week when Jack's Lumber comes."

Brenda grinned while Banks and the others grumbled.

June smiled at "her" residents. Everyone began to grab their planes, as it was getting close to lunchtime, so they needed to move the table back to its spot in the middle of the room and clean up their mess. She asked Banks to grab one bag of trash as she picked up the other. They walked into the kitchen, and Banks volunteered to take both bags outside to the bins on the other side of the garage.

June watched Banks for a minute, making sure he made it down the back steps safely. She took a quick drink from her water bottle and was headed for the broom closet in the hall when she heard someone call her name quietly.

Turning, she expected to see Banks.

Instead, she saw Tim entering the kitchen through the back door.

Instinctively looking down at her watch—which was silly, because she already knew it was nearly lunchtime—June saw it was twelve-fifteen. About three hours before Tim was supposed to be there.

"June," he said again, more forcefully.

She looked back up at him. "What are you doing—"

She didn't have a chance to get the last word out before a deafening bang echoed through the kitchen.

June stumbled backward as a pain like she'd never felt bloomed in her chest.

She lurched a second time when the same loud noise rang in her ears again, followed by more blinding pain in her chest.

Instinctively, she knew she had to get away. She staggered through the doorway to the dining room. She managed to stay on her feet long enough to see the shocked expressions of the residents before she tripped over her feet, or maybe it was simply that she didn't have the strength to stand anymore, and fell to the floor.

People were screaming all around her, but June couldn't do anything but stare up at the ceiling. Her hands went to her chest as she struggled to breathe. She vaguely wondered if this was how Cal felt when he was a POW. When his captors were cutting him.

"June!" Jara shouted as she knelt beside her.

Turning her head, June wanted to tell the old woman that she shouldn't be on the floor, that Austin would have to come and help her up, but no words left her lips, only a small groan.

"Oh, June!" Jara whimpered as she stared at her chest.

Lifting one of her hands, June frowned in confusion. It was covered in red paint. Who had brought the paint, and why was it on her hand?

"Pressure!" a male voice said urgently right before pain engulfed her once more. So much pain, June's vision went black for a moment.

People were still shouting all around her, but she couldn't make out what anyone was saying. The searing ache in her chest was too bad.

Then she saw Austin's face above hers. He was pressing down on her chest so hard, she couldn't breathe. "No," she whispered.

Austin didn't seem to hear her. He was yelling at someone else, telling them to call 9-1-1.

Then Meg's voice, shouting at someone from the direction of the kitchen.

"Is she going to die?" someone else cried.

"Not if I have anything to say about it," Austin said firmly. "You're not going to die," he told June. "You hear me?"

She did, but she didn't understand what was happening.

"Cal," she said . . . or at least she tried to, but no sound came out. She was hurt, confused, scared, and all she could think about was Cal. He'd make everything better. She had no doubt about that.

She coughed, and once more, pain shot through her.

"Shit, she's coughing up blood. Her lung was probably hit. Is the ambulance coming?" Austin asked someone frantically. "They need to get here *now*!"

Chapter Twenty-Two

Cal had just parked and was walking toward Hill's House when he heard a gunshot that was way too close to be anything other than trouble. They heard shots all the time from hunters while in the mountains, but this one wasn't coming from the woods.

Then it came again.

And it was coming from inside Hill's House.

Dropping the bag from Granny's Burgers, he ran toward the front door at an all-out sprint. He hit the door hard and grabbed the knob, but it didn't turn. Locked. He remembered then that Meg kept the house locked at all times for the safety of the residents.

He hit it hard with his fist but didn't wait for someone to open it for him. He could hear people screaming inside. Whatever was happening was bad and extremely chaotic.

Running around the house, Cal prayed the kitchen door would be unlocked. He knew from what June had told him in the past that Margaret didn't always lock the door because she liked to open it when she was cooking to air out the kitchen.

He vaguely noted a bag of trash lying on the ground near the garage but ignored it. Relieved when he saw the screen door, Cal wrenched it open and ran inside.

A man was lying on the kitchen floor with blood pouring out of his nose, and it looked like he was out cold. Meg was standing over him, pointing a gun at his head. Scott was standing beside the entry between the kitchen and the dining room, while Jeremy and Sofia were just inside the dining room, both holding what looked like lacrosse sticks and appearing more than ready to beat the crap out of the man on the ground if he so much as moved.

Banks was sitting in a chair at the dining room table looking shell shocked, his knuckles bleeding slightly. Brenda was on the phone, and Jara was on her knees on the floor next to Austin, who was kneeling over someone.

It took him a moment to understand what he was seeing.

Austin was hovering over June.

She was covered in blood. So much blood, it was obscene.

The floor under her was a puddle that was growing larger even as he stood there and watched. Her white blouse was awash in red.

Scenes from when he was in the Army flashed through his head. Of civilians who'd been shot and had bled out before help could arrive. Of servicemen and women who'd been caught in an IED blast and had limbs blown off.

For a moment he was frozen. Caught between the past and present.

"I'm calling JJ," Brenda said. "The police and ambulance are on their way."

Her words brought Cal back to the moment. He ran toward June, lying so still and pale on the floor. He slipped in her blood but didn't even feel the pain as his knees hit the wooden planks beneath him.

Without thought, he stripped off his shirt, wadding it up and shoving Austin's hands out of the way before pressing it to the wounds on June's chest.

He heard a gasp of surprise from Jara and knew what it was about, but he ignored her. The last thing he was worried about right now was other people's reactions to seeing his mangled flesh. All he cared about was the woman bleeding on the floor.

"June?!" he said in disbelief.

Her eyes opened, and Cal felt light headed with relief.

But it was short lived as Austin said, "Keep the pressure on or she'll bleed out. I need to go get my medical bag. I'll be right back."

The thought of watching the woman he loved more than life die was too much to bear.

"Hi," June said faintly as she stared up at him. Then her eyes closed once more.

"No!" he yelled in a panic. "Don't close your eyes. Look at me, June. Right now!"

To his relief, she opened her eyes once more. Her lips moved, but he couldn't hear what she said.

"What?" he asked, moving his head toward her lips so he could hear her better.

"Hurts," she whispered.

"I know, princess. I'm so sorry. But help is coming. Hear me?"

She stared up at him with a blank look.

He was losing her.

Instinctively, Cal knew she was dying, and he'd never felt as much agonizing pain as he did now. Even when the arseholes were cutting him to ribbons, he hadn't hurt half as much as he did at that moment.

"You know what Carlise told me today? I saw her before I left to get us lunch. She was there to see Chappy. She laughed and told me she was right, that she knew I'd find my Cinderella—and I did. I love you, June. You can't leave me!"

"My prince," she said, then coughed. Blood sprayed from her lips, and Cal winced. Her eyes went to her own chest, where he was still putting as much pressure as he dared on her wounds. "Scar . . ."

"We'll get a plastic surgeon to fix it, so you'll never know anything happened," Cal told her. "I don't care about a bloody scar. It doesn't change anything between us."

But she shook her head. "Now . . . now you . . . know . . . how I feel about you," she managed to get out, her words labored.

It hit Cal like a freight train. Exactly how stupid he'd been—and not just with June. Of *course*, she didn't care if she had a scar. Just as she didn't care about his imperfections. Or his money. Or his title. She loved him exactly how he was.

But he'd fought with himself for so long. Kneeling here, with her life literally in his hands, he finally understood what June had always insisted. What his friends had tried to tell him for years. What his parents had told him. What the therapists he'd gone to had claimed.

The scars didn't define who he was. They told a story about what he'd survived. That was it. No more, no less. And if someone treated him differently because of them, that was their issue, not his.

June's eyes closed again, and his panic reared up once more. He leaned down and practically yelled in her face. "Open your eyes!"

They popped open immediately. Cal could see the pain there. The absolute agony. He literally saw her life slipping away, and his own eyes filled with tears. He hadn't cried in years. Probably a decade or more, but he couldn't stop himself from doing so right now if his life depended on it.

"You hang on, June. Hear me? Do *not* give up. I don't care what kind of lights you see, you turn away. Come back to me. I can't live without you! I just found you, and I can't lose you now. Fight for me, princess, understand? No matter what, you *fight*. I did, and now you can as well."

"Cal," she said. It was more a movement of her lips than an actual sound, but he understood.

"I've waited my entire life for you. We have so much to live for. Marriage. Babies. Love. *Do not leave me.* Please, I need you so bloody much!"

She nodded once, then her eyes closed again.

"June!" Cal shouted. But her eyes didn't open. "June! Wake up. Stay with me!"

"Move aside, sir," a woman said as she knelt next to him. She forcibly moved his hands and peered under the bloody T-shirt balled up on June's chest before pressing it back down again and turning to her partner. "Load and go," she ordered. "Get the gurney over here."

Cal hadn't heard the EMTs arrive, but now that they had, the room seemed full of people. There was Chief Rutkey, some of his officers, and even all three of his friends.

JJ took his arm and pulled him to his feet, towing him off to the side. Cal fought him viciously for a moment before Chappy took hold of his other arm.

"Let them help her," he said firmly.

Tears still rolled down Cal's face as he watched the EMTs fasten restraints around June's legs and hips before rushing her toward the front door.

He tried to follow, not wanting to let June out of his sight, but JJ and Chappy held on firmly.

"Let me go. I need to go with her!"

"You can't. We'll take you to the hospital. Calm down, Cal," Bob ordered.

But he couldn't. This might be the last time he saw June—he couldn't let her go.

"I mean it," Bob said more forcefully, getting up in his face. "You aren't going to do her any good getting arrested. She's in the best hands she can be in right now. Chill the hell out."

Looking down, Cal saw his hands were covered in blood. June's blood.

She couldn't die. She was too big a force in his life. His light. He needed her. He was a better person with her.

Without her, he was nothing.

"What the hell happened?" JJ asked, keeping a firm grip on Cal.

"He just came in and shot her," Brenda said, her voice trembling.

Turning, Cal saw she was as white as a sheet.

"Tim. We didn't see it, we just heard the shots. He shot her in the kitchen. She stumbled in here and Banks . . . Lord love a duck, I didn't believe him when he said he was a boxer! We all thought he was making it up. But he was faster than I've ever seen him move. Flew back into the kitchen from the yard and knocked Tim out with one punch!" Brenda's hand shook violently as she placed it over her heart. "He fell right to the floor. Then Meg grabbed the gun in case he came to, and the others grabbed the lacrosse sticks we were going to use this afternoon for some game June was going to show us . . ."

Brenda started crying then, and Cal's attention shifted to the police chief, who was handcuffing a groggy Tim.

He lunged in their direction, but once again his friends held him fast.

"*No.* June needs you. Alfred will deal with him. You need to concentrate on June, not on kicking his ass," JJ said.

It was the hardest thing Cal had ever done. He wanted to kill the son of a bitch for hurting his woman, but JJ was right. June needed him.

"Let's get to the hospital," JJ said.

"They're going to airlift her to Portland," Austin interjected. He looked as pale as Brenda and was covered in just as much blood as Cal.

"Thank you," he whispered. "If you weren't here . . ."

"I didn't do much. Not enough. Thank God Newton is so small and the EMTs got here so fast."

Austin might not think he'd done much, but his fast action of putting pressure on the bullet holes in June's chest could have potentially saved her life.

"Come on, we need to get to Portland," Chappy said, pulling Cal toward the front door. He let himself be led like a child. At the moment, he couldn't think. Couldn't make any decisions. He felt numb. Lost.

He and his friends were well aware how deadly bullets could be. And June had been shot in the chest—twice. It would be a miracle if she survived. And Cal desperately needed that miracle.

"The Rolls," he managed to say as his friends practically held him upright. "It's the fastest."

"I'm driving," Bob said. "You guys get in the back with him."

"We should stop and get him a shirt," Chappy said. "Let him clean up."

"No! We need to get to the hospital!" Cal swore, struggling anew in his friends' grasp.

"All right, calm down, Cal. We're going."

Cal sagged again. He felt as if his head was in a fog. All he could think about was getting to June's side.

Cal stared into space in the small private waiting room they'd been led to upon arriving at the level-one trauma center in Portland. It took way too long to get there, even with how fast Bob drove. He'd wanted to see June as soon as they arrived but was informed that she was already in surgery.

Someone had found a scrubs top for him to wear, and JJ marched him into the bathroom and made him wash his hands. As the red water swirled down the drain, Cal started crying again. He didn't make a sound, but the tears fell unchecked.

He couldn't fix this. No amount of money, no family connections, no royal edict . . . nothing he had to offer could make June whole again. He had to rely on the skills of the surgeons currently trying to put the love of his life back together.

Waiting was the worst part. The not knowing. All the what-ifs that ran through Cal's head. What if he'd left work five minutes earlier? What if he'd skipped Granny's Burgers and gone straight to Hill's House?

What if, what if, what if . . .

Cal didn't know how long he'd been in the waiting room when April sat beside him, holding out his phone. He stared at it, wondering where the hell she'd gotten it, why she even had it. Hell, he didn't even know when she and Carlise had arrived.

He was surrounded by the best friends he'd ever had, and he still felt so damn alone.

"It's your mom," April said gently, as she nodded toward the cell.

The tears, which had finally dried up, started once more. He took the phone and brought it up to his ear. April didn't leave his side, putting her hand on his knee and squeezing hard. Carlise sat on his other side, putting her arm around his shoulders.

"Mom . . . ," he choked out when he could finally speak.

"Oh, son. I heard what happened. I'm so sorry. What do you need?"

"I need her to live," Cal sobbed. "I love her so much, Mom. She's the best thing that ever happened to me, and if she dies . . . I don't know what I'll do!"

"We're on our way," his mom told him, and fresh tears rolled down Cal's face. "Your father has already called the pilot, and they're readying the jet. We'll be there as soon as we can. What else can we do?"

"The man who did this, Tim Dotson—I need to know why." He closed his eyes briefly, his voice lower when he continued. "The police here are good, but if you can use any of your connections to figure this out . . . to make sure June isn't in any more danger . . ."

"We're already moving on that," his mom reassured him.

"I can't lose her," Cal said again with a sob. "This hurts so much more than when I was tortured. I'd do anything to trade places. She shouldn't have to go through this. She's the light to my dark. She's so good, Mom."

"Oh, my love . . ."

He and his mom cried together for a long moment before she cleared her throat. "I'm coming, son. I can't wait to meet her. Have faith, you hear me? If this woman loves you as much as you love her, she's going to hang on. She's going to pull through. I know it."

"I hope so," Cal told her.

"I *know* so. We'll be there as soon as we can. I love you."

"Love you too, Mom."

He clicked off the phone and dropped his chin to his chest.

"Tim's singing like a canary," JJ said quietly as he entered the room.

Cal wiped his cheek with his shoulder as he looked up at his friend. It was almost weird how dissociated he felt. He wanted to know why this happened, why Tim had shot June, especially when she'd never been anything but nice to the man. But at the moment, all his energy was going toward praying for his woman. It's why he'd asked his mom to look into things. His parents would do whatever it took to make sure June was safe from anyone who meant her harm.

"Claims he was acting on orders from her stepmother," JJ said.

Cal shut his eyes.

Jesus. He'd fucked up. He hadn't taken Carla's obsession with marrying him seriously enough. Not nearly. Had assumed once they'd left town, she'd move on. Find another mark.

He should've known better.

"Not only that, but you were right about your suspicions. He's claiming Elaine killed her second husband, June's dad. Poisoned him. Says he has a recording of the conversation when she told him. She's going down," JJ said firmly. "No matter what I have to do, what markers I have to call in, she and that bitch daughter are *both* going down."

Cal nodded. He was glad to have his friends at his back.

"Any word about June?" JJ asked.

"I'll go ask again," April said, patting Cal's knee as she stood.

As more time passed, Cal tuned out everything around him. His head felt like it was stuffed with cotton. As if he was watching himself from high above.

Two hours later, the door to the waiting room opened, and six pairs of eyes lifted to the exhausted-looking surgeon standing in the doorway.

"Friends and family of Juniper Rose?" she asked.

Cal stood, swaying on his feet. He tried to read what the surgeon was about to tell them from her expression, but she'd clearly been doing this far too long to give away any hints to worried loved ones.

"How is she?" Cal almost shouted.

"She's stable. It was touch and go for a while, and we lost her twice on the table, but she's a fighter. She's in the ICU, so you won't be able to see her for at least twelve hours as we continue to monitor her progress. But in my professional opinion, she's going to pull through."

Cal's knees gave out, and he landed hard in the seat behind him. He closed his eyes and lowered his head. No tears fell now—he was all cried out. But he'd never been so relieved to hear anything in all his life. Not even when he and his team realized the sounds they heard from their cell were their rescue party coming for them, mowing down anyone who stood in their way.

He vaguely heard the doctor explaining that the first bullet had gone straight through her right lung, and the second had missed her heart by less than a centimeter. Her heart had stopped twice while they were operating to repair the damage, but they'd been able to get it started again.

June had done what he'd begged her to do. She'd fought. Was *still* fighting. She hadn't left him.

He'd never been so grateful that his woman was so tough. Cal wasn't happy that he couldn't see her for a long while yet, but for the first time in hours, he felt as if he could breathe.

He'd make sure a day never went by without June knowing how much he loved her. They'd had a way too close call today, and he was more appreciative than he could put into words that he had a second chance with her. To live. To love.

Chapter Twenty-Three

"I'm not going to break, Cal," June complained.

"Humor me," Cal said adamantly. The last two weeks had been exceedingly difficult. Seeing her in the ICU, hooked up to so many machines with bandages on her chest, had been almost as bad as seeing her lying on the dining room floor of Hill's House covered in blood.

Almost.

He'd been at the hospital every day, sitting with her, entertaining her, keeping her calm when the pain was overwhelming, and generally trying to be her rock.

She was going home today, and Cal was excited and terrified at the same time. He'd wanted her to stay longer, to make sure she was completely healed, because he was paranoid of her moving the wrong way and tearing something inside that the doctor had expertly stitched together.

But June was more than ready to leave, and she hadn't been quiet about it.

He'd backed up the nurse's insistence that they use a wheelchair to get her to the car, and now he carefully settled her in the Rolls. When they began the long drive to Newton, she fell asleep almost immediately. Cal couldn't help but keep looking over at her. She was a miracle. *His* miracle. She shouldn't have survived being shot twice in the chest, and yet, here she was.

She napped for about an hour and a half and woke up when they had about an hour left to go.

"Cal?"

"Yeah, princess?"

"I love you."

Cal smiled. "I love you too."

"I heard you, you know," she said quietly.

"What did you hear, and when?" he asked.

"You were yelling at me. Telling me not to go, that you couldn't live without me. I told you that I was tired, and I hurt, but you told me I had to fight. Not to go toward the light. But . . ."

Cal stiffened, unsure he wanted to know what followed that "but."

"I saw my dad," she whispered. "He looked amazing. Exactly like I remembered. He smiled at me, and when I reached for him, he shook his head and stepped back. Told me he was just there to see me, but it wasn't time for us to be reunited. That I had to go back. You needed me."

Cal had cried more in the last two weeks than he had in his entire life, and he found his eyes once more filling with tears. He pulled over to the side of the road so he wouldn't wreck. He turned toward June.

"You told me to fight, so I did," June said calmly.

Cal palmed her cheek and closed his eyes for a moment. He felt her fingers wiping away the tears that had fallen. He turned his head and kissed her palm, then looked into her eyes. "You're the best thing that's ever happened to me. Thank you for coming back to me."

"Were you serious—"

"Yes."

She grinned. "You have no idea what I'm even asking about," she complained.

Cal shrugged. "If I said it, I was serious."

"About kids. A family."

"Absolutely."

"Good," June said with a small smile as she rested her head against the seat behind her. "Because I want two."

"Boys or girls?" Cal asked fondly.

"Doesn't matter."

He didn't think his love for this woman could get any bigger, but she'd just proved him wrong.

She studied her left hand, and her lips quirked. "I still can't believe we're married," she breathed.

Cal picked up her hand and kissed the ring he'd put on her finger a week ago. Once she'd woken up in the hospital and was cognizant, he proposed, she said yes, and he'd promptly brought in someone who could marry them immediately.

"Your parents were really good about everything."

Cal nodded. They were. His parents had shown up at the hospital as promised, and Cal had cried in his mother's arms as if he was a boy again.

He hadn't cried when she'd flown to Germany to see him in the military hospital. He hadn't cried when he'd seen himself in a mirror for the first time after his rescue. But seeing his mom when he'd just experienced the scariest thing he could imagine—almost losing the woman he loved—had been too much.

He wasn't surprised when she and June got on as if they'd known each other their entire lives. Even lying in a bed, doped up on painkillers, June had his mom wrapped around her finger within minutes of meeting her when she asked how their flight had been, if they had gotten any sleep, and if she was hungry.

His June, always worried about other people.

As for his father, he'd just given Cal a knowing grin and said when it came to love, he'd always suspected the apple didn't fall far from the tree.

His parents had given their blessing to marry and told him they'd make sure June was added to the royal family tree. Though his mother *had* warned him that, while she and his father didn't care if he and June had a laid-back civil ceremony, the people of Liechtenstein would expect some sort of public celebration of their marriage, if not a second ceremony in their homeland.

"They loved you," Cal told June.

"And I really liked them. You look just like your dad."

Cal smiled, leaned over, and kissed her gently before getting back on the road.

"Will you talk to me about what's going on with Tim?" she asked quietly.

Cal sighed. He hadn't wanted to mar the day with talk about the man who'd tried to murder her, but she had a right to know.

"He spilled his guts about everything," Cal told her. "You already know that Elaine and Carla hired him to stalk you. They had some warped idea that if there was proof of a stalker, I'd somehow go back to DC or something. Honestly, their plan seemed confusing and sense-less. Regardless, we know they were paying him to stalk you—to leave threatening notes, dead animals, things like that—to punish you for 'stealing' me."

"But he didn't," June said with a frown.

"Yeah, he was conning her. And Elaine was so gullible, she paid him every time he sent her a picture of a note on a door or whatever. The cops have the photos and proof of the money transfers, implicating Elaine without any doubt. His plan all along was to kill you for a big payout Elaine promised. He was just biding his time, milking her."

Cal's jaw clenched as anger filled him. "Another reason he didn't carry out his end of the bargain was to avoid putting you, and me, on guard. It would've been harder to get to you if we were constantly on alert."

"It worked. He was able to simply walk into Hill's House and shoot me," June said.

Cal shivered. "Yeah."

"So he's in prison? And will stay there?"

"Yes," Cal said, not mentioning the markers he and the rest of his team had pulled to make sure Tim wasn't living a quiet life behind bars. And if he eventually got out . . . he'd still not find any peace.

"And my stepmother? Carla?"

"You remember what we talked about in the hospital?" Cal asked gently.

She nodded. "Yeah. She killed my dad," June said flatly.

He sighed. "It's looking that way, yes. The detectives in DC are moving forward with exhuming your dad's body to test for poison. Even though Tim's an arsehole, he was smart enough to record their calls. Including the one where she admitted killing your dad with succinylcholine. She even suggested he do the same to you. Poison you, that is.

"And you were right to throw those brownies away. He took a page from Carla's book and laced them with enough synthetic drugs that it's possible, depending on how many you ate, they could've killed you."

June pressed her lips together. "Yeah."

"Anyway, there's a lot of evidence against Elaine. Carla? Not so much. Everyone believes she knew what was happening, that she agreed to her mom's plan, but without proof that she actually did anything wrong, she probably won't get charged," Cal told her.

June simply shrugged. "Karma will have her way."

She wasn't wrong. From what Cal understood from talking to JJ, thanks to the news coverage surrounding the events, June's stepsister had been dropped by her agent, abandoned by her so-called friends, and was essentially on her own.

And their former SEAL friend, Tex, the tech genius who'd hacked her computer for Cal, had made good use of some of Carla's webcam videos, the ones where she took her clothes off for money . . . and more. While none of the videos were illegal, she was currently in trouble for tax evasion, since she hadn't reported any of the money she'd made. He'd also ensured she'd been blacklisted, and no legitimate modeling agency would touch her with a ten-foot pole.

"I'm sorry about the house," Cal said gently. "Even though DC law enforcement now believes you were tricked into signing the papers that gave the house and your dad's insurance to Elaine, you were eighteen, technically an adult, and it was your signature."

"I know. And you know what . . . it's okay. I don't ever want to go back, and I've got the memories of my dad and me being happy there before he married Elaine."

Cal squeezed her hand tightly.

She smiled over at him. "Enough about that. But you'll keep me up to date on what's going on with their trials and stuff?"

"Of course. Do you want to go?"

June thought about it for a moment, then shook her head. "I don't think so. I just want to move on with my life. With you."

Cal was relieved with her decision. He didn't want her to have to relive any of the torment she'd been through with her stepmother, in front of a judge and jury, or talk about that awful day she'd almost died.

"I love you," Cal said. He couldn't count the number of times he'd told her that over the last two weeks.

"I love you too," she returned, as she always did.

The rest of the drive to Newton was uneventful, but instead of heading for his house, he turned toward town. "Do you mind if we make a quick stop before going home?" he asked.

"Of course not."

Doing his best to hide his smile—he knew she'd say that, had counted on it actually—Cal parked in a convenient spot right in front of Granny's Burgers. He jogged around the car to open the door for June and wrapped an arm around her waist as he led her toward the restaurant.

Knowing what was on the other side of the door, Cal finally let his smile loose as he pulled it open and urged June to walk ahead of him.

"Welcome home!" the more than two dozen people inside yelled as soon as she walked in.

June blinked in surprise at seeing all their friends, then immediately turned and buried her face in Cal's chest. He wrapped his arms around her, holding her tightly as she did her best to gain control over her emotions.

She soon lifted her head and stared at him. "You did this, didn't you?" she asked.

Cal shrugged. "Not really. Everyone wanted to do something for you, let you know how happy and relieved they are that you're one tough chick. They all wanted to see you, and it just made sense to have a welcome home party."

"I love you," she whispered.

"And I love you," he returned, wiping her tears from her cheeks. "You good now?"

She nodded.

"Don't overdo it. I'll be watching, and when I think you've had enough, we're leaving. And no amount of pleading or puppy-dog eyes or pouts will change my mind," he warned.

June smiled. "Okay."

"Okay," he echoed. Then he turned her to face everyone who was patiently waiting for her to regain her composure.

An hour later, June glanced around at everyone in the restaurant, still in awe that they'd all come for *her*. The woman who hadn't had a real friend in more years than she could count. Of course, JJ, Bob, Chappy, Carlise, and April were there. But all of the Hill's House residents and employees had shown up as well. And Chief Rutkey. And the EMTs who'd worked on her that awful day.

She even saw Cal's mom and dad standing against a wall, taking in the scene and smiling. Not only that, but several residents of Newton whom she'd met in passing—waved and smiled at but had barely spoken to—were there as well.

The last two weeks had sucked—but she was alive, she was married to the man she loved more than life itself, and she was determined to put the past behind her. It was hard to wrap her head around the fact that her stepmother had put out a *hit* on her and that she'd actually been shot—twice. But it *had* happened, and she was moving on.

She wasn't surprised when she learned she'd technically died twice on the operating table. She'd told Cal about seeing her dad during one of those times . . . but she hadn't yet told him what happened the other time. She'd share it with him one day, when the time was right.

She'd seen a bright white light . . . and she was drawn toward it. The pain had disappeared, and she felt lighter than air. Happy. Peaceful. Calm. But then she remembered a voice, almost like an echo. Cal's voice, telling her that he couldn't live without her. Ordering her to fight.

She didn't want to at the time. Had known if she ignored the light, she'd have to go back and feel the pain.

Then she'd seen a woman—someone she only knew from pictures. Her mom.

She'd smiled so lovingly at June. Told her she was beautiful . . . how happy she was to see her. June had stepped toward her, but the woman held up a hand. "It's not your time, love," she'd said. "Your man needs you."

"But I want to be with you, Mom," June had begged.

"I know, and you will. One day. But today is not that day. You need to go back to him. Your two little girls need you to return. They're going to do amazing things. Things you can't even imagine. They're going to be important not only to you and their father but to all of mankind."

"They are?" June had asked, mystified.

"Yes. You're an amazing woman, June—and I'm so proud of you."

Then she'd faded away, and the pain had returned full force.

June recalled their conversation as if it was yesterday. Children with Cal would be a dream come true, but knowing that their kids would grow up to do something important for the world was something she was still trying to fathom.

"Hey," Banks said as he walked up to the table where June was sitting.

"We'll talk more later," Granny said, hugging June before leaving her with the man.

"Banks," June said, tears springing to her eyes. She cried at the drop of a hat lately, but since no one seemed to mind, she tried not to worry too much about it.

She hugged the older man as tightly as she could, which wasn't very tight. Too much movement caused her chest to twinge with pain, but she didn't care. She'd deal with the consequences for now and take a pain pill later.

"I heard what you did," June said when she pulled back. "I guess you weren't lying about that boxing championship thing, huh?" she teased.

Banks chuckled. "Nope."

"I can't believe you just went up to a man with a gun, who obviously wasn't afraid to use it, and punched him."

Banks shrugged. "He wasn't interested in shooting me. He was focused completely on you." His voice lowered. "He was going to shoot you again. I couldn't let that happen, June."

She blinked in surprise. She hadn't heard that before. If Tim had shot her a third time, it was likely she wouldn't have survived.

"You knocked him out. With *one punch*," she choked out. "You're my hero, Banks. I mean it."

She wasn't surprised when he shrugged off her words. "Anyone would've done it."

"But anyone didn't. *You* did," June told him.

Banks refused to let her linger on what he'd done. "At least those lacrosse sticks came in handy for more than throwing a ball of paper around," he joked. "I wish you could've seen those guys holding 'em like clubs, ready to smack Tim if he dared get up."

June smiled fondly. She wished she could've seen that as well. She'd gotten the lacrosse idea from her stay in the hotel with Cal, after they'd fled DC.

She was proud of her Hill's House family. From what she'd heard, every single one of them had done their part in taking control of the horrible situation.

"When are you coming back?" Banks asked. "Because I have to say, things are fairly boring. We miss your activities. And Brenda keeps talking about being first to take a ride on the sled."

"She'll be back as soon as she's healed up enough," Cal said from behind her.

Tilting her head back, June smiled up at her husband.

"It's time to head home," he said gently.

She frowned. "So soon?"

"It's been an hour, princess. You're tired, and I need to get a pain pill in you because you've been frowning a lot."

He wasn't wrong. June had tried to hide the pain she was in because she was having too much fun talking with their friends, but, of course, Cal would notice.

"Oh, all right," she whined.

Banks laughed. Cal helped her to her feet and wrapped a firm arm around her waist once more. It took a long time to get to the door, as they had to stop and say goodbye to everyone they passed. They all told her again how relieved and happy they were that she was all right. By the time Cal got her into the front seat of his SUV, she was half-asleep.

"I can't believe your parents are back already," she told him once they were on the way to his house.

"They wouldn't have missed your homecoming for anything."

"Your mom talked to me tonight about visiting Liechtenstein," she said.

"Bloody hell," Cal swore.

June smiled. "Honestly? It scares me to death. Meeting your people, the king and queen, and being in the spotlight like that. But with you by my side, I can do it."

"Of course, you can," Cal said immediately. "You can do anything. But don't let my mom run roughshod over you. She's used to getting her way. If you don't want to do the vow renewal ceremony, we won't do it."

June stared over at him. "Honestly . . . ?" She let her voice trail off.

"Yeah?" he asked when she didn't respond.

"I've always loved the movie *Cinderella*. The most recent one. Where she wore that blue dress? I mean, I don't have near her body type, but I've always dreamt about wearing something like that and dancing with my own Prince Charming."

The look of love in Cal's eyes as he glanced at her made June want to pinch herself all over again.

"Then that's what you'll have. And your body is perfect, princess. You're *my* Cinderella. My beautiful princess. We'll go to Liechtenstein, have a ceremony for the press and my people, then we'll come home and settle back into our boring life here in Maine."

"That sounds like a dream come true. Although I'm thinking once our kids arrive, it won't be so boring."

"Very true," he said with a small smile. "But no baby making for a while . . . not until the doctor gives the okay."

"Darn it," June said with a mock pout.

Truthfully, she wasn't anywhere near ready for Cal's brand of lovemaking yet, but she'd heal. She'd already stopped taking her birth control pills, because it wasn't as if she was even thinking of them her first several days in the hospital.

She didn't know what Cal's timetable for having a baby might be, but she was more than ready to get on with the rest of her life . . . with Cal and their family.

Epilogue

The second the door shut behind them, Cal let out a whoosh of air when June practically tackled him. She pushed him against the wall, then used her hands to desperately shove his T-shirt up his chest.

It had been a long, frustrating two months for both of them since she'd been shot, and they'd just gotten back from the doctor. He'd finally given June the go-ahead to return to all normal activities. Work, exercise—and sex.

Cal had planned a romantic evening, with a nice dinner, a massage, and maybe a bath, then slow, tender lovemaking. But it looked like his wife had other ideas.

He chuckled as she growled when he didn't move fast enough for her liking, but the laugh was cut off when she got his shirt off, then went to her knees and fumbled with his belt.

"Easy, princess," he murmured.

"I want you, Cal. And you've been so stubborn," she complained. "I told you over and over that I was fine, that you wouldn't hurt me, but you wouldn't let me do *anything*."

A groan left his mouth as she got his jeans undone and shoved them down his hips, along with his boxers, and practically swallowed him whole.

He fisted her hair and watched as she sucked his cock deep into her mouth. She made a satisfied noise in the back of her throat when he immediately began to harden. The humming sound only stimulated him more. Cal had jacked off in the shower more in the last month than he had in his entire life. Holding back from his wife had been torture, but he'd refused to do anything that might hinder her recovery.

June's head bobbed up and down on his cock as she slurped and sucked him. Her gaze moved upward, and he couldn't take his eyes from hers as she gave him the best blow job he'd ever had.

"I want all of you," she said, taking her mouth off him long enough to speak. Her hand continued stroking him, keeping him primed as he leaned against the wall for support.

"Yes," he breathed.

The satisfied smile on her face was worth every penny he had in the bank. She lowered her head again and went to work bringing him pleasure. Even though he'd masturbated just that morning, Cal found himself on the edge way too soon. He couldn't hold back, not with the sight of her lips stretched over him and the way she caressed his bollocks as she took him deep into her mouth.

"I'm going to come!" he warned. This was the first time he'd ever let her finish him like this. But from here on out, anything his wife wanted, she'd get. Besides, coming now would hopefully make him last longer later, so he could worship her well into the night without worrying about coming prematurely.

In response, she sucked harder, her cheeks hollowing as she did so. Kneeling at his feet, fully dressed, so needy for him that she couldn't even wait for them to get to their bed . . . it was all so carnal, so erotic, Cal couldn't wait any longer.

A burst of come left his cock, and then he let go fully. He came so hard and so long that June couldn't take all of him. She swallowed twice, then pulled her head back as he continued to shoot ropes of come from his dick. His essence splashed onto her neck and chin, and he watched, entranced, as she used her hand to squeeze out every last drop.

When she looked up at him with such pride and lust, it was all Cal could do not to push her onto her back right there in the foyer and take her. He reached out and wiped some of his come off her cheek, then held his hand to her mouth. She opened for him, sucking his finger in deep, running her tongue around the digit as if it was a mini cock.

That was it. Cal was done. He toed off his shoes, chucked his pants and underwear, then, naked as the day he was born and not for one second feeling self-conscious about his scars, he reached down and hauled June to her feet. He swung her into his arms and headed for the stairs.

June latched onto his neck, licking and sucking, marking him as she went. He dropped her feet when they arrived next to their bed. "Clothes. Off," he ordered gruffly.

With a huge smile, June complied, and was soon just as naked as he was.

Cal pushed her onto the bed and immediately settled over her once she was on her back. He ran a finger over the long scar on her chest, where the surgeon had opened her up to save her life.

"You're so beautiful." He looked into her eyes. "It took me a long time, but I finally understand."

"Understand what?" June asked, holding onto his arms tightly as he hovered over her.

"That scars aren't ugly. They're just a road map to our past. They tell others what we've survived. And we're both survivors, you and I," he told her. "We've been to hell and back, but nothing could keep us from finding each other."

"I love you," she whispered.

"And I love you," he returned.

"Will you shut up and make love to your wife already?" she pleaded.

Cal smiled. "Yes, ma'am."

"Good. Oh, and one more thing," she said with a sly grin.

"I thought you wanted me to shut up and get on with it," he teased.

"I asked the doc something while you were getting the car."

When she didn't continue, Cal raised a brow in question.

"I wanted to make sure it was okay if I got pregnant. That our baby wouldn't be in danger or anything. That I could deliver naturally without any problems from the surgery."

Cal froze. "And?"

"He said yes. That I was completely healed, and he didn't think there would be any complications whatsoever. And you know that I haven't been taking my pill for a while now, so . . ." She grinned again as her words faded.

Cal couldn't think. He was dumbstruck. Of course, he knew she hadn't been taking precautions against pregnancy while she was healing, but for some reason, he hadn't given thought to what that meant once she was cleared for normal activities.

"I want your baby, Cal," she whispered. "Today. Right now."

He'd intended to go down on her. To worship every inch of her body. To show her how much he loved her. How he couldn't live without her. But now, all he could think about was getting inside her and filling her with his come, over and over again, until he knocked her up.

His cock hardened almost painfully, and he grunted like an animal as he moved into position, pushing her thighs apart and notching the head of his cock to her opening.

It wasn't until he'd bottomed out, until he could feel her pubic hair meshing with his own, until he felt her contract around him that he realized what he'd done. He hadn't even made sure she was ready for him.

"Feck!" he swore.

June giggled, and he felt it on his cock.

"Someone likes the idea of making a baby," she teased.

He didn't like it—he *loved* it. June would be even more beautiful pregnant than she was right now. And he couldn't wait to meet their baby. To watch her breastfeed, to see her holding their son or daughter. He wanted to experience it all. The crying, the rocking, the diaper changing. It was almost ridiculous how ready he was to be a dad.

"I love you," he whispered. "You have no idea how much."

"Of course, I do," she retorted. "I cheated death, twice, to get back to you."

She wasn't wrong.

She'd finally told him about the second near-death experience she'd had on the operating table, and the thought of them having two little girls was enough to bring him to his knees. Cal was positive her mom was trying to tell June that their daughters would cure cancer or be the first female president of the United States or achieve some other hugely important accomplishment. But even if they never left Newton and became servers at Granny's Burgers, he knew they'd be the best waitresses anyone had ever known.

He began to move in and out of her slowly, showing her without words how much he revered her, how important she was to him, how much he loved her. Their gazes remained locked on each other as they moved, and Cal wasn't the least bit surprised when they came together. He rolled until she was lying on top of him, his semihard cock still planted deep within her body.

"If you think you're getting out of this bed anytime in the near future, you're dreaming," he informed her.

June lifted her head and smiled at him. "I can take whatever you dish out, Prince Charming."

"My Cinderella," he murmured, then rolled them again. He pulled out, reluctantly, and moved down her body. "I didn't get a chance to do all the things I wanted to earlier."

June spread her arms and legs with abandon and smiled up at the ceiling. "Do to me what you want, husband. I'm all yours."

Yes, she certainly was.

~

Bob was bored. Again. He loved co-owning a business with his friends. He enjoyed the fresh air here in Newton and leading hikers on the AT. But deep down, he craved more excitement.

He'd loved being a Special Forces soldier. Lived for the adrenaline rushes that went with the missions. Thrived in busy places teeming with life. If he'd won that game of Rochambeau during their captivity, his choice of where they'd have moved when they got out of the Army was New York City.

He wasn't upset that they'd ended up in Maine, but his restlessness had soon gotten the better of him . . . and after living there for just a year, he'd given in and contacted a man in the FBI whose name had been passed to him by a team of men who lived in Indianapolis.

Gregory Willis worked with former military members, sending them into situations around the globe to rescue people who needed the kind of help no one else could provide. Some were hostages, others were runaways, some found themselves in the sex trade. Still others were people who'd gotten in over their heads with foreign law agencies, with no way to get back to the States.

It was dangerous work but exciting. And fulfilling. It allowed Bob to not lose his mind from monotony.

Of course, his friends—his very best friends in all the world—had no idea. He knew they wouldn't approve. It was JJ who'd been adamant that they not start a business that had anything to do with security.

And here he was, going behind their backs and doing just that.

How he'd managed to keep it a secret for two years was a mystery, but he'd gotten to a point now where it was almost impossible to come clean. They'd be hurt that he hadn't told them sooner, that he was keeping such a huge secret from them, and upset that he was putting his life on the line without allowing them to watch his back.

When his phone rang, Bob jerked. He chuckled a little and shook his head. He shouldn't be so jumpy, and yet with what he'd been doing on the side, he wasn't surprised. He'd made some enemies over the last two years, people who would love to end him, to make sure he didn't stick his nose in their business ever again. But Bob wasn't worried. He could take care of himself, had proved it time and time again.

"Evans," he said into his phone.

"Got another job for you," Willis said without preamble.

Adrenaline immediately shot through Bob's veins. Yes! He needed to do something. It was closing in on midsummer, and while Jack's

Lumber was busy—as was their guide service on the Appalachian Trail—it wasn't enough. He was itching for more excitement.

"I'm in," he told his contact.

"Don't you want to know what it is?"

It didn't really matter to Bob, but he said yes anyway.

"Thailand. A woman found herself incarcerated on a drug charge. Her brother claims it's bogus. But since she's not a celebrity or anyone notable, the press hasn't paid much attention."

Bob scowled. That part of the world wasn't his favorite place to attempt to infiltrate. First, he didn't exactly blend in with the locals. Second, the weather sucked. Hot and humid wasn't his favorite atmosphere for a mission. And third, the justice system, like many of the police officers, was totally corrupt. "What's the plan?"

"Depends on what you want. Do you want stealthy or expedient?"

"Expedient," Bob said without hesitation. So far, lying to his friends by saying his elderly aunt needed assistance—an aunt he didn't have—and that he was helping to take care of her since they didn't have any other family had worked as an excuse for leaving town every now and then for a week or two. Anything longer and Bob knew they'd start getting more suspicious . . . if they weren't already.

Bob listened, shaking his head as Willis gave him intel about his target and outlined the plan. There was so much wrong with what Willis had put together, it wasn't even funny. But dealing with the Thai police and government didn't leave them with a lot of options. "When am I leaving?" he asked.

"Day after tomorrow," his contact said. "You'll fly from Bangor to Chicago to Los Angeles to Beijing to Bangkok. We've got an inside source, and he'll meet you at the airport."

Bob took a deep breath. This mission was happening extremely fast. But he was glad. He hoped to get there, find this Marlowe woman, and get the hell out. The stress and excitement of such a crazy mission should be enough to tide him over for months.

"Sounds good."

"I'll send the info packet tonight, and you'll get a package in the mail tomorrow. I'm working on setting up the underground network to get you and Marlowe out, but it'll be tricky. You'll have to cross into Cambodia . . . creatively."

Bob knew what that meant. They wouldn't be waltzing across any of the official checkpoints. They'd probably have to cross at a remote, out-of-the-way location, which upped the chances they could get caught. "Understood."

"Payment will be made once the mission is complete, as always. If you have any questions, you know how to get me. Good luck."

Bob let out a snort when Gregory Willis hung up without giving him a chance to speak again. He clicked off the phone and stared into space for a moment, then got up off the couch. He had some preparations to make, an info packet to read, and lies he had to perfect so his friends didn't worry about him.

Guilt made him frown, but Bob pushed the feeling aside.

The last thing he wanted to do was let down JJ, Chappy, and Cal, but his friends were otherwise occupied with their women. Even though JJ and April weren't officially a couple, Bob had no doubt they soon would be. The chemistry between the two sent sparks flying every time they were together. It was simply a matter of time before they broke down and did something about it.

He was thrilled for his friends, but he wasn't ready to settle down. And now he had someone else he could help with the skills he'd perfected over the years.

He'd rescue Marlowe Kennedy so she could get on with her life, and his restless soul would be appeased once more . . . at least for a while.

Determination settled around him as Bob headed to his room to pack.

~

Marlowe Kennedy huddled over the sewing machine she'd been assigned, sighing heavily. She'd been in this hellhole for almost a month, with the first two weeks in solitary confinement to make sure she didn't have any viruses that could spread to the other inmates. The prison was overcrowded, and the air of misery and dejection was overwhelming.

She shared a "room" with two hundred other prisoners. She slept on a thin mat with women touching her on either side. The food was awful, and Marlowe knew she'd already lost too much weight.

When she'd been arrested, she'd begged and pleaded with the police. Told them she had no idea how the pills they'd found in her bag had gotten there. But it hadn't done any good. She'd been forced to sign a document that she couldn't even read, driven to this prison, and locked away without a second glance.

She'd been "interrogated" for hours—which simply meant she was screamed at in a language she didn't speak—but hadn't been given a chance to tell her side of the story. She was allowed no phone calls or legal counsel. She'd been in Thailand working on an archaeological dig, minding her own business, and the next thing she knew, her tent was being searched, and drugs—that were *not* hers—were found.

She'd cried for days, but now, no more tears would come. She'd been thrown away, forgotten.

She didn't understand what anyone was saying, and the trustees—prisoners who'd been there long enough to be given responsibilities over their fellow inmates—didn't like her simply because she was American.

Thinking about her brother was the only thing that kept Marlowe from completely breaking down. She'd begged the site boss to call him when she was being dragged away, knowing her brother would do what he could to help. He was five years older and had always been protective of her, even more so after their parents had been killed in a hit-and-run accident when she was fourteen.

Tony would figure out what happened, how to get her out. He had the connections to help her, thanks to working in politics for years. He wouldn't stop until he got the charges against her overturned and she was released.

Yet, despite that conviction, with each day that passed, her faith and confidence took another small hit. Every single day felt like it lasted a week, and it was difficult to maintain her belief that she'd get out of here one day soon.

She was pretty sure she knew *who* had set her up, but it wasn't as if she could do anything about it while stuck in this place. She desperately needed her brother.

"I need you, Tony," she whispered out loud. "Please get me out."

But, of course, her words disappeared into the noise of the large, overly hot room. No one magically appeared to apologize and tell her the arrest had been a huge misunderstanding.

Marlowe closed her eyes for a moment. She wasn't famous . . . wasn't a star athlete or a politician or an actress. She was a nobody. And it was that fact that made her fear she'd die in this dark, dank prison, with no one other than her brother to care.

If by some miracle she got out of here, she was going to make changes in her life. Was going to try to be more outgoing. Was going to get married. Maybe have kids—she wasn't sure about that part yet. Be a better aunt to Tony's kids, definitely. Stop taking such dangerous assignments.

And she'd be forever grateful to whoever managed to get her out of here. A lawyer, a negotiator, some badass mercenary—she didn't care. Hell, she'd marry the person and devote her entire life to them . . . if only they could provide her a second chance.

Sighing again, Marlowe took a deep breath and opened her eyes. She was required to finish a certain number of blouses each day, and if she didn't get them done, she'd be punished by the trustees.

In her scant free time, she made sure to exercise. She had to keep up her strength. Just in case she somehow managed to get out, she wanted to be ready for anything. To run, climb, swim, hike hundreds of miles to the border . . . whatever it took, she was going to be in the best shape she could, weight loss be damned.

"Please, Tony," she said out loud again as she hunched over the material on her table. "Please help me."

Help is definitely on the way for poor Marlowe. She needs a hero right about now. Bob might never see himself that way, but he'd be wrong. Look for the next book in the Game of Chance series, *The Hero*. Keep reading for a sneak peek of the first chapter.

THE HERO

GAME OF CHANCE SERIES, BOOK 3

Chapter One

Marlowe Kennedy jerked in surprise when one of the trustees yelled her name loudly enough to be heard over the noise of the hundreds of sewing machines in the room.

Turning, she saw Yanisa scowling at her from just inside the door. She didn't immediately move, because the last thing Marlowe wanted was to get in trouble.

Trustees were prisoners who'd been given a bit of power over their peers. One word from any of them to the guards and a prisoner could find herself in solitary. Most of the inmates were scared of the trustees, and Marlowe couldn't blame them.

The ratio of guards to prisoners in this massive Thai prison was something like twenty to a thousand. It was sheer terror—or simply a lack of will—on the prisoners' part that kept them from uprising. Most of the women here had been sentenced to life. Same as Marlowe.

It was unbelievable that a month ago, Marlowe had been an esteemed archaeologist working on a dig not too far from Bangkok. She'd been respected and considered an expert in her field. Now look at her. She was a convicted drug dealer, according to the Thai government, and had been thrown away as if she were a piece of trash.

Her days were spent hunched over a sewing machine, stitching cheap blouses, and her nights spent sleeping in a room crammed with a couple hundred other women, lying shoulder to shoulder on thin mats that didn't do a damn thing to cushion her from the hard concrete floor.

"Marlowe!" Yanisa yelled again, more impatiently this time. She gestured with her hand for her to come.

Standing, Marlowe made her way through the other women, none of them curious in the least as to why she'd been called out by the trustee. Or maybe they just knew better than to draw any attention to themselves by stopping what they were doing.

When Marlowe got close to Yanisa, the woman reached out and grabbed the front of her light-blue prison shirt in her fist, shaking her violently.

Marlowe's first instinct was to smack the woman's hand away, to fight back, but if she did that, she'd go straight to solitary. It was forbidden for any of the prisoners to touch a trustee. But of course, that didn't go both ways. The trustees could do whatever they wanted to the women in their charge. They frequently hit, punched, kicked, and sometimes sexually assaulted others in the dark of the night.

Such was life in this overcrowded and underfunded prison.

Yanisa turned, Marlowe's shirt still in her fist, and started walking toward the administrative building.

Dread rolled through Marlowe. She didn't like anything about the main building on the prison grounds. It was where the guards hung out. And where interrogations were done.

Marlowe had already spent more than enough time in one of the small rooms in the large brick building. When she'd first arrived at the women's prison from the dig site, she assumed she'd just explain that the yaba pills found in her belongings weren't hers. She thought she'd get a chance to tell her side.

Including how she suspected Ian West was the one who'd planted them.

But that hadn't happened. Instead, she'd been yelled at for hours in Thai. She couldn't understand a word they were saying. She begged for an interpreter. For something to eat and drink. To use the bathroom. If anyone understood her, they ignored her pleas.

She had no idea how long she was in the room, but finally a woman came in who spoke English. Marlowe had never been so relieved in her life to meet someone she could understand and who could understand her.

The woman explained that she was being charged with drug trafficking, that she needed to sign an affidavit of some sort. It was in Thai, and Marlowe couldn't understand a word of it. She'd refused at first, but the woman had explained that if she didn't sign, she'd be found guilty on the spot and sentenced to death.

It was a nightmare she'd had no idea how to get out of. She knew it wasn't smart to sign something without reading it first, but the woman had been so reassuring. And by that point, Marlowe was hungry, exhausted, and terrified. She'd seen the way the male guards drank in her body while interrogating her. She'd heard the horror stories of women being assaulted in Thai prisons.

In the end, she'd signed the papers.

She'd been brought into a room, her clothes were taken away, and she'd been forced to change into the light-blue shirt and dark-blue skirt all the prisoners wore, before she was taken to solitary confinement. Where she stayed for two weeks.

So yeah . . . needless to say, she didn't have good memories of the administrative building Yanisa was currently dragging her toward. At just five-four, Marlowe wasn't a large woman, and with the amount of weight she'd lost since her incarceration, she was even more slight. Generally, Thai women weren't all that much taller, but Yanisa was an exception, which was probably part of the reason she was a trustee. She easily yanked Marlowe behind her as they walked, and it was all she could do to stay on her feet.

To Marlowe's immense relief, instead of being taken to one of the small interrogation rooms, she was dragged toward the visitors' area.

For a brief moment, hope bloomed in Marlowe's chest. Was Tony here? Had her brother finally navigated through all the red tape to get in and see her? She felt almost dizzy with relief. Tony would get her out.

Her big brother was her most fierce protector. As a US senator, he had friends in high places, as cliché as that seemed. If anyone could figure this mess out, it was him.

Yanisa jerked to a stop and practically threw Marlowe into a chair sitting in front of a chain-link fence. The setup for the prisoners to talk to visitors wasn't ideal. She sat in front of one fence, with another fence standing about eight feet beyond the first, and behind *that*, the visitors sat. There was absolutely no chance of them being able to touch, to talk privately. Given the size of the room, and with a dozen other women talking to visitors, it was almost impossible to hear what anyone was saying.

"Five minutes," Yanisa told her gruffly, then turned and stomped away.

No one was sitting in the chair on the other side of the large gap, opposite where she was sitting, and Marlowe frowned in confusion. Then she looked eagerly toward the door on the left side of the room when it opened, expecting to see Tony.

But the man who entered wasn't anyone Marlowe had ever seen before. He stood out like a sore thumb from everyone else. He was taller than the guards. Had thick dark hair and a scowl on his face and was dressed impeccably in a white dress shirt, a blue tie, and a pair of khaki pants. He carried a briefcase, which he set on the ground as soon as he got to the space in front of where she was sitting.

He didn't lower himself into the chair. He simply frowned at her through both fences.

His lips moved, but Marlowe couldn't hear what he was saying.

"I'm sorry, what?" she practically yelled.

His lips moved again with what Marlowe thought was a swear word, before he raised his voice. She could just hear him over the din. And English—American, unaccented English—had never sounded so good.

"Marlowe Kennedy?"

She nodded.

"I'm your lawyer."

Marlowe blinked. This man didn't look like any lawyer she'd ever seen. Granted, she wasn't exactly an expert, but he seemed too . . . rough? She wasn't sure what gave her that impression. Maybe it was the edgy look in his eyes or the huge muscles she could see bulging under his white shirt. But never in a million years would she have pegged this man as a lawyer.

"Did you hear me?" he yelled through the fence.

Marlowe nodded again.

"I'm going to get you out of here. Understand?"

She didn't. Not really. But she couldn't deny having someone on her side felt good.

She nodded yet again.

"You need to be ready," he told her, his dark eyes boring into hers. She had a feeling he was trying to tell her something, but she had no idea what. "In the meantime, keep your head down, don't bring attention to yourself. When the time is right, you'll know."

Marlowe tilted her head slightly and studied the man across the gap. He hadn't asked for her side of the story. Hadn't pulled out any papers, or mentioned her charge, or done anything she expected a lawyer would do when meeting a client for the first time. Granted, this wasn't exactly a normal circumstance. It wasn't as if they were meeting at a conference table, where they could have a serious conversation.

Suddenly, she needed to know this man's name. She wasn't convinced he could help her, didn't know if *anyone* could at this point. The Thai government was in a war against drugs that it couldn't win, but it was willing to make an example out of anyone caught with any substance, no matter how small the amount. Especially foreigners. It was why the prison was as overcrowded as it was.

But for some reason, looking into this man's eyes, she felt a deep-seated urge to trust him.

She stood slowly, not wanting to alarm Yanisa or any of the other trustees or guards in the room with a sudden movement. She gripped the metal fence in front of her so tightly, her fingers turned white. "What's your name?" she yelled.

The man stared at her for a beat before saying, "Kendric."

Kendric.

It fit him. Marlowe hadn't met anyone with that name before. His deep voice rumbled around in her brain as his name echoed. *Kendric. Kendric. Kendric.*

"How are you holding up?" he asked.

Marlowe shrugged. She knew better than to complain. She had no idea if Yanisa or anyone else could hear her over the other loud voices, but she wasn't going to take a chance that they might.

Kendric frowned again. Then said, "I just need you to hold on a little longer. Can you do that for me?"

Marlowe wanted to say yes, but the truth was, she wasn't sure. This was the worst experience of her life, and she was nearing her breaking point. The thought of spending the rest of her days here was demoralizing to the point that she'd do anything, *anything*, to get out.

"Did Tony send you?" she shouted instead of answering his question.

"Yes."

His answer was immediate, and the relief that swamped her made Marlowe feel light headed.

"Is he okay? Is he here?"

"He's fine. Worried about you. And no, he's not here. He sent me," Kendric said. His gaze moved from hers, slightly to her right.

Marlowe turned her head to see what he was looking at and saw Yanisa headed her way. She gripped the fence tighter. She didn't want to go back to the sewing room. She wanted to stay here, talking to Kendric. He was a link to her brother. To freedom. And she didn't want to lose it.

If she lost sight of Kendric, she somehow knew she'd fall right back into the pit of despair she'd been living in for what seemed like years instead of weeks.

As if he could read her mind, Kendric yelled, "Look at me, Marlowe."

She immediately turned her gaze back to him.

"I'm getting you out of here. You just have to be ready. For anything. When the unexpected happens, I'll be there. Understand? You just have to be brave enough to move."

Marlowe had no idea what he was talking about.

Yanisa grabbed her upper arm and said something in Thai.

Marlowe held on to the fence, not letting go. Not wanting to leave Kendric.

"Can you do that?" he shouted.

There was an urgency to his question that Marlowe didn't understand.

"Marlowe!" he called as Yanisa pried her fingers off the fence. "When the time comes, be like Forrest Gump . . ."

He said something else, but the words were lost in the noise of everyone else yelling to be able to reach their visitors.

Marlowe was so confused. Kendric couldn't have actually said "Forrest Gump" . . . could he?

But he had. She knew it.

Looking back before Yanisa pulled her out of the visitors' room, Marlowe saw Kendric standing exactly where he'd been before. He hadn't moved. He was holding on to the fence, much as she had, staring at her intently as Yanisa manhandled her out of the room. In her last glimpse, she saw him mouth something to her.

The door slammed behind her, and Marlowe was once more being yanked along the grounds toward the sewing room. Yanisa was mumbling under her breath, and Marlowe was actually relieved she couldn't understand what she was saying. When they arrived back at the sweatshop, which was what Marlowe considered it, Yanisa threw her toward the door.

Not expecting the violent move, Marlowe flew forward and hit the door hard, barely avoiding smacking her face against the metal.

"Get work!" Yanisa growled.

Moving as fast as she could, Marlowe fumbled with the knob and managed to get it open. The air inside the room was stifling, and the familiar smell of body odor assaulted her senses.

It wasn't until she was once again seated at her sewing machine and struggling with the material, trying to get the stitches straight, that Marlowe realized what Kendric had mouthed at her when she was being hauled away.

Run.

Was that the reference to Forrest Gump that he was trying to make? It made sense . . . but then again, it didn't. Run? To where? There wasn't anywhere to run *to*. And while there weren't a lot of guards at the prison, the walls were high, covered in barbed wire, and the bullets in the rifles of the men guarding the walls were faster than Marlowe.

She must've read his last word wrong.

She supposed it didn't really matter. She now knew her brother was doing what he could to help her, and she had to have faith that eventually she'd be released. *Someone* would figure out that the yaba pills in her belongings weren't her own.

She frowned at the thought. Shoot, she didn't get a chance to tell Kendric to look into Ian West. He was the reason she was in prison— she was sure of it. But if the man was smart, he'd be long gone from Thailand by now.

A sharp pain in her side made Marlowe grunt. Turning, she saw another of the trustees standing next to her, yelling and pointing at the sewing machine. The woman had kicked her because she was staring into space instead of working.

Lowering her head, Marlowe did her best to concentrate. She remembered what Kendric had said. Not to bring any attention to herself. She had no idea what he was doing to free her, but she wasn't going to be a hindrance in any way. Not when her freedom was at stake.

She could survive for a little while longer. She just hoped it wouldn't be months before Kendric and Tony could work through the red tape and get her the hell out of here.

About the Author

Susan Stoker is a *New York Times, USA Today,* and *Wall Street Journal* bestselling author whose series include Badge of Honor: Texas Heroes, SEAL of Protection, and Delta Force Heroes. Married to a retired Army noncommissioned officer, Stoker has lived all over the country—from Missouri and California to Colorado, Texas, and Tennessee—and currently lives in the beautiful wilds of Maine. A true believer in happily ever after, Stoker enjoys writing novels in which romance turns to love. To learn more about the author and her work, visit her website, www.stokeraces.com, or find her on Facebook at www.facebook.com/authorsusanstoker.

Connect with Susan Online

SUSAN'S FACEBOOK PROFILE AND PAGE

www.facebook.com/authorsstoker

www.facebook.com/authorsusanstoker

FOLLOW SUSAN ON TWITTER

www.twitter.com/susan_stoker

FIND SUSAN'S BOOKS ON GOODREADS

www.goodreads.com/susanstoker

EMAIL

susan@stokeraces.com

WEBSITE

www.stokeraces.com